Heart in the Highlands

To all lovers of Scotland~
Slàinte mhòr agàd!

One Sweet Kiss

He reached for a strand of her hair and coiled it slowly around his finger, staring deeply into her eyes, two green jewels made brilliant by the sun.

She couldn't move, mesmerized by his gaze and his presence.

Tempted, he lowered his head. Just one kiss.

Her heart pounded. He was going to kiss her again.

All of a sudden, the fire in his eyes died away and his expression altered. For no reason he pulled back, releasing his hold upon her arm.

She felt confused and wanted to cry out, "What have I done?" but didn't possess the courage.

GALLANTRY BOOKS
Burning Rose Press
www.burningrosepress.com

ISBN-13: 978-0615715827
ISBN-10: 0615715826

Heart in the Highlands

Highland Hope

Highland Dream

Amy P. Kennedy

Contents

Heart in the Highlands ~ *Highland Hope*
"Faith is the substance of things hoped for"

"Wherever I wander, wherever I rove,
My heart's in the Highlands, wherever I go"
-Robert Burns, *My Heart's in the Highlands*

Clan Map of Scotland

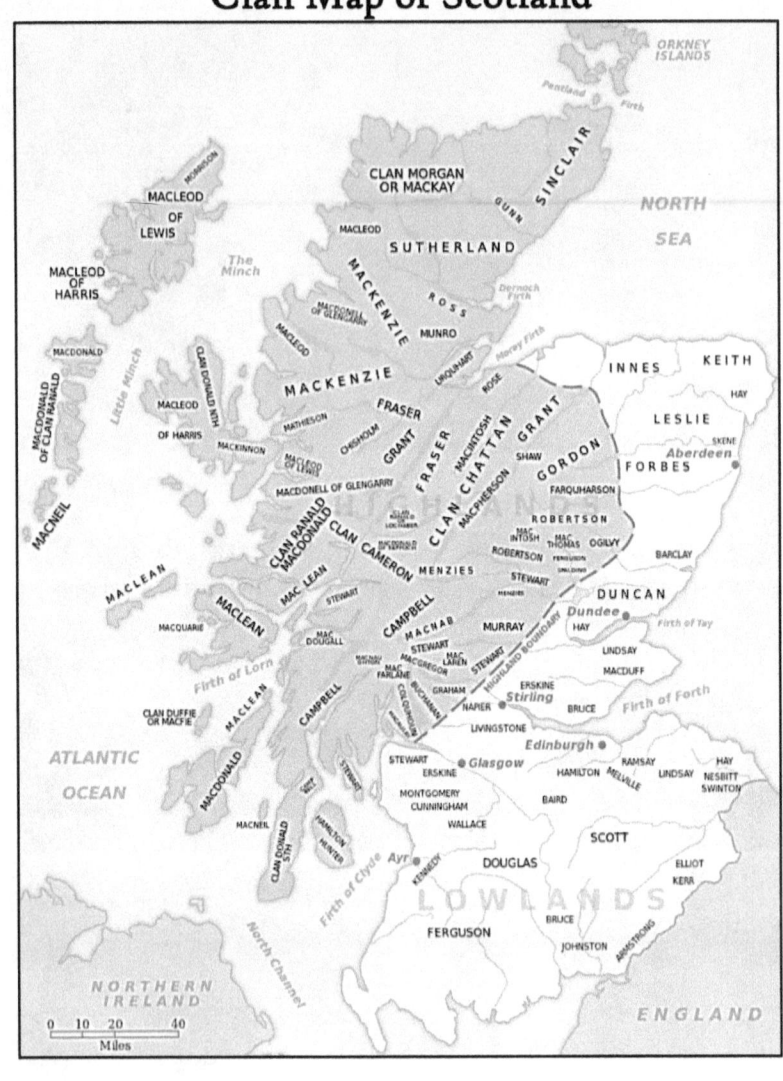

McCallum♥MacDougall Family Tree

McCallum

Laird Raibeart Eobhann Mac Chailuim
(Robert Ewen McCallum)
Of Dunchalum, Argyll, Scotland
Wed 1728
To Lady Aileanna Muireall Nic Kinnon
(Alanna Muriel McKinnon)
Daughter of John dhu McKinnon of Skye

MacDougall

Laird Donnochadh Alasdair Mac Dhùghaill
(Duncan Alistair MacDougall)
Of Dunolly, Argyll, Scotland
Wed 1718
To Lady Grairh Ealasaid Camphbeul
(Grear Elizabeth Campbell)
Daughter of Ian Angus Campbell of Balloch

1750

Raibeart Ailean Mac Chailuim, 1729
(Robert Allan McCallum)

Coinneas Eubh Nic Chailuim, 1729
(Kennis Eve McCallum)

Màiri Gilsoral Nic Chailuim, 1738
(Mary Grace McCallum)

Alasdair Dughlas Mac Dhùghaill, 1720
(Alistair Duglas MacDougall)

Dunnochadh Seumas Mac Dùghaill, 1728
(Duncan James MacDougall)

Ona Milread Nic Dùghaill, 1731
(Anna Mildred MacDougall)

Highland Hope

"Faith is the substance of things hoped for"
Hebrews 11:1

Argyll, Scotland, April 1746

Prologue

"The Bonnie Prince needs me more, lass."

A shroud of silver mist lingered on the Highland loch in the cool spring morning, a grey portent hovering over the wild beauty of its solitary banks. In firm opposition to the threatening shade overhead, the blue-black water sloshing against the loam remained steady; change of any kind had yet to mar or defeat its timeless rhythm. Deep in conversation, two figures ambled along the pebbled shore, heedless of the coming transformation to the land.

She choked back sharp words of denial that quickly rose to her lips. The pervasive, heady scent of fresh cut pine mingled with wet earth, moldering leaves and peat served as a potent reminder that some thoughts should remain unspoken. War was never glorious and a young man like Robbie was susceptible to the ravings of foolish men.

"Don't leave, Robbie." Her nails dug into the soft flesh of his strong forearm. "We need you here!" If only she could persuade him to stay home, far from the raging conflict, everything would turn out right in the end.

Silent, he pried her cold fingers loose, smoothing them gently before tucking her arm into the crook of his own.

Bagpipes skirled in the distance, their colorful voices echoing across the wooded hills and glens. *Alba gu brath,* the pipes cried on a proud note, *Scotland forever!,* calling men to arise to defend their homeland from the tyranny of the English.

Bonnie Prince Charlie, claiming the thrones of Scotland and England on behalf of his father, James Stewart, had raised the royal standard at Glenfinnan, proclaiming him King. In the months preceding his arrival, numerous councils convened across the nation to discuss and pledge allegiance to the Prince, pitting clans against one another. Now, the Scots' ongoing battle for freedom was on the verge of being determined as the clans marched to war, brother in opposition to brother.

"But Father's leaving, and so are the men from the villages." She shivered in the chill air, the fearsome thought of parting forever seeping into her bones. "What are we to do, who will protect the women and the children? I can't bear to think of the hurt our clan may suffer," she raised her eyes to his, "and what if the Cause is lost?" A dark shadow cast by the towering castle overhead lengthened over the fog-curtained loch, seeming to confirm her words.

"Lost." Robbie's brows lifted in disbelief. "Have you so little faith in us, Kennis, to win out over the English?"

"We're vastly outnumbered," she said, not willing to yield the point, "and the English have a far superior force." She kicked a loose stone on the path into the dark indigo water in frustration.

He cocked an eyebrow in amusement. "Listened to the council meeting, eh? You shouldn't concern yourself with such details, nor take to heart the rash words you heard spoken."

"I fully comprehend the situation, Robbie, don't patronize me." She felt annoyed at his evaluation of her understanding. "The English have wealth, skill, and men. What do we possess that will enable us to win this conflict? Besides," she said stubbornly, "willing hearts don't necessarily win real battles or fill empty stomachs."

"We have one another," he said with confidence. "'Tis enough. There's power in what a man believes, lass, and in his words. We're of one mind."

"Not all. Father said so, I heard him. Some even believe the country will fare better under English law."

"Never." He was adamant. "Besides, Charlie's already won the first round of skirmishes. He's victorious at Prestonpans and Falkirk, and is in Edinburgh now." His handsome countenance lit with excitement. "He entered Holyrood without striking a blow, Kennis, and when he marches on London, we'll be there to put a final end to the plague of English domination." A militant gleam shone in his eyes. "You'll see, it will be a grand victory and the *Sassenachs* will trouble us no more. We'll have a Scottish King, one of our own blood on the throne, and live the Highland way without interference from meddling lowlanders."

She brushed away hot, sudden tears. "Have you considered the possibility that you or Father may be killed? What then?"

"To die fighting for what a man believes 'tis honorable, Kennis. If death claims me," he said gravely, "then rejoice that I didn't remain home a coward, and will find my place in heaven among our ancestors." He covered her trembling hand with his strong warm one in reassurance. "Don't worry, lass, all will be well, and we'll be home in a month."

"I find no comfort in your words." Regardless of a heavenly reward, she was deeply worried over the prospect of being alone without him, and of the very real possibility that he might die. "I listened closely to the debate last week, and the chiefs are divided. 'Tis not the proper time to fight, we need clan unity in Scotland right now. This war will bring division and pain, and more people will suffer. Honor and glory have little to do with it, Robbie. Our greatest hope lies in peace." She straightened, looking him directly in the eye. "I question whether or not this war 'tis truly in the best interests of our people."

His fair brow wrinkled in disappointment at her censure. She usually supported his ventures with enthusiasm. "I'm surprised at you, Kennis. The English must be stopped. They'll exploit our land, send our men off to fight their king's foreign wars. We must fight, there's no alternative." He paused. "I thought you'd be glad Father's allowing me to stand with him, to fight at his side."

"There are other men who'll stand with him. Of a truth, I've no doubt you're capable but the people who remain behind need you here since Father is departing. Why don't you stay?" She seized the front of his leather jack. "Mam, Mairi and I need you."

"Mam will defend the keep, if necessary," he reminded her. "You'll be well protected behind the walls of Dunchalum, and by the lads that remain behind. Besides, it will never come to such a pass. We'll win this battle. Fear not for me, lass."

Her sea green eyes, almost identical to his, clouded. "A handful of old men and a few women defending a Highland keep? You must stay, Robbie, make your stand here with the clan. No one will think less of you, and Mam's burden will be lightened."

He shook his head, unswayed. "I canna." A cannon boomed in the distance. "'Tis the signal. I must go now, Kennis." He leaned forward to plant a kiss on her cheek. "Fare well."

The brilliance of the morning sun rising behind him diffused the early morning haze but not her heartfelt distress. "Fare well, Robbie." She fervently returned his embrace. "May God go with you and protect you always."

America to Scotland, Spring of 1750

Chapter 1

New Journeys

She thrashed in the darkness, pushing away the invisible hand stifling her breath.

Bagpipes skirled throughout the misty hills, drums boomed in the distance. Frantic over his decision to leave the safety of home and kin, she urged him to stay—*Please don't go, Robbie, we need you here!* and nearly strangled on the words.

Kennis McCallum awoke in a tangle of bedclothes, heart pounding and gasping for air. Moist tendrils of hair were pasted to her cheeks and cold sweat dampened her cotton chemise. She sat up in the small bed, weary from a restless sleep. "The Bonnie Prince needs me more, lass," she bitterly repeated aloud. "We'll be home in a month." His parting words haunted her dreams. She begged him not to go, and he'd not returned.

Throwing back the covers, she swung her feet to the cold floor and slipped them into her leather mules. The fire in the hearth had died and she shivered, missing its warmth as she reached for her worn flannel wrapper.

The door creaked open. "I've brought ye some warm water t' wash, miss." Glenda, the housemaid, opened the plain muslin curtains to reveal the sunrise. "Is there anything else ye need?"

"Has Mr. Gilmore come down to breakfast yet, Glenda?"

"He's there right now, miss, havin' his coffee. Would ye like one o' the lads t' come and light this fire?"

"Nay, that won't be necessary. Please have it lit and a bath ready for when I return at seven."

She bobbed a curtsey before retreating from the room. "Very well, miss."

Kennis dressed quickly, glancing at her reflection in the looking glass. Satisfied with her appearance, she stepped into the dimly lit hall. It simply would not do to tramp along the docks dressed as if she were going to church. Besides, today could be the day her prayers were answered. She must run her errand and return before her young charges were awake.

Pausing to listen to the stirring household, she then tiptoed to the servant's stair in her stocking feet. After a careful descent into the nether regions of the old house, she opened the lower door into the redolent kitchen. Martha rested in the rocking chair by the hearth from her early morning labors, and Kennis smiled as she slipped past the immobile figure.

"Good mornin', miss." Martha was kind in her gruff way. "I didn't see ye walk by now, jus' remember tha'."

Kennis jumped at the sound of her voice. The old woman never missed a trick. "Good morn," she returned, reaching for an oat scone from the stoneware platter on the table and tucking it into her pocket. She pulled on her boots, ignoring Martha's grumbles, and then opened the side door to step onto the wooden stoop. Munching on the scone, she skipped down the narrow steps. The fresh morning air took her breath away. She shivered, and quickly swathed herself in a large brown shawl to drive out the chill as she hurried down the cobbled street.

On the wharf, a handful of sailors tossed bundles dockside and a few passengers waited to board. Her pulse quickened in anticipation. Tonight was her turn to sail. She was going home! A sudden movement among the crates caught her attention. Deciding to investigate, she discovered a half-starved child gnawing on a dry crust of bread. She walked slowly toward him and broke the fresh baked scone in two, offering him half of her meager breakfast.

He stepped forward, one foot at a time, never taking his wary eyes from her face.

"Please take it." Her heart wrenched in dismay at his haggard appearance. How many hungry children were there in the world? Compared to the Highlands of Scotland in the aftermath of war, America was a land of plenty. This boy should have a better chance at life, a sturdy roof over his head and plenty of nourishing food to eat. "One day," she determined, continuing on her way, "I'm going to make a difference in the lives of the poor."

After completing her routine search of the quay, she retraced her steps along the cobbled street and let herself in at the Gilmore's kitchen door. Sadly, she didn't have time to do more. She slipped off her boots and carried them, mounting the stairs two at a time. A steaming bath awaited her by the hearth. She'd best enjoy it now; the ship held no such luxuries, at least not for the likes of her.

Knock, knock, knock. "Kennis! Are you in there?" a childish voice trilled. "Cause if you are, I need you."

Kennis groaned. "Aye, but I'm in the bath."

"But you're s'posed to be packing my things!"

"Don't fret, Jennie, 'tis almost done. Now let me finish, and I'll be with you in a *twink*."

"Oh, alright." She skipped down the hall to the room that she shared with her little sister, Molly.

That child. Kennis shook her head, rising from the wooden tub. She enjoyed her job as companion to Mrs. Gilmore and governess to the children. Distant relatives, the Gilmores provided her with room and board, treating her with kindness and respect, and she enjoyed being a valued member of the family. Still, her wages could not provide for her in the manner to which she was accustomed and the gold coins that her mother had given her at the beginning of her journey were nearly gone, spent on necessities.

Although the post wasn't difficult, her initial excitement about traveling to America had waned and she was eager to be home. Fortunately, the female members of the family rose late, making her responsibilities less tiresome. Mr. Gilmore, however, rose at dawn and she often broke her fast with him. The conversations they enjoyed reminded her of her own dear father on more than one occasion.

Her toilette complete, she stepped out into the narrow passage. The door to the girls' cozy little room stood ajar and she peeked inside. "Come, girls, your mother will be waiting for us." She pushed the door completely open and paused on the threshold, eyeing the clothes strewn about the room and her two charges, playing in their night rails. "Why aren't you dressed, Jennie?" she said. She moved forward, picking up garments she'd folded the evening before. "And look at the mess you've both made!"

Shaking her head at the rueful silence that followed, she helped each child into cotton undergarments and woolen frock. Jennie tugged a brush through her riotous curls while Kennis tied a pretty riband in a neat bow at the top of Molly's soft hair.

"There," she said, satisfied with her handiwork, "now you're presentable. Let's go down to breakfast." She took each child by the hand and carefully descended the narrow steps.

Their mother awaited in the dining room. "Good morning, Kennis, girls." Mrs. Gilmore opened her arms wide and the children ran into her warm embrace.

Kennis seated Molly at the table first. "Good morning, Mrs. Gilmore."

"Mam," Jennie pouted, "Kennis still isn't finished packing my trunk."

Buttering her toast, Kennis said nothing. The mess above stairs was enough to consume her energies for half of the morning. At least her own meager belongings were in good order and already stowed away in her trunk.

Mrs. Gilmore smiled lovingly at her daughter. "Patience, my love, there's plenty of time. Leave Kennis be and she'll be finished sooner."

"But the wagons are coming." Jennie's little brow wrinkled in concern.

"The wagons are already here." Mr. Gilmore entered the room. "We're loading the household crates first, Jennie lass, and the rest this afternoon. Don't worry, child, we won't leave anything behind." He pulled a chair out from the table and sat down. "Kennis," he said with a lift of his brow, "you were out early this morning."

"Aye, sir," she replied truthfully. Mr. Gilmore knew of her many jaunts to the harbor and of her search for her brother. After all, the main reason she agreed to work for the family and travel to North Carolina from Scotland was in the hopes of locating Robbie. The possibility existed that a shopkeeper or a dockhand might remember him, with his fair good looks and large stature. The ship that he'd sailed upon unloaded its human cargo in Cape Hatteras. The indentured men were disbursed as manrent to plantation owners or anyone who could afford to purchase and provide for them over a ten-year period of service. Robbie could be anywhere in the Americas now.

"And have you any news, lass?" His eyes were full of compassion.

She shook her head in the negative. Had she really expected to find anything? Over the last few years, she'd exhausted every possible lead, and now she wondered if her family would ever be reunited again.

"I'm sorry you haven't been able to discover Rob's whereabouts, but we've certainly been fortunate to have your company, eh, Ailis?"

Mrs. Gilmore nodded. "I don't know what we would have done without you, Kennis, truly."

"I appreciate your kind words and it's been a pleasure to work for you, but I confess I'm disappointed that I've found out so little about Robbie or any of the men from the clan. Although our information was good, apparently it wasn't enough."

"Well, these things have a way of working themselves out," Mr. Gilmore said wisely. "I'm sure we'll know the truth of the matter soon, and the journey's been worthwhile for us since I've landed such a fine position in Argyll. 'Tis not what I expected, but a blessing all the same. In the meantime, we'd all best finish our chores, eh? Or we'll not make the launch this evening."

Mr. Gilmore had recently received an offer to be steward to the powerful Duke of Argyll in Western Scotland. He concluded that aside from his excellent qualifications, it must be due to the moderate wages he requested since the duke was well known by all for his miserly ways.

"Then we're definitely sailing tonight?" Kennis' heart leapt with joy. Although she had little news for her mother, it would be grand to be home.

"Aye, the weather's fine," Mr. Gilmore said. "I've spoken with the Captain. We just need to have our possessions at the dock by mid-afternoon, and be ready to sail with the eventide."

After breakfast, Kennis spent the remainder of the morning and the early afternoon packing, helping with children, and running errands. When she finally stood on the sidewalk and stared one last time at the narrow brick house that she'd called home for the last four years, she marveled. Time passed so quickly yet here she was, an experienced young woman of twenty-one instead of a naïve girl of sixteen.

Considering how much she'd altered over the last few years, what would Robbie be like? Would she know her own brother when she found him? Time and difficulty changed people forever. She'd heard more than one horror story about the battle of Culloden and couldn't imagine the effect it must have had on Robbie. Moreover, it was possible that she might never see him again.

She climbed into the carriage with the Gilmore family and soon enough, the white-capped harbor came into view. Stepping onto the quay, she marveled again. Four years. She just celebrated her birthday in America and longed to be home but dreaded the lengthy journey across the tossing sea.

The rippling waves crashed against the hull of the ship and she shuddered. Time to board. With mixed emotions, she followed the Gilmores up the gangplank.

Her main task aboard ship was to care for the children and keep them occupied. With Jennie, that meant keeping the child out of the mischief that seemed to find her everywhere that she went.

"Jennie, where are you?" Kennis scurried about the cabin, peeking under the bunks, making a game of the search with Molly. The child wasn't in the room. Again. Why could she not stay put and do as she was told? Taking Molly by the hand, she walked down the hall and softly knocked on the door of Mrs. Gilmores's chamber.

Molly slipped in when it opened and Ailis appeared. "What is it now, Kennis?" She was well aware of her eldest daughter's antics.

"Jennie left the cabin again, Mrs. Gilmore, I'm going to see if Cook has seen her. She loves to visit him for treats."

"I'll tell her father when he returns."

She nodded. A lot of good that would do—Mr. Gilmore would probably laugh, call her a naughty puss and tell her not to do it again. What the child really needed was a good *skelping*. She turned, skipped down the steps and disappeared into the galley.

Her intuition was right. She discovered the girl hobnobbing with the ship's cook and munching on an apple. "Jennie," she scolded, "you're not supposed to leave the room by yourself or be here without permission."

"But Kennis, Cook says—" Jennie tried to explain.

"I don't care what Cook says," Kennis interrupted, seizing her hand. "Come, I'm taking you to your mother right now."

After she safely delivered the child to Mrs. Gilmore, she ran to her cabin, grabbed her shawl and hurried up the steps to the weather deck. Jennie's disappearance had kept her from this daily pleasure and now a storm brewed overhead.

Chapter 2

Stormy Seas

A sharp gust of wind whipped across her body, flinging her tawny hair about her shoulders.

Breathless, she closed her eyes and tilted her head back, deeply inhaling the tangy scent of the sea. The cool morning drafts danced over her cheeks and she reveled in the sensation. This, she exulted, was what drew her out on deck every morning.

The ship's cabins were dry and stuffy, confining to a Highland bred girl accustomed to roving freely among the trees and the heather. Gazing again at the choppy sea, she spread her arms wide and spun in a circle, laughter spilling from her mouth in pure joy. When raindrops splattered onto the tip of her lightly freckled nose, she frowned up at the changing sky in dismay.

The heavens rumbled, and the vibrant banner of color displayed on the horizon rapidly faded. The sails of the *Faioleag*[1] ballooned when a fierce wind threatened to rip the thick cloth from the masts. Cresting with white foam, the emerald waters peaked and crashed against the ship as ominous grey clouds pelted everyone on deck with freezing rain.

---

[1] *Sea gull*

Off balance, Kennis struggled to grasp the rail and maintain her foothold on the slippery floorboards. A wall of frigid seawater raised high above the bulwark and flooded the heaving deck. The relentless wind drove her closer to the torrent of rushing water. She grabbed at a dangling rope and fought to hold on. The loosened knot gave way, and she screamed. The rushing water tore at her; she was about to wash overboard! All of a sudden, a strong hand reached out and pulled her close.

"Mercy," she breathed out in relief, safe within the circle of muscular arms. "Thank you kindly, sir." Shaken, she clung to her rescuer, staring wide-eyed up at him.

He gave her a cursory glance, his attention riveted on the drama unfolding before him. "Donal," he barked at a crewman nearby, "tie down the ropes! Knot them good, lad, we don't want to lose the men above in the rigging."

Crushed against his warmth in the icy rain, Kennis studied his lean rugged profile and her feminine interest awakened. A thick lock of jet-black hair, loosed from his queue, fell over his brow into penetrating dark eyes. Impatient, he swept it away. The persistent wind thrust the heavy lock back onto his forehead, and he scowled.

Unable to resist, she giggled.

A kindred spark of amusement flashed across his face, softening the rigid set of his mouth.

The moment passed, his expression hardened again and the warm feeling of camaraderie vanished. "You've no business on deck in this gale, mistress. Have you no more sense than a bairn?" The rain continued to bombard them with icy drops, seeming to confirm his words as he sheltered her from the downpour. His fingers bit into her shoulders as he turned her around and thrust her ahead of him. "Go on, I'll see you safely to your cabin before you're washed overboard."

In this modern world of 1750, men were still lord and master, expecting complete obedience and respect without question. Not surprised by his censure, she opened her mouth to defend herself but grey clouds overhead interrupted, thundering like the boom of cannon fire in a heated battle upon the open sea.

Wave upon wave rolled over and tossed the helpless vessel, crashing against the timber and sailcloth. Thrust from side to side and knee deep in the rushing water, the pair made slow progress across the deck to the safety of the arched doorway that led to the cabins below.

Her mind raced as she clung to him. Who was he? He'd not sailed from the Americas with the other passengers. The ship, skirting the coast of England, stopped at various ports to pick up passengers and unload precious cargo as it traveled to the island of Islay on the western coast of Scotland.

Huddled within the comfort of his embrace, she trembled with cold as brilliant streaks of lightning zigzagged across the sky. His stubbly chin brushed her forehead and she glanced up, searching his face for reassurance as the wind howled, a sea demon loosed from the cavernous pit of hell.

A man of action, Alistair quickly evaluated their perilous position, pulling her close to shield her from a sudden cascade of water. Without warning, he swept her into his arms, tossing her over his shoulder with no more consideration than he might show a meal-sack.

Of all the impudence! Taken by surprise, she struggled to be free from his strong grip. "Unhand me, knave," she cried, kicking her feet and pummeling his back with her fists as the wood planking beneath her bobbed up and down.

"Be still, lass," he gritted, holding tighter, "if you know what's good for you."

His hard shoulder dug into her chest, cutting short her breath as a sharp pain stabbed her ribs. Out of the corner of her eye, she glimpsed the waves continuing to spill over the port side of the ship where she'd stood only moments before, frothing water wetting everything in its path.

He pushed forward, striving against the wind. Kicking open the narrow door to the passenger cabins, he carried her through and set her down.

Finally, she was out of the violent gale and on her own two feet. "You take far more liberty than what is your due, sir. I didn't need your—"

"Gallant rescue?" He cut her short, arching a black brow. "God's truth, mistress," he said. "I could add dauntless, heroic, and any number of fine words to describe my actions but what about yours? You placed yourself in serious danger, idling on deck before a storm."

She stared at him, reading the mockery in his dark eyes. True, she was grateful for his aid but his high-handed treatment of her, combined with the trauma of their ordeal, stirred her lively temper.

Hands on hips, he waited for her apology, expecting her to behave like a proper young lady. When she said nothing, he continued. "You're supposed to apologize, lass," he said gently.

Kennis sensed the cold steel beneath his deceptively calm manner. She pressed her lips together, resisting the urge to speak her mind. And then, in a surprising moment of clarity, understanding washed over her. He meant well, and she felt drawn to him despite his arrogance. Her thoughts raced on in an attempt to understand him more completely. At the very least, he was what, formidable?

She studied him for a moment longer. Aye, he was definitely alarming, especially with that glower darkening his handsome face. Yet her intuition told her that he was more than what he appeared to be, she just couldn't explain why.

On top of it all, her unruly heart insisted that she take his full measure, to discover if he possessed qualities that would set him apart from ordinary men. She immediately dismissed the thought. She'd encountered his type before. In the end, he'd prove to be exactly what he was—a flesh and blood man, just like any other.

The startling revelations quickly passed. Bristling, she glared at him, blurting the first words that popped into her mind. Highland words. Her words, and those of her McCallum kin. "My behavior! Nay, I dinna agree, wi' ye, sir." She rubbed her aching ribs where his hard shoulder had probably bruised her. "Gal'ant an' heroic, indeed," she huffed. "Ye fair near killed me, ye meddlesom' *howtowdie*."[2]

---

[2] *A young unmarried woman: fig., a hen who has not begun to lay*

Alistair gazed at her, wondering what could possibly be running through her mind. She was an open book; he read worry and resentment, mixed with something else that he couldn't identify. At least not yet. Perhaps she'd come to her senses in a few more minutes.

His grim expression gave her pause but patience wasn't her virtue. More than once, her mother counseled her to reign in her temper. All she had to do, Mam said, was ask God to help her, then wait and listen for His still, small voice. Mam was right, as always—small, it was, and so still that she'd missed it altogether.

In any case, the rogue had taken liberties with her, even if he'd come to her rescue. She felt justified taking him to task for his behavior, and surely Mam would agree if she'd witnessed the scene. Wouldn't she? Her doubts surfaced again.

Kennis feared that she'd never be a real lady, demure and refined; she was far too impulsive. Untamed, Grandad said, like the land. 'Twas in her blood, sang its own Highland melody and could never be removed.

Much to her chagrin, she began to shake with cold. Rivulets of seawater trickled down her face and the dripping garments formed a small puddle at her feet. The man didn't care that she was freezing or that the drenching might be the death of her. Acutely aware of her condition, she noted that he was equally wet through. His windswept appearance, however, only seemed to enhance his good looks, making him more appealing than ever.

How unfair! she wanted to scream. Instead she grasped her soggy skirts with shaking hands. "No one," she muttered, wringing out the heavy layers, "has the right to treat me like a piece of baggage or an old meal-sack." She'd not give him the satisfaction of being right by acting like the foolish bairn he'd called her earlier.

Amused, Alistair's ready sense of humor erupted in low laughter, his long-idle interest awakening. He reached out, took hold of her skirts from waist to hem, and gave them a hard wringing twist.

She gasped as he pulled her forward. What might he do next? She crossed her arms over her chest to protect herself.

A smile lingered at the corner of his mouth. He dropped the heavy garments, and his gaze slid down her face as an unfamiliar air played on the strings of his heart. The top of her pert head barely reached his shoulder. Beneath her fair brow, speaking green eyes, framed with thick lashes, met a lightly freckled nose that turned up a little at the tip. Oddly pleased, he leaned toward her, resting a bronzed hand on the low beam above her head.

Her senses reeled and she drew in a sharp breath. His laughing eyes were mere inches from her face. Was he actually going to kiss her? Surprised, her mouth dropped open.

"I fear the cold's muddled your brain, lass," he said, containing his mirth and eyeing her parted lips. "'Tisn't possible for me to be a *howtowdie*, and impolite of you to say such a thing. You'd better get out of those wet skirts and wrap yourself in a warm plaid before the chill you've taken permanently jumbles your thoughts."

He reached out to touch the sodden curls plastered to her cheeks. "Here," his resonant voice lowered, "let me help you." Squeezing a cold trickle of water from both locks, he gently tucked a limp tendril behind each ear. "That's better," he said, satisfied with his handiwork. "I could fetch a plaid if you have need." His eyes sparked with mischief. "We could share."

She bit down hard, struggling not to say something that she might regret later. Too late. Heart pounding, she stepped back, flattening her body against the rough plank wall. "Impolite of me? Ye still had no cause or, or right, sir," she insisted, stammering, "t' heave me o'er your shoulder without so much as a by-your-leave. A proper gentleman would behave wi' more courtesy, an' I've ev'ry intent of reportin' ye t' Captain Murray for plaguin' me." She finished in a rush, thrusting out her chin in defiance.

With a gleam in his eye, he closed the short distance between them. Slowly tracing a line down her cheek with one finger, he cupped her chin in his hand, and waited.

She wriggled uncomfortably, wanting to escape but still he held her captive. He was much too close for comfort and she dared not look into his eyes.

"Did you expect me to bow politely and ask your leave while we were blown away?" He scoffed at her empty threat and open disdain.

She peeped up at him, and involuntarily shivered at his expression. This was going too far. What could he mean by it? She was a gently bred female, mostly used to the men in her immediate family and clan at home in the Highlands. Even during her time in America with the Gilmores, her social life had been limited.

"I've every right, mistress, since the Captain ordered me to keep his passengers safe. *Losh*," his Scots' burr lilted in exasperation, "you were nearly washed overboard. I've a good mind to *skelp* you right here and now, first for being on deck in the storm and then for kicking me after I so gallantly saved you. 'Tis obvious someone needs to teach you a much needed lesson."

Her eyes widened in astonishment. "You wouldn't dare!"

"Wouldn't I?" Holding her stare with a compelling one of his own, he let the stern words sink in. Satisfied that she was finally listening to him, he continued. "Fortunately for you, I'm a reasonable man so I'll offer you a choice—either stay in your cabin like you're told," he smoothly challenged, "or pay a forfeit for your impertinence now." He waited expectantly, hoping she would accept his teasing offer.

Kennis was mortified. "Pay a forfeit?" she repeated, misunderstanding him. "What do you mean, sir? Your help was timely and I'm grateful, but I do object to the mode of your service. 'Twas," her cheeks grew hot, "unseemly."

Some gentleman he turned out to be, expecting a reward. Never had she been treated with so little respect or consideration in her entire life. Thoroughly flustered, she fully betrayed her overwrought emotions, blushing at the reminder of his warm touch. For some reason that she couldn't fathom, it mattered. A lot. She simply must restore her sense of dignity, her womanly pride demanded it.

On impulse, she reached into the folds of her skirt, drew forth a slim leather pouch and shook the few remaining silver coins into the palm of her hand. "Here, take this in payment for your trouble. I'm fully able to take care of myself and don't require your assistance any further."

Hearing a low rumble akin to a growl, she quickly looked up at him in alarm. His smoldering gaze burned through her as she thrust the coins at him. Lowering her eyes in confusion, the glinting links of a gold chain drew her gaze. A small cross, Celtic in design, slipped from its hiding place beneath the collar of his white linen shirt.

A pang of disappointment stole over him at her refusal, and despite his irritation at her offer of coin, Alistair's sense of the ridiculous won out. "Are you certain?" A hint of a smile appeared. "Then I won't trouble you any further. However," he jingled the silver coins in his hand, "I'm truly grieved by your lack of faith in me. 'Tisn't the sort of payment I had in mind." He deliberately lowered his arm from the beam overhead and stared down at her from his full height.

The temperature in the cold passage went up several more degrees. "Let me offer you a wee bit of sound advice—never return a gentleman's aid with coin. He might feel insulted, and you may reap the serious consequences of his displeasure." He glanced down the passage at an approaching sailor. "But I suppose we'll have to wait for a more fitting moment to continue this lesson." He paused, reiterating. "Both of your lessons."

The lurking twinkle in his black coffee eyes deepened as he lightly tossed her the coins. "Keep your silver, lass, you might have need of it before long." His dark gaze shifted from her face to the gold riband threaded through her hair. "In lieu of the forfeit, I'll take this bauble instead and wear it next to my heart to remember you."

He untangled the wet, knotted silk from her sodden hair and stuffed it beneath his shirt. Resuming his earlier stance, he smiled, slowly leaning forward until his face was within an inch of hers.

She gulped. Escape was impossible, he was so close she could see the tiny crow's feet at the corner of his eyes, feel his warm breath on her cheek.

"Better yet, I'll tuck it under my pillow, eh, lass?"

Speechless, she gaped at him, her heart racing.

Eyes dancing, he drew back and reached for her hand, gently stroking her knuckles with his thumb. "God speed and Fare well," he pressed a warm kiss onto her chilled fingers, "until we meet again." Releasing her, he turned on his heel and strode away.

A man just like any other. Dumbfounded, Kennis stood motionless as he retreated around the corner, his soft laughter ringing in her ears. What could she have been thinking? His warm look nearly made her heart stop. The back of her hand still tingled from his kiss and she pressed the spot to her lips. The rogue! He'd deliberately baited her, throwing down a heady gauntlet in the subtle game of flirtation.

His firm tread upon the wooden steps at the end of the passage jerked her back into reality and her temporary confusion turned into disappointment. "I must be fated to meet his kind," she muttered, cross. "Men are the same all over the world, it seems." Bending at the waist, she retrieved the precious coins that had fallen to the floorboards and stalked down the narrow passage to the small cabin she shared with her charges, Jennie and Molly Gilmore. She yanked open the door and glanced quickly around. Much to her relief, neither girl was present in the room.

She stripped off her wet clothing and drew a fresh shift from the trunk. Slipping a dry blouse over her head, she tucked it into her woolen skirts. "If I ever meet the man again," she vowed to no one in particular, "I'll settle the score." Smiling at various ways that she could repay his impertinence, she flung a woolen shawl around her shoulders and secured it with her buckle.

Once the shawl had been an *arisaid*, a bright tartan plaid buckling in the front and winding around her body, Highland style. Now it was a drab yellow brown, dyed with a brew made from the lichen that she collected herself near her Highland home. The silver buckle, a thistle of Scotland set within a circlet of amethysts, seemed out of place on the plain garment. She fingered it with love, a precious gift received from her father on her fourteenth birthday. A family heirloom, the buckle passed from generation to generation of young McCallum women.

Sighing, she lay down on the bed, staring blankly at the wall. "What kind of life, Lord," she said aloud, "to what kind of Scotland am I returning? Home is in the Highlands, not on the tip of an island." Her mother now resided on the Isle of Lewis with Morrison kin. Sir Hugh Morrison had offered her a home at Dun Eistein, following the uprising in 1745 and extradition of Jacobite rebels. The McCallum ancestral home, Dunchalum Castle, lay nestled in the heights of Argyll overlooking Lochangless on the mainland of Scotland.

She fixed her gaze on the rough beams overhead, lost in memory. The horror of the night that she, her mother and sister were driven from their home was permanently imprinted upon her mind. Awakened in the wee hours of the morning by urgent voices, she jumped up from her bed and pushed a chest beneath the small window in her tower bedchamber. Climbing onto it, she opened the shutter to peer out into the gloom of the night, trying to get a glimpse of the man pounding at the gate. In the distance, the sky glowed with an unnatural reddish light above the whispering trees.

"The redcoats are comin'," he shouted, panting for breath from his footrace to the castle. "Tell the mistress to flee without delay."

Her breath caught in her throat— Dear God, the man looked like Calum McCallum. Was the battle over then? Her heart nearly stopped beating and sudden fear gripped her. Where were Father and Robbie? She leapt from the chest and grabbed her shift from the hook, quickly dressing.

Her small pack lay on the floor. She stuffed it with a few necessities, hoping to return to gather more of her belongings. She picked up a small book of prayers and carefully tucked it between her clothes. A sense of foreboding overcame her; she would never return. Shaking off the distressing thought, she pulled on her boots. The door flew open and she rose to her feet.

"Kennis," her mother called. "Kennis, love, we must make haste. We're leaving now, bring only what you can carry."

"I heard the messenger, Mam, I'm ready." She followed her mother into the passage.

"Help Mairi while I see to the others," she said, anxious. "They're burning the village and we must go without delay."

Kennis grabbed her arm as she turned to leave. "But what of Father and Robbie?"

Tears filled her mother's eyes. "Not now, Kennis. Say nothing to your sister, and please hurry."

Knotted rope dug painfully into her back through the thin mattress on her bunk aboard the *Faoileag*. Only God could redeem lost time, but she would never abandon her search for her beloved brother. She sat up, restless, wondering if the winds had abated or if there was merely a lull in the storm. Soon her feet would touch solid ground and she looked forward to the moment with pleasure.

She yearned to roam through wooded glens and splash in the shallow burn that flowed into Lochangless. She would climb the *clach dion*[3] in the hillside near the water that she and Robbie dubbed *Castle Rock*. The flat-topped boulder narrowed to two sharp points, creating twin platforms that jutted out over the water.

As children, the two shared marvelous adventures in the hidden passage beneath, real and imagined, from a simple meal of bread and cheese to pretending to be outlaws or pirates hiding stolen treasure. Occasionally, Robbie was the heroic knight and Kennis, the fair damsel in distress.

---

[3] *Shelter stone*

"Robbie, lad, where are you now," she worried, her brows knit together. "Are you well, are you even alive? God forbid such a thought!" After the Scottish defeat on Culloden Moor in April of 1746, her father, Robert, was executed for his participation in the uprising against the King of England. Robbie's fate was less certain; imprisoned at Dumbarton, the McCallum family received no word of him until the English government published lists of deported Jacobite prisoners.

Disheartened, she considered fellow Scots she'd met on her journey. Most were displaced, robbed of home and country forever with little to no hope of return. The determined spirit that drove them, a will to succeed in spite of hardship, amazed her. Encouraged, a new resolve grew within her to help the poor and needy. How to support such a venture was in question, but she knew exactly where to begin. What place could be more fitting than the Highlands?

Clans all over Scotland suffered in the aftermath of the uprising. The widespread destitution and the resulting need staggered her mind. Providing food, clothing and shelter for the multitudes was an enormous task. She would begin with one person or clan at a time, and trust God to use her as an instrument of His healing and provision. God is the source of every need and would use her, Kennis McCallum, to demonstrate His love to the people. She would rally others to do the same, making a difference in the lives of the poor Highlanders.

The tempest raged on. Shaken from her daydream by an ear-splitting thunderbolt and the sound of cracking wood, Kennis jumped up from the cot. "Lord, what's happening?" She tottered to the door and opened it, peering down the empty passage. She debated on the wisdom of venturing to the Gilmore's cabin in the midst of the storm.

The vessel pitched as she stepped out of her cabin. She fell to the rough floorboards with a hard smack. Pushing herself off the floor and onto her knees, she looked directly at a pair of black boots. "Mr. Gilmore." Surprised, she gazed up into his face. "I was just coming to see you, sir."

"Here, lass, give me your hand." He placed his own on the wall for support as the ship continued to heave, then reached out and pulled her to her feet. "You'd best stay in your cabin, Kennis, unless you need our company. 'Tis a fearsome storm."

"I know." She rubbed her elbow, and winced. "I was caught on deck earlier."

"So I heard."

Taken aback, she looked at him sharply. "From whom had you such news?"

His eyes twinkled with good humor. "I went in search of you and bumped into a gentleman of my acquaintance. He said he'd just returned from rescuing a fair maiden who was almost washed overboard."

She flushed. Hmph, swept overboard indeed! "Hardly, sir. The water seemed calm enough when I went out to take the air. The wind was strong, but I'd have made it inside by myself, given the opportunity."

He grinned at her denial and said nothing in return.

Kennis knew that in his silence Mr. Gilmore, having heard the tale from the rogue himself, was naturally more inclined to believe the man. Such was the way of the world.

He spoke again as she turned back to her door. "You should know by now that the calm before a storm is a warning, lass, after our travels. No respecter of anyone, or anything, the wind. Of a truth," he wagged his head, "a body can be washed overboard in a *twink* by rough water, and I'm glad you're still with us. I don't think I could've faced your mother without you." He smiled encouragingly. "I'll bring the girls by later. I came to tell you that we're invited to a farewell supper with the captain tonight, if the weather clears."

"Very well, sir. I'll stay here until then." Returning to her cabin, she threw herself onto the bed. Weary, she closed her eyes and fell into a troubled sleep, instantly transported to a distant shore.

Shadows lay deep along the ancient wooded footpath that led to the dark waters of the loch early in the Highland morning. A cold mist swirled upward and enshrouded the shoreline, dampening her woolen plaid and ankle-length garments. Moistened tendrils of wheat-colored hair clung to her temples.

Ten minutes more and the inky water would be within view. Longing welled up within her breast for the sight and the sound of the gently lapping tide, followed by an unprecedented joy. Would the place of her heart's desire be the same as she remembered it, or had her dreams and imaginations created a feigned reality? Trudging through these woods, familiar scenes and voices from both a recent and distant past floated upon the air, speaking her name.

She carefully descended the rugged terrain of the hillside, hearing the voices more distinctly. Only moments, and she would break free from the trees; the heather on the high hill before her would cast a purplish hue onto the gray shadow of the castle looming overhead as its honeyed sweetness, wafting on the breeze, mingled with the smell of fresh water and earth.

Dawn broke; the castle battlements became visible. The rays of the sun diffused the mist, clearing it away, as diamonds twinkled upon the rippling water at its foot. She heard a faint rustling made by some creature, perhaps on the hunt, hoping even as she hoped that this search was not in vain. Again the voices—nearer to her, urging her on—or maybe it was merely the echo of her wishing heart. She must hurry lest she miss the sunrise and the vision about to unfold before her eyes.

She awoke with a start and brushed her hand across her eyes, trying to focus. Beads of perspiration dampened her brow, reminiscent of the mist in her dream. The dream, she puzzled, what did it portend? This was the third time it had occurred since her departure from America.

Chapter 3

Carefully Laid Plans

"I've arranged a rendezvous with that villain Denoon tonight."

Alistair MacDougall stood before the Captain's desk examining numerous maps and charts. The evening sun streamed through the window behind his imposing figure. "Have you collected new information concerning our Jacobites? I'd hoped to hear a good report about your findings."

"Nay, Alistair," Donald Murray, captain of the *Faioleag*, replied. "I've made discreet inquiries at every port between Bristol and Dundee. The hawkers are careful and don't want to talk." He puffed an imperfect ring of smoke into the air. "I hear they're keeping quiet for fear of reprisal from the king's men."

He snorted. "Afraid of George, are they? The Duke of Cumberland's agents more like, although it's been four years since Culloden. Tell me," he abruptly changed the subject, "how many pounds have you expended to gain information on the three men we're picking up tonight?"

The Captain smiled. "Not enough. Consider it my contribution to a worthy cause."

"You shouldn't, Donald." Alistair frowned. "I'm well able to cover the expenses incurred for this venture."

"And you shouldn't be set on paying for the freedom of every slave in the market, Scot or no," he argued, "it will break you. The numbers are large, notwithstanding the added burden of the widows and children."

"Nonsense." Alistair turned over the paper in his hand, dismissing the thought. "As soon as possible, I'll introduce a plan to his grace to aid the survivors of Culloden and their families, as well as put an end to slavery in Scotland."

"You mean what survivors are left, and not forced to depart their own country." Captain Murray eyed him skeptically. "An enormous task for one man, I still say. And you firmly believe Argyll will sympathize with you?"

"Why shouldn't he?" He glanced at his friend and compatriot. "Not unless he's thick with the likes of men like Denoon."

"Denoon's a Campbell *sept*[4] of Argyll, but go ahead and believe what you will, 'tis your kin and your gold." Donald shrugged, and blew a double ring of smoke before picking up a letter that was lying on his desk. "Jacobite rebels have no place in the halls of the Campbells."

"True," Alistair nodded, "but the uprising's over. Too many men have been sentenced, died untimely deaths. I don't believe the duke's involved in the slave trade. He's an honorable man in that regard, I'm certain."

"I won't argue with you, lad. I'm not acquainted with the man personally, only by report." He scrutinized the document spread out on his lap and muttered aloud. "I still don't know what to make of this."

"Make of what?" Alistair continued to study the chart he'd pulled from the bottom of the pile. He regarded it intently, memorizing every line and navigational marking.

"This letter." He nodded at the parchment on his lap. "I received it at my last stop in Jamaica, before I returned to England. 'Tis a list of names, commoners and noblemen alike. The writer, a Captain Grahame, claims that the men whose names are recorded here are in the slave business."

Alistair looked up from the chart he perused. "Sounds interesting. May I see it?"

"Thought you might be curious." Donald handed him the parchment.

---

[4] *A clan family name*

"How did this come to you? This Captain Grahame must be a rascal, to accuse these men of slaving, and treason."

"A man brought it to the ship, said he'd received a shilling to deliver it. I never saw him, and Sutton said he wouldn't give his name. What puzzles me," he added, "'tis how he knew to bring it to me."

Alistair looked at him squarely. "I'd like to know the answer to that riddle as well. Do you think we're discovered?" His dark brows drew together as he studied the missive. "There's one name on this list that intrigues me."

"And who might that be?"

"Cameron Campbell of Argyll."

"Ho," his friend snickered, "and you're sure his grace has no interest in the business?"

"Aye," he said, "Cameron Campbell's a devious man. He may be the duke's kinsman, in fact," he smiled, "a relation of mine as well but his most obvious ploy is to insinuate himself into the circle of men of influence. I don't trust him."

"I see." Donald rose, stepped past Alistair and opened a small window. "I'll have Sutton ask the men, find out if they knew the fellow." He tapped his pipe against the wood sill, emptying its contents into the water below. "Are you coming to supper tonight? You'll need to change your attire."

"Nay, I can't, I must rendezvous in a timely manner or lose the rewards of our hard earned labor." He crossed his arms, pensive. So much rested on tonight's journey. He could ill afford a delay and aside from his errand, his men were counting on him. "But you can greet Peyton Gilmore's lovely charge for me, and give her my congratulations at not being washed overboard during the storm." The corner of his mouth curved upward in a crooked smile.

"You can tell her yourself." Donald joined him at the door and peered out the portal glass onto the weather deck. "It appears that my guests are arriving."

"Then I'll be going." Alistair slowly lifted the latch. "'Tis a pity I must, I've no time to spend with the lass now, when I promised I would with the utmost sincerity." He grinned, recalling the fair-haired lass he first watched twirling on the quarterdeck, oblivious to the approaching storm. Bonnie, she was, and if time permitted, he'd gladly fulfill his vow to pursue his forfeit. He chuckled over their brief encounter, knowing that he caused her considerable annoyance and confusion. "Alas," he placed his feathered bonnet over his heart, "duty calleth."

Donald laughed and followed him to the door. "That chick is well guarded, lad. You'll have your hands full if you pursue her too closely."

"Exactly," he said, joining in the Captain's laughter.

"Someday, Alistair, you'll go too far and find yourself in parson's mousetrap before you're wishing it." He clasped his shoulder. "God go with you, lad."

"Aye, and in His name, Donald, I'll succeed in this venture of ours for Him."

Chapter 4

Stowaway

Childish voices interrupted Kennis' solitude as Jennie, the elder and livelier of her two charges, burst into the cabin like a small whirlwind. Sweet Molly quietly followed in the wake of her rambunctious elder sister.

"Kennis," Jennie cried, "Papa said you'd be back soon." She danced around the room. "Did you know Mam's seasick? Cook says 'tis from the storm. And, Cook says that Molly and me are good sailors 'cause we weren't sick even a wee little bit *and*," she crowed, "he's making us a special treat!"

"Not sick one wee little bit," echoed Molly. Her pink cheeks dimpled as her mouth turned upward into a soft smile. "A special treat!" She clapped her pudgy hands happily together.

"You're not supposed to leave the cabin alone, Jennie," Kennis reminded her.

"I know, I'm sorry." The child bounced onto the lower bunk, golden curls flying. "But I need to tell you something important! We met a *braw* Highlander during the storm and guess what?" Her blue eyes sparkled. "Papa told him what you looked like and asked him if he'd seen you. He said Aye, and I couldn't hear the rest." Pouting, she crossed her arms. "I wanted to hear what he said about you."

"Laughed, did he?" Annoyed, Kennis glanced down at the stocking she'd just finished darning. What insolence. But then, she had no reason to be surprised based on his previous behavior and as far as she was concerned, a *braw* laddie had best mind his manners as an ugly one. "You heard nothing more of their conversation?"

"Nay," she sulked. "I don't think they wanted me to hear a thing."

Jennie continued to chatter and Kennis' mind wandered. The dark stranger had picked her up as if she were lighter than a feather, which she knew that she was not. Her heart pounded fiercely, remembering the feel of his strong arms about her, the warmth of his breath misting over her cold skin as his face drew near to her own. Rosy color appeared on each of her cheeks at the thought.

She slowly rubbed the back of her hand where his lips had softly caressed her skin. The spot still seemed to tingle of its own accord. "What a foolish girl I am!" she muttered. No girl with any sense of self-respect should want to be kissed by a complete stranger, especially a man who was merely playing games, but he'd been so close and— She closed her eyes briefly, her imagination soaring. It was wanton; he held her captive in his arms for a few moments and she submitted to her ardor.

A knock on the door brought her back to her senses. She stood, pulling it open. "Mr. Gilmore," she said, scanning the hall. He was alone. "Good evening. I trust Mrs. Gilmore 'tis recovering from her illness?"

"Aye, that she is, lass. She'll be well soon enough."

"Can I do anything for her, sir?" she said in earnest. "Sit with her awhile perhaps? I've plenty of free time at my disposal."

"That's kind of you, Kennis, but she'll be all the better for a wee respite." He eyed the three girls, displeased. "Och, I thought you'd all be dressed for the Captain's supper by now. I'd best be off while you put on your finery. We mustn't be late."

"What about us, Papa?" Jennie interrupted eagerly. "Are Molly and me invited to sup with the Captain, too?"

"Aye, of course you are, lassie," he said, pinching her chin, "so be sure to wear the blue dress your mother had made up for you." The child looked at him, an innocent question in her eyes. "It brings out the bonnie color of your eyes, love, like the heather in full bloom." Her face glowed with pleasure at the compliment.

Molly tugged on his sleeve. "And me, Papa, what shall I wear?"

"Oh, the green, little one," he tweaked her nose, "makes your eyes glisten like twin emeralds staring out from your pert face." Mr. Gilmore's reward was swift; the two little girls embraced him with fervor.

With a pang in her heart, Kennis wondered what Mairi, her little sister, was like now. She'd not seen her in almost four years and of course, Robbie and her father were long gone. Aside from Grandad, the men in her immediate family were in short supply.

Hackles rising, her thoughts returned to the rogue who teased her without mercy. No doubt he would be among the invited guests at the Captain's dinner party. Her gold-flecked eyes flashed, sparking with indignation at the memory of how he manhandled her.

To her way of thinking, courtesy and honor pronounced the gentleman, so he most certainly didn't qualify. In fact, he'd proven quite the opposite, and now she discovered that he'd mocked her in front of her charges. Grimacing, she felt equally dissatisfied with her own behavior. Her actions were far from circumspect, so she'd best stop pointing the finger.

When Mr. Gilmore returned promptly at seven, the cabin door flew open before he could knock. "Jennie lass, are you that hungry? You're supposed to make a gentleman wait for you."

She flung her arms about him. "I can't wait, Papa, I'm too excited!"

He smoothed her golden curls and she beamed at him. "We'd best be going then," he said, chuckling. "I must say, you're all fine as pence tonight. I wonder how many hearts you'll conquer."

Amused, Kennis decided that she'd enjoy conquering only one, just for a wee bit of playful revenge. It wasn't likely to happen, and he probably wouldn't even be present at table tonight. Just as well. He'd be sure to tease her about something.

"Fuil lass," she said, in a quandary as the girls followed Mr. Gilmore from the room. "Why can you not think straight about the man?" Pausing at her looking glass, she stared at her reflection. The familiar green of her eyes sparkled with life. But privately, she felt that her expression and temperament had grown serious since Robbie and her father went away to war.

Wondering what the future would bring, she hummed a tune while fluffing her hair one last time, then closed the door behind her. She trailed behind Mr. Gilmore and the girls, minding her steps on the rough deck, when a chorus of male voices rose in dissent as the foursome neared the Captain's cabin.

"I say we never should've let the villains aboard. Look at what's come of it."

"Silence, Alan, we've company." The discussion ceased and two of the men quickly departed. The other members of the group, passengers of the *Faioleag*, nodded to Mr. Gilmore as he and the girls passed.

"I wonder what that was about," Mr. Gilmore remarked when the four were safely out of earshot. "Not promising, eh?" He grasped Molly's hand and continued to walk across the deck.

"Nay, sir," Kennis agreed. "Upset about demands upon their coin, no doubt." Her lively curiosity awakened at the possibilities and she peeked over her shoulder at the men one last time. "Mr. Gilmore, do you know all of those gentlemen?"

"Aye, most of them." He gazed away from her for a moment toward the retreating men. Kennis wished he would be more forthcoming but Mr. Gilmore generally held his own counsel. "Ah, here we are at Captain Murray's cabin. Perhaps we'll discover what's amiss over supper."

Four pairs of eyes turned to the paneled door as he raised his hand to knock. Without warning, the door squeaked open as if by magick, and out stepped the man who had occupied her thoughts for the better portion of the day.

She scanned him with a grudging yet admiring eye. The faded hunter green jacket that he wore suited his rugged appearance, and black leather breeks hugged muscular thighs. A single white feather dangled from the cockaded bonnet that he held in one hand and a travel-stained wool cloak, slung hastily across his shoulders to keep out unwanted cold, seemed in peril of falling to the planks.

The tooled grip of a *skean dhu*, a Highland dagger, peeking out from the top of his tall boot added to the aura of danger about his tall person. He was clearly not a man to trifle with and she wondered about his departure, at what circumstance drew him away before the Captain's farewell supper had even begun.

He bowed to Mr. Gilmore. "Good evening, sir."

"Good evening, Laird." Mr. Gilmore returned the polite gesture. "You're not staying for supper tonight? The ladies will be sorely disappointed."

His eyes held a glimmer of a smile. "Unfortunately, business that I can't delay has called me ashore tonight. A galley awaits me even now." He glanced at Kennis, slowly surveying her figure from head to toe as he spoke to Mr. Gilmore. "I'm sorry the ladies will be disappointed, and I sincerely regret not furthering our acquaintance." He met and held her eyes, studying her face for a brief moment. "But I can't avoid it."

Her color rose at his deliberate scrutiny. Ooo, the impertinence of the man.

"Then accept our good wishes for a pleasant journey."

"All of you, sir?" His dark gaze remained on Kennis.

Mr. Gilmore laughed aloud as she glared at him.

He grinned. "Now I must be off," he said, inclining his head in farewell. "Good evening, and God speed." With long strides, he crossed the deck and quickly disappeared from view.

"Don't *fash* yourself, Kennis," Mr. Gilmore said, "'tis to be expected. Move along now, girls." He gave them a gentle shove. "We'd best not keep the Captain waiting."

"To be expected, sir," she repeated. "But why?" She met her kinsman's eyes squarely. "Mr. Gilmore, we've not been properly introduced, and I expect a gentleman to behave like one. I think he's rude," she said frankly, glancing across the deck. Just then, the laird's resonant voice carried on the wind as he shouted orders to his waiting men.

"I know, lass," Mr. Gilmore said, eyes gleaming with amusement, "but if you wanted to be made acquainted, you should've asked me earlier in the day. Why, he's none other than—" The roar of an exploding firearm cut him off mid-sentence. "What the deuce!" he exclaimed, thrusting the girls behind him as the cabin door flew open and Captain Murray hurried out, thrusting his cap onto his head.

The Captain quickly strode across the deck. "Ahoy, Donal! What's going forward?"

"I don't know, sir," Donal bellowed in return. "Blew off the starboard!"

Mr. Gilmore hustled the girls into the Captain's cabin. While he reassured the little ones, Kennis peered out the door, trying to discover the cause of the gunfire. The crew rushed from their quarters below the forecastle and her curiosity peaked when she saw her tormentor reappear on deck. What was he up to now? She imagined the adventures that she could have if she were a man.

Society was certainly less forgiving of women. A woman's virtue was too easily compromised. Her brows drew together in a thoughtful frown. But why not a man's? It was such a ridiculous double standard. Men should be held equally accountable for their behavior, and morals.

"Kennis," Mr. Gilmore said firmly, interrupting her musings. "Come away from that door."

Reluctant, she obeyed, stealing one last look. "Are you going to go and see what's happening, sir?" She stood before him in eager anticipation, hoping he'd attempt to discover what was happening outside.

"Nay, the Captain's more than able to take care of this matter without my interference." His firm tone indicated that he would stand no nonsense from her. "I must stay and look to you all, and leave the Captain's business to himself."

Disappointed, she gazed around the Captain's cabin, surprised at its generous proportion and elegant furnishings. The rich, warm woods, crimson draperies, and book-lined shelves stood in sharp contrast to the starkness of the cabin she shared with the girls. A long table, complete with place settings of fine china and silver on a white linen cloth caught her eye. She helped Molly to a chair and Jennie followed suit. Although her first priority was to care for the children, her mind wandered. She longed to know what occurred at this very moment elsewhere on the ship.

Before long, the door opened and Captain Murray stepped into the spacious room. "I beg your pardon, ladies and gentlemen, but you must excuse me for a while longer. My first officer, Mr. Sutton, will be your host while I'm away." He bowed and hurriedly left the room.

"'Tis our pleasure," Mr. Gilmore murmured. Intent on polite conversation, he added, "I'm sorry that my wife is unable to attend this evening, Mr. Sutton. She took sick when the storm set in, never was a good sailor."

"There are many folks not meant to grace the sea, sir, who are otherwise most charming," he returned cordially. "On behalf of the Captain, may I say, we'll miss your lady tonight."

Kennis listened to this exchange of pleasantries in frustration. Altogether, the entire group was unconcerned about what interested her the most. She awaited Captain Murray's return to the dinner party with impatience. Fueled by her curiosity, a plan to determine what was happening on the ship took shape in her mind. Not able to stand the suspense any longer, she rose from the table, urged on by a whim.

"Mr. Gilmore," she said sweetly, "pardon my intrusion, sir. I must seek the privacy of my chamber."

He nodded, half-listening, failing to see the sparkle in her eyes before returning to his conversation with the gentleman to his right.

Politely excusing herself to the other guests, she eagerly slipped out of the cabin.

Kennis shivered in the cool night air, wrapping her shawl tightly about her shoulders. She paused, listening for the firm tread of the sentries making their rounds. The flickering light cast by the torches eerily illuminated the darkness, her figure an indistinct shadow on the moonless deck.

Gathering her skirts together to prevent the telltale swishing sound, she tiptoed down the creaky steps and stole across the freshly swabbed boards to the piles of cargo stacked against the gunwale. She slipped around the corner as two men lowered a crate over the side of the ship. Careful to avoid the torch light, she hid in the gloom until Splash! A crate dropped to the depths below.

"Ho, lads," a voice grated into the night. "We can't afford to lose them all to the sea! Get another and we'll be off."

She couldn't place the voice although she recognized the Scots' burr easily enough. Concealed in the stacks, she searched for an avenue of escape. Lud, the footsteps were coming directly toward her! To her dismay, two men quickly advanced. She pressed closer to one crate and it shifted; the lid was loose! *Should I?* On impulse, she raised it several inches and climbed inside. As she settled herself on a prickly bed of straw, the shuffling of brogues and the hush of whispered voices was unmistakable.

"Look, we done the Cap'n's biddin' and I'm not goin' back empty-handed, see?" a rough voice threatened.

"Don't be stupid, ye lackey. Ye'll blow m' cover on this tub an' our plans will be for naught. Ye leave the lassies alone, ye hear me?" He grabbed the smaller man by the collar and shoved him against the crate.

Kennis jumped and stifled a scream as the two bumped against her hiding place.

"The Cap'n's got plans, see, and his blackness'll pay fer his impert'nence."

"Git your hands off me! An' how's tha' t' happen, eh? The man's no *gowk*[5]."

---

[5] *Fool, idiot*

49

"Through ol' Crooknose, lad." He thumped him on the head. "Use your noggin t' think fer once and let's git out o' here!" The villain dragged his unwilling comrade off by the collar.

Kennis sat motionless, listening to the men reveal the threads of some nefarious plot. Fortunately, they had no idea that she was privy to their conversation. How silly she was to suppose she'd get away with a little sleuthing of her own.

Several more minutes passed, the whispers ceased, and the night grew still except for the noises rising from the men on the galley below. Breathing a sigh of relief, she placed her hand on the lid above. Suddenly, footsteps sounded on the boards and the crate tipped over. She crashed hard against the side and groaned. The villains had returned and if they found her, they might do unspeakable things. But what if she was stuck inside the crate, she worried, in turmoil about what to do. Another frightening thought occurred to her. And what if no one found her, either?

"Wha' was tha' noise, Rab?" a man exclaimed, lifting a corner of the crate. "Och, 'tis a heavy one."

"I dinna hear nothin', Jocko."

"Come on, lads, quit chatterin' up there!" A shout rose from the galley waiting below. "We don't have all night."

"Well, heavy or no, we've got t' get this crate onto the galley." He lifted the corner again and his companion slid the rope underneath, securing it with a tight knot.

The crate swayed and Kennis felt dizzy, knowing that she was hanging in the air over the open sea. If the crate missed its mark on the vessel, no one would ever know that she'd sunk to a watery grave. Frozen in place, she clung desperately to the walls of her small prison, incapable of screaming, terrified to make a sudden movement that might tip it, and her, into the icy depths below.

Thud, the crate hit the wooden belly of the waiting galley. "Ow, that hurt." She rubbed her aching shoulder, berating herself for her stupidity and resolving to put an immediate end to her dilemma.

Discovery was certain, and if she didn't reveal herself soon, she'd sail away from the *Faioleag* to an obscure destination with strange companions, provided she didn't suffocate first. She started to push upward when a familiar voice rang out into the still night.

"Shove off, lads," a rich voice boomed. "We've an appointment with old Nick himself tonight!" The men laughed raucously.

The Highland galley pitched in the water and her heart lurched. Worried, she searched for a knothole and finding none, pushed gently upward again, peeping out of the crack. Fresh air rushed in, filling her lungs, and she realized that she sat conspicuously in the center of the boat next to the tall mast.

The moon and stars shone bright in the clear night sky, shedding light on the galley and the oarsmen. The wind whipped the sail as the oars sliced through the water in a steady rhythm. Men to her left and right conversed, occasional footsteps shuffled alongside.

Time passed slowly and sleep was impossible, giving her ample time to consider the dialogue she'd overheard. What betrayal were those vile men planning? If only she knew what their vague words intended, she could warn *His Blackness*, whoever he was, unless he too was a villain and deserved his fate.

Every man deserves a chance to be forgiven, Kennis lass.

With familiar clarity, her father's voice intruded into her thoughts, reminding her of God's love for all men. Tears welled up in her eyes at the memory, and feeling suddenly overwhelmed with sorrow and unbearably cramped to boot, she fought her rising panic.

Her legs tingled, on fire with growing numbness, and she anxiously wiggled her toes. Time was running out, she just knew it, and she desperately wondered how to explain her conduct when a firm voice interrupted her thoughts.

"Almost at the rendezvous, lads, a few more miles and we'll stop and have a drink."

A drink! The horrid man didn't realize how much his words tormented her. But how could he, when he had no idea she was aboard the galley? She was fair parched, and the sloshing oars only increased her need to quench her thirst. Choking on a sob, she inhaled the fine dust in the crate and managed to smother a cough. Her tickling nose finally betrayed her. "Achoo!" she softly sneezed.

"Rab, did ye hear sneezin'?" Jocko asked his long-time friend. He jerked his head toward the crate at his elbow.

"Hearin' a ghostie, Jocko?" Rab teased.

"Nay," he said, affronted. "I'm no *gowk*."

Listening, Kennis grew still, dreading the inevitable confrontation. Perhaps she should reveal her presence now. Nay, she wavered, maybe she'd wait. Escape was certain at the next destination. All of a sudden, strumming fingers rolled like thunder on the wooden lid above her head, and she gasped.

"What are you chattering about, lads?" The rogue's resonant voice boomed in her ears.

Her heart pounded, certain discovery loomed directly above. *Oh, mercy.* She shut her eyes tight and still his mocking gaze appeared. He would probably *skelp* her, especially since he'd threatened to do so once already. It was a common enough practice, unfortunately, and she'd been victim of her own impertinence enough times to recognize the difference between a promise and a threat.

Rab nodded toward the crate. "Jocko here says he heard sneezin' in yon box, Laird."

"Sneezing," Alistair repeated, incredulous, "in the crate? Impossible, I checked it myself before we hauled it aboard."

He shrugged. "If ye say so, Laird."

Kennis braced herself, staring resolutely into the darkness, caught in her own net. He would never believe that she was there by accident, that she'd overheard important information about a plot endangering a man's life.

"Here Rab, bring me that lantern." He started to pry the lid open, found it loose and tossed it aside. While Rab held the lantern aloft, he peered inside. "Well, what have we here?"

The light spilled into the crate, revealing the top of her golden head as the cool night air swept over her. She shivered. The dread moment had arrived and she reluctantly lifted her face. Her heart sank to her toes when his forbidding gaze slammed into hers.

"Seems we've got a stowaway, lads." He reached in, pulled her to her feet and swung her easily out of the box. When he let go of her hands, she sank to her knees, her weakened legs buckling beneath her.

He leaned over and surprisingly gentle, helped her to sit upright. "Lost your legs, eh lass?" he said. "Serves you right for sneaking aboard." Kneeling beside her, he reached out to lift her skirts above her ankles.

Humiliated, she smacked his hand away. She'd never demean herself by sneaking aboard his or any other man's boat. "It wasn't intentional." She looked away, and sniffed.

"No?" He cocked a dark brow. "I hope not, for your sake. Here now," he said, impassive, "I only mean to help restore your circulation, so be still like a good lass." He pressed his quivering lips together. "But don't think I won't discover what you're doing aboard. Rab," he said to the man holding the lantern, "fetch the lass a drink." He set himself to the task of easing the cramping pain in her legs.

Kennis gratefully accepted the proffered mug and thirstily gulped down its contents.

"Easy, mistress," he said, "'tisn't water."

"You could've warned me," she choked. "I thought—"

"No matter, drink it and you'll feel better." He appraised her condition. "Are you hungry?"

She shook her head. "Nay." She'd never request a boon of him under the circumstances if she could help it. The light pressure he exerted with his kneading fingers on her bare right calf, then the left, embarrassed her enough. She scowled. The *fuil* stocking would fall down.

"Feel better?" She nodded. "Good." He rose to his feet, towering over her. "Can you walk?"

Kennis tried to stand, failed miserably and was swept into his strong arms once again. He set her down on a thick plaid in the bow of the cruising galley. "Now," he said curtly, tossing her another to wrap up in, "suppose you tell me why I find you on my galley in the middle of the night on the open sea, in a crate I brought from England." He stood with arms folded, waiting.

She winced and gave him a fleeting glance, hesitating to speak at his stern tone. "Well, I—" The words constricted in her throat.

"You what?" he said, impatient. "Come now, lass, I want the truth." He gazed at her, intent on his purpose.

She raised her head, warmth spreading through her from the brew she'd consumed. "It was a mistake," she said simply.

A flash of annoyance crossed his face. "Your mistake, mistress, is in not telling me exactly what I want to know. I should've skelped you before, to keep you from such foolish behavior." He leaned over, tightly gripping her arms as he pulled her to her feet. The plaid fell from her shoulders to the wooden planking.

"Now out with it before I lose my patience entirely."

Irrationally angered, she jerked away from his stronger grip and on impulse raised her hand, palm up, to slap him.

His eyes glinted mirthlessly. "I wouldn't if I were you."

Dropping her hand, she stepped back, turning to face the dark rippling water. "I was curious about what was happening on the *Faioleag*," she began in her own defense. "After the gun fired, Captain Murray was absent most of the evening. When he finally returned," she shrugged, "he told the company assembled in his cabin nothing. After consigning us to the care of Mr. Sutton, he left again. I excused myself and went to see what was going forward. I heard voices and hid behind the crates." She pursed her lips, reluctant to continue, knowing how silly the tale must sound to him. "Then, before I knew what was happening, I heard footsteps coming toward me and there was no avenue of escape. I didn't want to be caught, so I lifted the lid on the crate and climbed in. Faith," she said, exasperated. "I never intended to stow away on your vessel. Why would I?"

"I don't know. You tell me," he said sardonically. "God's truth, mistress, you'd have me believe that you were caught snooping, made a poor decision, and nothing more?" He lightly grasped her chin with strong fingers and turned her face upward, staring doubtfully into her eyes.

Kennis' heart fluttered, held captive by the soft touch of his fingertips. She wondered if he felt the same quiver at her nearness. "I already told you what I was doing. In fact," she suddenly recalled, "those two men—"

"Do you realize," he interrupted, unable to pull himself away from the blue-green depths of her eyes, "what might have happened to you if the rope had broken? Did you see the other crate come loose and sink to the bottom of the sea?"

Alistair wanted to shake her, stunned by her thoughtless negligence. He dropped his hand and tightly gripped her shoulders.

"What am I to do with you? I have important business to conduct tonight and I can't drag you into the middle of it. Did you stop to consider Captain Murray's responsibility toward you, and the feelings of Mr. and Mrs. Gilmore and their family? Don't look so surprised, I make it my business to know who I travel with when I go abroad, which is more than I can say for you."

He leered at her. "How do you know I won't ravish you, mistress, or allow my men to take advantage of you? You're a foolish bairn, wandering about and putting your nose where it doesn't belong. If Captain Murray had wanted to apprise you of his affairs, he would have made them your concern. Do you expect me to believe that nonsensical story you so glibly recanted? I assure you, I'm no fool." He dropped his hands from her shoulders and stood glaring down at her. "Well, what do you have to say for yourself?"

Mortified, she forgot about the plot she'd uncovered and stepped back, astonished that he would berate her so abominably. She'd not received such a tongue-lashing since her father, Robert, sternly admonished her for taking a sailboat out on rough water, unaccompanied and without his permission.

"Afraid? You should be." He clearly misunderstood her retreat. "Be glad I've enough restraint not to turn you over my knee right now."

He railed on, and she ceased to be dismayed at his effrontery. Her remorse quickly faded, along with the apology she almost uttered. At his unjust estimation of her character and the disavowal of her honest account of why she stood before him on the galley, her Highland temper flamed. Obstinate *fuil* man! He was obviously past due for a good set down. Perhaps no one dared to challenge his authority often enough, if ever. Well, she wasn't the Black McKinnon's granddaughter for naught.

She clenched her fists at her side. "I'm nae afraid o' ye! Only a churl would treat a lady in th' unco' way ye've treated me. I've endeavored t' be truthful but still ye accuse me falsely. Ye've insulted me ev'ry way conceivable," her volume rose exponentially, "an' hae th' audacity t' treat me as tho' I've nae a brain t' think wi' or a tongue t' answer ye forthwith. Furthermore, my actions canna be o' no real concern t' ye." Kennis shook with the violence of her emotions, knowing and not caring that she'd overstepped the line of propriety.

"No concern to me?" he bellowed. "Haven't you heard a word I've said to you?"

She flinched, expecting the worst, not worrying about the outcome. She'd paid dearly for her impudence more than once before this wretched confrontation.

The wind caught at his hair and thrust a black lock into his eyes. Annoyed, he pushed it away and she giggled. The scorching look she received from him in return nearly undid her. All of a sudden, the tension of the last few hours caught up with her in a rush, breaking down her resistance. Irrepressible laughter consumed her and she clapped both hands over her mouth.

"Beg your pardon, Laird," a gravelly voice cut in. "We're at the landin'."

Thunderstruck, Alistair stared at her, sharply answering the newcomer. "Have we received a signal yet?" he barked over his shoulder, never taking his eyes from her.

"Aye, a minute ago," said the man.

"Signal our response. We'll put ashore as planned." He faced Kennis squarely, hands on hips. "This doesn't mean I'm through with you, mistress."

His frigid tone cut her to the quick and her hilarity stilled as quickly as it erupted. "Well, I'm through with *ye*," she blurted out, finding her voice and crossing her arms over her chest in defiance. "I've nothin' more to say, either."

His dark eyes burned through her. "I've plenty left to say to you but it will have to wait. If this meeting goes ill, if you say one word out of turn, I vow I'll—"

"Ye'll what?" she demanded, unafraid. Her sea green eyes glittered, reflecting the turbulence of the emotional waters swirling within her soul.

"Don't tempt me to show you," he growled. "Farrell, take charge of the lass. See that she makes no mischief." He turned abruptly and shouted orders to his men.

Farrell glanced uncertainly at Kennis and awaited instructions. "What am I to do with her, Laird?"

"I can't leave her alone on the galley, we need every man ashore." He frowned, considering his options. "Bring her in the last boat."

"Aye, sir," Farrell acknowledged as the laird climbed over the side of the vessel to the waiting *scaff* below. His gaze settled on Kennis. "A fine kettle o' fish ye've boiled, lass. I canna imagine what possessed ye." He continued to shake his head. "Ye should've let him have his say and been done with it. I suspect we'll return to the ship tonight now, and hope for your sake that the lads willna be upset." Seeing the dismay on her face, he spoke more kindly. "Dinna worry that bonnie head of yours. 'Twill come about right, always does. Just do as ye're told now, will ye?"

His calm words soothed her ruffled feathers. "Aye," she said. "I'm sorry for causing you so much trouble." Hesitant to ask for his favor, she plowed ahead. "May I call you Farrell?" Her brogue faded along with her sudden fury.

He smiled and nodded. "I'll be happy to serve ye, lass."

"Thank you," she breathed out in relief and sat down upon the thick plaid, weary from the traumatic events that had unexpectedly overtaken the evening. Suddenly, she remembered the plot she'd overheard aboard the *Faioleag.* "Oh, Farrell, please wait." She scrambled to her feet. "I've something important to tell you." He turned around, a hint of impatience in his eyes. She related the brief conversation she overheard while imprisoned in the crate.

His thick brows drew together. "Hm. Ye're a good lass, now rest a short while before we put to shore."

Nodding, she tried to make herself comfortable on the hard boards, snuggling deep into the heavy folds of the warm plaid. The gentle ocean breeze blew her tawny curls across her cheeks. Deep in thought, she twisted one damp strand about her finger. Although the future remained unclear and shadows from the past still lingered, the significance of the current events deeply impressed her. In fact, the present adventure called out to her with a loud voice. A slow smile spread across her face. Scotland. Home at last.

Chapter 5

Uncharted Waters

Peyton Gilmore opened Captain Donald Murray's cabin door, staring out into the peaceful night.

His brow puckered as he stared at the quiet deck below. The ship groaned, pushing ahead as the whish of breakers splashed against the hull and unintelligible, muffled voices drifted on the air. Small fingers tugged insistently upon his waistcoat. "Papa, where's Kennis?" Jennie yawned sleepily, leaning her golden head against his elbow. "I want to go to bed."

He smiled at his small daughter. "What, retire early? Jennie lass, I'm surprised at you." He gave the company a cursory glance, wondering where his young cousin had disappeared to this time. "Since Kennis hasn't come back, I'll take you and Molly to your mother."

Captain Murray, noting his anxious look, approached him. "May I be of service to you, Mr. Gilmore?"

"I hope so." The corners of Peyton's mouth turned down in displeasure. "Our Kennis went to her cabin earlier and hasn't returned. She's been gone nearly an hour."

"I see," the Captain said, "but I doubt any harm has come to the lass. I'll attend to the matter, if you'll meet me here after you take your daughters below."

Peyton's scowl lessened. "Of course." Several minutes later, he deposited Jennie and Molly into their mother's arms. "Ailis, love," he said, kissing her cheek. "I'm returning to the Captain's quarters. I have business to attend to." She nodded and he bid her good night, knowing that he'd not sleep a wink until news of Kennis was forthcoming. She was like a daughter to him, entrusted to his care by his cousin, Lady Alanna McCallum, for the journey to the Americas.

Worried despite Captain Murray's reassurances, he climbed the narrow steps to the deck. What if her disappearance was connected to the dispute among the sailors tonight? The Captain had given his undivided attention to it for half of the evening, so it must be serious. He hurried forward, his arrival coinciding with the Captain's.

Donald Murray nodded to Peyton and opened the door. "After you, Mr. Gilmore."

He stepped into the now empty room, determined to learn the reason for the incident earlier in the evening. "Well, Captain," he said bluntly. "What have you discovered?"

"Nothing so far, I'm afraid." Donald directed him a probing look. "The ship is still being searched."

He eyed the Captain shrewdly. "How could this happen? Something's afoot, I'm sure of it. We've been on this ship for months without incident, and now my young cousin disappears when we're nearly at port." Hands clenched behind his back, he began to pace the room. "Are you going to tell me what's going on, or not?'

"I've a theory, but no proof." Donald watched him out of the corner of his eye, calmly picking up his pipe to fill with tobacco. "Unfortunately, I'm not at liberty to disclose the details."

"What!" Peyton was incredulous, pausing to stare hard at the Captain. "This is intolerable, and I demand an explanation. I'm responsible for the lass, sir, she's not merely an employee, but 'tis my kinswoman."

He ended on a raised note and Donald removed his pipe from his mouth. "Perhaps so, but there is some mystery attached to the girl, and you're keeping secrets about her."

"Secrets?" he scoffed. "The lass 'tis none of your business. On the other hand, *you* are responsible for what happens aboard this ship. I hold you accountable, sir."

Donald considered his options. Due to the serious nature of the girl's disappearance and the night's peculiar activities, he decided to take a step of faith. "Mr. Gilmore," he said after a brief silence, "I believe you're an honorable man. I trust that the small bit of information I am about to divulge will go no further than this room."

Peyton visibly relaxed. "You may depend upon my honor and silence, Captain."

"Very well, then. Please," he said, extending his hand, "call me Donald."

* * *

Warm and cozy under a thick plaid in the bow of Alistair's galley, Kennis contemplated the events of her day. A deep sense of remorse troubled her heart. The Gilmores must be anxious over her disappearance. Furthermore, Captain Murray, his entire crew and the passengers of the ship would search for her and when she wasn't found— She could hardly bear to think of it, there was no hiding her folly.

She deliberately turned her thoughts in a more pleasant direction. It would be so wonderful to be home again. Fergus and Daly, her long-time friends and attendants, always bailed her out of serious trouble. In fact, Farrell reminded her of the two men and soon she would reunite with them and her family, too. Comforted, she returned to her present dilemma, and the rogue who didn't even have the courtesy to tell her his name.

He could be the laird of any number of clans in the West of Scotland and if the gunshot hadn't exploded on the *Faioleag*, starting the chain of the night's unsettling events, she'd never have ventured onto the deck or been tempted to get into the crate. Now, here she was at the mercy of his black temper, wondering what fate awaited her when she returned to the ship. To make things worse, her presence on the galley disturbed his crew. She sighed. Oh well, when the time came, she'd just have to summon the courage to face her punishment.

Farrell interrupted her musings to instruct her about the night's activities. "Mistress, we're goin' ashore now, so stay close to me. The Laird'll hae my head if there's trouble, and ye dinna want to invite his wrath down upon yourself a second time." The rising alarm on her face stirred his sympathy. "I've known him since we were lads, lass. Dinna fear, his bark's bigger than his bite. Have ye a cloak?"

She rose to her feet. "Only this shawl."

"Here then, put this on," he handed her an oilcloth, "and keep your head and face covered. We dinna want those pirates to know we've a lass in tow."

His tone convinced her of the serious nature of the midnight errand and her heart leapt in eager anticipation. She could almost feel the smooth sand between her toes and despite her initial dismay, her chance undertaking was proving to be quite an adventure. Something important was at stake here; she could feel it in her bones. However, she'd wait and see if her help was needed.

"The crates are a payment of a sort," Farrell explained further, "and ye came mighty close to bein' part of the booty." He glanced at her clothing. "Ye'll have to roll up your skirts under the cloak and take off the fancy slippers. I'll help ye to shore the best I can," he continued, "in the dark it willna be easy."

She climbed into the *scaff* after Farrell and a few men followed. Soon, the light boat scraped bottom close to shore. Farrell slid over the side and handed her into the knee-deep water. "Lud, 'tis freezing!" she exclaimed. Cold water and squishy sand met her calves and feet, and he held her fast against the rough breakers.

"Aye," he said, "now shush, lass."

Splashing to shore with the laird's men, joy bubbled up in her soul. Solid ground for the first time in weeks! She wanted to shout her happiness into the stillness of the night, and the bright stars overhead seemed to agree, twinkling merrily in the velvet sky.

Farrell chuckled. "Ye'll have to contain yourself awhile longer, lass."

She peeked out from under the hood, eyes sparkling. "I will," she whispered, crossing her heart in earnest. "I promise. It's been weeks since I've stood on the shore, and I feel like running and shouting."

Without warning, a deep voice spoke menacingly into her ear. Alistair tightly grasped her elbow for a brief moment. "You'll do nothing of the kind, mistress, if you know what's good for you. Now be still and be quiet." He released her and turned away. "Jocko," he called. "Any sign of them yet?"

She made a face behind his back, rolling her eyes. Farrell suppressed a grin. The bonnie lass had no idea of the black temper of his master, and he didn't want to encourage her sauce. He'd never seen the man bested by a lass yet; the experience might do him good.

"By the rocks, Laird."

"Come with me, Jocko. Farrell?"

"Sir?" he said.

"You'll know what to do if anything goes wrong."

"Aye, that I will." He gently pushed Kennis to the rear of the group and smiled at her in reassurance.

She shrugged in return and clasped her full skirts, pulling the oilcloth tight about her slim figure.

Alistair led the men onto the beach, confidence in every stride. "Denoon, where are you?" he bellowed. "Show yourself, you villain!" Torch upraised, he scanned the shoreline.

Across the strand, more torches sprang to life, lit by the opposing crew. The flames cast an eerie, wavering glow over the two groups of men standing warily behind their leaders on the beach. Suddenly, the moon peeked through a bank of clouds, illuminating the dark shore.

Kennis peered around the men blocking her view, trying to get a better look at the man called Denoon. A scar ran the length of his broad forehead, continuing in a jagged line from his pug nose to square chin. In spite of his disfigured face, his eyes, glittering with malevolence, caught her attention. Mercy, she'd almost fallen into the clutches of this monster.

Farrell stood beside her, gripping her arm. "Easy now, lass, steady," he said softly, feeling her quiver beneath his fingertips.

"Show me the purchase, Denoon." Alistair wasted no words.

"Isn't that likes ye, your blackness," Denoon sniggered. "Always so high 'n mighty, never respectin' a man's honest business. Gimme a reason to show ye me goods."

Startled, Kennis looked quickly from one man to the other. Your blackness? Her brow puckered. Hm, the title the two villains on the ship had bestowed upon their intended victim. She tugged on Farrell's sleeve, glancing up at him. Who was ol' Crooknose, then?

He squeezed her arm in understanding but said nothing. The fewer words spoken now, the better.

Alistair signaled to his men and they tugged on the slack ropes in their hands, dragging a crate forward where the two men stood, facing one another. "Open it," he ordered. Once the lid was off, he motioned to Denoon.

"Better be no trickery," Denoon sneered.

"See for yourself," he retorted. "Step back, men."

Denoon crept forward slowly, keeping an eye upon Alistair and Jocko. His henchman followed, ready to defend him. He held a torch over the crate and fished away the straw, pulled out an object and unwrapped its covering. Although the booty glistened in the flickering torchlight, Kennis couldn't make it out. Satisfied, Denoon returned it to the crate.

"There's supposed to be two," Denoon said. "Where's the other? I willna hands over me goods till I sees it."

"It's here, you scoundrel." Alistair's lip curled, and he motioned to his men to pull the second crate near the first.

"Open it."

"Not until you show me what I've purchased," Alistair countered. "I've yet to see evidence that you have them here." He stood his ground, relentless in his pursuit.

Kennis listened intently, confused by his words. What kind of object was he referring to, or was some ill-fated creature caught in a web of violence between the two men? In answer to her unspoken questions, three large sacks were roughly tossed before him upon the wet sand.

"Open them." Alistair glared at Denoon. His men stood at his side, poised to act in the event of trouble.

"Open 'em yourself," jeered the villain.

With grudging respect, she admired the laird's forbearance, his command over himself and his crew. Shows he has some character, she thought wryly. More than you realize, her conscience whispered. *Hush, you.*

"Jocko, untie those sacks and see what's inside." Menace saturated his voice. "I hope for your sake these goods aren't damaged, Denoon."

Denoon guffawed. "Not permanently, eh, lads? They wasn't in very good shape when I gots 'em." He shrugged. "Ye can take 'em or leave 'em to rot fer all I care. They're no use to me in their condition. Ye're a fool, your blackness." He gloated as Jocko emptied each sack. "Just remember, a deal's a deal."

A lump rose in Kennis' throat and her heart constricted. Three battered men lay unmoving on the sand. Were they alive? She peered over Farrell's shoulder. If only she could see their faces. Her heart leapt as a new thought occurred to her. Maybe, just maybe....

Taking great care, Jocko examined each man. "They're alive, sir, just barely." The tension among the men visibly increased.

"Before you haul off them unfortunates," Denoon began, "I expects to have a look-see in that other box."

"Do what you like, Denoon." Alistair's thinly veiled restraint vanished. "I'm taking these men regardless. Like you said, we have a bargain. Jocko, Rab, get these men to the galley." His eyes flickered over the three men lying on the sand. "Go easy on them, lads."

Denoon busied himself opening the second crate. Jocko and Rab gently lifted each man onto a makeshift litter and four more of the laird's men hurried forward to carry them away. When the first litter passed Kennis, the injured man's head lolled toward her and the torchlight revealed the lean contours of his bruised face.

She sucked in a breath. "Davis!" she squeaked, startled into sudden recognition.

"Shush, lassie," Farrell hissed, covering her mouth with his big hand.

Denoon's head shot up, hearing a female voice. "So, ye gots a wench with ye, your blackness, what's she like, eh? We're nae particular though, are we lads." He turned a greedy eye on Alistair. "Give ye a fair price." The pirates sniggered.

"Not a wench, Denoon, 'tis a young lad." Alistair's eyes narrowed in suspicion. "Or doesn't it matter to you?" His taut voice was heavy with implication.

At that moment, Kennis saw the danger she'd narrowly escaped mirrored in Denoon's black eyes and she shuddered.

"I knows a wench when I hears one," Denoon muttered, ignoring him as he continued to rifle through the crate. He paused, fixing beady eyes upon his adversary. "Prove it to me."

Alistair tensed, glaring at him. "Nay."

Farrell gripped Kennis' arm and pushed her toward the waiting *scaff*. She needed little persuasion and took a hasty step, fumbling with her skirts. The white undergarments and shimmering green dress slipped through her fingers and dropped to the sand. Desperate, she looked up at Farrell. He helped her to gather the voluminous garments, handing her the bundle as he hustled her along. "I'm sorry," she whispered.

He grunted, and pulled her quickly along behind him.

Watching through veiled eyes, Denoon dropped the silver piece in his hands and ran forward. "'Tis a wench," he cried. "After her, lads!" Two of his opponents blocked his mad dash and he waved his arm in the air, signaling his men. Reinforcements sprang from hidden places among the rocks.

Treachery! Alistair drew his pistol and fired at the villains racing towards him. The loud report of the blasts echoed in the bay, creating a random explosion of lights across the dark beach. Kennis and Farrell arrived at the *scaff*, jumped in, and rowed hard. When they reached the galley, Farrell shoved her over the side, pulling himself up and in to safety. Most of the men had reached the craft by now, except for Alistair and two more of his men.

"To the boats, lads," Denoon cried out. "To the boats!"

The three remaining men splashed their way to the galley in the choppy water. Once released, the sail caught the blustery wind and the vessel lurched forward, easily cutting through the whitecaps. Skillful hands maneuvered the craft around the rocks and out into the open sea, speedily leaving the villain and his foul crew in their wake as Providence, in the form of a light fog, enveloped them in the haze.

Kennis sat still, not daring to move a muscle. The men were quiet, rowing with the wind to put as much distance between themselves and Denoon as possible. Farrell tended the wounded and she longed to help him, to discover if she truly had seen Davis McCallum, one of her people from Kilcalum on the beach. Was she imagining things? Four years had passed since Culloden; her memory could be at fault. Her courage rose and she cast aside the plaid to make her way to Farrell's side. Without a word, he handed her a cloth dipped in wyche hazel to bathe their battered faces.

She knelt by the man who was either Davis McCallum or his twin. He moaned, and she gently applied the compress. He reached up and gripped her wrist. "Mistress Kennis," the weakened man whispered. "Am I dreamin'? God be praised."

"Hush, Davis," she softly admonished, sure of him now. "You mustn't say my name." In his condition, she hoped that he understood the importance of keeping her identity a secret.

"Aye," he murmured groggily, closing his eyes in sleep. She stole a look at Farrell, wondering if he heard the brief exchange.

He lifted his head to meet her gaze, his expression unreadable.

Ill at ease, she returned her attention to her long-lost kinsman. After several hours and weary from the night's labors, she sought her plaid and fell fast asleep.

Daybreak came bright and early. She awoke with a start, the previous day's events hazy in her mind. A rope lay coiled at her feet and the brine of the sea assaulted her nostrils.

Throwing aside the heavy plaid, she rolled over onto her back, suddenly remembering the disturbing events that had brought her here. Oh my! She gazed up into the laird's dark eyes and her unpredictable heart thudded in betrayal.

The corner of his mouth lifted in a knowing smile and he greeted her in dulcet tones. "Sleep well, mistress?" He leaned easily against the bulwark, gazing down at her.

She continued to stare up at him while she collected her thoughts. Now what was she to do? After yesterday's disastrous events, this day was sure to bring more disagreeable surprises.

"You'd best stretch a bit or else you'll be stiff and sore." He offered her his hands and she automatically grasped them, allowing him to pull her to her feet. "We're almost in the ship's path and should be meeting her soon. I hope you understand what that means."

She gathered the warm plaid from the planks and flipped it over her shoulders, warming her chilled body. "Nay, I don't." The imp within her had fully awakened. "Perhaps you'd better explain what that means, sir, and how it will affect *me*."

"Tempting me to violence, eh?" His steady regard never wavered. "Since you constantly need instruction," he lifted a brow, noting her embarrassment at the brief reminder of their first meeting, "I'll tell you exactly what's going to occur when we reach the ship."

Seeing an added spark in her eye, he spoke firmly. "Don't be foolish enough to argue with me, lass. You will go immediately to the Captain's quarters where you will meet with him, Mr. Gilmore, and me to render an accurate and complete account of this foolish escapade of yours. I will then quit the room, and the two of them may see fit to do with you whatever they choose." His eyes gleamed. "If it were up to me, I would turn you over my knee and give you the thrashing you so justly deserve."

"I don't believe you." A rosy flush warmed her cheeks. "You're merely baiting me."

He laughed. "Care to find out?" He reached for her, holding her hands in a tight clasp.

"Nay," she said, trying to pull away. "Let go of me."

"Coward," he taunted.

"I'm not afraid of you," she said simply. "I don't give in to foolish jests."

He pulled her closer to him. "I'm not jesting."

Staring into his dark eyes, her resistance vanished, and she was tempted to melt into his embrace. It would be so easy to give in, to let him kiss her.

Feeling her response, he leaned toward her and then drew back, thinking better of it. Her relatives might consider the journey aboard his galley with only his men to act as chaperon a compromise of her virtue, though it wasn't his doing. She had little notion of the jeopardy she'd placed them both in. Hopefully her family wouldn't demand satisfaction, meaning an unwanted marriage for both of them. Peyton Gilmore seemed like a reasonable man and he placed his hopes in that comforting thought. Releasing her, he turned away to stand in the bow of the vessel.

Kennis watched his dark hair ruffle in the wind for a few seconds, her heart aflutter. Finally, she mustered the nerve to stand beside him and was rewarded by the sight of a golden riband peeking out from beneath his collar.

Surprised by her sudden appearance at his side, he looked down at her, and his eyes softened. "You have need of something, mistress?"

"You're wearing my riband," she marveled, staring up at him as a splash of color leapt into the sky. Dawn broke upon the horizon and in her mind's eye, she saw a cold mist swirl upward, surrounding them in its smoky wake. Did he feel it, too? Something tangible yet unseen surged in the air and she waited expectantly beside him. Surely, a mystery of great proportion was about to be revealed.

Alistair ignored the keen awareness rising up between them, nearly overpowering his senses. A refreshing, tangy breeze washed over him from head to foot but he shook off the feeling of awakening. "I told you I would, and I keep my promises."

"Meaning I don't?"

"Only you know the answer to that question."

"I didn't think you'd keep the bauble, let alone wear it." Puzzled, she studied his chiseled profile. For a brief moment, they seemed as one. What had happened? Lowering her gaze, she noticed a dark stain on his shirtsleeve. "You're wounded." She reached out, hesitating, before touching the soiled cloth. "I can dress it for you, if you like."

"'Tis only a scratch." His eyes warmed at her genuine concern. "Worried about me, lass?"

"I don't want to see you hurt on my account."

A teasing note entered his voice. "Ah, so you do care." He reached for her, resting his hand in the small of her back.

The heat from his palm seeped through the cloth and she trembled at his touch. She sighed. "Are you ever serious?"

"Always," he said promptly, "when a fair lass offers to tend my wounds."

Suddenly shy, and not meeting his eyes, she changed the subject. "How were you able to find these men?"

He fell silent, weighing his options. Should he tell her anything at all about himself or his quest? An unfamiliar insistence that he share his thoughts tugged at his heart. "A man has many resources."

"Aye," she said, annoyed, "and so do I when it pertains to my family circle and our connections. But these men in particular, where are they from and who is Denoon?" She lifted questioning eyes to his, searching for answers.

He wrestled with the desire to disclose his plans, his passionate pursuit of the men held captive by the English. "He's a villain, not an acquaintance for such a one as you." He removed his hand from her back and pulled her to face him, leaning back against the wooden bow of the galley. She fit comfortably, too comfortably, within the loose circle of his arms. The ocean spray rose up behind him, spattering them both with a fine mist. "Can I trust you, lass, not to give away our secrets? I can't tell you all, but perhaps a wee bit will set your mind to rest."

Kennis wanted to know everything but decided that this crumb might be all she would receive. "Aye," she said in earnest, "please tell me whatever you can."

"Denoon is a smuggler," he began. "I've known him most of my life. He's not particular about who he sells in the slave market, Scot or no, women, children. I received word from an acquaintance that he'd picked up indentured men from the colonies, and decided to purchase their freedom."

She stood up straighter, her heart pounding against her ribs. Perhaps he could help her to find Robbie! "But from whom?" she demanded. "How can I find out about such things?"

His brows drew together in consternation. "You want a slave? 'Tis legal enough in Scotland."

"Don't patronize me." She glared at him. "Of course I don't want a slave."

Alistair eyed her thoughtfully. "Then what do you want?"

Desiring to confide her hopes, Kennis wavered. He'd entrusted her with his secret, perhaps she should return his confidence. Surprised at herself, she realized that she wanted to tell him about Robbie, to pour out the whole story about how much she'd lost because of the war. He would understand her feelings and her desire to find her brother. Staring him directly in the eye, she took the first step. "I'm searching for someone."

Amused, he struggled not to smile in the face of her obvious inner debate. She had no idea how much every emotion played on her face, but she was right in assuming that she'd found a sympathetic listener. "A lover perhaps?"

She laughed, embarrassed. "Nay, though 'tis no business of yours. This person is a relative."

"Person?" he prompted, curious and enjoying her discomfiture.

"Well, a man, if you must know."

"I thought so," he said, smug. "Perhaps I can be of service to you in your quest."

She looked at him, incredulous. "I'm sorry, I can't allow that although I appreciate your kind offer." She shifted, wondering what else was passing through his mind as he tightened his hold on her. "If you could point me in the right direction, supply contacts?"

"Nay," he said. "It wouldn't be seemly."

"But I have friends who will help me," she clutched the sleeve of his leather jack, "men that will go to any lengths to restore this friend to me. We can pay you well."

Annoyed and disappointed, his eyes hardened. "Do you think I do this for money? I'm no mercenary." He thrust her hand away. "That's the second time you've insulted me. What kind of man do you think I am?"

"I don't know what kind of man you are," she scowled, "or who you are. I don't even know your name."

He snorted. "And you've no reason to know it."

Abruptly, Jocko's voice rang out, ill-timed, interrupting their conversation. "Ship ahoy!"

It was the *Faioleag*. Kennis' brief adventure was over and now she awaited the reckoning for her actions. On top of it all, she still hadn't discovered the aggravating man's name. He was more of a villain than Denoon.

* * *

The meeting on board the ship was brief. The laird escorted her to the Captain's cabin where she met with the three men and recounted her story. The only prevarication she felt compelled to make concerned Davis McCallum.

The varying emotions that played upon the face of each of her listeners were a remarkable sight. Kennis faced their wrath with a determination to receive her due punishment without flinching. None, to her astonishment and relief, was forthcoming. Captain Murray accepted her apology on behalf of his crew and passengers. Mr. Gilmore expected her to repeat the story to her grandfather and mother, confessing her guilt, and to honor her promise when she returned home. She agreed to obey his terms and gave him her word after he lectured her for a full hour.

"Well, lass, I suppose you've had enough of an ear beating for one day," he paused from his remonstrations, "so I'll not say any more on the subject. You'll hear nothing from Ailis or the girls, either." He smiled kindly. "We're all glad you're safe and sound." He shook his head again in amazement over her escapade. "Just remember that not everyone will be so forgiving."

"What do you mean, sir?"

He reached out and tapped her gently on the forehead with his finger. "You didn't think, Kennis. More than one lass has been forced to marry under less compromising circumstances."

"Marry!" she said, aghast at the thought, "but why? Nothing untoward happened."

"You and I know that, as do the Captain and the Laird himself who, fortunately, is an honorable man. But the fact remains that you spent a night alone without a female companion and only a boatload of rough seamen for company."

At her continued protests, he raised his hand. "'Tis over for now, just don't do anything so foolish again." He gave her a stern look. "I'm not your father, but there are men more old-fashioned than me who would insist upon a wedding. I confess that I'm hard-pressed not to, and you've my Ailis to thank for your good fortune. She won't see you pushed into a loveless marriage. Enough said, now off with you, and have a good rest. Looks like you've need of it."

After he'd gone, Kennis drew a bucket of fresh water from a barrel and returned to the stuffy little cabin. There were so many things to think about that her mind was in a whirl. Davis, and Robbie, and her narrow escape. She berated herself for the thousandth time, glad that her ordeal was over and doubly glad that she wasn't being married this very minute. She'd heard of girls in similar situations forced to marry against their will. It had simply not occurred to her at all until Mr. Gilmore pointed out the obvious.

"Oh no," she groaned. *He* must have thought about it. His every action showed his restraint and consideration for her well-being. No wonder he'd not kissed her, especially in front of his men. "What a stupid girl you are, Kennis McCallum," she muttered. Eyes shut tight, she wished the memory would go away. Not a chance. With any luck she'd never have to face him again.

Her jumbled thoughts flitted here and there as she slowly bathed. Foremost in her mind were Davis McCallum, her homecoming and Robbie, and of course her almost-groom, the sometimes mocking, sometimes irresistible laird. Despite her present woes and for some reason unknown to her, she couldn't erase the man from her mind.

Chapter 6

Rendezvous

A cloaked figure sped down the lamp lit street, pulling a woolen hood securely about his face.

He dashed to the next corner, turning right into a dark alley. Like a specter melting into the flickering shadows of a grey twilight, his muffled footsteps blended with the sound of seawater lapping against the many wooden boats moored in the harbor.

The rendezvous point—with any luck, the men would arrive at the designated hour. Scanning the lane ahead of him, he saw a lone figure make its stealthy way toward the abandoned warehouse. Optimistic, he assumed that it was another of the crew on his way to the meeting. Arriving at a weather-beaten door, he rapped thrice. Almost immediately, the door opened a crack and a deep voice grated into the night. "*Deus refugeum nostrum.*"

"*In ardua petit,*" he answered confidently.

"Aye, come in then, lad." The grizzled old man opened the door wide.

He quickly slipped in and followed the man down the passage. The light in the room that he entered was poor, the air stuffy and malodorous; several men stood in the shadows along the walls.

"Where is Patrick?" he asked, examining the room.

One of the lounging men stepped forward. "Not here yet, Captain Grahame."

"He should've been here by now, confound that Irishman!" The color rose in his lean cheeks. "I just hope nothing's happened to him, or all of our effort will have been for naught."

"Oh, he'll be here, lad," the grizzled man said. "Soon enough."

"He'd better be, that pirate, when we're so close to achieving our goal."

A redheaded man, whistling cheerfully, poked his head into the room and greeted the assembly even as the Captain uttered the words. "Evenin' lads, you all look like ye're goin' to a wake, with those gloomy mugs o' yours."

"It's about time, Patrick," the Captain said, impatient.

"Aye, but I had a bit o' business to take care o' before I came here for this meetin'," Patrick replied. "I stopped to see Mags—"

"You're going to get us caught, Gallagher, if you continue to see that wench at the tavern," he interrupted. "What have you told her, anything? Because if you have, I'll throttle you myself."

"Told the gel? Not I, lad," he protested. "Don't *fash* yourself."

Not convinced, Captain Grahame threw back his grey hood. "Well then, gentlemen, you know enough of the plan for now, so I'll provide more details when we reach our destination. The rest is up to Patrick here, who claims to have obtained the goods we need to complete this journey." He turned to Patrick. "What about our prisoner, how does he fare?"

"Well eno'," Patrick grinned, "dinna even put up a fight."

"I hope you haven't damaged him," the Captain said with a grim smile. "At least not too much."

"Nay, your honor," he assured. "Me and the lads only cleaned up the mess, so to speak."

"Explain yourself."

Patrick leaned forward. "The wicked man was soused. All we had to do was pick him up off the floor and lug him down the back stairs." He made a face. "Foul, it was, I'll have you know." The men surrounding him sniggered. The Irishman had recently given up drink, the result of his newly found religion.

"And where is he now?"

"Where the likes o' him belongs, lad," Patrick said. "In a safe place behind bars."

The Captain wordlessly concurred, relieved that the deed was done, and addressed the group of men. "Have you men completed the tasks appointed to you?"

Ayes rang out around the room as each man reported on his progress. Satisfied with their response, he nodded. "Well done. Now return to your posts, and we'll be underway on the morrow. You're dismissed, gentlemen."

Aboard ship once again, Captain Grahame sat up late stewing over the events of the last several days. Many thoughts occupied his mind, one more than the rest. He contemplated the lovely young woman he observed earlier on the wharf. Plainly clothed and obviously with little enough to spare, she shared her breakfast with an urchin. Eyes narrowing, he shook his head. "Impossible." Still perplexed, he finished the tumbler of the amber liquid he'd poured and dozed off, exhausted from the day's exertions. Waking long enough to rise and stagger away from the table, he pulled off his boots and flopped onto the canopied bed. Moments later, someone pounded on his door.

"Captain," a shrill voice insisted. "Captain!"

When he awoke, he thought he was in a dream, or was the pounding a part of the dream? He rose unsteadily and staggered toward the door. "What is it, Jake?" he mumbled. His head ached. He'd tossed and turned all night, his sleep disturbed again by that infamous dream. What did it portend, if indeed, it meant anything at all? This was the third time it had recurred in the past fortnight.

"Captain, sir, there's a boatload of redcoats comin' our way!" Young Jake squeaked out, raising his voice a notch in his attempt to wake his captain.

He yanked the door open. "In the middle of the night? Are you sure, lad?"

"'Tis mornin'," the boy cheerfully replied. "If ye'll let me in, sir, I'll open up the windows for ye and air the room."

Morning. The night was far spent and the day close at hand. "I'll be right there, Jake. Run and tell Gallagher to pull up anchor. We can't afford to be boarded." He watched Jake wheel about and run down the passage. "Especially not with our *guest* aboard," he muttered bitterly, closing the door. "At least he won't be living in luxury on this voyage. It will be my pleasure to insure just the opposite."

Chapter 7

Alba gu Brath!

Kennis stood on the bridge of the *Faioleag* comparing the rippling aquamarine water to the storm-ridden sea of a few short days ago.

She shivered. Though the warm sun cloaked her shoulders, she still couldn't seem to forget her ordeal. The fearsome storm and the ferocity of the roiling waters had captured her imagination. Or perhaps, she grudgingly admitted, 'tisn't the water at all. An image flashed before her eyes. In truth, a certain man of like temperament inspired her thoughts. She tugged on her shawl, securely gathering its loose ends about her slender frame as the wind swirled about her.

Captain Murray pointed to a misty shore ahead and she eagerly leaned forward, squinting through the bright glare at the jagged peaks and rocky coast of her homeland outlined in the distance. Port Eilidh, her final destination, was south of the mainland on the Isle of Islay.

The ship was alive with the tramping and scuffling noises associated with docking, and the activity increased as a tall figure strode with purpose across the deck. She glanced away from the water, prudently observing the roguish laird from a distance, all the while telling herself that she'd not have any more to do with him. The aggravating man didn't even have the courtesy to tell her his name.

After her brief voyage aboard his galley, she'd scarcely seen him and didn't dare inquire as to his whereabouts. Common sense told her to beware his teasing charm; he was probably not the marrying kind. Ruggedly handsome, his craggy brow, deep-set eyes and prominent nose made her feel— Her heart beat more rapidly. Hm. She slowly examined him from head to foot. His stature was impressive, and thick wavy hair rested atop his broad shoulders, black locks rippling in the wind. "Foolish girl," she said to herself.

An air of confidence hung about him like a heavy cloak, his inborn vitality creating an intense awareness within her. She felt uncomfortable in his presence and he knew it. Watching him lift crates and toss light bundles to his fellows gave her ample opportunity to observe him.

He was a man of authority, she conceded, and not merely because of his title. The manner in which the men jumped to do his bidding, his haughty bearing when he confronted the slaver Denoon, lent credence to the idea that he was accustomed to command. And, she lifted a fair brow, to be obeyed without question. Having experienced his wrath, she wasn't surprised that his men seemed eager to do so. Well, he was somewhat intimidating, perhaps, but not unconquerable. She had yet to decide whether it was wise or even her true desire to rise to the challenge of winning his heart.

Just then, he glanced up and met her disapproving gaze. Sweeping off his feathered bonnet, he executed a courtly bow amidst a roar of laughter that rose to mock her.

Her bosom swelled, her face growing hot in embarrassment. Equality between the sexes was nearly unheard of in an age that favored men. She yearned for a companion who would treat her with respect but it was clear that in his eyes they weren't equal. She was merely a source of amusement to him.

For a fleeting moment on the galley, he'd awakened a desire in her to know him better. After sharing his plans, she took a bold step in telling him about her pursuit of her brother, a secret that she dared not speak of elsewhere. Her emotions about him were mixed, disturbing.

She forced herself to look away but not before Farrell tipped his hat to her. She waved back. A stab of annoyance pierced her afresh when his watching master grinned and spoke a few words to him, making Farrell laugh in return. Evidently the rogue made her appear ridiculous again.

Captain Murray glanced at her, the gravity in his voice belied by his twinkling grey eyes. "Don't let him worry you, miss. You're a comely lass, and the Laird's a good man."

She shrugged. It was pointless to argue with him. "Thank you for allowing me to join you on the bridge. Good day, Captain." Leaving his side, she skipped down the steps, joining the Gilmores on the main deck. She intended to enjoy the rest of the lovely day, made even more beautiful by the fact that she would be home soon.

"Kennis," Jennie eagerly greeted her, "there you are. We've been watching the sailors ready the gangplank. I can't wait to go ashore!" She hopped up and down, doing a little dance, first on one foot and then the other.

Kennis smiled at her bird-like antics. "Aye," she said, scanning the busy quay before her, hoping to see a familiar face.

All of a sudden, Jennie grabbed her arm. "Look, look," the child cried.

Her gaze followed Jennie's pointing finger. With glee, she noted that the laird had slipped on the gangplank and was desperately trying not to lose his balance. He dropped a large parcel and roars of laughter greeted her ears. Farrell managed to pull him back, saving him from a quick plunge into the cold depths below.

Jennie clapped her hands. "Oh, I'm so glad he didn't fall in!"

"Are you?" She looked over the child's head at Mr. Gilmore with a mischievous sparkle in her eye. "I confess, I'm rather disappointed. I'd liked to have seen it."

He laughed. "I fancy you would, lass, but you'll have to excuse me. I must take my leave of the Laird now. Shall I bid farewell on your behalf?"

"Aye." She flashed a saucy grin. "Please send my compliments to both he and Farrell at having avoided a wetting, and my deepest regrets at having missed the pleasure of seeing *him* receive one."

Peyton laughed aloud as he strode toward his new acquaintance. If only the lass knew whom she teased, she might think differently about antagonizing the man. Nevertheless, he delivered the provocative message. To his amazement, the laird received it calmly, yet his arched brow and decided smirk left Peyton with an uneasy feeling in his gut.

* * *

"Donald, our thanks for an excellent voyage," Peyton said to Donald Murray, the ship's captain. "I'm grateful for your help." He glanced meaningfully at Kennis.

"You're welcome." Donald extended his hand and the two men firmly shook, parting in good faith. "I hope you've not been too hard on the lass. Shows a bit of courage, I think. We need our women to be strong in times like these."

"She's a good lass, sir, and I depend upon her to do as I've asked." Turning to his little daughters, he said, "Well, have you lassies naught to say for yourselves?"

Jennie and Molly, dressed alike in traveling clothes, bobbed dual curtseys. "Captain Murray," Jennie piped with her usual enthusiasm, "thank you for inviting us to your party." Shy Molly gazed up at the Captain, wide-eyed beneath her bonnet, and echoed her sister. She then promptly hid behind her mother's skirts.

Jennie tugged on the Captain's sleeve one last time. "Please sir, can you tell me more about the Laird?"

"Jennie," Mr. Gilmore admonished.

Donald grinned. "You'll have to ask your father about him, lassie. It appears, sir," he said to Peyton, "that our friend has an admirer on board."

"More than one if I'm not mistaken."

"If I take your meaning, I fancy 'tis mutual. Health to you, Peyton."

"And to you, Donald. Fare well." Peyton returned the customary salute and moved on.

Kennis followed Mrs. Gilmore, pretending not to hear their conversation. She dropped a curtsey before stretching out her hand to the Captain. "I, too, thank you, Captain Murray for a pleasant voyage. I confess that I'm happy to be home again."

He smiled. "Aye, 'tis grand to arrive in your home port after a long journey. God speed, mistress." He nodded, tipping his hat to her and to the waiting Gilmore family in a final show of respect.

"God speed, sir."

It was a fitting day for their arrival. The sun shone brightly in the clear blue sky and the gulls circled above, squawking over cast-off morsels of food lying on the splintered boards of the pier. A crowd had gathered; women eagerly awaited their menfolk and the seamen, in turn, rushed to greet their loved ones.

Walking down the gangplank, Kennis strained to see over the heads of people in front of her. How she envied Robbie his height. He resembled their father in every way and she wanted to be more like him, to possess the freedoms with which men were liberally endowed.

When her foot finally touched down on the ground, her heart sang its own joyful song. Oh, happy day, to stand on Scottish soil. Although Islay wasn't the mainland where she was born, it was still Scotland. *Alba gu brath*—yes, Scotland forever! She drank in the familiar sights around her. It was so *muckle*[6] good.

On impulse, she climbed onto a squat barrel, hoping to get a better view of the busy port and with any luck, her friends. Without warning, her bottle green skirts and full-sleeved saffron blouse billowed out, caught by drafts of cool air. She hastily pushed them down; she'd worn her favorite colors to represent her clan for her homecoming. Although the English banished the tartan plaid in an attempt to destroy the Scottish way of life, hope remained in her that someday the right to freely wear the tartan would be restored to all Scots.

---

[6] *Much, big*

The brilliance of the early spring sunshine crowned her tawny hair with light, transforming her into a golden sentinel standing watch over the small harbor. She eagerly searched the crowd, lifting one slim hand to shield her vibrant green eyes from the blinding sun.

Unknown to her, an inner sweetness shone from her, enhancing her God-given outward beauty. Having sat at her mother's knee often as a child, she listened attentively to her instruction about the goodness of God and heeded her mother's prayers. This was her covering and heritage in the Lord. Now, at the age of twenty-one, the seed planted early in the springtime of her young life took root in a new and living way at the close of a long, bitter winter.

She continued to search for the clansmen her mother had sent to meet her. In the event the ship's arrival did not coincide with the business the men transacted for their mistress, she'd travel to the mainland with the Gilmores until her passage home could be arranged.

At last she spied Fergus Love and Daly McCallum in the crowd, her lifelong guardians, nay, friends, and madly waved to gain their attention. The two men were a very important part of her extended clan family. Daly put her on her first pony, the sheltie she named Snowdrop because of his white spots and Fergus, the huge man-at-arms, was always nearby when she needed rescue.

It seemed an age since she departed the Isle of Lewis, left the protection of Dun Eistein and her mother and Morrison kin behind, and traveled to Port Eilidh with the Gilmores to catch their ship to America.

Fergus and Daly were reluctant to let her travel alone at the time, pleading with her mother to allow them to accompany her to North Carolina. Lady McCallum refused, and her two forlorn henchmen stood waving a final good-by from the wharf until the ship sailed from the harbor. Now here she was in Scotland, home again and none the worse, despite their fears.

She watched Mr. Gilmore attend to his lady while his servant, Brieve, went ahead to secure lodgings for the night. The Gilmore family would travel to Argyll instead of to their home on the Isle of Lewis. Once there, Mr. Gilmore would assume his new position as steward to Inveraray Castle, the stronghold of the Campbell clan and the home of Archibald, the powerful Duke of Argyll. After four years abroad, he felt fortunate to receive such a fine opportunity.

The current political and economic situation in Scotland was difficult, and although he possessed excellent credentials, he wasn't a Campbell or related to Campbells. The Duke feathered his own nest by currying the favor of the King with his outward obedience to the new laws. Peyton was merely another tool in his capable hand.

The old clan system where the chief cared and provided for his people was broken after the uprising in the '45 and the resulting battle at Culloden. Argyll wouldn't miss a chance to continue to secure his own success. Employing one man from another clan made no threat to his long-range plans.

Waiting for her friends, Kennis noticed a man with sandy hair casually leaning against a post, one hand tucked into the vest of his russet jack, boldly staring at her. He nodded, and she looked away, ignoring his impertinence.

Daly reached her first and lifted her down. "Ye're a bonnie sight to see, standin' there all golden." His eyes misted over, betraying his soft heart. "We've missed ye, lassie, and your mother and wee Mairi send their luve." He encircled her in his arms, squeezing tight as Kennis giggled, feeling like a child again.

"Hold onto your bonnet now," he whispered before releasing her. "See the lad movin' our way? 'Tis your long-lost cousin, Eavan Malcolmson of Kilmartin." He wiggled his brows and she lifted hers in mock horror. "Aye, ye heard me right. We're all surprised, eh, Ferg?" He glanced at the silent, big man nodding in agreement. "'Ware, here he comes."

She followed his gaze, filled with sudden misgiving. The brazen man in the russet jack strolled confidently toward them.

He swept a polite bow as Daly performed the introductions. "'Tis a pleasure, Cousin, to meet you at last. I've heard much of your kind ways and beauty from the folk at Kilcalum. I'm here today in the hope of renewing a sense of goodwill between our two families."

She rose from her curtsey. "And I, sir, am surprised and pleased to make your acquaintance." Her fair brows knit together. "I have a faint memory of you from somewhere." Her skin prickled as she uttered the words. *And that tells me you're more than what you appear.*

"I hope 'tis a good one," he said with a quick smile. "'Twould be disappointing to know otherwise."

Smooth-tongued rascal. Wary, she appraised him further, wondering about his intentions.

He laughed at her scrutiny, and waited for her to complete her examination of him.

The pleasant rumble of his laughter awakened an unmerited desire to know him better. For some time, she'd felt anxious about her future—Robbie was gone, her father too. Perhaps this surprising twist of fate and the developments at which Daly hinted would help to answer the questions in her heart.

With a clatter, the carriage arrived and Brieve, the Gilmore servant, jumped down from his roost to load the vehicle with baggage, interrupting their exchange. Fergus nudged Daly, who reached into his leather jerkin and pulled out a letter. "Lass, I've a note from your mother. Once you've bid the Gilmores farewell, you can read what the mistress has to say." He jerked his head in Eavan's direction. "We're travelin' with him."

She arched a brow, startled, but having no reason to doubt his word. Pocketing the letter, she walked down the strand with the Gilmores. Molly clung to her with chubby arms and tears filled Jennie's eyes.

"When will we see you again, Kennis?" Sniffling, she wiped them away with the back of her hand. "I'll miss you something fearsome!"

"We shall indeed," Mrs. Gilmore echoed, enveloping her in a motherly embrace. "You're truly a blessing, Kennis. I hope we'll see you again soon. Greet your dear mother and sister for us. I must write to her at once to express our gratitude for sharing you with us for so long."

"Mrs. Gilmore, the pleasure has been mine. Molly, Jennie, I'll miss you both." Kennis returned their affectionate farewell. "You must come and visit us on Lewis. I'm sure Mairi will be delighted to have two more sisters." Molly's smile brightened her tear-stained cheeks.

The most difficult time had arrived all too soon. The girls climbed into the carriage as Mr. Gilmore gave Kennis a warm, strong hug. "Kennis, lass, I'll miss you, too. Come to see us when you feel the need to escape the island."

"I will, sir," she said, delighted by the invitation. "Nothing compares to the Highlands, and I so dislike saying good-bye."

"As do we all, lass. Well then, we'll look to see you at Inveraray. Bring your family, if they'll come. Good bye for now, lass, Health to you," he said, turning to step into the carriage. The girls poked their heads and arms out of the window to wave as it rumbled away.

She lifted her hand and called out. "Good bye, Health to you!" The coach disappeared around the corner and she turned to face the men awaiting her. *Four years of my life have swiftly passed*, she reflected. *I've been across the Atlantic twice, to America and home again.* A quiver of excitement ran through her. *What new adventures lay ahead, I wonder?*

Chapter 8

Port Eilidh, Islay

The pungent odor and loud noise of the shipyard faded, replaced by the general racket of the busy town.

Sitting aboard the rumbling wagon, Kennis rode down the crowded street toward the market with her three companions. The strident cries of vendors filled the square, the aroma of freshly baked bread making her mouth water. Her stomach growled just as she spied a candy maker.

"Daly," she said, breaking the silence that had fallen over the group. "Can we stop here for a moment? I'd like to make a purchase." The sweets would be a welcome snack on the journey home and a gift for her little sister.

"Aye, lass, sure ye can." He nodded to Fergus, who pulled on the reins of the plodding carthorse. "Not home for an hour and ye're shoppin' already."

She grinned at the grumblings of her old friend. Some things never changed.

Eavan jumped down from the wagon, turned expectantly toward her and held out his hand.

Still wary, she was nevertheless polite. "Thank you kindly, sir."

His formal tone matched hers. "You're welcome, mistress."

Kennis smirked. His manners were more suited to a ballroom than the open street. What was he up to, really?

"May I escort you to yon vendor's booth?"

She played his game, taking his proffered arm the short distance to the booth. "Indeed, sir, you may."

"Wha' can I get for ye, mistress?" The plump woman in the stall eyed her hopefully.

Smiling, she stopped at the booth and greeted the woman in her native tongue. Mairi would enjoy the cinnamon flavored treat but to her, the brief interaction with a fellow Scot was sweet enough after being away from home for so long.

"I'd like a half pound of the cinnamon *gundy*[7], and a quarter of the anise, please." She watched the woman carefully measure out the sweets.

"Aye, now show me your *siller*[8]." The woman wrapped up the sweets after Kennis handed her the coins. "Thank ye kindly, Good day." She bobbed a curtsey.

"You're welcome," Kennis said, unable to hide her pleasure. "Good day."

Eavan hovered at her elbow as she strolled through the bustling thoroughfare. The inn stood on the opposite side of the street where Daly impatiently waited at the door for her and for Fergus, who drove the wagon containing her trunks.

When Kennis and Eavan crossed the rough cobblestones to stand before him, Daly cleared his throat. She cast him a fleeting glance, brows lifted in mute question. He was up to his old tricks, no doubt he meant for her to watch her tongue. She dipped her chin in response to his quizzical look. Eavan's family and her own hadn't been on speaking terms for many years. Aware of the tension between the two families, she wasn't privy to the cause of the separation.

A weathered sign hung above the entrance to the Auld Bane Inn, and the creaky door banged hard against the wall from the constant coming and going of its patrons. Eavan opened the door, barely avoiding the low hanging sign. "After you, mistress," he said. "Be sure to watch your bonnie head."

---

[7] *A hard cinnamon or anise flavored candy*

[8] *Money*

She colored, quickly releasing his arm. All of a sudden, two figures walking down the busy street caught her attention. "I'll be right back," she announced.

"Here now," Eavan began, "don't go running off. 'Tisn't safe." He walked briskly after her, reaching her side in time to see her hand a scruffy urchin some of her newly purchased sweets.

"Oh, Eavan, I'm glad you've come." She gave him a hopeful look. "I've spent my last pennies on the gundy. Have you a coin to give this poor woman? I'll pay you back when we reach home."

A ragged woman stood nearby with her child, watching with a speculative gleam in her eye.

"If you wish it, of course." He dug into his leather jack and produced the desired coin.

After he handed it to the poor woman, she promptly bit into it. "Thank 'ee kindly, Laird," she said, satisfied with his offering. Bidding the child to follow, she hobbled off. The little boy waved to Kennis as he followed his mother down the busy thoroughfare.

She heaved a sigh, watching them. Her heart was resolute; someday she would make a bigger difference in the lives of the poor. *Help me, God.*

"A penny for your thoughts, lass." Eavan said, waiting at her side.

"Thank you, Eavan," she said, shaken from her musings. "You have no idea how pleased I am to offer such a small gift to the needy. I wish I could do more."

He nodded. "'Tis a worthy cause but you can't feed them all, no one can."

"Aye, but we can do our part, and if everyone did just a wee bit there would be more full bellies and clothed backs in this world. I believe such troubles can be resolved."

He shrugged. It wasn't his concern. "Not unless the entire world has a change of mind and heart. And now," he gave her a lop-sided grin, "if I'm not to expire of hunger, have a heart for me. Let's return to the inn and partake of our luncheon." He drew her arm through the crook of his own and led her away.

The proprietor of the inn warmly greeted them upon their entrance. "*Failte*[9], milady." He turned to Eavan. "Laird, I've prepared all ye requested. Please follow me." He led the way to a private parlor.

"Have you a chamber where I might refresh myself?" Kennis asked.

"Aye, one of the maids'll wait on ye."

"Thank you." She turned to her attendants. "Daly, Fergus, I'd like a word with you." She crossed to a narrow window and the men followed.

"There's also a room for your use, sir."

Eavan pulled out a chair at the oak table in the center of the room. "Aye, soon enough, but drinks for the lads first, MacDonald."

"That I will, sir. Do ye require anything else?"

"Are there any messages for me?"

"I'll look into it." MacDonald left the room. Within minutes, he brought a serving tray laden with a pitcher and ale-filled tankards, and set it down. He then pulled a grimy piece of paper out of his worn apron pocket. "'Twas left by a man earlier today, Laird."

Eavan set down his tumbler and reached for the note. "At what time, do you recall?"

"Och, mid-mornin', I reckon."

"I see," he said, considering. "Did another man accompany the lad who delivered this?" The sunlight streamed into the parlor through the double window. He glanced at Kennis and her men, quietly conversing by the window.

"Naught tha' I know of, sir, but he said he'd return at noon, and await ye in the common room.

Eavan nodded. "Thank you for your trouble."

"Ye're surely welcome, 'tis my pleasure to serve."

---

[9] *Welcome*

Eavan flipped him a gold coin before perusing the spidery scrawl on the brief missive. What did the villain want from him now? So far, the information he'd gained wasn't enough to make the tiresome partnership worthwhile. An uneasy feeling stole over him; he needed to make alternate plans immediately. When he returned to Malcolm House, he would arrange a meeting with Conor Malcolm, to see what news was available.

He glanced toward the window to find Daly watching him. Eavan invited the men to drink with him, and Fergus and Daly gladly accepted. When Kennis released them, they reached for the proffered mugs, concluding after a sip that the finest brew came from the Highlands.

Kennis followed the landlord, laughing at her two friends. After all, their prejudices concerning their homeland were only natural. She climbed the narrow stairs and waited as he opened a door on the left side of the hall. "I hope this'll do," he said, intent to please. "There's hot water and towels, everythin' for your ablutions. If ye need anythin' else, just ring the bell and Lena will wait on ye."

"Thank you, sir, for your trouble."

"'Tis all in a day's work. Good day to ye."

Kennis smiled. "Good day." A drab chamber greeted her, the walls bare and the furniture utilitarian. At least it was clean and the necessities provided for her comfort. She opened her small portmanteau and drew out her hairbrush. Picking up the pitcher on the washstand, she poured the tepid water into the flat basin, and dashed it over her face and neck.

Tidying her hair, she tucked wayward strands into the loose coil, wondering what minor miracle had occurred to cause her mother and cousin Hugh to be reconciled to Eavan and his family. She puzzled over her response to him at their first meeting, trying to recall something important from the past. Troubled, she rose from the stool and exited the room.

At the foot of the steps, a firm hand took possession of her elbow from behind, startling her out of her deliberations. Her senses reeled. That faint spicy citrus scent belonged to only one man.

"We meet again, so soon," he murmured, his warm breath tickling her ear. "I trust you're able to stay out of mischief now that you're ashore."

She raised her chin, attempting to pull away and brush past him. "I don't see why it should concern you, sir. You don't even have the courtesy to properly introduce yourself. For all I know, you're as much of a rogue as De—"

He lightly pressed his finger over her lips before she could utter the name.

"Be still, lass," he said softly. "Don't speak of the villain in here, you'll cause me trouble. Unless, of course, 'tis your intent."

She shook off the hand resting too familiarly on her shoulder. "No matter what I say, you willfully misjudge me."

"I hoped you'd enough sense not to chat about my affairs in public," he said, unperturbed. "Perhaps my first assessment of you was correct."

"Oh?" she said. "And just exactly what was that?"

He looked at her in mock disbelief. "You don't remember my words to you on the galley?"

She tossed her glossy braid over her shoulder, moving away from him. "Nay," she said, pert. "There were far too many. Besides, why should I remember when you behaved so horribly, and falsely accused me of being some kind of spy?"

"Now lass, you mistook my noble intent." He crossed his arms and leaned against the door, blocking her path so that she couldn't escape. "You needed someone to point out the error of your foolish ways."

Her mouth fell open in disbelief. "You call ripping my character to shreds *noble*? You also dubbed me a regular bairn." She faced him squarely. "Admit it. You were an insufferable boor."

"You don't expect me to take that fish bait, do you, lass?" He uncrossed his arms, his body taut with impatience. "I had to know what you were doing aboard."

"So you do admit that you were unreasonable." Her eyes gleamed, challenging him to disagree.

"Of course not," he denied. The corner of his mouth tilted in a crooked smile, adding to his roguish charm. "Do you take delight in opposing me? I'll have to teach you otherwise." He reached for her, his dark eyes softening. "You didn't say a proper farewell," his voice grew husky, "and now you'll have to pay a forfeit."

"Again?" Her brows knit in confusion. "You teased me about that once before, but you're the one who didn't bother to say good-bye. Most ungentlemanly of you, sir. Besides, Mr. Gilmore assured me that he'd deliver my parting message. Did you not receive it?"

"Aye, I did, and a saucy one it was." His eyes were alight with glee. "There's no help for it, you'll have to pay a double forfeit for your audacity."

"Nay, I've already given up a silk riband." She held him at arm's length. Her heart hammered so hard that she felt sure everyone in the room could hear it reverberate upon the walls. "Besides, I merely returned the favor of the compliment you sent to me through Mr. Gilmore, after we were nearly washed overboard."

He shrugged and drew closer. "I'll buy you another, one to match your bonnie eyes but first, I must teach you a new lesson. Taunting a man to his face has its own price, lass."

"I did no such thing." She tried to move away but he wouldn't yield. "I've said nothing that isn't true. Lud, sir," she said in exasperation, her temper rising, "you mocked me in front of your men. What's the difference between the two?" Annoying rogue!

"Nonsense, don't change the subject. We were speaking of Mr. Gilmore and the polite compliments you sent to me via that gentleman."

"Aye, wasn't I uncommon clever?" She relented slightly, pleased with her own wit. "I hope you and Farrell were entertained, 'twas far better than the *fine for me and not for you* game you play."

Tired of wrangling, he answered by sweeping her none too gently into his arms.

Desperate to untangle herself, she pushed hard against his chest but made the mistake of stealing an upward glance. Caught by the warmth in his eyes, she stopped struggling and melted into his embrace, forgetting that she stood in a public inn.

He tightened his hold upon her and lowered his head.

She trembled, her heart pounding.

Feeling the ripple of her emotion, he drew in a sharp breath before gently brushing his lips against hers in a feathery kiss. "That barely qualifies for the first forfeit, lass," he murmured unsteadily. "Ready for the second?"

Jarred out of her temporary insanity by the sound of his voice, she stiffened. "Nay, unhand me, you, you—"

"Villain," he readily supplied, "knave, poltroon? You seem to have run out of sweet nothings for me, lass. Just remember," he said, not unkindly, "a man knows when a kiss is welcome and freely given. Now, about that second forfeit," he said lazily, his eyes darkening in anticipation, "to insure you've learned your lesson." At her affronted look, he grinned. "Think of it as a small token of my affection."

Token of his affection and love lessons? The scoundrel! She attempted to wrench herself free. "One undeserved *token* is enough, I assure you, ill-gotten as it was. I must go." She tried to step back a second time.

Reluctant to let go, he released her. "Faint-hearted?" He lifted a mocking brow.

"You repeat yourself, sir. I'm no coward, and you'd best remember it."

"I won't," he said. "Nor will I forget your indebtedness to me."

"Only in your imagination," she declared. "I'm not beholden to you."

"Ah, but you are," he laughed, warm and low, "and you'd best remember that I always collect my due." He took her hand into his and planted a light kiss upon the inside of her wrist. "Until we have the pleasure of meeting again, sweet. Fare well and God speed."

Heat flooded her cheeks. She jerked her tingling hand away and fled amidst the laughter of a handful of the male patrons of the inn who witnessed the scene. Flustered, she entered the chamber occupied by Eavan, Daly and Fergus, who were in the midst of a discussion about their traveling plans. The three men rose from their seats as Kennis pulled up a chair, her pulse erratic. *Settle yourself, ye gowk.*

"MacDonald will be back in a trice, lass," Daly said. "In the meantime, I'd like to have a wee talk with ye about our journey."

Eavan remained standing. "What would you like to drink, Kennis? I'll fetch it for you."

She was pleasantly surprised by his offer. "Oh, something cold other than ale, if there's anything to be had, Eavan, and thank you."

He nodded and retreated down the hall, the heels of his boots clicking on the wooden floor.

"What's to do, lass?" Daly noted her flushed countenance.

"Nothing," she blurted too quickly, averting her eyes. She dropped the subject and he didn't pursue it but sat watching her for several minutes.

* * *

Eavan stepped from the room, glad for Kennis' timely interruption. He strode down the short passage and paused, scanning the entrance before crossing into the public room on the opposite side. In the far corner, a large, black-haired man sat with his profile to the door. Across the table, his companion drank a mug of ale. Eavan stiffened and took in a sharp breath, recognizing the face. Looking away, he searched the room for Niall Malcolm, his kinsman, and discovered him sitting at the opposite end of the long room in a dark alcove, smoking his pipe. When Niall began to rise, he motioned to him. Eavan slid into a chair and got straight to the point. "I see we have unexpected company."

"Aye, Laird, he came in a few minutes ago," Niall replied.

"Have you been here all morning?" Eavan cast a furtive glance around. Something just didn't feel right; his plans were going to go awry, he just knew it.

"Off and on. I posted two men to send for me when ye came."

"I got your message but I can't stay long." He glanced toward his long-time nemesis, seated by the door. "I wonder what he's doing here."

Niall shrugged. "I dinna know, they just arrived."

"Well, I need to hurry. They're expecting me back soon."

Niall produced a folded note and handed it to his master. "It arrived yesterday evenin'."

Eavan broke the seal and perused the contents written in a bold hand. *Events are proceeding as planned. I will rendezvous with you on the 10th of October to finalize and to bring you news. Be there. Yours, etc.*

"Blast the man," he cursed. "Can he never be more specific? Be there, he says. Events are proceeding as planned. Bah!" He crumpled the piece of paper and threw it into the fire. "Does he take me for a complete fool? At any rate," he said, calming down, "I also have some good news. I'm gaining favor with my long lost relations. Everything's in place, including the documents. The only trouble now is the girl."

Niall, waiting patiently, raised his brows. "The girl?"

"Aye, my cousin has returned from America. What am I to do with her?" He raked his hand through sandy locks. "I'm expected to take her to the McKinnon on Skye, although she and her henchmen think they're traveling to Lewis."

"To the McKinnon, sir?" Niall frowned. "What have ye to do with him?"

"Haven't you been listening?" Eavan glanced furtively around. "He's her grandfather."

"Well, if that's so, then he should be grateful to ye," Niall said. "Is she a comely wench?"

He smirked. "Aye, that she is. What do you have in mind?"

"Marry the lass. Seal it right and tight, legal-like. 'Twould make it easier to get hold of everything ye're tryin' to recover."

"And thwart our noble accomplice?" Eavan rubbed his chin. "I like it. I like the lass, too, come to think of it." He stood abruptly. "I need to go. You can return home while I'm off to Skye." He paused, considering more options. "What of Conor Malcolm?"

"Nae heard from him," Niall replied. "Seems he's occupied with other business of late."

"I see." He contemplated the information. "I'll be in touch soon." He rose and slowly made his way out of the room, stealing a cautious glance at the two men seated in the opposite corner.

Chapter 9

The Letter

He kissed me and I kissed him back.

Kennis squirmed in her chair, barely hearing Daly explain their traveling plans.

"We'll begin our journey today," Daly explained, "spend the night in Kilcreag and come mornin', sail up the Sound into the Firth o' Lorne. The crossin's rough, so we'll pass Skye to avoid the open waters o' the Minch.

Maps and distances usually interested her but her thoughts were in turmoil after her brief encounter with the laird. "We'll not see Eavan's home?" she said, disappointed and forcing her thoughts to attend to the matter at hand. "I'll admit I'm curious about him."

"Malcolm House is further inland, southeast of the Bay of Craignish, lass. We canna risk goin' so far." His broad fist pounded the table. "We need to stay as far away from Campbell lands as we can!"

"Are the Campbells still troublesome, Daly?" Worry laced her voice. "I'd hoped to hear otherwise upon my return home." The Uprising was over but people didn't change quite so easily. There were too many enemies abroad and without her father and Robbie to protect her, she was an easy mark for anyone with a vendetta against her clan.

"Aye, *fasheous* enough. When Fergus and I traveled to Argyll, our reception was far from friendly, except for the lassies." He winked and she laughed. "But I think 'tis the lads that might worry ye more, lass."

"Whatever in the world do you mean?"

"Take that Eavan Malcolmson now," he countered shrewdly. "Seems to have taken a shine to ye."

Her cheeks grew warm. "We're barely acquainted. Besides, I know very little about him."

"That's my point," he said.

Dismayed, she stared at him. "Are you saying he's not to be trusted?"

"Just a gut feelin', lass."

"Why bring him with you then?" She eyed him and Fergus, who sat quietly listening to the other two. "Didn't Mam send him? She must have confidence in him to allow him to accompany you here."

"After he persuaded your cousin, Sir Hugh, aye."

"What do you mean, Daly McCallum?" she demanded, strumming her fingers on the table. "I want a straight answer. What about Grandad?"

He glanced at the doorway. "The McKinnon's yet to meet him." The shuffle of several pairs of feet sounded on the wooden floorboards. "Not now, lass. Read the letter I gave ye from your mother first."

She leaned back in her chair, peering into the short hall, and sat up straight as Eavan reentered the room, a glass of lemonade in hand.

He set it down in front of her. "I'm sorry to keep you waiting, mistress."

"'Tis no trouble at all, sir," she said, a spark of mischief in her eye. "I'm fair near parched to death, but I thank you all the same."

"In that case, I'll see to it that you receive an extra glass," he said gravely, his twinkling grey-green eyes in stark contrast to the solemnity of his voice. "I can't have such a lovely lass expire of thirst on my account."

During their simple exchange of pleasantries, the landlord and maidservant laid out a generous portion of food on the table. Throughout the meal, Kennis couldn't help but notice how frequently Eavan's eyes gravitated in her direction, but his examination of her didn't impede her enjoyment of the simple fare. A slab of cheese, fried herrings, and fresh barley bannocks graced the table. To make her happiness complete, in a day or two she would see her mother and sister.

The meal passed all too quickly and soon Daly urged them to hurry. "We've a long journey ahead, are ye finished, lass? Wrap that bannock up and take it along, if ye're that hungry."

She laughed. "I'm not hungry at all. I'm absolutely stuffed, but I'll take it with me for a snack later."

"Take 'em all if you like. But mind, ye'll have to share."

"What for? If I carry them, then they're all mine!"

He lifted a sandy brow in mock horror at her lack of good manners as they ambled through the narrow passage. "Don't sass now, or I'll turn ye over my knee like I did when ye were a bairn."

"Is that so?" she scoffed. "Fergus," she said sweetly, "are you going to let him talk to me like that?" She clutched his arm and smiled up at him.

The big man shook his curly head. "Ye know I wouldna let any man do such a cruel thing to ye, lass."

The laughing trio enjoyed their easy camaraderie, failing to see Eavan's glare as he entered behind them. His old nemesis, Alistair MacDougall, Laird of Dunolly, walked into the vestibule from the public room. The two men stopped short in their tracks and stared at one another.

The laughter died on Kennis' lips as she watched the two men and listened, fascinated, to their conversation.

"Malcolmson." Alistair's harsh tone sounded his dislike.

"Haven't changed at all, have you, Alistair," Eavan returned, razor sharp.

"We've no reason to love one another," Alistair said coldly. "What brings a weasel like you out of his hole?"

"No, we don't," Eavan returned evenly, ignoring the insult and controlling his temper. "And none of your business. But for the record, I'm escorting my fair kinswoman home to her family on Lewis."

Kennis' eyes flew to Alistair's. In his, she read a mixture of astonishment and revulsion.

"You've chosen yourself a fine traveling companion, mistress," he said. "Had I known, I might have left you to Denoon. 'Tis all you deserve."

She fumed, affronted and not deserving such cruelty. Eavan's escort wasn't her doing. In fact, she was barely acquainted with him. "How dare you insult me so, sir? I've done nothing to merit such scorn." After their intimacy earlier, how could he be so unfeeling? Her sensibilities wounded, she defended herself. "I am at the disposal of my kinsmen and obedient to my family's will, besides, I hardly know—"

"'Tis no excuse," he said, curt. "You should have refused his escort. You'll receive your just desserts if you continue to associate with such a one as he." His dark eyes glittered with unconcealed anger.

"Here now, that's no way to talk to the lassie." Daly's protest fell on disbelieving ears.

"No? And who are you, another of her misbegotten kinsman?"

All activity in the lobby ceased as the confrontation escalated.

Daly's face turned beet red and his fists clenched at his side. Equally insulted, Fergus growled, stepping into the fray.

"Stop it, all of you!" Kennis stamped her foot. "There is no reason for this madness." She briskly walked toward the door and swung it open. "Let's go, Daly, Fergus," she commanded. "Are you coming Eavan, or not?"

Seeing an end in sight to the altercation, the interested patrons of the inn resumed their activity.

Eavan stood rooted to the floor, listening to their dialogue. He threw her a cursory glance. "Aye, I'm coming." He wisely said nothing more, glowering at Alistair as he passed through the open door.

Daly lowered his fist and Fergus wore a long face.

Behind Alistair, Farrell studied the assembled company. "Laird," he said calmly, breaking the silence. "The lads are here with the wagon." He caught Kennis' eye, all the while appraising her two companions.

She flushed under his careful scrutiny although she'd done nothing wrong. *Alistair,* she realized too late. *His name is Alistair.* Desperate, she sought his face. His expression stabbed her heart like a cold, hard blade. His dark eyes glittered with anger. The tenderness that filled them only a short hour ago had vanished, now replaced by loathing and disdain.

Salvaging her pride, Kennis squared her shoulders and raised her chin, returning stare for stare as she walked out the door, her two cohorts silently following in her wake.

* * *

The day was still young when Kennis and her companions stepped into the Highland galley to begin their journey home. Although she enjoyed sailing, this trip would be the last she planned for a while. Autumn was here and she, Mam and Mairi were going to enjoy every possible minute of the remaining fine weather before the cold winter arrived.

Sitting on the hard wooden bench, she fumed over the incident at the inn. *Alistair.* How dare he accuse her and treat her with such contempt, berating Eavan so cruelly, too? *Alistair,* the name echoed in her mind. She shifted uncomfortably, snagging her finger on the rough wood. Ouch, a splinter had embedded itself into her soft flesh. Her brows met in frustration, wondering what had caused the rift between the two men, and what prompted her mother to have confidence in a Malcolmson cousin with whom she was not well acquainted.

Alistair obviously mistrusted Eavan, nay, despised him. Unfortunate that she was now involved in their dispute by default, assumed party to it because of her kinship to the man. Almost immediately, she remembered the letter Daly had given to her at the wharf in Port Eilidh.

Breaking the seal, her heart leapt wildly. In her mother's fine handwriting, she read,

My dearest Kennis,

I trust this letter finds you well and in the care of our beloved kinsmen, Fergus and Daly. As you know by now, your cousin Eavan Malcolmson has become a trusted friend and ally. I can hardly begin to tell you in this simple letter all that he has done for our people, daughter. In time, I shall. He is a kind hearted man, and generous. He came unexpectedly to Dun Eistein three months ago to see me. Hugh welcomed him and spoke for me at first. Eavan understood since your father and his were not on friendly terms. When Hugh was convinced that he meant well, he sent for me and explained the reason for Eavan's visit.

He brings news of our Robbie, my dear. I confess that I was utterly astonished and could not say a word! Eavan claims that it is a surety he will be released from his servitude and returned to us. Robbie has been in Jamaica, not America. It is no wonder you could find no trace or record of him. Even more wondrous is the possibility that Dunchalum will be restored to us. It is not yet certain.

You must know that your father was at peace with Argyll although they had bitter words. Argyll counseled him not to follow the Bonnie Prince. However, what is done, is done. There is no going back. Campbell of Fraoch Eilean is Constable on Argyll's behalf of Dunchalum. This has been a recent development. I am sorry I did not tell you sooner, my dear one, but I simply did not want to give you more pain.

Eavan showed Hugh and me very convincing documents to assert that the information he possesses is accurate and true. I believe you are in safe hands with Eavan. He is a noble and charming young man.

How I look forward to sharing in this joy with you! We will meet soon now, "May the Lord bless thee and keep thee, make His face to shine upon thee, be gracious unto thee and lift up His countenance upon thee, and give thee peace[10]."

Mairi sends her love and I close with mine,
Your Loving Mother

---

[10] *Numbers 6:24-26; KJV, paraphrased*

The galley swiftly cut through the water, the gusting winds propelling it forward. Kennis took a deep breath in an attempt to still her shaking hands and ease the sudden throbbing in her temples. To have Robbie home and Dunchalum restored seemed incredible. Glancing up, she saw Eavan watching her. He obviously knew the contents of the letter and guessed what raced through her mind as she read.

To his credit, he was discreet in referring to her as a Morrison cousin on their short journey. Gilmore was a Morrison *sept,* and while Kennis traveled with Peyton, Ailis and the girls, the name provided a measure of protection in itself. The Gilmores were kin on her mother's side of the family and the Morrisons of Lewis had little to do with Culloden. Only those who went out to join the prince in the '45 suffered much grief in the aftermath.

Her hidden identity was important to the safety of her father's clan and to Robbie's future recovery. Kennis, Mam, and Grandad McKinnon laid careful plans to find him before she left for America. She couldn't afford discovery now. The documents Eavan possessed must be of tremendous import.

She held the letter open in her hand, vacantly staring at the rippling, white-capped sea. Perusing the missive once again, she wondered how Eavan had acquired his information. Sir Hugh and Mam were satisfied that the documents were legitimate. Surely, the two wouldn't ignore the slightest twinge of doubt about the origin of Eavan's information persuaded by hope in men alone. Perhaps they were hoping against all hope, placing confidence in false evidence and disregarding the warning in their hearts.

Hope is often misguided without faith in God. It can even make the human heart sick. Trust in God is different, and faith is much more than the stuff of heavenly dreams. Faith is apparent in the tangible and intangible, the ordinary transformed into the extraordinary in such a way that a person not only can hear and see, but experience all five senses in a supernatural way.

On a practical level, Eavan's family wasn't out in the '45, and he might have reliable connections. Participation in the uprising was a matter of choices and his father made the wiser one. Still, she questioned the motive behind his decision to help find Robbie now. She must ask him why he'd chosen to become involved in their lives after so many years of disharmony in the family.

Kennis gazed at Knapdale to her right; to the left loomed the crags and peaks of the fog-encircled Isle of Jura, visible even at this distance. She knew these islands well, recognized various points and curves in the coastline. Her father, Robert Ewen McCallum, taught her as a young girl. She learned about the sea and sailing from him at the same time as her brother Robbie.

Kennis was a determined child—anything Robbie could do, she could do better. Amused by her resolution, Robert humored her and taught her the art of sailing. Conversation during their outings generally centered on nature, the sea and wildlife or foliage native to Scotland, and God.

"I love to see the hills from the sea, Papa. I can almost smell the heather and feel it beneath my feet. Do you think there'll be heather on the hills in heaven?"

Laughing, Robert said, "Aye, lassie, I do. Now what kind of place would heaven be without at least a wee bit o' the sweet stuff? I'm sure every good Scot believes 'tis there, else one would insist upon takin' it with him! Can ye imagine the archangel Gabriel at the pearly gate, trumpet in hand, tryin' to make one of us leave the weed behind?"

"But the Bible says that we can't take anything with us."

"Aye and no, but ye have to admit 'tis a bonnie flowerin' plant. I suppose ye could compare a Scot's hope in seein' it there to faith, in a simple way."

"But how?" she asked.

"Faith is the ground on which we believe in Christ, and I think that what we're hopin' for is like the heather. We canna see if 'tis there in heaven or no right now, but we hope, and someday we'll see the Bonnie Man, face to Face. 'Tis a wee reminder that what we hope for isna always something to be seen with our eyes, just believed in our hearts."

Oh, how she missed him, and the special times together. Kennis shared her mother's heartache. The only hope remaining was that Robbie still lived somewhere in the colonies. No, that wasn't exactly true. Alanna McCallum's strong faith in God carried her and her daughters through this horrible period of their lives. Kennis hoped that her faith would stay strong like her parents. If she ever married and had bairns of her own, she would impart the same confidence in God to them.

* * *

Alistair glowered, his gaze following Kennis and her henchmen vacating the inn. "Farrell," he said, gruff. "Where are the lads?"

"Out back in the alley, Laird."

He jerked his head toward the door. "Did you send Jocko to follow them?"

"Aye," he affirmed.

"Good. We'll see what mischief Malcolmson's brewing and what the girl has to do with him." Farrell's solemn countenance gave him pause. "Well, out with it, man."

Farrell considered his words well. "Don't ye think ye were a bit rough on the lass?"

"Rough?" Alistair snorted. "I don't think I was blunt enough."

"I thought ye were," Farrell said. "Brutally so,"

"Now I'm a brute, eh?" He was visibly annoyed. Alistair had never worn his irritation well or tried to hide his fierce pride. "We'll see who proves to be, me or that villain."

"I know how ye feel about him, lad, none better, but none of us can help the blood relatives we have, including the lass."

"Moralizing over me, are you? I'm afraid I'm a lost cause, Farrell," he admitted. "I've the devil of a temper."

"Aye, sir," Farrell said. "I'm well acquainted with it."

His smile was grim. "Indeed." He looked away, his attention caught by Jocko running toward them.

Jocko stopped to catch his breath. "They've sailed off, Laird, and none stayed behind."

"Then let's ride," he said, "for Craignish and Dunolly, Farrell, before I'm off to Inveraray to visit his grace." He led the way out the back door to the narrow lane, down the alley to the quay, avoiding the people that made their abode in the deteriorating tenements. A lone figure stole after them, taking a protracted look at the Laird of the MacDougalls.

Alistair glanced over his shoulder, eyes narrowing. He scanned the road ahead and behind. Must have been his imagination. *Losh,* he'd been imagining far too many things of late. Before long, the group drew near to Rab and the moored galley. After loading the vessel, the men rowed out into the Sound of Jura, hoping the wind would be in their favor.

Standing in the fore, his arms rested on the dipping bow, the salty spray misting over him. He mulled over the events of the last few days and hours, passing the time in thoughtful silence.

One kiss. He'd not really intended anything more, a wee flirtation, that's all. One kiss had shaken his practiced reserve. Long ago, he'd given up courting females, waiting for the right one. Growing disinterested in marriage, he was convinced he would never meet a lass in whose company he'd care to spend a full week, let alone a lifetime. One kiss? Alistair shook his head in patent disbelief.

He heaved a sigh, setting aside matters of the heart as he prepared to disembark the galley.

Chapter 10

Fox and Huntsman

What a fool I am.

Alistair sat in the duke's well-appointed library brooding over the sudden turn of events. The fire in the large hearth crackled, reflecting his uncertain temper. Somehow he'd fallen into a well-laid snare, one set especially for him. Although he promised the duke nothing, his future hung precariously in the balance.

The imperious summons three days before to Inveraray Castle, home of the Chief of Clan Campbell, failed to stir petty emotion in his heart. A lesser man might have been afraid. The duke had sought his opinion or requested that he perform a special task on more than one occasion. He owed his allegiance to Argyll; he deserved the respect due to the head of his mother's kin.

In addition, the duke was instrumental in the return of precious MacDougall lands to him and his clan, sealing their alliance. Considering what the MacDougalls had won and lost in years past, to be in the favor of Archibald Campbell, the Duke of Argyll and presently the most powerful man in Scotland, was an added boon.

Persuaded by Argyll, he'd not fought in the uprising of 1745. A few of the MacDougall clansmen had gone out anyway, including Duncan, his younger brother.

He was chief of his clan, he could have stopped the young men but to see Scotland set free from English tyranny was the heartfelt desire of all true-blooded Scots. As for himself, he'd fight for Scotland despite Argyll's opinion if he chose to do so. Unfortunately, the Bonnie Prince was vain, and charm alone would not win battles.

Argyll, fighting for the English King against his own countrymen, used his influence to restore Duncan to his family after the Battle of Culloden. Locating Duncan had been no easy task. Moreover, smuggling the young man through the Highlands and home to Dunolly took a considerable effort. He grimaced. Another reason to be grateful to the duke. This further obligation made him uneasy but his will remained firm. His conscience wouldn't allow persuasive arguments to alter his personal convictions.

That spring, Argyll offered the return of Dunolly Castle and MacDougall lands along Loch Etive and a new acquisition, Craignish Castle, south of Oban, in exchange for his promise not to fight the English. How could he refuse? Argyll argued against Alistair's participation in what he believed to be a lost cause. Had the MacDougalls not suffered enough humiliation and defeat in years past? Overall, the duke gave prudent counsel, and Alistair and his clan greatly benefited from his wisdom.

The implication that he was disloyal to Scotland bothered him the most. He wasn't the only Scot who resisted taking up this Cause. Prominent men from all over the country abstained from this war on England in an effort to rid the country of the old ways that pressed the people into abject poverty.

And just as many were willing to risk all—their lives, their lands and the well-being of the clan family for the Cause. The McKinnon of McKinnon, for one, was a fierce opponent to anything English and Alistair respected the old man's opinions. His arguments were just, yet Alistair felt compelled to protect his family and to see Scotland free of the tyranny of poverty.

Secret Jacobite meetings in Edinburgh were held before the prince landed in Scotland, and those who didn't support Charlie's Cause were accused of treason. The McKinnon came to his rescue in the midst of a heated debate.

"Well, lads," the McKinnon said, after the room at the inn had quieted. "I canna blame the MacDougall here for nae wantin' to go out. We've all our clans to consider and the man has little enough left after the '15. 'Tis a serious business, and ye'd best think well on it ere ye make a hasty and enthusiastic decision. If ye're willin' to become an outcast and subject your entire clan to the same, then so be it, but dinna condemn the rest who disagree with ye for concern o'er the people. Scotland wouldna be Scotland without 'em!"

Hearing of the fiery old chief's release from prison after the '45[11], Alistair was greatly relieved. *I'd like to visit with the McKinnon, to see how he fares.* His frown deepened as he contemplated the duke's displeasure. *A puppet on a string, that's what I'll become if I'm not careful.* It was past time to sever this close tie or at the very least, loosen the knot before he became hopelessly entangled. He must distance himself from Argyll's sphere of influence.

The noose Argyll presently connived to place about his neck had little to do with the art of warfare or political intrigue. It was the tightest of all, a promise of intent to marry. He'd gain wealth and lands through this particular alliance but Argyll assumed too much. He wasn't agreeable to an arranged marriage. He preferred to select his own bride; gaining wealth wasn't equal to this personal sacrifice. He was determined not to be manipulated through marriage or to be bought with lands and gold.

Power and position were vital to Argyll, and Alistair seriously questioned his own heart before accepting the duke's first offer. Though it meant restoring precious MacDougall lands, what would be the ultimate cost to him and to his clan family? They depended on him to make the right decision in all matters. How far was he willing to be obligated to the Campbells, kin or no, and not only to Argyll but to Campbell of Breadalbane? He'd much prefer to strengthen ties utilizing some other method.

---

[11] *Historically, after the '15. See Author's Notes.*

Aye, the Lady Vanora Campbell was a comely wench but not in his style. She seemed mercenary; her cold, pale beauty didn't appeal to him. She neither loved nor cared for him any more than he felt any of the more tender feelings for her. Marriage was her object, and being the eldest daughter in a family of several daughters only increased her desire to become contracted. Fortunately her father, the Earl of Breadalbane, was well endowed enough to provide a handsome dowry for her in spite of his numerous offspring, not usually the case with one daughter, let alone with four or five.

When there were several sons, normally the law of gavel applied. A chief portioned out his land to his sons as tenants and they likewise did the same with their sons, securing lands and the highest rank and position within the clan to the chief's immediate family.

He scowled. Why did he postpone the inevitable? He needed to provide an heir; his family, his clan, expected it of him as their Chief. In spite of the new laws conspiring to break down the clan family, he remained the father figure to those remaining in his care.

He pondered the virtues he desired in a woman. He believed himself to be an honorable, God-fearing man, as were most Highlanders. A pair of wide, soft green eyes, intruded on his thoughts. Leaning forward, he cupped his chin in his hand. Her outrage was justified; he'd treated her cavalierly. Smiling, he remembered her every expression, and when he looked deeply into her eyes, the warmth and sweetness of spirit reflected there enticed him to know more of her. And then, he kissed her. He sighed, shaking his head in denial. What was wrong with him?

He was hard on her aboard the galley and she'd taken his scolding, nay, bullying, according to Farrell, well. In fact, seldom had anyone responded to his rantings without fear. Maybe she was just plain obstinate or foolish but her courage, a quality he sought in a woman, impressed him. Did she also possess honor?

His keen, black eyes narrowed. Something seemed extremely familiar about the girl. Surely he'd seen her or someone very like her at some other time. After all, most men wouldn't forget her lovely countenance. Or maybe it was the kiss. He recalled with dissatisfaction the manner in which he'd spoken to her at the inn. He wasn't in the habit of browbeating women but Eavan Malcolmson's presence outraged and puzzled him.

His thoughts grew darker; he was no closer to figuring out the riddle now than before. Peyton Gilmore would give little information concerning the lass other than her name, Kennis Morrison of the Isle of Lewis. She was the daughter of a cousin, entrusted to his care as a companion to his daughters.

He was aware of Peyton's appointment as Argyll's new steward since John Campbell remained as factor of Kintyre. Highly recommended by MacLeod of Lewis, he came to Argyll on a trial basis. Not having fought at Culloden seemed to be an important part of any recommendation these days. Otherwise, MacLeod wouldn't have recommended him nor would Argyll have considered him.

Perhaps through Peyton he might discover more about the girl. He was surprised at the persistence of his own wayward thoughts. 'Tisn't the moment to seek out any woman, his reason insisted, beautiful eyes or sweet kisses. His resolve finally won out. "Nay," he said firmly. "I must avoid the engagement trap. I'm my own master and intend to stay that way."

His dark thoughts moved in another direction altogether as he considered his present dilemma. There was a fine line between intention and actual marriage. Hopefully Breadalbane and his daughter would take the hint without a direct confrontation. If he paid little attention to the Lady Vanora and ignored an invitation to visit her home, false expectations might not arise to plague him. Her father was just as wily as the fox Argyll. He resolved to speak with his mother upon his return to Dunolly. The need for caution was great.

The door squeaked opened and the Duke of Argyll entered the dimly lit library. Ree, the duke's large deerhound, bounded into the room. The hound sensed his mood and rubbed his huge face against Alistair's thigh.

"Alistair, my lad, sitting here by yourself on such a fine afternoon? Ree and I took an invigorating walk and would have been glad of your company. The ladies are wondering exactly where you've disappeared to, and the Lady Vanora in particular enquired after you in a most pleasing way. I do hope you're considering well what we discussed this morning."

Argyll paused, surveying his quarry. "You'd be doing yourself a tremendous favor, lad, as well as strengthening ties with your Campbell kin. Breadalbane," he continued, "is well breeched and will provide the girl with an excellent dowry. He's mentioned some fine property, Alistair, as well as a liberal financial settlement. I was quite pleased and considered it a compliment to you as well as a favor to me. You can do no better elsewhere. She's a fair lassie, wouldn't you agree? An additional benefit, I must say."

Alistair rose from his chair and greeted the duke. "I hope you're not endeavoring to further this cause," he began, carefully choosing his words. "She's a comely enough wench, sir, I won't deny. However, I don't wish to give the lady a false impression of my intentions toward her, and I hope, no disrespect intended to you, that you'll understand me when I say that I don't desire for this marriage to be contracted now or ever."

"Well, well, 'tisn't so very bad to tie the knot, my lad, as distasteful as it may be to you now. I was young once, you know. But why the objection? I'm sure if you desire a marriage of convenience, it can be arranged." Argyll watched him through hooded eyes. "The girl will do as she's told and won't object. No need to wait until you're older when such a splendid opportunity for advancement is staring you in the eye. Your own father married late, I'll grant, but that's—"

"No reason for me to do so?" Alistair finished for him. "On the contrary, to me it becomes all the more imperative to wait, in spite of *splendid opportunities*."

"But why?" Argyll said, exasperated. "You must provide an heir, surely you don't object to a Campbell alliance?"

"Nay, I don't," he said. "To suggest such a thing is absurd, your grace. I'm half Campbell myself. I've no desire for a marriage of convenience. I have personal reasons for not wishing to become engaged or contract a marriage at this time."

Ree, lying on the carpet at his feet, raised his large head. Alistair gazed at the beast, thinking that the dog was well-named. The dog's kingly, less complicated life was preferable to his own current situation.

"Personal reasons!" Argyll exclaimed. "You must know that the earl will take this personally, as do I! I personally invited the man, his wife and his two eldest daughters, believing that you were seriously considering taking a bride."

"I can't imagine what I've said to induce you to believe so," he interrupted. A log hissed on the fire in echo of his sore temper.

"You don't recall, eh, lad?" Argyll was irritated. "How convenient for you and unfortunate for me, is that it? You didn't object when I raised the question to you a fortnight ago. Why did you say nothing contrary to the suggestion then? You could've saved me, and yourself, I might add, an enormous amount of trouble," he said ominously, "and gold!"

Hands clenched behind his back, he paced back and forth before the fireplace. Stopping abruptly, he eyed Alistair with his well-known icy blue stare. "I'm displeased, Alistair, very displeased." He retreated into sarcasm. "Do you propose to tell Breadalbane and his daughter outright that they're not wanted here," he lifted a brow, "by me or by you?"

"I don't propose anything," Alistair said honestly. "And I didn't object when I saw you last because I wasn't aware that my marriage was an important consideration at that time. Nor was I aware that it was of interest to anyone but myself, except perhaps my mother. I truly didn't take the matter seriously." He paused, thinking aloud. "Let this visit take a natural course. Better to say nothing than to become embroiled in a situation from which I want nothing, and they can expect even less. I must return to Dunolly today on business, anyway."

"Hah!" Argyll said, smug. "We'll see, my lad. I don't think the lady will give in so easily. She's set her cap in your direction and intends to have you, willing or no. If you resist, I advise you to tread warily, Alistair. The lady's father is cunning and the daughter appears to have inherited the trait from him." He flashed a superior smile. "This could prove to be very entertaining after all."

"I'm not amused," Alistair gritted. "Don't underestimate me, sir. I will outwit the fox at his own game and win out in the end. I must go. I'll be sure to extend your invitation to my mother and sister. A pleasant day to you, your grace." He bowed stiffly, quitting the room upon the heels of the duke's cynical laughter.

He briskly strode down the cold hallway, his heeled boots clicking on the slate floor. He passed through the massive oaken doors, held open for him by Argyll's kilted servants. The groom awaited, walking his sable horse in the bailey. Mounting the steed, his thoughts were as black as his brow. Argyll was earnest, and not entirely amused by the situation. He'd bide his time, wait for one faulty move of Alistair's and then corner him like a wounded creature. The man was exceptionally clever; outwitting him would be a difficult task.

There was one definite way to defeat Argyll's purpose but that would be his last defense. He smiled as the plan took shape in his mind. On the long ride to Dunolly, he considered his options. A competent strategist must consult with his advisors. An old proverb entered his mind—*In a multitude of counselors, there is wisdom.*

Farrell McConacher, his first, would assist him to play this game. The man was a right canny Scot. He must also inform his mother that he wasn't in favor of this marriage. Most importantly, the final play in this game must belong to him.

Chapter 11

Castle Moil

Castle Moil remained a poignant testimony to the ways of auld Scotland, boldly jutting into the clear blue sky overhead, battlements on guard and towers keeping watch.

The castle stood sentry to the ancient passageway between the Isle of Skye and the mainland. The guards on the watchtower signaled, acknowledging the travelers' arrival.

Kennis glanced upward, occupied with thoughts of the surprise that lay in store for Grandad McKinnon, and the pleasure it would bring her to see him again after so long of a separation. She smiled to herself as they drew near to the shore, recalling the pride in her grandfather's voice as he recanted stories of his ancestors.

"Care to share the jest, mistress?" Eavan inquired at her obvious distraction.

She turned to face him. "Jest? Oh no, merely a bit of family history. But more than that, Grandad's manner when he related it to me."

"And?" he persisted.

She recited like a schoolgirl. "The story goes something like this—Findanus, the fourth McKinnon chief, married a Norse princess with the nickname of Saucy Mary around the year of our Lord 900. Well, to make a long story a wee bit shorter, Castle Moil stands between Skye and the mainland, commanding the narrow sound through which all ships must pass or else attempt the stormy waters of the Minch. My enterprising ancestors ran a heavy chain across the sound and levied a toll upon all ships passing up and down the waterway." She shrugged. "I've always thought the tale amusing."

"Well, the McKinnons are a clever lot, if I do say so m'self," Fergus said loyally.

"For my part, I canna imagine what life must be like married to a lass with the name o' Saucy Mary," Daly ventured. "Do ye think she was the one responsible for the chain and the toll?"

"I don't know." She sat up, startled by his observation. "I never thought about it. Why do you think it was Saucy Mary and not Findanus who had the idea to charge to use the passage?"

He leaned forward, hands on his knees. "Sakes, lass, whenever there's a chain and a fee, there's bound to be a woman involved. Beggin' your pardon, but ye ken this to be true."

The men on the galley hooted with laughter. "Got ye there, lassie," Fergus chortled with glee.

"I ken nothing of the kind." She made a face at the men. "I begin to understand you better, Daly McCallum. Now I know why you aren't married, and Fergus too, I'll wager. Well, I'll definitely have to see to it as soon as I see Mam."

"Dinna be findin' me a wife, lass, I'm nae lookin'," Fergus declared. "I've barely escaped on more than one occasion. I am a happy man."

"And I, blithe indeed," Daly added. "Besides, I'm searchin' out a wife for him."

"I think it would be good for *both* of you and I'm determined to see it through." Kennis grinned. "He who finds a wife findeth a good thing[12]," she quoted. The two groaned and the other men joined in the laughter.

The McKinnon village of Kilmoil was scattered along the rocky hillside near the castle, a random grouping of stone and thatch blackhouses. At the crown of a tall, grassy knoll stood Castle Moil, seat of the McKinnon of McKinnon. The flagstone road wound upward in a spiral pattern until it reached the iron gates of the castle. An impregnable fortress, a ship could not approach or land troops on the shore without being sighted by those looking on from above. The rocky landscape created a natural defense against unwanted visitors and enemies.

Kennis gazed upon her ancestral fortress with pride as Eavan's voice rose over the sound of the water lapping against the side of the rocking boat. "Lower the row boats, lads. Carrick, come with me. Mac, select a guard for the boat and the rest of you take turns. I'll send Carrick later with additional orders."

The small boats splashed as they hit the surface of the water. Eavan ordered Myles, a gillie, to run ahead, announce their arrival and request an escort with additional horses for Kennis and himself. Meanwhile, the rest of the party would make their way to shore in the two small *scaffs*, unload trunks and gear, and await a much-anticipated welcome.

Eavan glanced at Kennis, admiring the sunny highlights in her hair. "Ready to go ashore?"

"Aye, I'm looking forward to getting out of this boat." Eavan's warm glance was lost upon her. Gazing up at the castle above, she sheltered her eyes with one hand from the bright sun.

He continued his pursuit with trivial conversation. "Not much of a sailor, are you?"

"On the contrary, sir, it's just been awhile since I've had my feet on solid ground for more than a few hours at a time." An airy breeze gusted about them, whistling its merry tune and hinting at mischief.

---

[12] *...and finds favor from the Lord." Proverbs 18:22*

"Well then, jump down and we'll see to it that you have the opportunity to do so immediately. Just don't fall in the water," he added deliberately, watching for her reaction.

"I won't," Kennis laughed, oblivious to his overtures. "What makes you think I would?"

Eavan's eyes gleamed. "Just wanted to hear the sound of your laugh, lass. It gives me pleasure."

Taken aback, she looked away in embarrassment and busied herself by climbing over the side of the galley into the waiting *scaff*. When his laughter rumbled above her, she winced, hoping that no one was paying attention to his nonsense.

"Let me give you a hand," he said, "else you'll take a wetting for sure."

She took hold of his strong grip and warmed toward him as he handed her into the boat. The sooner she arrived at Castle Moil and to the protective arms of her Grandad and McKinnon kin, the better.

The McKinnons, not unlike the other supporters of Bonnie Prince Charlie, suffered greatly since the '45, harassed by the English redcoats and unsympathetic fellow Scots. Throughout the nation's history, vigilance was a way of life in the Highlands and Islands of Scotland. To protect and to defend the clan lands and the extended clan family members was their priority in life.

Some things in this world are constant and noble, and cannot be destroyed; the greatest of these is love. For the Scot, this kind of love yields an enduring and undying loyalty to family and friend as well as a sense of honor toward a foe.

An hour later, the gillie returned, bringing McKinnon clansmen, horses, and a cart for Kennis' trunk. The McKinnons stationed themselves around the group, keeping a careful watch as the wagon was loaded. She recognized her grandfather's foremost man-at-arms and promptly greeted him. "Hallo, Murdoch! What news of Granddad?"

He tipped his bonnet. "Welcome, Mistress Kennis. The McKinnon sends his greetin' to ye," his dour countenance relaxed into a half-smile, "and he bids ye come quick-like since his supper's waitin'."

She laughed. "Oh, how like him." Turning to Fergus and Daly, she said, "Did you hear? Supper's waiting. Is the wagon loaded?"

Aye," Daly confirmed. "Shall I give ye a leg up into the saddle, lass?"

"Please do, and then find yourself a ride and we'll be off." She turned her back to the emerald water sparkling in the sunlight, gazing ahead to the short road before her, eager to travel on to Castle Moil.

Once in the saddle, she entertained Eavan with local tales, superstitions and more of McKinnon history. Such tales, left to the clan bards, were recanted all over Scotland. She wondered what had happened to Angus, the McCallum family bard. Had he been killed at Culloden, too, like so many of her kinsmen or was he a prisoner of the king, enslaved in the colonies? Remembering Davis McCallum, she grew silent. The memory also brought to mind another man with eyes like midnight, a stolen kiss and heavenly embrace. She could almost feel his strong arms about her and—

Eavan interrupted her reverie. "You've grown quiet, mistress."

"I'm sorry, Eavan, I was daydreaming." She glanced at him, comparing his fair coloring to that of the darkly handsome man she couldn't forget. "What did you say?"

"I wondered what's occupied your thoughts for so long."

"Just thinking about the ghost of Castle Moil." She grasped at the first random thought that came to mind.

"Scotland is full of haunts," he said. "One's pretty much like the next."

"Ah, but our ghost has a penchant for golden-haired maidens. When I was a child, Robbie draped himself in a sheet and chased me down the halls. Sometimes," she chuckled, "he'd stand at the foot of my bed in the wee hours of the night, hoot and howl, and scare the wits out of me. He was very convincing."

"I wouldn't worry that yellow head about it if I were you. I'll gladly protect you from the local haunts and bogles, if need be."

"Unnecessary, since I don't believe in ghosts, do you? The Kirk doesn't encourage belief in the old ways."

He shrugged. "I'm not a religious man, lass."

"You don't believe in God, then?"

"I didn't say that," he protested. "I believe in God just as much as any man."

"But you don't make an issue of it, take your faith seriously, I mean."

"I wouldn't put it quite like that," he said, his brow puckering. "More like, I'm a God-fearing man but as I said, I'm not religious." He shifted uncomfortably in his saddle.

"Meaning, perhaps, that you don't go to Kirk or make a practice of reading the Bible?" Kennis listened closely, wondering at his answer.

"Aye, that sounds like a reasonable description."

She paused as the wind caught her hair and whipped it over her shoulder. "I see," she said simply.

"You object?" Eavan shot a look at her.

She carefully weighed her words. "'Tis a good thing, I think, to practice your beliefs in many ways. Going to Kirk, and reading the Bible are just two of them."

"Well, if that's how you feel, then by all means, do so." He gave her sidelong glance. "But as for me, I'm content to believe there is a God, and leave my fate in His hands."

Kennis was dissatisfied with his reply and said nothing in return. Fate had little to do with it. In her experience, people who blamed God for their problems or who were unwilling to change usually said the same. They rode on, climbing the grassy hillside. The blue sky overhead turned a shade greyer at his words. She took her faith seriously, calling to mind the words of her own dear father once again.

"Faith, lassie, the kind that can move mountains is a tiny seed growin' inside of a person," he said, when they were on one of their sailing outings. "'Tis creative, and when it sprouts and takes root, when ye really believe in Him and His Word and all that He did on the Cross for us, then it will cause whate'er ye're prayin' for to come to pass. God answers prayer. It's just that sometimes the answer is a Nay when we expect an Aye, or a wait, when we think we canna wait any longer."

He smiled in understanding. "Ye're too much like your father, Kennis lass. Always ready to jump into the middle of a thing before ye know what ye're about. Ye need be more like your dear mother, listen to God speakin' to your heart. I know 'tis there inside ye, lass, and someday ye'll understand, hear God's voice for yourself."

Each of the weary travelers approaching the gates of Castle Moil that afternoon possessed a certain kind of expectation upon their arrival. Most thought of a hot meal or a cozy bed, and good company. Those with foresight considered the next road to travel at the end of this road before the final destination is reached and all journeys are at an end.

After all, life contains a thread of homely goodness, weaving its pattern through our dreams and experiences, an indefinable something to return to when all great adventures real or imagined are at an end. Every road has some type of destination, a result of the action taken upon it whether the conclusion is satisfactory or not. We must run the race, and as we draw near the finish line, possess a *knowing* instead of a mere hope that we are deserving of a *well done!* for our faith and endurance in the events which have passed in our lives.

Faith is incomplete without supernatural works that are proof to it, and good works performed by human hands are empty of meaning without the evidence of faith at work in our hearts. Our lives must be an active, living demonstration of the creative power of faith at work in and through us every day.

Chapter 12

Knight or Pawn

Alistair returned to Dunolly House, weary in mind and body from his long journey to Inveraray Castle.

He trotted through the familiar gates into the flagged courtyard and threw his reins to the waiting groom. The iron-studded wooden doors flew open as he ascended the white granite steps.

"Owen, send word to the men's quarters that I wish to see Captain McConacher immediately."

"Aye, my lord." Owen, the butler, bowed and withdrew to deliver the message to a footman. He returned a few moments later with a tankard of ale. "Will you want supper at the usual hour, my lord, or something lighter for the time being?"

"Nothing now, Owen, supper as usual will do. Is my brother at home?"

"He is not, sir," the butler replied. "Master Duncan did not return for luncheon. He has been out hunting the Stag all day. Perhaps he's cornered the animal at last?"

"Cornered the Great Stag Chalum?" He lifted both brows in disbelief. "Not likely. He'd better be careful or the beast will gore him. He charged a lad once who came upon him in the woods. I was nearby, let fly an arrow, and missed. At least the lad was able to shinny up a tree." He smiled at the memory. "I confess I was forced to do the same. The creature's wise, Owen, a very knowing one, Duncan will never track him. Whatever put the notion into his head?" He turned as the door opened.

"I apologize, Laird." The deep gravel voice of Farrell McConacher, captain of Alistair's personal guard, interrupted from the doorway. "I confess that I'm the culprit."

Alistair welcomed him with a smile and leaned against the desk, arms folded, one leg crossed in front of the other. "You, Farrell? How so?"

Rueful, Farrell regarded his master. Alistair possessed a quick sense of humor as well as a black temper. "Well, the men and I were havin' a muckle good time the other evenin' shootin' the gab. I'd had a couple of pints and recalled a time, sir, when ye were a wee bit younger and on a dare undertook pursuit of the Great Stag into the hills."

He lifted an eyebrow. "Go on, lad."

"To make the long of it a wee bit shorter, I told the lads how ye tracked the beast, worked so hard to set the perfect trap, but in the end got caught in the midst of it." He chuckled. "I can still see ye shinnyin' up that tree faster n' ye can say *auld clootie*[13] and end fallin' into the loch."

"I hope the men were entertained by the story, but what has this to do with Duncan?" Amused, he awaited Farrell's reply.

"The lad overheard and decided he'd outdo ye. He's determined to track the beastie, and do what ye couldna." On this final note, his face crumpled and the two men burst into hearty laughter.

"I'd like to see it." Alistair wiped his streaming eyes. "Duncan thinks too highly of himself these days, Farrell. And did he take any of the men with him, or was he foolish enough to go by himself?"

"Aye, he took Jamie, my nephew, and a couple of the other young 'uns." He grinned. "What good he thinks they'll do him, I dinna know."

"Well, a little humility goes a long way. Perhaps it will be a good lesson for the lot of them. We'll see." Alistair stroked his chin abstractedly, his eyes giving away the perturbation of his soul. When at last he addressed Farrell again, he requested a report of all that had transpired during his brief absence.

---

[13] *Old devil*

Farrell sensed Alistair's mood with the understanding of long friendship. He recanted the ordinary news of the household first. "I've collected a bit of information concernin' the matter ye laid before me. I canna say if serious trouble's brewin' or naught. Malcolmson of Kilmartin traveled a few times toward Fraoch Eilean with a wagon of goods. Since he wasna involved in the '45, I canna imagine why he'd be involved with renegade Jacobites now."

"Nor can I, but I still don't trust him. Our source of information was too good. Some devilry is brewing, I'm sure of it." He shook his head. "You know our history. We attended university in Edinburgh together. He was present at the Jacobite meetings in Edinburgh before the '45 and disputed with the older Chiefs too harshly for my tastes." His dark brow clouded over. "I don't like the man. He lacks a certain something in his soul that gives him the appearance of strength, but he's weak spirited. Put to the test, he fails to do what is just. We must find out what he's been up to, Farrell. I'll leave this matter in your capable hands."

"I'll look into it." Farrell paused. "Have ye heard more of the Morrison lass since Port Eilidh, sir?"

Alistair looked at him sharply. "No, why?"

He scratched his head. "I've been stewin' over a few things. Ye remember when Denoon shouted there was a wench with us."

Alistair nodded. "Aye, after the lass cried out." He felt a twinge of renewed irritation.

"She dinna just speak out random, Laird, she recognized one of the men."

"Did she, indeed." He arched one dark brow. "And you're just now telling me this?"

Farrell's cheeks reddened. "There's been no opportunity to speak to ye proper," he admitted. "Moreover, when she helped nurse the man on the galley, I'll swear he knew her, too. Called her by her given name, like I would speak to Lady Ona."

"And then? What did he call her?"

"She shushed him, and spoke so soft I couldna hear. He called her Mistress Kennis, but it was the way he said it, if ye know what I mean."

Alistair did know. A common clansman would treat the mistress of the castle with respect or else he would pay dearly for his impertinence. "You said there were two things. What else haven't you told me?"

Farrell trod warily. "Ye remember the two lads who accompanied her at the inn, other than Malcolmson? I know I've seen the likes of them before, especially the tow-headed one." He shook his head. "If I dinna know better, I'd say he was a McCallum of Dunchalum."

"But do you know better, Farrell?" Alistair's curiosity increased tenfold. "I'm sure there are plenty of men masquerading under assumed identities since the '45."

"Aye, sir, but this one was a personal servant to the laird's household, I'm sure of it."

"So you believe the lass 'tis a relative or," he said as a new idea occurred to him, "perhaps even Robert McCallum's daughter?"

"'Tis possible. Did he have a daughter?"

"I don't know. I only know of the lad, Robbie." He frowned, trying to solve the mystery. "Who was Robert's wife? I remember a dark-haired woman, but I don't know her maiden surname. The lass certainly doesn't resemble her."

"Nay," Farrell agreed, "but Laird Robert was a fair-complexioned man, as was the lad."

Thunderstruck, Alistair stopped short. Why had he not seen it before? The resemblance was remarkable. "Confound it! I should have realized who she is, knowing Robert and the lad. She's as near identical to Robbie McCallum as a lass could be." He laughed in self-derision at his own stupidity. "That's the answer to the riddle. Why would she be with Eavan Malcolmson? The McCallum and Malcomson clans are blood relatives. This is a fine muddle!"

"How so, Laird?" Farrell puzzled. "We need have nothin' to do with the man."

"Nay, but how involved is he with the family, moreover, what mischief is he brewing?" His temper quickly rose. "After all our efforts to redeem the lad, I'll not have them wasted on the blackguard." He ran his fingers through his raven hair.

"There's a wee bit more," Farrell plunged ahead, "and one final thing the lass told me on the galley."

Alistair's mouth turned down in a grim smile. "Confessing your sins, Farrell? I'm no man of the cloth, though I abide by His rules as much as a man possibly can, within reason."

"I ken ye're a God-fearin' man but He expects us to trust in Him, nae reason. That's trustin' in ourselves."

Alistair raised both brows. "And the lass, Farrell, if you're done with your sermonizing."

Farrell grinned. "She overheard a couple of Denoon's henchmen talkin' about ye aboard the *Faioleag*, some mischief that Crooknose's plottin'."

"My beloved kinsman," Alistair said sardonically. "Now why doesn't that surprise me?"

"'Tis a riddle, to be sure," Farrell said, troubled. "The day before yesterday, a band of men traveled on foot toward Loch Awe. Angus tracked them to Dunstaffnage, keepin' to the wood. They disappeared on a track in yon Highlands when a *haar*[14] moved in. He turned home so he wouldna be lost in the mist."

The faint scowl on Alistair's face deepened, his black brows drawing together in a straight line. "They were strangers, no distinguishing clothing or weapons?"

"Nay, Laird, he couldna get close enough to see their mugs."

"How many men, Farrell, and were they armed?" His concern for Duncan's safety and the next journey to Inveraray grew considerably.

"Twenty, give or take a few, and armed to the teeth."

"We'll have to be very watchful on the road. If Argyll hadn't commanded it, I wouldn't take my mother and sister to Inveraray just now. You're sure they weren't Malcolmson's men?"

"I canna say," Farrell replied. "'Tis possible."

Alistair grunted in response. "Just keep an eye open and your ear to the ground while I'm gone."

---

[14] *Drizzling rain, heavy mist from the sea*

"I'll keep both eyes and ears fully open, sir," he said with a glimmer of a smile.

"Very well, Farrell." Alistair's countenance lightened at Farrell's gentle wit. "Perhaps you'd best reserve one eye for that scamp of a brother of mine. If something important develops, send a gillie with a message to me at Inveraray. I'm returning with my mother and sister for the All Saint's week of festivities. I'd prefer to have you with me on the road but under the circumstances, I need you here."

He smiled at the crestfallen look on his henchman's face. "I'm taking most of the guard with me on the journey. See to it that they're ready at the end of the week to ride to Inveraray."

"I will, Laird." Farrell began to bow himself out of the room.

"Oh, and Farrell—"

He straightened. "Aye, sir?"

"What would you think of journeying to Skye with me tomorrow, to visit the McKinnon?" Alistair gladly invited his oldest friend. "The man's been much on my mind. I'd like to see if he fares well."

Farrell nodded his head in the affirmative. "I'll make preparations. What about the lass?"

"I'll inquire of MacLeod what he knows of the Morrisons of Lewis. Sir Hugh Morrison is Laird of Dun Eistein. He may be a relation." Alistair determined that it was time to settle his unfinished business with the duke and the lass. His delay in returning to Inveraray had proved costly. The new plan forming in his mind to avoid marriage to the Lady Vanora Campbell might become a necessity. Perhaps he'd travel to Dun Eistein and speak with Hugh Morrison after his visit with the McKinnon. He rubbed his chin, staring at but not seeing the fire.

Farrell opened his mouth to speak but thought wiser of it. He quietly slipped out the door.

Alistair considered what he hoped to gain versus the possible outcome of his maneuvering. If he inquired too close after the lass, Hugh might have some expectation of him and require a pledge of intent toward a betrothal. He must present his case as a matter of business concerning her ill-advised journey aboard his galley, playing this game with great care. One mistake and he'd find himself in the very trap he wished to avoid.

On the positive side, his thoughts brightened, he'd be making his own choice. He would visit the jeweler on his way to Lewis and be prepared in the event his plan went awry. He laughed. Sweet Jesu and sweet lass—she'd be astonished to discover an impending betrothal to him, and Argyll would be furious. My fate could be worse, he ruefully admitted, deciding to go through with his plan. Forfeits, indeed.

Chapter 13

Ceud Mile Failte!

"Och, man, I can do it myself!"

The man-at-arms stepped back from the McKinnon, knowing the black temper of the once powerful Chief of Clan MacFhionghuin.

Hailed by sentries at the heavy gate, the traveling party drew rein and waited admittance to the McKinnon stronghold. The chains grated and creaked, the portcullis lifted, and Kennis' heart hammered in anticipation at its opening. Castle Moil was now her home and the McKinnons her nearest kin. More important, at the end of this long journey was her maternal grandfather, one of the few surviving male relatives she possessed.

At last, it was time to ride through the massive gates. Dismounting, she watched John Dhu beneath the grey stone arch inscribed with the clan motto in a bold script, *Audentes fortuna juvat*. It was a nice sentiment but *Fortune Assists the Daring?* It might be true of her mother's clan, but not her father's. The McCallum's had paid dearly for their reckless bravado.

"*Ceud mile failte*[15], my bairn!" John Dhu McKinnon greeted his granddaughter. "I'm right pleased to have ye home." He wrapped her in a snug embrace and she tightened her arms about his sturdy frame.

---

[15] *A hundred thousand welcomes*

Clicking his tongue, he tilted her chin upward. "Let me have a look at ye. How proud your Father'd be to see ye bloomin' like a white rose." His voice grew husky, tears threatened to overflow. "Ye certainly hae the look of him." His keen dark eyes grew suddenly merry. "Every laddie in the Americas must've been wooin' ye, my bonnie lass."

Smiling, she shook her head in the negative.

"Come now," he said, shocked. "Ye canna tell me no lads courted such a fair maid! Och, hae they no eyes in their *coof*[6] heads?" He patted her cheek. "Well, I suppose there's plenty of time for that, and I'm sure we'll find ye a braw lad, indeed."

She emerged from his hearty embrace, eyes glistening with unshed tears.

John Dhu turned to Eavan and greeted him. "And ye're Eavan Malcolmson, I take it. I've heard about ye from Alanna."

"Honored, sir." Eavan extended his hand.

"I'm pleased to welcome ye," he said, gripping Eavan's hand firmly, "and my thanks for bringin' the lass home safe." He turned to Kennis and winked. "Here's a braw laddie," he teased, nudging Eavan. "What say ye, eh?"

Eavan grinned, his warm laughter and even warmer glance making her cheeks grow hot.

Together they walked up the grey stone steps leading into the Great Hall. "Grandad, I've only just arrived and you're trying to be rid of me already?"

"Nay lass, I'm simply lookin' out for my own. I could invite the young MacDougall chief to meet ye, too. Perhaps he'd be more to your likin', albeit," his brow furrowed, "he dinna support the Bonnie Prince, and the unfortunate young man's related to those Greedy Campbells. He canna help it, poor lad, and the MacDougalls've had their own hard times. Would ye believe they'd desert a fine castle like Dunolly to build a manor house? A house! I think his widder mother must've had a say in that. Young Alistair has Craignish on his hands as well now."

---

[6] *Fool*

Her ears perked up at the name *Alistair.* Nay, surely it couldn't be—Alistair was a common enough name in Scotland. She must remember to ask her grandfather later, even if he teased her without mercy.

At that moment, the double doors of the castle swung wide in greeting. The huge fire burning on the grate heated the Great Hall and engulfed them in its warmth. Colorful tapestries depicting the ancient glories of past McKinnons adorned the walls, and shimmered in the flickering blaze. *So much like us now.* She gazed upon the furnishings and reflected on the Psalm she heard at church before her long journey home. "Life is a mere handsbreath, one quick intake of breath and it is over." What, she wondered, is reflected in me? I must make the most of my time now. See Mam and Mairi, find Robbie—

John Dhu's voice broke into her musings. "Here's another to greet ye, lassie."

A sudden chill washed over her as a slim figure emerged from the shadows. "Mam! Oh, Mam!" She flew into her mother's arms. The two embraced until Kennis pulled back slightly.

"Where's Mairi?" she asked. A split second later, the child rushed into the room and nearly bowled her over.

"Kenni!" she shouted, a brilliant smile lighting her face. "I'm so glad you're home!"

Relieved, Kennis hugged her baby sister, no longer afraid that Mairi wouldn't remember her since she'd been away for so long.

Just then, she recalled Eavan's presence as their joyous laughter faded. On impulse, she stretched out both of her hands.

With a satisfied look, he clasped her hands in return.

"Oh thank you, Eavan," she said happily. "You knew they'd be here, didn't you? How I wish you'd told me!"

He smiled. "Aye, but your mother requested that her plan be kept secret in the event she couldn't come, not wishing you to suffer a disappointment. I wasn't sure myself until we arrived."

"Well, 'tis the best surprise I've had in a very long time." Her eyes shone in appreciation. "How can I ever find the words to thank you?"

His possessive grip on her tightened. "You already have, Kennis."

Stunned by the warmth in his voice, the irregular beating of her own heart equally astonished her.

Alanna intervened, stating in her quiet way that their rooms were prepared and refreshments awaited. "I'd like for you to come with me, my dear. The maidservant will have your bath ready by now. I've had your favorite room prepared for you." She acknowledged Eavan, smiling a dismissal. "Daly can assist you to the same, Eavan, and then you may join Father here while Kennis and I enjoy a cup of hot tea together before supper." She rang the bell and Daly appeared, ever ready to serve.

Eavan bowed before following Daly from the room.

John Dhu's keen gaze rested on Alanna. "Well, daughter," he said. "Ye canna keep her hidden away forever."

"I don't intend to, Father, but there is plenty of time left for courting. We have four years to relive together, and I plan to make the very most of the time. Please make Eavan welcome," she commanded. "We'll see you at dinner. Come, Kennis."

"May I come with you, Mam?" Mairi eagerly asked.

"No, Mairi, stay and keep your Grandad company for a while. I won't keep her too long today."

* * *

The recently freshened chamber was the same as Kennis remembered. Her favorite green adorned the windows, keeping out the chill. Heavy brocade curtained the four-poster bed; even so, she preferred to sleep with the windows open, enjoying the fresh air and cool breeze that wafted its way into the room, filling it with the tangy scent of the sea, the heather, and the night.

Alanna followed her into the room. "'Tis such a relief to have you home again, Kennis. Mairi and I have missed you."

"Oh, Mam, when I saw you in the hall, I thought my heart would burst." Her eyes misted. "Yet somehow, I knew you were here, though I brushed the feeling aside. And when Mairi came running in, there was only one other thing I wished for to make it complete."

"I know, my love, if only Robbie was here with us. I don't have enough time right now to tell you the whole. Perhaps tonight after supper we can have a cozy chat. We'll retire early, the men won't notice. They'll be awake half the night celebrating." Alanna moved toward the wardrobe and her eyes sparkled as she opened the doors. "Come, love, take a look and see what I've brought you. I hope you like them."

"Ooo!" Kennis squealed in delight at the display of color peeking out from the wardrobe. "I confess, I've been so weary of these old rags." She spread wide her brown skirts revealing the neat hand-stitched patches and made a face.

Alanna laughed. "Of course you have, my love. I never expected you to wear them forever. I've saved what I could for you, and your Grandfather has been most generous in providing the rest. You must remember to thank him, although he'll act like 'twas was nothing at all. Here now, don't cry. I don't think we've shed this many tears in a long time."

"I can't help it," she sniffed. "I'm so very happy to be home, to be with you, Mairi and Grandad that I hardly know what to say."

"I know, but for now a *Thank you* would be nice," Alanna teased. "Really, I think we must hurry. The men will be waiting and when it comes to a meal, men should never be kept waiting. But I confess, I've been eager to see these gowns on you. After you've bathed, you must try this one first, and then the slippers to match."

Emerging from the bedchamber together, mother and daughter descended the broad flight of stairs that entered the Great Hall and were gratified by the admiring glances sent their way as they drew near the bottom arm in arm.

Kennis' new gown of amber silk with a white underdress, trimmed at the neck and sleeve in white gold-tipped lace set off her figure admirably, and the ocher *snood*[17] adorning her hair complemented the elegant garment. A delicate gold collar of aquamarines graced her smooth neck. Matching earbobs, a gift from her mother, completed her toilette.

---

[17] *A ribbon*

Alanna's crimson velvet gown accentuated her dark beauty. A ruby pendant, looped around her neck, sparkled in the candlelight. In contrast, the rich color set afire the gold tones of Kennis' ensemble and countenance. The men present that evening congratulated John Dhu on the beauty of his womenfolk.

Supper that evening was a grand celebration. In a festive mood, Kennis felt quite the fashionable lady in her new gown. The conversation at table was jovial, the Great Hall bright and cheery, and the fire blazed and crackled on the hearth. The men gathered at the long table feasted upon a haunch of roasted venison and traditional Island dishes. She sat at the dais with her family and Eavan; the McKinnon still clung to many of the old ways.

I almost feel like a prodigal returning home. She looked at her family and the McKinnons gathered around her, suddenly content with life.

In defiance of the new law, John Dhu wore his tartan and called for his bard. "I've paid my dues at Tilbury, and shall do as I please at my own table," he declared. "Tonight we celebrate the reunion of my family, and I look to the day verra soon when I shall welcome my grandson to Castle Moil and the fellowship of the McKinnons!"

He stood, threw back his chair and climbed onto it, resting his right foot upon the edge of the table and raised his glass. Following suit, the guests arose as he pronounced in clear tones, "Now lads and lassies, a toast. *Here's ta the heath, the hill and the heather, the bonnet, the plaidie, the kilt and the feather! Here's ta the song that Auld Scotland can boast, May her name nev'r die!-that's an Islandman's toast!*[18] And no one shall drink from this glass again!" With these final words, he flung his glass over his left shoulder.

The glass shattered amid the many Ayes and the loud cheer, mixed with the squeal of the pipes, resounded to the rafters. No thought was wasted on the law prohibiting such an action. It was as much a part of each one of them as the air they breathed and the red blood that flowed through their veins. Alba gu brath! Scotland for ever— May her name never die!

---

[18] *Orig. Highlandman's toast*

"Proud words, and brave ones," Eavan remarked to Kennis as they were seated. "I only hope that everyone in this room tonight is trustworthy."

"What do you mean?" Her fierce sense of loyalty to her kin rose to the challenge. "Why wouldn't they be—they're all McKinnons, and friends. How could you even think such a thing?"

"Well, lass, these are treacherous times," he said reasonably, "and with your Grandfather breaking the law, there's always the possibility someone could use it against him."

"Breaking the law, 'tis a *fuil* law and you know it, Eavan Malcolmson. As if any harm ever came from playing the pipes. Instrument of war indeed!" She hotly defended her family and countrymen. "Whose ridiculous idea was it to ban them in the first place? The English, that's who. And not only the pipes, but the wearing of the tartan itself. 'Tis an absolute disgrace!"

"I'm not disagreeing with you, Kennis. I'm as much a Scot as any man here, but the pipes do rally our people in times of conflict. It concerns me to see him in flagrant disobedience to English law. 'Tis dangerous in these times."

She gave him a sidelong glance. "I suppose 'tisn't dangerous or unlawful for you or your men to bear arms though, is it?"

"Now, as to having a good dirk handy, I canna say." He smiled winningly at her, a dimple peeping through at the corner of his mouth. "You know, lass, you'd best watch that shrewish tongue of yours, if you ever expect to catch a husband."

She primly tipped her nose into the air. "I don't see how that can be any concern of yours, sir. We weren't discussing my prospects. *Your* prospects were the topic of conversation if I recall correctly, as to whether or not you may be apprehended by your own overt disobedience to English law."

"Indeed, how so?" He wore a mask of innocence. "A man must be able to defend himself properly, not only from Englishmen but from beauteous wenches who hide sharp tongues like weapons, and draw them when a man is defenseless against their wiles."

Her color heightened. "I take it you have much experience of wenches, sir, particularly those with dirks hidden in their laces?"

"Oh, not just any wench, lass, didn't you hear me? Beauteous wenches only. The dirk in my boot I keep in reserve for the English and the Campbells."

When his laughter rang out, Kennis jumped to her feet, annoyed. Alistair's ruggedly handsome face flashed across her mind's eye. Again. He'd probably behave the same or worse, she fumed, chasing his image from her mind. "Oh, you're just like the rest of them." She slammed her mug onto the table, pushed back her chair and walked away to converse with other guests who congregated around the blazing hearth. Conscious of the fact that Eavan's eyes followed her across the room, she made a point not to return his warm gaze.

"Och, dinna take it to heart, lad, she'll come round." John Dhu's eyes twinkled with his ever-present humor. "She's a canny lass with a lot of spirit. Canna imagine who she takes after."

"As to that, sir, I can't say that I mind." He was in hot pursuit of his quarry and glad to be so well entertained. "If I have your permission, sir?" The hopeful note in his voice persuaded John Dhu.

"Aye, that ye do, lad, that ye do. I expect, though, that she'll lead ye a merry chase."

"Well, I'm up for it," he said, laughing. "Now if you'll excuse me, I think I'll go and warm myself by the fire."

"Do that, laddie," he replied as Eavan walked away.

Angus, the McKinnon bard, was telling tales. Eavan approached the piper and drew him aside, speaking softly. He then approached Kennis and bowed low while Angus winded the instrument. A fast-paced Highland reel soon skirled forth from the piper's skilled hand.

"May I have the honor of a dance?" he requested. "I promise I'll behave, lass."

"Will you?" she said with some misgiving. "Somehow I doubt it."

"Cross my heart," he said meekly. "Word of a gentleman."

"Are you up to some mischief, Eavan Malcolmson?" she asked, suspicious, the expression on his face giving her pause. "Humility doesn't suit you well at present."

He grinned, pulling her to her feet before she could change her mind. She placed her hand on his arm and he led her onto the floor. The small group by the fire joined in the fun. The bagpipes droned and Angus increased the tempo. Each time the music swelled, Eavan spun her around faster and she matched his steps.

It was a wild dance, inappropriate for a lady, and when the music ceased Eavan bent his head toward hers. Breathless from the exertion, she stared up at him oddly and pulled away. This she'd not expected. If he were someone else maybe, but—Confused, her brows knit together. The onlookers burst into applause and Kennis recalled herself. Red-faced, they took their bows and retreated from the floor.

Alanna watched the two deep in conversation after the dance as she advanced toward John Dhu's table. "Father, what have you been up to? I saw Kennis flounce away a few minutes ago, and now this outrageous display." She glanced at the young couple across the room.

"'Naught me, luve, 'twas young Eavan there." He winked. "Taken a fancy to our lass, he has. Look how he dances with her."

"I see, but I wish you wouldn't encourage him all the same. All they've accomplished is to make a spectacle of themselves."

He placed his hand over hers in comfort. "Dinna worry, daughter, naught harm will come of it. 'Tis good for the lass to have a wee flirtation to occupy her for a time."

Watching Kennis and Eavan across the hall, Alanna hoped that a little flirtation was all that either had in mind. She wasn't quite ready to give up her eldest daughter in marriage to Eavan Malcolmson or to any other man.

Chapter 14

Enter the Phantom

"Well, Jamie, what do you think?"

Duncan MacDougall examined the ground on which he stood with a keen eye. "Our quarry has escaped us again. He's certainly giving us a merry chase."

"We should move on, Master Duncan." Jamie McConacher, Farrell's nephew, reminded him for the second time. "We're on McCallum lands, ye know."

"I'm not worried about that. They're Campbell lands now, we've nothing to fear."

"'Tis wiser nae to tempt fate," Jamie said in disapproval. "I'm sure the McCallum's wouldna agree with ye."

"I don't disagree, Jamie, but I can't do anything about the way the McCallum clan's been treated. They aren't the only clan in Scotland who's suffered since the '45. If I'd known the consequences, I wouldn't have gone out myself. I barely made it home alive, and that was thanks to Argyll, truth be told. I can't speak of it without being horrified and angered at the same time." His gaze returned to the track they were following. "Back to the hunt, what say you?"

"I'm willin' to go, if ye're wishin' it. Do we return to Dunolly tonight, or do we make camp in the woods?"

"I think we'll go on while we have a trail to follow, and see if we're any closer to chasing the stag down. Alistair returns tonight from Inveraray, and I need to speak with him. Once he leaves, I'll be free to pursue the beast."

When the men rode on, a shadowy figure hidden from sight by the dense underbrush observed from beneath the trees. The ghostly form flitted, soundless, across the uneven terrain, following the riders to the village that lay beyond.

"How far are we from Dunchalum, Jamie? I wonder if there's a village or a shieling nearby where we might get news of the stag."

"A short way up this track." He gestured toward the wood. "I came here a few times with m' Uncle Farrell when I was a lad."

Ascending a steep hill through the peaceful forest, the men rode in silence for several minutes. The track, overgrown by foliage, showed months of disuse. A few half-burned, deserted cottages greeted them, a grim reminder of the violent aftermath of the uprising against the English and the following desecration of Scotland.

Although there was always talk of rebellion, there would be no more uprisings. In spite of the bloodshed and loss of life and property, *the king over the water*[19] still held a loyal, albeit small following. The majority of Scots didn't have the means to support another war. Through the unification of England and Scotland, the English government was doing its best to destroy the remnants of the clan system that divided the two nations.

The track widened and Duncan urged his mount forward. The glen opened before them all of a sudden, and the somber, empty landscape saddened the men. A few shielings boasted peat fires and smoke drifted on the air, yet not a soul welcomed the riders. Since Highland hospitality was notable, the men were surprised.

"Well, isna this a morbid place? Ye'd think a visitor'd be welcome, way out here." Jamie marveled at the cold silence. "Someone must be about. Ye can smell the peat burnin'."

"Let's investigate." Duncan dismounted. "If there's some mystery, we need to solve it. Come, Jamie, let's have a look. Andrew, look after the horses. Young Rab and Big Coll, stand guard and keep your eyes open. I don't like the looks of this."

---

[19] *James Stewart in France*

Cautiously approaching one of the stone shielings where smoke trickled out of the thatched roof, he rapped on the door. "Hallo, anyone there?" A sudden rustle inside the hut silenced him. When no one responded, Duncan nodded to Jamie. Silently drawing weapons and counting to three, the two men burst into the cottage, dirks upraised. A shriek greeted their ears as a little girl and boy dove for cover under a pile of heather.

Duncan and Jamie glanced at one another. Grinning, Jamie walked over to the makeshift bed and knelt, pushing aside the fragrant plants. "Here now. Come out, ye urchins. We mean ye no harm. Come, I say! Have ye naught to give a thirsty traveler?" Without warning, a hand popped out from the midst of the heather and grabbed his hair. An even smaller hand quickly snatched at and tweaked his nose.

Jamie cried out while Duncan burst into laughter. "Well, Jamie, what have you caught or maybe I should say, what's caught you?"

Hearing laughter, the hand let go and Jamie pulled back. Childish giggles erupted from under the pile. Duncan motioned to Jamie. He stood to his feet, rubbing his injured nose. Together they shoved the bundled plants aside to reveal Jamie's small tormentors. Their childish giggles faded as they fearfully gazed at their captors.

The two men soberly regarded the two children. Ragged clothing hung on thin, underfed frames, their faces gaunt. They were also barefoot, a common practice among Highlanders.

Duncan smiled in a friendly way. "Good day."

The small girl was encouraged enough to step forward. "Granny told us t' stay put an' nae open the door." She put one finger to her lips, and whispered. "Can ye keep a secret?"

Duncan nodded as she whispered again.

"Granny said someone's gonna die 'cause the phantom o' the dead Laird Robert's walkin' the woods in the glen. The menfolk went out lookin' fer him, t' try and scare him back whar he come from!"

"The Laird? Who are you talking about?" he said, perplexed. "Surely you don't mean a ghost?"

"Shh. Ye're nae s'posed t' be talkin' aboot him, master. He might come here fer us!" The child shivered and her blue eyes, which seemed too large for her small face, clouded in fear.

"Who told you such a thing? It's not true, so don't be frightened."

"But Granny Jean said sae," the girl insisted. "Mam sae Granny Jean knows all about bogles an' phantoms."

"Well, clearly she doesn't know everything," Duncan retorted. "Where did they go? Is there anyone else in the village?"

"Aye, sir," Jamie piped up. "I stepped out while ye were busy with them. There're more than two here, I'm sure."

Interrupted by a shriek and a holler, he darted outside. Andrew had a tight hold on a boy who looked to be about twelve years old.

"Tried to sneck off wi' m' bag, he did," Andrew said. "I caught him just as I turned around." The boy struggled against the firm grip on his collar.

"Well laddie, what have you to say for yourself?" Duncan asked sternly. "Stealing is a serious charge."

"But I dinna mean t', Laird, I mean, I wasna gang t' snitch it fer guid."

"Then what were you doing?"

Hanging his head, the boy admitted his need. "'Twas only lookin' fer a morsel t' eat, Laird." He rubbed his stomach. "I'd no meal fer two or three days. Like as naught, I'm gang t' expire o' hunger." His lean face and skinny body bore witness to his malnourished state.

Duncan studied the boy for a moment, grieved. "Andrew, see what you can do for him. If you've nothing left, look for oatcakes in the other packs."

More of the village inhabitants, curious to see the visitors, arrived on the scene. A small crowd gathered around the group of men, mostly women and children. "Where are your menfolk?" Duncan asked, although he believed he knew the answer to his question.

"Dead. Naught but a few left," offered an old granny. "The rest air chasin' the phantom."

"Phantom? What's the auld woman goin' on about?" Jamie asked. Duncan told him. "Well, that canna be right. I dinna hold with such *havers*[20]."

"Right or no, they seem to believe it." Turning to the old granny, he spoke kindly. "There's nothing we can do about this phantom of yours, but how long has it been since you've had good food to eat?"

"Och, two weeks or mair since the Laird o' Kilmartin come by. We do wha' we can in the meantime. Thar's plenty o' game, when we can git it."

"The Laird of Kilmartin," he repeated. His voice took on a hard edge. "You mean Eavan Malcolmson?"

"Aye, the one an' the same," she said matter-of-factly. "He comes once a month, brings meal, flour." She offered the information freely. "Afore tha' we'd little eno' t' fill our stomachs."

Duncan and Jamie glanced at one another. The McCallum clan was a known sympathizer to the Jacobite cause but no threat existed here. There would be little to report to Alistair at Dunolly in that regard. He felt a tug on his sleeve and glanced down. It was the little girl from the first cottage.

"Who air ye, Laird? Air ye goin t' help us?"

Amused by the child yet saddened by the plight of the villagers, the insistent tug on his heart to help them increased. "My apologies. I've neglected to properly introduce myself." He doffed his cap and bowed low, and she giggled. "Duncan MacDougall of Dunolly, mistress, at your service." He motioned to his men. "This is my henchman, Jamie McConacher. By the horses is Andrew MacDougall and two others are hereabouts by name of Big Coll McColl and Young Rab Colquhoun. And if I can, I'll help you. I must speak first with the Laird, my brother, Alistair MacDougall. Does that satisfy you?" He smiled down at the child and she returned it. "What's your name, lassie?"

"Meggie," she replied. "Meggie McCallum. My da died in the fightin'. Did ye go t' the fightin', Laird?"

---

[20] *Nonsense*

"Aye, I did." Duncan's voice was grim. Changing the subject, he asked for information about the Great Stag. The children pointed north, chattering about the paths to seek but none of the assembled company noticed the slight movement in the nearby bushes. The horses softly whinnied at the shadowy figure lurking in the woods.

With great interest, the phantom watched the entire scene unfold. He noted the number of the company and their armaments and without a sound, swiftly departed, unnoticed by all.

Duncan and his men prepared to ride. Mounting his chestnut stallion, he waved farewell to Meggie and her little brother, Davy, and trotted through the village. Viewing the abject poverty, he made a silent vow to return and to aid the people as soon as possible.

Across the glen, a hill track rose and forked. If they chose left, the steep track climbed to the Highlands where Dunchalum fortress, former stronghold of the McCallum's, stood uninhabited. The right path led to a rushing burn near the String of Lorne, a drover's lonely track leading all the way to the shore of Loch Awe. The Great Stag, the villagers claimed, often wandered through these very hills.

"The rumor of a phantom would spread like wildfire in these parts, in fact, in any part of Scotland," Duncan remarked to Jamie, his brows knit together. "What exactly is the meaning of it, do you think?"

Jamie snorted. "I dinna hold with superstition, sir. 'Tis naught but some devilish trick to hide another Jacobite plot behind."

"Maybe, but what plot? These people are too poor to support a rebellion, Jamie. They barely have the means to survive. Besides, there are hardly any men, mostly women and bairns."

Continuing the discussion, the men failed to see a silver flash of light deep in the forest. A shrill, eerie wail pierced the air, and the horses beneath them sidled and neighed. "What in the name of God Almighty was that?" Duncan exclaimed, bringing his mount under control.

"Screamin' like a banshee!" Jamie's eyes widened as he stared intently into the trees.

"What direction did it come from? Andrew, Young Rab, Big Coll, did you see anything?"

Before they could reply, the Great Stag Chalum boldly leapt across the path and into the woods beyond.

"After him!" Duncan shouted gleefully, forgetting about the unnatural howl. He dug his heels into the flanks of his mount and raced after the fleeing stag. He sped on, full tilt, his men trailed behind. Up, up, and down the narrow deer track they flew.

"'Tis a brutal pace, Master Duncan," Jamie called out. "We canna keep up with the beast!" Branches slapped the riders in the face as the horses dodged numerous stumps and dead trees, careering through the dense underbrush. The horses were blowing hard and sliding in the loose scree that covered the hillside before Duncan pulled up and came to a halt.

He gazed ahead with regret. "Well, lads, I expect that stag is great for more reasons than his size. What a brute! I don't think I've ever been led on such a grand chase. Let's ride for Dunolly and a warm bed, instead of settling for the hard, cold ground tonight."

The men cantered at a more sedate pace. Descending from the mountainous region, a flat moor appeared in the glen below. Picking up speed and hoping to reach Dunolly before the shadows fell, the ground thundered and shook beneath the horses' hooves. The forest was behind, the road ahead; every mile passed by quickly but not unnoticed.

Each young man possessed a keen eye, aware that on every side lay a potential danger. At present the country was unsafe and in their estimation, might never be with the English roving about. But their desire wasn't for a safe haven. Driven to explore new ground, the spirit of adventure captivated each heart. And when the home fires beckoned, a longing arose within each one to dig in and to dig deeper for a season.

Chapter 15

Late Nights and Summer Skye

The hour was late when Kennis and Alanna bid goodnight to the men now seated at the trestle table.

The servants brought chopins of ale and decanters of whiskey along with trays piled high with scones to spread with creamy butter and honey.

Alanna slipped her arm around Kennis' shoulders as the two slowly made their way upstairs. "Are you tired, love? It would be grand to have a long talk tonight. The men will be occupied for hours, and we may do as we choose."

Kennis yawned in response. "That would be lovely, Mam. My room or yours?"

"Oh, yours, I think. Mairi's room is next to mine, and she is sure to hear us talking."

Kennis shook her head in mild disbelief. "I can't believe how she's grown. I knew she would, but I suppose I've gotten used to Jennie and Molly." A deep sense of peace washed over her. "I'm glad to be home."

"Aye," was all Alanna could find to say, gazing at her daughter, hardly believing they were a united family again. "I'll meet you in a few minutes."

She strolled to her room, undressed, and slipped on her flannel wrapper. A soft knock at the door gave her pause. "Who is it?" she said.

"'Tis Flora, your maidservant, mistress. I've brought th' tea and scones Lady Alanna ordered. Do ye need anythin' else? If not, I'll turn down th' covers and be off t' my own bed."

"That will be fine, Flora," she nodded to the young girl. "Thank you."

"I'm to wait on ye while ye're here, miss," she said. "Jus' pull the bell if ye need me."

"I'll do that." Flora bobbed a curtsey and gave Kennis a knowing look. "He's a braw laddie." She turned and opened the door, leaving Kennis speechless.

Alanna stood in the hall, hand extended toward the latch.

"Evenin', milady."

She nodded to the girl. "Good evening, Flora." Alanna turned to Kennis as the maid hurried off. "I see our wee nibble is here."

"I'm ravenous, though I ate enough for a horse this evening," Kennis declared. "Shall I pour the tea?"

"Please do, love. It's no wonder you're hungry," her mother said wryly, "with all of the dancing and flirting to work up an appetite."

"Oh, Mam! I wasn't so very bad."

"A little naughty, I think. 'Twas obvious to me."

"I guess it was obvious to a few others, too," she said, annoyed. "Did you hear what Flora said to me on her way out? Impudent girl!"

Alanna lifted a brow in question.

"I lost my temper with Eavan," she confessed, "but he goaded me into it. I love to dance, and couldn't resist when he asked me. There weren't many opportunities to do so while I was away." She frowned. "And I wasn't very successful at finding Robbie either, not that it seems to matter at this point."

"Not if our information is correct, no." Alanna looked thoughtful. "Still, Cameron Campbell has never been a friend to the McCallum's. He's been appointed by Argyll to handle this matter, but I can't say I like it. Fortunately, we've had unexpected help in our long lost kinsman."

"Eavan, you mean."

Alanna nodded.

"I'm still amazed at the help he's been to us, Mam, and to our clan in Argyll. I thought his family was our enemy, especially after all of the stories I've heard from Fergus and Daly. What really happened to cause the rift?"

Alanna chose her words with care. "If you must hear the tale, understand that many hard words were spoken between the Malcolmson's and the McCallum's, kin or no. Cruel deeds were done out of greed and a lust for power. Much of it happened in times past. Your Father, however, maintained a distance because he didn't trust Eavan's father or grandfather. He believed that in a real time of need, neither of them would have the strength to do what was honorable. Past situations and alliances had already proved them false. No doubt that's why Daly and Fergus spoke so harshly."

"Fergus told me once about a betrayal to the Campbells involving one of our clansmen. He said it caused the deaths of the man's entire family. Is it true?"

"Aye, as far as I know. Don't worry over old sorrows, Kennis. There are so many wounds needing healed in Scotland right now that we must put aside our differences, and forgive. I believe we're on the road to healing through Eavan right now. Wouldn't you agree?"

Kennis knew that Alanna spoke well but her loyalties to her own clan were strong. A new resolve had grown within her during her brief sojourn in America. Being in Scotland again strengthened it. She must do something to ease the suffering, and to serve not only her own people but also any person in need that she encountered. Not one soul would be denied assistance if it were within her power to aid them. How to accomplish such a monumental task or on what path she would find her direction, she didn't know. The desire to restore unity among her brethren and to heal their wounds was nearly overwhelming.

"I hope you're right. My heart wants to believe it. Mam, do you think 'tis possible to help not only our people, but also other needy folk in Scotland who have been hurt by the terrible events of the last several years? I have a longing, right here," she held her fist to her breast, "and I don't know how to express how I feel or bring it to pass."

"All things are possible with God, Kennis." She looked at her daughter with motherly concern. "But I'd like to know about something else of importance that concerns my eldest daughter." The corners of her mouth tilted upward in an attempt at a smile. "What do you feel about Eavan, love," she quietly asked. "Or wouldn't you care to say?"

"I'm not sure. I don't know him well enough." Kennis hungrily munched on a scone. "I like him, and so far I've enjoyed his company. I know no evil of him, plus," she grinned suddenly, her eyes brimming with mischief, "I think he's handsome, don't you?"

Alanna laughed aloud. "Aye, but I wonder about his desire to know God for himself. Have you ever asked him about his beliefs?"

Kennis washed the scone down with a mouthful of tea. "Not exactly. We had a brief discussion on the ride to the Castle, and he didn't have a very clear idea about spiritual things. It made me wonder, I confess. I don't think he has a very deep personal conviction. The remarks he made were general, anyone could say what he did about believing in God."

Alanna's brow creased. "Maybe you need to be more direct. I suppose you weren't specific?"

"Nay, I wasn't," she said, her mouth full again. "I figured if he understood what I meant, he'd say so." She sipped her tea and lathered another scone with creamy butter.

Alanna chuckled. "Poor man! I begin to feel sorry for him. Many people think they understand what it means to have faith in God, Kennis, but they choose their own path. I'm sure you'll discover the truth eventually."

She sighed. "I'm sure I will, but I have the feeling that I'm going to dislike it." She set down the butter knife, drew the dipper from the honey pot and held it over another scone, drowning it in the golden syrup. "Mam, how do you know when you're really in love?"

"Heavens! We are traveling the world tonight, aren't we?" Surprised, Alanna eyed her daughter. "While I'm curious about the gentleman you have in mind, I'd rather postpone that topic for a moment. I'd like to hear about your desire to help our countrymen."

"Don't worry, there isn't anyone in particular," she blurted out. Uninvited, a picture of Alistair popped into her mind as a pang of guilt stole over her. Here she sat telling tales to her mother when she felt sure that the rogue didn't love her. Furthermore, he'd not had the civility to tell her his Christian name.

Her temper uncertain, she took a deep breath and exhaled, considering the notion of love. Did she love Alistair or was it mere attraction? Love at first sight was excessively romantic but not very practical, and now she had Eavan to consider. He, too, intrigued her but his character and she admitted, his motive, was in question. A sense of disquiet fell over her.

"I had a talk with Father once," she began, "about faith being a seed that takes root in the heart and grows in the soul. I pray for our clan, but I'd like God to speak to me about the work He's doing in the hearts of people, who they are and how I can help. Do you think 'tis possible?"

"Aye, love, I do," she encouraged. "Please continue."

"I want to feed hungry folk and clothe the needy," she said, intent on her vision. "I also want to pray for the wounded and ailing as the Lord did, healing all who suffer, body and soul."

"How came you by such thoughts, Kennis?" Alanna marveled at her daughter.

"I had many discussions with Mr. Gilmore, Mam, and he encouraged me to read the Bible for myself, not only to listen to sermons. In fact, so did Father when he was alive."

"You should still listen to the minister, Kennis."

"I do, I assure you," she said, sincere. "I've discovered that the scriptures are much more than I ever realized. Surely you understand?"

Alanna nodded. "I'm glad you've discovered His truths for yourself. Shall we pray before we retire for the night?"

Kennis grinned. "You mean, morning."

"So 'tis, and you may pray first for that remark."

"Gladly."

Both women bowed their heads. Each gave thanks in silence for a moment, and then voiced aloud to God the concerns that weighed heavily upon their hearts. Considerably later, each sought her own bed with pleasure. In their own lives, weeping had endured through a long night but a new joy was awakening, breaking through to a morning filled with the light of a new dawn.

* * *

"Kenni! Kenni! Look over here!" Climbing rocks, Mairi pointed to a bird's nest she'd spied in the crevices.

"Do be careful, Mairi! Don't disturb the eggs else the gulls will be down on you," Kennis called to her little sister. She turned to Eavan, who had accompanied them to the shore for a picnic. "I'm glad you came this morning. Isn't it lovely?"

Eavan fixed his eyes upon her. "Aye, 'tis a beautiful morning, and so is the view." His warm gaze never wavered from her face.

Almost a caress. Suddenly shy, she turned away. "Shall we go for a walk?" she asked, hoping to distract him. "Fergus will see to Mairi."

"I'd be delighted," he replied. "I've something to say to you for which I don't require an audience." He glanced meaningfully at Fergus and Mairi. "You know that I'm sailing tomorrow."

"So soon?" Disappointed, she looked away toward the sea and watched the whitecaps crest upon the breaking water.

"Aye, lass." A glimmer of hope shone in his grey-green eyes. "I hope that means you'll miss me," he began, the tone of his voice changing. "Kennis, a man has a lot of responsibility and—"

She interrupted him. "Please, before you say any more, I want to thank you on behalf of our clan. I confess I'm amazed at what you've done for them, the aid you've provided...." Her voice trailed off as he raised his hand to silence her.

"They were very needy," he said, not desiring her praise and knowing that he didn't deserve it. "How could a man not help them if he'd the means? Many of the people are gone, some have moved south to Kilmartin, others have emigrated to America or the islands. I'm sorry, lass, to have to give you such a poor reckoning. They have suffered much. Even Argyll couldn't protect them from every marauder after Culloden. Most of the folks who remain are simply too old to move, or women who lost their men. One Granny Jean inquired about you, but at that time I had no words of comfort to offer her."

Kennis smiled through her tears—Granny Jean, one of her oldest friends among the people. She fondly remembered the day they met. Running errands in the village for the first time by herself, she'd taken *manchet* loaves of bread to the elderly. It seemed like only yesterday that Granny warmly welcomed her into her home.

Knock-knock-knock. "I'm comin' noo, hae patience wi' an auld woman!" Granny opened the door. "Och, lassie, ye're a fair sight fer these tired auld eyes." She looked Kennis up and down. "*Failte*, child, and close the door behind ye. The peats air burnin' low, an' the heat'll be flowin' free oot the door," the old woman cackled.

They were fast friends. Kennis returned often, collecting peats for her to burn in her hearth, carrying them in a large *kreel*[21] on her back.

Eavan's rumbling voice shook her out of her daydream. "Your people love and respect you, Kennis, for your many kindnesses. I've been asked many times how you fared, and if I'd news of you. I began to know you before we ever met face to face." He stopped, unexpected emotion darkening his grey eyes to smoke. "Kennis, I know 'tis early—"

Thundering hooves echoed down the castle track, interrupting him as Daly swiftly rode toward them along the shore. "I'm sorry to disturb ye," he shouted, "but the mistress sent me. A messenger arrived an hour ago, lassie. Ye're wanted at the castle."

---

[21] *Basket*

"A messenger! From who, where?" She turned sharply about. "Have you any idea, Eavan?"

"Nay, I don't," he said, an interested look on his face as he questioned Daly further. "Is that all, lad, anything else?"

Daly returned his intent gaze with a suspicious one of his own. "Only that ye're both to come as soon as possible. Any word for the mistress?"

"Please tell her we'll be there within the hour."

"Aye, lassie, I will." Daly turned his horse around and sped off.

Kennis repacked the picnic basket, glad for the respite. Had Eavan been about to declare himself? "I'm sorry, Eavan, we'll have to go back sooner than I'd planned."

"Will you walk with me later this evening in the garden?" he said in earnest. "I'd like a private word with you, lass, if I may have it."

Gazing into his eyes, she wondered what he desired in life. Right now, she was in a season of discovery. Would it be right for either of them to pursue a relationship at such an uncertain time as this, if ever?

"Very well, Eavan, you may have it."

Pleased, he lifted her into her saddle and then easily swung into his own. They rode in silence, each absorbed with thoughts about the future. She meditated upon the conversation she and Alanna shared the evening of her return. Her own cause, to see her home restored and family reunited seemed paltry in comparison to the suffering of the Scottish people as a whole. Their entire history was one desecration after another, clan warring against clan. The aftermath of Culloden was even worse.

The Duke of Cumberland, Butcher Cumberland as he was known, had given the Scots no quarter on the battlefield. He paraded through the towns afterward, allowing his troops to burn and to murder the people who stood on the streets—men, women, and children. After that, the English redcoats became marauders, roving the countryside and terrorizing anyone who stood in their path. Many lay dead, homes burned, husbands, wives and children brutalized.

Her vision was clear about her role in helping people. The greater question at present was whether Eavan was destined to be her partner in life and in a mutual pursuit of God. He seemed to have an interest in caring for people, similar to her own.

And what about Alistair? She'd not forgotten him in the last few weeks in spite of Eavan's presence. He ruffled her composure more than she liked to admit, and his temper seemed volatile in contrast to Eavan's quiet manner. However, she couldn't forget his passionate quest for his enslaved countrymen; saving even one life from slavery was a worthy cause. Despite her feelings for him, she was confused, and admitted that she knew neither of them well enough to make a reasonable evaluation.

Before long, the grassy slopes leveled out and the towers of Castle Moil rose to the sky. The horses clattered into the stone bailey and she eagerly slid from her mount.

Eavan caught her, dragging her close.

Breathless, she gave herself a mental shake and pushed away.

She found her mother in the library with Grandad, discussing the contents of a sheet of parchment spread on the broad oaken desk before him.

Eavan followed close on her heels.

"I canna like it, Alanna," John Dhu said, doubt edging his voice, "sounds too muckle good to be the truth. Ye know the lad's like a son to me and I've no heir except for my Charlie, and he's far off in Antigua." He turned as Kennis and Eavan came into the room. "Och, lassie, ye're back. We've news of Robbie at last, the poor lad! This letter comes from Campbell of Fraoch Eilean, who's newly appointed constable of Dunchalum. He says the lad's on his way home to us, but I dinna know, seems unlikely to me as I've been tellin' your dear mother. I've a natterin' feelin' about this."

"But why, Grandad, is it because the letter is from Cameron Campbell? I've never met the man." Worried about more delays, she wanted to plow ahead and not miss any opportunity to see her beloved brother returned to Scotland and to her, Mam and Mairi.

"Nay, ye've no reason to meet him. I wouldna let a wicked man like that near any of the womenfolk in my household, includin' a widder daughter with a twenty-one year old bairn of her own," he declared. "The man's nae to be trusted with the lassies, girl, ye remember that! On top of his notorious philanderin', he happens to be a Campbell and I'll ne'er trust a Campbell again!" His voice grew loud. "Greedy Campbells, and called so for good reason!" He slammed his fist on the desk.

The firelight cast a shadow behind him, adding height to his sturdy frame. He was a dark Scot, dubbed John Dhu for the mercurial temper he possessed, not for the dark coloring that he'd passed on to his only daughter sitting before him. However, Kennis and Robbie had seen past the tough veneer to the merry soul beneath many times.

"May I see the letter, sir?" Eavan asked.

John Dhu handed him the single sheet.

He perused the missive. "Well, he doesn't give any reason for lending his aid, to be sure. Can you fulfill these requirements he mentions? Except for that, the rest of it seems to be in order. There have been a few others released, sir, and their lands restored, including yourself."

It was a valid point. John Dhu eyed him closely. "Aye,'tis true. But I'm an auld man, and there wasna much for me to do in prison but take up needed space. Robbie's a strong young lad, I'd think they'd work him a bit more. The McCallum's are nae a large clan nor powerful, as ye know, bein' one yourself. He's little threat to the Crown and none to Argyll."

"I'm returning to the mainland the day after tomorrow. I can investigate this matter and send word after I've made careful inquiry as to whether this information is legitimate or not. Would you agree, sir, madam?" He waited for John Dhu and Alanna to confirm his request.

John Dhu pressed his lips together, wondering how far he could trust the young man. So far he'd proved to be reliable. "Hm," he said at last. "I will. Alanna?"

"Aye." She dipped her chin in agreement.

He held Eavan's gaze. "And will you shake on it, lad?"

"Aye, sir." Eavan returned his steady regard and reached out his hand. John Dhu grasped it firmly. The four agreed that before the McKinnon acted upon any of the instructions in the letter, Eavan would investigate and send news. For the time being, it seemed to be the most reasonable course of action.

The opportunity for Kennis to walk in the garden with Eavan never arrived. A violent storm shook the castle, rain flooded the garden, and the wind howled through the corridors. The evening passed slowly in conversation until the candles guttered in their holders.

The following day the sky grew dark and threatening as Eavan prepared to leave Castle Moil. Forced to say final good-byes in front of everyone with no opportunity for private conversation, Kennis bid Eavan a cousinly farewell as he and his men departed early the next morning.

Chapter 16

Dunolly House

"Where is Duncan?" Alistair wondered aloud.

Donning the woolen jacket and trews of a Highland gentleman, he studied his reflection in the mirror. A sober face returned his gaze. "The young fool had better not get himself into trouble."

"Any orders, sir?" Farrell interrupted his abstraction. "Supper'll be served within the hour."

"Nay, Farrell, go and have your dinner. I'll call if I need you later."

"The young master's come home, Laird. I thought ye might like to know."

"Good." Alistair's expression lightened at the news. "Thank you, Farrell."

"Aye, ye're welcome." Farrell departed from the room.

Alistair followed soon after, pausing on the landing just as a clear voice rang out below.

"You should've seen him, Owen. He was magnificent! Powerful hinds and a great rack upon his head. Where is Alistair? I must see him!" Duncan's youthful enthusiasm bounced off the walls as Alistair moved toward the stairs.

"I hear you've been hunting, lad." Leaning on the banister, his voice sounded out into the vestibule. "I'd like to know what you've been about, but you'd best go and change your clothes. I'll have dinner set back a half-hour and even then, the kitchen and the ladies won't be happy."

"Oh, they'll do as their told, and be glad enough," Duncan retorted, smiling up at him. "Besides, Mother never complains." Mounting the stairs two at time, he joined him at the top.

"Fortunately for you, that's true." Alistair gazed at his brother for a moment, and then continued down the steps to the parlor below where the ladies waited for him.

"Good evening, Alistair," his mother greeted. "How good to have you home again. I trust your journey was successful?" Lady Grear MacDougall lifted her face to him as he leaned over to kiss her on the cheek.

Glancing at Ona, he saw her blue eyes sparkle with mischief. "Well, madam," he answered, giving his younger sister a quizzical look, "Argyll certainly has grander plans for me than I do."

"Indeed, I rather thought something of a specific nature was in the wind." Lady Grear waited expectantly. "We've heard many interesting rumors of late." She glanced at Ona who sat snickering beside her, then back to Alistair. "Have you news for us, my dear? How does Argyll fare, in any event?"

"'Tis rare when his grace doesn't fare well," he said bluntly. "He's shrewd and testy as ever."

Ona watched her eldest brother with idle amusement. "You must understand, dear brother, we've had a most instructive house guest of late."

"Have you indeed? And may I ask the name of this person?"

"Why Alistair, I'd thought that *you* of all people would know of whom I speak," she said with feigned innocence. "What do you think made Duncan ride off so abruptly?"

"I was under the distinct impression the Great Stag was the reason for his rash departure."

"Oh, I hadn't heard. Has the Stag been sighted? Lady Breadalbane assured us, that is, Duncan, Mother, and me that—"

"Lady Breadalbane was here? Confound the woman!" A black scowl darkened his face as his temper rose. "She has no business snooping about here."

"Alistair, love, you mustn't be so angry over a mere visit." Lady Grear gently reproached her eldest son. "We may not be on the best of terms, but she is my kinswoman."

"Kin or no, the woman's an infernal gossip." He transferred his stern gaze to his sister. "Now, what were you going to say a minute ago?"

"Do you mean before you so very *rudely* interrupted me? There's no need to snap my nose off." Ona peeked at him through her lashes. "As I was saying, Lady Breadalbane assured us that we would all be most welcome to visit Kilchurn Castle. She looked forward to her return because she expected good news concerning the nuptials of one of her numerous daughters, and to welcome us as family."

Alistair controlled himself with an effort as Lady Grear intervened. "You mustn't listen to Ona chatter, my dear. Effie Campbell hasn't an ounce of common sense. If she did, she wouldn't speak so freely of many things."

"Yet she did speak of something of importance to you, didn't she? I desired to speak with you about this before rumors spread abroad. We'll discuss it after dinner." His tone of voice brooked no argument, even from his mother. "And as for you, lass," he turned to Ona and noted that Duncan had quietly entered the room. "I'll deal with your impertinence later." He offered his mother his arm as she rose from her seat by the fire.

Duncan took Ona's hand, giving her a brotherly squeeze as the four exited the room.

Over supper, Duncan entertained them with the tale of his hunt. He told of the plight of the McCallum's, drawing compassionate remarks from his mother and sister.

Alistair listened intently, concerned for their neighbors.

"Well, brother," Duncan finally said. "Do you think we might aid them? The entire village is destitute. I'd be willing to take the responsibility to deliver assistance and supplies. My men will go with me." He'd already decided to help the poor Highlanders whether his elder brother agreed or not.

Ona's sense of compassion stirred. "I'd like to go with you, Duncan."

"'Tis dangerous country, Ona."

Alistair set his tankard down on the table. "You know, Duncan, that's still Jacobite territory. What will Argyll say if he learns of it? Is he not the administrator of those lands for the Crown?"

"Aye, but if we don't do something for them, Alistair, who will? 'Tis mostly women and children, anyhow. What harm will come of assuring they don't starve to death? They have little enough, in spite of the fact Eavan Malcolmson brings them a cart load of supplies here and again."

"Eavan Malcolmson." Alistair's voice grew cold. "I'm surprised you didn't say as much before. You know I can't abide the man." His dark brows met. "That would account for Farrell's report."

"How so?" Duncan asked as Alistair nodded. "What else has happened?"

"Only that Malcolmson traveled north with a cart load of goods recently." He helped himself to another serving of eel. "I've had the road from here to Loch Awe watched, as well as the well-traveled drove roads. Unfortunately, I can't see all of the activity on every deer path in the vicinity."

"Do you really believe those rebels are planning another uprising, Alistair? It doesn't seem very likely. Besides, Malcolmson is a relative of the McCallum's, isn't he?"

Alistair stopped eating for a moment and sat back in his chair. "Aye, he is. As to an uprising, 'tis doubtful, lad," he said quietly. "We've had reports that the Lairds in exile are still plotting rebellion but their people here are unwilling to pay them more rents."

"I don't blame them! They'd be paying twice then, and how many of them can afford it? Those poor McCallum women can't."

He shook his head. "I wouldn't think anyone could afford paying double rents. In fact, with most of their properties being held by the Crown, they have no real reason to expect such support any more."

"Alistair," Lady Grear interrupted. "Are you certain there is nothing we can do for the McCallum's? Perhaps Argyll would permit our intervention if I requested it of him."

Alistair was surprised by her question. "I can't say for certain, Mother. If you wish, I can ask him when next we are at Inveraray."

"Perhaps it would be better received if I made a personal request. Once," she explained further, "I was well acquainted with the Dunchalum family. I'd like to assist them in a needy hour."

"If you prefer to ask Argyll, I've no objection. But if he proves difficult, I'll be glad to intervene." He gazed at her in speculation. "Perhaps I should have consulted you first about what happens in the neighborhood. Evidently you know things I've never thought to ask."

Lady Grear chuckled. "My dear, you may ask but certain information 'tis not to be divulged. Besides, since when have the men in this family taken serious advice from the women? That would be a wondrous occasion indeed!"

Alistair and Duncan laughed. "'Tis all too true, I'm afraid. But you must admit, now's as good a time as any to begin. So if you've aught to say, then please do so."

"Well," she acknowledged, rising, "*that* is an admission not to be forgot. And we won't, Ona, so you must help me to remind these gentlemen of so courageous a declaration."

"Fear not, we'll leave you two with secrets, I expect, that you won't share in front of me."

"Nay, lassie, and what could we tell?" He shrugged. "We'll join you ladies shortly and leave you to discuss the only secret I know, which really isn't one at all."

Lady Grear nodded in agreement. "Come, Ona, I'll tell you the surprise in store for you. I hope you'll be happy."

The ladies departed, leaving Alistair and Duncan alone in the room. Alistair broke the silence, his voice stern. "Well, Duncan, what have you to say for yourself? Running away when there are not only guests in the house, but when I and most of the guard, am absent? I'm not pleased, lad. I left you in charge."

Duncan looked away, a repentant tone in his voice. "I know, Alistair, it truly was wrong of me. I happened to hear Farrell telling a story about you and the Stag, and I couldn't resist the temptation. Couple that with Lady Breadalbane's constant hints about that rabbit-toothed daughter of hers, I simply had to flee."

"Hints about her daughter? I thought they were all reserved for me."

"Hardly. It seems his lordship has made plans for you with Argyll, but his lady made her own the moment she clapped eyes on me, right after she arrived to promote family unity. You may well imagine why I fled."

"I can, Duncan," he laughed mirthlessly, "but you must learn to think of others first and be responsible for their well-being. 'Tis your duty, whether you like it or not. We live in dangerous times and what you don't know is that I've received reports of an unknown band of armed men in the area. If you'd been here, you could have assisted Farrell in taking more prudent measures."

He paused. "As it was, he secured the household while you were completely unaware of the situation. You not only endangered the household but your men, and abandoned your responsibility to the care of another."

"I'm sorry, Alistair," Duncan said, ashamed. "I guess I've been too eager to prove to you that I can do anything you can, but I've only succeeded in doing exactly the opposite." He lowered his eyes and studied the patterned carpet. "Do you have any idea who these men are, and how many?"

"Farrell estimated around twenty. They headed inland, traveling from the coast. But we don't know who they are or what they're doing here. They're dressed as common Highlanders and heavily armed." He paused. "You won't go after the Stag again, Duncan, or take supplies to the McCallum's until I find out more about this devilry." He demanded Duncan's cooperation and obedience. "I don't want to discourage our mother, but I can't allow you or anyone else to venture into Jacobite territory. 'Tisn't safe to be abroad in small numbers."

"So Ona was right, and you do have secrets with which to acquaint me."

Alistair ignored his flippant attitude. "Promise me, Duncan, that you'll not do anything foolish while I'm away with Mother and Ona at Inveraray."

"More secrets?" Duncan arched a brow. "I promise. I didn't know the three of you were going to visit the duke."

"'Tis at the duke's request that I'm returning with them for the week. I believe he wants to use them to persuade me to wed the fair Lady Vanora Campbell."

"If she's so fine then why don't you wed her? It would certainly remove a tremendous burden from my mind." He went down on one knee and clapped his hands to his breast. "I beg of you, O Noble Laird, save me from this dreadful plight."

"Get up, Duncan, don't be ridiculous. You can't possibly mean you wouldn't want to step into my boots one day?"

"And why should I? I'm very comfortable as I am, thank you. I have you to depend on, a roof over my head and a full belly. What more can a man need, aside from a wench now and then to warm his bed. If you have the lovely Campbell lass to wife, with her father's help and Argyll's support, you'll never lack for anything and neither shall I."

"Ah, lad, that's where you're wrong." Alistair's eyes danced for a moment before he sobered again. "I've heard about your wenching too, Duncan. You don't need to go down that path, it only leads to trouble. But you're forgetting Breadalbane's other daughter. What did you call her?"

"Rabbit-toothed," Duncan said, disgusted. "You should've been here, Alistair. Parading the girl around as if she were a beauty. And to top it off, the creature followed me everywhere, no place was safe from her chatter or encroaching behavior."

He burst out laughing. "Well, lad, it looks like we need to put our heads together to avoid the marriage trap. Argyll's practically got me to the altar." His merriment over Duncan's discomfiture ceased.

"So, that's why he summoned you to Inveraray, is it? I gathered as much from her ladyship. She openly acknowledged her desire for a union with our family without saying what the plan was, exactly. Was Breadalbane there, too?"

"Aye, and the Lady Vanora."

"A trap, Alistair? How did you manage to get caught so easily?"

His irritation surfaced. "Not caught, little brother. Challenged, aye, so I'll have to be careful. Last month, Argyll mentioned to me the idea of a betrothal to one of Breadalbane's daughters to promote clan unity." His mouth turned down in a scowl. "I confess I didn't take him seriously and told him that I'd consider it, just to silence him at the time. Needless to say, he—"

Duncan whistled and finished for him. "He went ahead and made a proposal for you, didn't he? Alistair," he leaned forward, "how far has this gone? Breadalbane can't sue for breach of promise, can he?"

"Nay." He frowned. "At least, I don't believe he can. I didn't make the first overture or speak to the man, let alone to the lass." The feeling of inevitable doom descended over him like a cloud.

"But Argyll could, couldn't he? I mean, he could since he is the chief of Clan Campbell, and our kinsman?" Duncan leaned back in his chair and stretched out his legs. "We aren't Campbells, but we're closely related."

"Aye, he might try to make this soup a wee bit hot for me," he said, chagrined. "I must be very careful, Duncan. I mean to speak to mother and Ona about this. I hope they were discreet when Lady Breadalbane was here."

"I'm sure they were, but that Campbell girl couldn't be depended upon not to snoop around."

"Aye, the rabbit-toothed one."

"Alistair, please—"

He laughed. "I couldn't resist, lad. Nay, you can do a mite better than that, I'm sure. How about one of our MacDougall cousins? The one I'm thinking of squints a tad, but I'm told she possesses a handsome dowry. Just think, a fine castle in the Highlands of your very own and a winsome bonnie wife to grace it, all to yourself."

"How generous of you, dear brother. Perhaps you might want to consider such a good bargain for yourself, squint and all."

"Oh nay, laddie, I've got other plans for myself." He leaned back in his chair, hands behind his head. A vision of golden loveliness flashed before his mind's eye.

Startled, he dropped his hands. Her eyes and face seemed permanently imprinted upon his brain. 'Tis a good thing I'm not the marrying kind, he reflected, else I might be in serious danger. I'll have to be very careful when I visit Hugh Morrison. Her golden hair was much warmer, more tempting than flax, and he wanted to slowly undo her thick braid, run his hands through her honey tresses. He closed his eyes and took a quick breath. His heartbeat increased, remembering the fateful kiss—

What's this? Duncan watched Alistair in surprise. With a mischievous gleam in his eye, Duncan interrupted his brother's daydream. "So, who's the wench, Alistair?"

Annoyed, Alistair opened his eyes. "Now what are you blethering about?"

"I asked you twice if you were ready to join the ladies and you said nothing at all, just stared into space in a complete state of euphoria."

"What's that got to do with a wench?"

"It's got everything to do with one! Now come on, I'm tired of waiting. If you won't tell me, I'll have to find out for myself," he said, eyes glinting. "Maybe I'll even steal her away from you. She must be beautiful, indeed, for you to be dreaming about."

Alistair jumped up and grabbed him, wrestling him to the floor. "First of all, scapegrace, you'd best remember to respect your elders. Secondly, you can't steal away what don't exist but in dreams."

He loosened his grip, and Duncan rolled over and sat up, rubbing his arm. "I still think she does exist," he said, sly, "and when I find out, I'll—"

"You'll what?" Alistair stood to his feet, a smirk on his face. "Think you can beat me at my own game, do you? You'll have to work a little harder than that, lad. Come on." He extended a hand. "Stand up and make yourself presentable. We'll go see if mother and Ona haven't given us up and gone upstairs to bed."

On this easy note of camaraderie, the brothers raced one another up the stairs and arrived, out of breath, on the threshold of the small sitting in time to hear Ona's last remark.

"Well, Mother, I suppose you're right. I could—"

"She's always right, lass," Alistair interjected. "You should always listen to your mother."

"Oh, there you are at last. We were about to retire," Lady Grear said, pleased. "Ona and I were discussing our recent visitors before you entered."

Alistair and Duncan exchanged a look of misgiving. "And?" He raised a brow. "I hope you both realize this is a most precarious situation."

"Is it, now? You'd best treat me well, then." Ona lifted her chin, a mischievous expression on her face. "Now let me think," she said, tapping her cheek with her forefinger. "What can you do for me to require my silence and cooperation?"

"Blackmailer," Duncan said. "What, do you desire Mistress Rabbit-Tooth to be your sister-in-law, and her sister to be your other sister? Won't we all live happily ever after together."

"Oh, come now, my dear, the situation isn't quite so desperate," Lady Grear admonished. "Alistair, you must tell me more of your visit to Inveraray. You mentioned earlier that you have something of import to tell me."

"I do, and I'm beginning to feel very uneasy, if not desperate. It affects you also, Ona, so please listen carefully." He looked at his sister, expecting her obedience.

She bowed her head in acquiescence.

"As you know, his grace requests your presence at Inveraray for the All Saint's Eve festivities. Part of the reason for his invitation is that he expects to confirm and announce my betrothal to the Lady Vanora Campbell, daughter of the Earl of Breadalbane."

"What!" Ona exclaimed. "I haven't met her, have I? Grizel is very sweet, but she reminds me of a frightened rabbit more than anything."

Lady Grear's mouth twitched in appreciation. "That will do, Ona. Let Alistair finish without interruption."

"This whole affair wasn't my inspiration, and I'm counting on you ladies to discourage her and her father as much as possible. 'Tis imperative there's no mistake made about my intentions during this visit."

"I don't understand how this has come to such a pass," Lady Grear said, puzzled. "I hadn't gathered from our last conversation that any serious connection was in the wind. How came you to this place?"

"My Lord Argyll has been rather high-handed as usual. He mentioned this to me once before, as I told you earlier." Glowering, he crossed his arms tightly across his chest. "On this visit, nay summons, he informed me the deed was all but settled. He'd spoken with Breadalbane, talked betrothal and settlements without a word to me. The girl and her father await our return to Inveraray, and Argyll is gleefully rubbing his hands together in anticipation."

"Shall we play dumb, Alistair?" put in Ona. "I'll enjoy doing so immensely."

"Do you mean you have to *play* at it, dear sister?" Duncan teased. "I thought it came natural to you."

"That's enough, Duncan," his mother said. "That was unkind. You, of all people, should be thankful for her intervention on your behalf of late."

"I most humbly apologize. Your grateful servant, mistress." Removing his arm from its resting place on the mantel, he swept his sister a flourishing bow.

Playing the great lady, Ona lowered her head. "Your *humble* apology 'tis accepted, sir."

Alistair ignored them both. "I hope all of you understand the importance of this matter. Someday when I marry, it will be to a lass of my choosing, not Argyll's or anyone else."

"Of course, my dear, we're agreed. I believe God has someone very special for all of you." Lady Grear spoke with sincerity. "I've prayed for each of you to have your heart's desire in your marriages, and that He will richly bless you. He can, you know."

"Aye, Mother, we do know. You've taught us well." He suddenly smiled at her. "That's why I intend to wait and not have my hand forced now." Unbidden, a vision of the McCallum lass rose again to the forefront of his mind. *Losh*, his wretched heart. He drew in a sharp breath, quickly glancing around. Good, the others hadn't seemed to notice his mental lapse.

"I'm sure all will be well, my dear," Lady Grear comforted. "We'll give it to God and trust Him to keep our paths straight. In the meantime, we'll be on our guard at Inveraray, aware of the strategies of Argyll and outwit him at his own game."

"I sincerely hope so," he said with forced equanimity. "The Earl and his daughter are wily in their own right, Mother. You must regard them as equal adversaries."

"You sound as if we're going to war," she chuckled. "Surely this isn't going to be a battle?" Duncan and Ona laughed aloud, pleased at the challenge it presented.

"On the contrary," he said, brooding. "I expect serious opposition but what weapon will be aimed next, I don't know. The first round goes to Argyll. We must win the second."

Chapter 17

Confessions

"Now what are ye lookin' for, eh lass?" John Dhu teased his granddaughter.

Kennis stared, absentminded, at the choppy waves that crashed upon the rocks. One brief message from Eavan had arrived, stating that his search was unsuccessful. She wondered how hard he really tried.

"I thought ye weren't interested in any particular laddies yet."

She smiled at him, and continued to sift the warm sand through her fingers. True, she was disappointed that Eavan hadn't even sent her a greeting but perhaps it was for the best. "I fear 'tisn't quite time for me, Grandad, not till we have Robbie at home safe with us."

He looked out to sea and back again, measuring his words. "Well, lassie, I'd nae wait too long if the right one comes along," he said wisely. "Ye may have to make up your mind a wee bit sooner than Robbie's homecomin's likely to happen." He rose, patting her head before strolling down the rocky shore.

Mulling over his words, Kennis examined her heart. She agreed with him; the time wasn't quite ripe for her. However, she must find her brother. She simply couldn't sit still any longer, waiting for letters that might never arrive. Her determination arose, a plan formulating in her mind.

She'd leave a note explaining her intentions. Mam would understand, even if it made her upset. Fergus and Daly would go with her to McCallum lands, and Robbie would surely go to Dunchalum if he came home. It was possible that he might travel to Skye but not until he'd gone to see his clan. He was Chief of Clan McCallum now. The mainland was definitely his first destination.

With fresh resolve, she beckoned to Fergus, keeping watch nearby. He and Daly were usually eager conspirators and the three of them would carefully lay plans together. Fergus, in response to her summons, strolled to where she sat comfortably on a plaid. "Where is Daly, Fergus? I'd like to speak with both of you."

"He's nearby, lass. Threw a fishin' line in, I think, on the other side o' that rock. I'll fetch him if ye like."

"Please do." She drew a picture in the sand while she waited, content to sit and listen to the peaceful whoosh of the rolling waves.

He ambled off and returned in good time with Daly, who carried a bucket and was pleased with his good fortune.

"What do you have there, Daly?"

"A few choice salmon, lass. I've had a fine run this morning."

"I'm glad for it." She appreciated his enthusiasm. "I always feel like you two don't have enough time for yourself when I'm around."

"Nay, that's nae true, lass. We always manage to enjoy ourselves wherever we are, dinna we, Ferg?"

The big man agreed. "Aye, that we do. Besides, we'd plenty o' time to relax while ye were away. Now tell us what's on your mind."

"I hardly know how to begin. I've been sitting here stewing over this half the morning. There are two things I haven't told you," she admitted, "or Mam and Grandad. I've debated about what to do and I've come to no conclusion." She inhaled deeply. "I promised Mr. Gilmore to confess what I'd done, and so far I've not had the courage to tell Mam."

Not surprised by her admission, Daly and Fergus waited for her to speak. They knew only too well that Kennis could be a handful. "So, lass," Daly said, "what were ye supposed to confess?" He glanced down the beach at the McKinnon.

She related the tale about how she unintentionally stowed away on the laird's galley, leaving out the fact that his given name was Alistair. "You may imagine my surprise when I realized that the man wrapped in the blanket was Davis McCallum. I wasn't sure at first, but on the galley there could be no mistaking him. He recognized me, too, and I think the Laird's man heard him call out my name."

Daly whistled. "But ye dinna tell the Laird your name, did ye, lass?"

"Nay, I used the Morrison surname on my entire voyage."

"Then there's probably nothin' to worry about."

"But that's not all of it," she said contritely. She brushed away the sand picture and started a new one.

"I dinna think," he muttered. "Go on."

She looked up from her drawing. "You remember when we luncheoned at the inn at Port Eilidh? The man who spoke so rudely to us, and to Eavan?"

Daly's tanned face turned a deeper shade.

"Aye, I remember him," Fergus said, frowning.

"He's the Laird from aboard the galley. I don't know who he is, I could never discover his full name." She scowled, recalling his taunts. "The only clue I have is that Eavan called him Alistair. But there are a lot of Alistairs in Scotland."

"'Tis true," Fergus agreed, "but nae all the Lairds in Scotland are named such, so that narrows the field. Do ye really think it matters?"

"Of course it does!" she said, exasperated. "Don't you see? He may know how to find Robbie if he has connections with men like Denoon." *And it matters to me, too.*

"Why dinna ye ask Eavan Malcolmson?"

She grimaced. "I thought about it. The two of them weren't exactly on friendly terms. I wasn't sure I'd receive help from that quarter, and he would demand an explanation. She paused. "And then I'd have to tell Mam and Grandad the whole story and they might've told Eavan. 'Tis a hopeless tangle."

"Are ye goin' to tell the McKinnon and your mother what ye did, lass?" Daly asked. "A promise 'tis a promise."

"I should," she worried, "but I can't bring myself to tell them about Davis and I don't know why." Her insides twisted with remorse.

Daly and Fergus exchanged looks. "Leave that part to us. Ye honor your word to Mr. Gilmore and no one will know the difference."

Relieved, Kennis agreed to their offer. "Very well, but that's not all I wanted to discuss." She took a deep breath. "I'd like to know if you two are game to journey to Kilcalum and Dunchalum, to see the clan and gather news of Robbie. I'm not satisfied with this report from Cameron Campbell or Eavan, though I dislike admitting it."

Daly pressed his lips together. "Well-l, ye've taken the words from my mouth, lass. Fergus and I were thinkin' of goin' ourselves since our annual visit's o'erdue. Must ye go?"

Kennis eagerly jumped up and brushed off her skirt. "Aye, will you take me? I've been thinking about it for days."

The two men grinned. "Then let's go as soon as possible, since the weather willna wait for us. Fergus and I will take care o' the details. All ye'll have to do is gather what ye need." He paused. "One thing, lass. Ye have to do what we say, 'tis dangerous country and we need to be careful."

"I will," she said, exuberant. "I promise I'll obey every word!" All three laughed at this pronouncement, knowing that she possessed a stubborn streak.

A time to finalize their plans was set for the end of the week. Kennis' heart felt lighter from sharing her burden. That evening, she told mother and grandfather what she'd done on board the ship during her journey home from America, and her promise to Mr. Gilmore.

Sitting by the fire embroidering, Alanna dropped her tambour frame in shock.

Her grandfather guffawed during her confession. "Now who was this Laird, lass?" he asked, curious. "Seems to me he was mighty tolerant of your sauce."

"Tolerant?" Her mouth dropped open. "How can you sanction his behavior, sir, after what I've described to you?"

"Well, it depends upon your perspective. Ye gave him reason enough to turn ye over his knee and *skelp* ye, by my calculations."

"Grandad," she said, astonished, straightening in her chair. "I'm disappointed to hear that you believe I deserved such unjust treatment."

"Ye mustn't tempt a man to violence." His resolve was firm; he held up his hand to silence her as she began to protest. "Ye gave him cause to reprove your conduct, and I think ye know that already. Let it rest, lassie." He restated his previous question. "Now, tell me the man's name."

Kennis sat silent, gazing at him as he smoked his pipe. The opinion of the world definitely favored men. How would she, being a woman, accomplish her purpose in life if everything rested on the viewpoint of men? Disappointed, she finally answered. "All I know is that his name is Alistair, nothing more."

"Then what did he look like? Describe him to me."

Recalling Alistair's features and expressions, she described him fully, unaware that her own expression subtly altered.

The effect wasn't lost upon the perceptive John Dhu. He watched her with a keen eye, not moving a muscle. "Alistair, ye say."

"Aye," she said, a far off look in her eye. "Alistair."

John Dhu glanced at Alanna, and she held his gaze with slightly raised brows. "Kennis, love, I wish you'd told me about your adventure before this evening. You've been very close-mouthed about it."

She turned her gaze from the dancing flames in the hearth. "I was embarrassed, Mam. It was a silly thing to do, and although I promised Mr. Gilmore that I'd relate the whole, I couldn't bring myself to admit what I had done."

"And what of your young man?"

Kennis' eyes flew to her mother. "My young man?"

"Why, the Laird you spoke of, my love. Is there nothing more you can tell us about him?"

"Nay," she said, coloring. "Whatever for? And he's not my young man!"

Alanna smiled gently. "I'd like to give him my thanks for rescuing you from a most difficult situation. Have you no appreciation of the service he rendered you?"

"Service!" she said, indignant. "How can you say so? He was overbearing and uncouth."

"Ye dinna say that before, lass," John Dhu added shrewdly, observing the flush that accompanied her disavowal. "I had the impression ye were taken with the man."

"Taken with him! I'm amazed that the two of you would make such an assumption." She looked from one to the other, dumbfounded. "Faith, he threatened me, and behaved in a boorish manner. And you want me to thank him?"

"I think you owe him a great measure of appreciation," Alanna insisted. "In spite of what you deem his poor behavior, he seems to have preserved you from certain harm."

She blinked, incredulous, as John Dhu questioned her further. "I agree with your mother but I'll say no more for the present. Can ye not recall anythin' more about the man? What about his men, do ye remember any of them?"

"Aye, one in particular who was very kind to me."

"Who then?" he said, impatient. "What was his name?"

"'Twas Farrell." She recalled that Alistair used his surname on several occasions. "Farrell McConacher, I believe. He was very pleasant and patient with me, too. He helped me on the beach."

"Hmph," he grunted, and stood. Walking to the hearth, he tapped his pipe on the stone and emptied the ashes into the fire. "And how was his appearance?"

"He has dark hair and eyes, a sturdy man."

"And ye say he went about everywhere with this Alistair?"

"Aye, he did."

Alanna added her opinion. "It sounds to me as though he also deserves your gratitude, Kennis." She held her daughter's eyes for a moment then selected a red silken thread from her basket.

Kennis smiled at the mild reproof. "I did thank him, Mam. If anyone deserves my thanks on my journey aside from the Gilmores, it would be Farrell."

"So what think you, Father," Alanna asked. "Know you this man?"

"I might," he said, noncommittal. "I'll make a few inquiries and be sure to discover the name of Kennis' Laird, and what clan we're dealin' with first."

"He's not mine," she repeated, glancing at her mother.

"Nay?" he teased, his face alight with laughter. "Looks like our Eavan'll have some competition from the sound of it."

Flustered, Kennis rose from her chair by the fire. "I think I'll retire if you don't object, Mam, Grandad. Good night." She hurried toward the door and opened it.

"Good night, love," Alanna echoed.

"Evenin', lassie," John Dhu said, enjoying the moment. "Sweet dreams."

After Kennis departed the saloon, Alanna reproved him. "Father, you shouldn't tease her so."

"And why nae? I used to treat ye the same."

"I know," she said dryly. "That's exactly why."

"Och, she'll survive."

She laughed. "You're incorrigible, sir."

"I know." He joined her in a hearty laugh and slapped his knee. "That's just what your mother used to say. Anyway, I believe, daughter, that I know the identity of these men."

"You do?" she said, amazed. She stopped sewing and stared hard at her capricious father. "But I thought you needed to inquire more thoroughly."

"Nay, luve." He gave her a smug look. "I knew who she meant from the start. There's only one man in the West of Scotland who answers to the name Alistair and fits the description she so readily provided. And Farrell McConacher's his henchman, confirmin' my suspicions."

Alanna laid her embroidery aside, wishing that her father would be more forthcoming. "Then who is he? Don't keep me in suspense."

"You promise you willna tell the lass?"

"Not if you insist, Father, but why the secrecy?"

"Because I've a natterin' feelin' about it. If young Alistair wanted her to know, he'd have told her himself. He's a right canny Scot and a good man." He stroked his chin. "Now there's a man I'd be proud to own as a grandson, even by marriage."

"You still haven't told me who he is, sir." She rose and stood before him, hands on her hips. "Alistair who?"

"MacDougall. The MacDougall of Dunolly, now that his father's gone. 'Twould be a fine match for our lassie. He's the man to hold the reins tight." He cocked his head and looked up into the dark eyes so like his own. "Dinna stand there like a common wench, Alanna, it dinna become ye. Sit back down."

"I'll sit down when I'm ready to do so, sir." Her forehead creased. "Has the man a fierce temper?"

John Dhu sat back and pressed his fingertips together. "Aye, he's black enough but not any more so than I. Ye canna say that's a problem."

"Only if he's cruel." Alanna had seen the effect of abusive husbands on their wives too often in years past.

He shook his head in the negative. "Nay, not he. He's a better man than Eavan Malcolmson."

"How can you say such a thing?" she said, exasperated by her father's vagueness. "Have you known him long?"

"Since he was a lad. I met him at Dunolly many years ago, and he's visited here upon occasion, stopped by to drink a pint or two with an auld man like me. He's a good lad, a mite difficult, perhaps, but a man of integrity and purpose. I've a good mind to write him a letter, thankin' him for takin' care of the lass and for toleratin' her sauce."

Shaking her head and knowing what mischief he was capable of performing, Alanna resumed her seat, picking up her threaded needle and embroidery frame.

John Dhu rose and hobbled to the writing table in the corner. Pulling a thick sheet of ivory parchment from a vellum folder, he sat down on a spindly-legged chair and reached for the quill that sat in the inkstand. After carefully carving the tip, he uncorked the inkwell. Dipping the feather into the ink, he shook off the excess and slowly began to write. What he didn't tell Alanna was the plan forming in his mind. His old eyes gleamed, pleased with the turn of events that had taken the lass straight into the path of Alistair MacDougall.

Chapter 18

Megrims

Alistair lay awake in the wee hours of the morning disturbed by more than the howling wind that shook the house.

He stared at the dark canopy hanging over his head. *Almost a death shroud*, he thought gloomily. He knew that he could depend upon his mother and sister to discourage the pretensions of the Lady Vanora and her father. What bothered him the most was his standing with Argyll. "I should have foreseen this," he berated himself for the twentieth time. Argyll gave nothing away without expecting a return. "How have I managed to— Nay, I won't think of it any longer tonight. I must get some sleep and track the brigands tomorrow."

After a troubled night, he rose and pulled the bell cord to summon Farrell. He arrived in short order, bringing with him a hot pitcher of water for Alistair's ablutions. After setting it on the stand, he pulled back the bed curtains and awaited further instructions.

"Has Duncan been to breakfast yet, Farrell?" Alistair threw back the coverlet and rose from the large feather bed.

"Nay, Laird, I dinna think so. What clothes would ye hae me lay out, sir?"

"Riding breeks and my leather jack. I think I'll have a look about for these brigands, Farrell. Duncan will go with me." Alistair smiled at the man's hopeful expression. "And you, too. We'll take several of the lads and ride to the coast. Perhaps we'll hear more of them on the road to Inveraray, so I won't go in that direction today. While I'm away, under no circumstances is anyone to leave the premises without an escort. Is that understood?"

"Aye, sir. When do we leave?"

"Have the men and horses at the gate in thirty minutes. I'll break my fast before I go. Wake Duncan, too," he said, pulling on his boots. "The sluggard better be ready to ride when I am, else I'll drag him from his bed."

Ten minutes later, Duncan joined Alistair in the breakfast parlor. "Going to drag me from my bed, were you? For your information, I've been out and about since sunrise."

"A good morning to you, too," Alistair retorted, piling his plate high with another generous helping of the breakfast set before him on the warmers. "Doing what, may I ask?"

"I wanted to be ready before you were." Duncan was inordinately pleased with himself. "I figured you'd be off to spy out the land at first light."

"Very good, Duncan. You begin to understand me better."

He sat opposite his brother at the table. "Oh, I understand you better than you know, Alistair. Where do we ride this morning?"

"South along the coast. We'll ride to the old castle and take in the view from there, then wind our way down, covering as many tracks as possible. I don't think we need to check the road. This band isn't likely to travel out in the open."

"And what do you expect to find?"

"I honestly don't know," he admitted. "We'll see if we can find evidence as to who they are and where they've come from. Too easy by half to travel by land or sea here. Are you finished with your breakfast?"

Duncan stuffed his last bite into his mouth. "Aye, as you can see."

"Good, eh?" Alistair smiled. "Let's be off. I only have today so I want to make the most of it. I ride for Inveraray soon."

He arose from the table and Duncan joined him. The two men walked briskly across the room, through the hall and down the steps into the courtyard. His men walked the horses, ready for the journey. He mounted while Farrell issued his orders to the riders. The sun peeped over the horizon, and Alistair and Duncan led the riders out the gate, followed by Farrell, Jamie, and the rest of the tail.

Within minutes, Dunolly Castle came into view. Presently used as a quarry, the ancient structure stood proudly at the north end of Oban Bay. It was beginning to show the wear and tear of the work, a despoiling of its bleak kind of beauty.

Alistair rode through the open gates and dismounted, motioning for his men to follow suit. Within minutes, they scoured the premises, looking for signs of intruders. Satisfied that nothing out of the ordinary had occurred there, he swung into his saddle and rode back out, his heart pierced at the emptiness of the abode of his ancestors. Apparently, this desolation was the type of progress for which all of Scotland was destined.

He pondered the thought, knowing that the tumultuous events of the past five years that affected them all so deeply were impossible to recover or correct in the present. The changes that had taken place were vast and permanent. Those concerned for the welfare of the country were forced to make many adjustments and hopefully, the lot of some of the poorer folk would improve.

The day wore on, yielding no clue to the identity or whereabouts of the intruders. The countryside was quiet, the few birds that hadn't flown south sang in the late October sunshine. Soon it would be dusk, time to return home since tracking anything after dark was a futile endeavor. The men fanned out in one last effort before their return journey.

"Captain, o'er here!" Alistair's head shot up toward the voice of Jocko Dougall from the brush nearby. He turned his horse to the west and met Farrell head on, emerging from under a heavily laden branch. Near the shore, Jocko and Mac Tawesson crouched, examining the rough ground.

"What is it, lads?" he called out.

"'Tis what's left of a fire, sir," Jocko said, "and footprints, if you'll step carefully. Whoe'er was here wasna careful to hide the fact." He picked up a tattered piece of cloth and handed it up to Alistair. "'Tis this wee bit that's bamboozled me, now. I'd guess 'twas a piece of tartan, or a plaidie."

He dismounted, Farrell following close behind. Alistair handed Farrell the piece and he examined the rough cloth. "What do you make of it? I'm not sure."

"Could be a tartan, sir. 'Tis dirty, but there's a wee bit of blue and green peekin' through." Farrell inspected it more closely and rubbed it between his fingers. "What's more, the weave is that of a plaidie. If ye look closely at the footprints, I wager ye'll see a brogue or two, as well as a boot heel."

"Let's check thoroughly before dark. Jocko, you and Mac head north. Andrew, gather the others, while we head to the shore. Where's Duncan?"

"Right behind you, Alistair. Jamie and I have been to the shore. There's not much to see with the tide in."

Alistair studied his surroundings for another moment, frustrated. "Let's finish combing this area while we have daylight. Move on, lads," he ordered, mounting his horse. He looked out to sea before urging the animal forward along the rocky beachhead.

All leads exhausted, the weary men reached Dunolly at nightfall. Following supper, Alistair and Duncan removed to the library and sat companionably over a bottle of claret.

"Well, Duncan," Alistair said soberly. "I'm off to Inveraray in four days. Wish me well."

"You know I do, Alistair. Besides, if you marry the wench, it directly affects me." He looked at his brother in concern. "I have no desire, big brother, to see you tricked into a loveless marriage. I never thought I'd see the day you were outsmarted by anyone, although I confess that I've had moments when I thought it would be entertaining."

"Hopefully that day isn't upon you." He ran his hand through his wavy locks. "Are you sure you won't accompany us? I could make you, you know."

Duncan snickered. "I know you could, but you won't."

"Don't be too sure of that, Duncan. If I find myself in a tight spot I may send for you." He spoke half to himself, planning his route of escape. "Otherwise, I'll make a hasty retreat to Craignish, perhaps take Mother and Ona there for a change of scenery. I'm also leaving for Skye tonight."

"Skye?" Duncan repeated. "What in the world are you going there for? The place is a hotbed of Jacobites! You've no place there."

"On the contrary, I have important business to attend to," he said, a slow smile lighting his face. "There is one old friend, a Jacobite indeed, whom I desire to see. I trust that he's learned his lesson this time around."

"You're speaking of the McKinnon."

"Aye, the man's been on my mind. He's old, Duncan. I don't think he'd have gone out to follow Charlie if it weren't for his long-standing political ties."

"He's still a cursed rebel, Alistair," Duncan argued. "And every man that stands on the same ground with him on a daily basis is one and the same."

"Perhaps, but I choose to be his friend. He freely offered me his friendship, which is more than I can say for most men. I was relieved to have him safely removed from Tilbury. A prison is no place for such a one as he." His eyes glinted with sudden passion. "Besides, I may be more of a rebel than you know."

"You're being sentimental over the McKinnon. You wouldn't dare say you were a rebel to anyone else but me, I hope."

"I wouldn't, except to Farrell," he acknowledged. "He and I are alike, and I don't think I'm sentimental. Nay, brother, loyal to friendship and remember, the rebellion is over."

"Well, I hope you're right." Duncan was unconvinced. "How long do you plan to stay?"

"Naught but a day. I simply want to see how he fares, if with the return of his lands, he has sufficient wealth on which to live and support his own."

"I'll wait for you, then," Duncan said stubbornly. "If you don't return within a reasonable time, I'll bring the lads and come for you."

Alistair laughed. "What, do you fear for me, Duncan? I'll take Farrell with me. Don't worry, lad. All I need from you, is to do as I bid while I'm gone. Don't go chasing that stag. With the rumors flying abroad about marauders, we must still be on our guard."

Duncan still wasn't convinced. "And what about the McCallum's?" he reminded him.

"I'll speak to Argyll. I give you my word."

Chapter 19

Foiled

*T*oday is the day I return home.

The words had a familiar ring. She'd said the same on the day of her journey home to Scotland from the Americas. Moreover, she sneaked out of the house to search for news of Robbie one last time. This time, however, she went to meet Daly and Fergus to sail to the mainland.

Kennis quickly dressed and snuffed the lone candle. She opened and peeked out her door into the dark passage. All clear. With all of the stealth she could muster, she tiptoed down the passage in her stocking feet, carrying her boots as she descended the stairs to the kitchen below.

The castle slept and Daly awaited her, oilcloth in hand. "'Tis a wet mornin'." He handed her the oilcloth after she put on her boots. "We'd best be off. Fergus'll be at the boat by now. We packed everythin' last night." He examined her in the dim light. "Ready, lass?"

Kennis nodded and started to reach for an oat scone left on a platter from the previous night. Had she not done the same last April, too? Suddenly she remembered sharing her breakfast with a hungry child. Coincidence? Probably so. It only proved that she'd waited too long to resume her search for Robbie. It was a good thing that she was finally on her way.

She stepped onto the stone walk and shivered in the chill wind that perpetually blew around the castle. Excitement over the journey that lay ahead made her head spin. She looked forward to seeing Granny Jean and the other McCallum clansmen who remained near Dunchalum Castle.

The cobbled walk near the postern gate was empty. Daly looked quickly from left to right before he dashed ahead and hurriedly slipped the unwieldy key into the iron lock. He searched the dawn for prying eyes before stepping through the arch. The sentries shuffled overhead, making their rounds on the keep like clockwork. "Come on, lass," he whispered. He turned back to the gate and tucked the key into a crevice where the iron grill embedded into crumbling masonry. Dora, the kitchen maid, was sweet on him and would be along in a few minutes to collect the key and lock the door from the inside. Leaving the door unlocked left the castle vulnerable. He felt guilty using the girl, exposing her to censure.

"Daly," Kennis whispered, urging him on. "Come on, what's the matter? The sentry is returning this way! Do you think he heard us?" She glanced upward, seeing movement at the top of the battlements. The torch above them flickered in the gusting wind.

Daly lifted his finger to his lips, motioning for her to join him in the shadows. Pressed against the cold rock of the outer castle walls, the two held their breath as the sentry paused overhead. He stood there for what seemed an interminably long time, listening. Kennis hoped that the man's diligence wouldn't be their undoing. Finally, he turned and stalked away.

Daly grasped her arm and guided her toward a well-used track. The kitchen maids and stable hands that lived in the village often used this route to walk to the castle. Kennis could ill afford discovery. If this scheme was exposed, her efforts were in vain and the opportunity lost.

The sheltie ponies were tied to a tree as pre-arranged and the two made haste to unbind them and mount, urging the sure-footed little beasts forward. The track wound gently down the hillside and overhead, the tree limbs poised to enfold the riders in their giant, hoary arms.

The early morning air invigorated her, and she became impatient with the slow plod of the animal beneath her. Soon she'd be out of the saddle and sailing to the mainland. She peered ahead in the gloom. Two figures trudged up the hillside toward them, a bobbing torch lighting the way. She grew uneasy as the pair drew near. "Daly," she said quietly, "is there no other route we could take? I don't feel comfortable about this meeting."

"Dinna worry, lass," he replied. "I'm sure they're comin' to work at the stables. Ye know the lads and lasses use this path every mornin'."

"Perhaps, but they shouldn't see me out this early."

"I dinna think it matters, but we can turn off and pass by the cottages where," he said in a dry tone, "ye're more likely to meet someone."

She heard the exasperation in his voice. "I'd rather not see any McKinnons right now." She pushed a low, wet branch away from her face. "At least we can bypass the crofts and stay in the shadows."

Daly started to grumble, making a face that his mistress couldn't see in the dark. "Verra well. Let's turn off here, then. Follow me, and pull your cloak around your face. 'Twill be dawn soon."

She obeyed and steered her pony to the narrow path that he indicated. The ponies slowly picked their way over the rough ground. Ahead, lights glinted in the distance. The inhabitants of Kilmoil called the string of blackhouses and shielings a village but it was actually a series of the small, stone dome-like structures dispersed along the main track to the castle. The ground provided an uneven foundation, and most were neatly tucked into the hillside, sheltered by the leafy foliage and rocky terrain.

* * *

Alistair and Farrell heaved to on the oars of the small sailboat. The lack of a steady wind forced the men to row. The moon spread an aura of light over the rocky shoreline, revealing their destination before a dense bank of clouds shrouded it again in inky darkness.

"Should I light a torch, sir?" Farrell asked, peering into the gloom.

"Not yet," Alistair replied. "We should be able to put ashore without mishap. There's a track that leads straight up the hillside to Castle Moil."

The two resumed rowing and within moments, the hull of the vessel grated to a halt on the shore. Farrell jumped out and Alistair heaved their packs to him before leaping over the side, splashing into the ankle deep water. They beached the boat, pulling it high away from the tide and flipping it over to keep out unwanted intruders and rain.

"Let's go." Alistair strode toward the brambles and pushed aside the dry bracken. Before him, a little used path rose steadily higher. Farrell lit a small torch and handed it to him.

The pair silently trudged up the steep hill, glad the journey was nearly at an end. Lights shone warmly in the heights above, welcoming the two travelers from afar. Each concentrated on his footing; the ground was wet and slippery from the dew, and a light mist spiraled upward, limiting their visibility. Within minutes, the twinkling lights of the village of Kilmoil appeared. Hushed voices drifted on the air from the awakening inhabitants.

Alistair halted. Farrell stopped short behind him, a question in his eyes. He pointed up the track at two ponies trekking downward. Abruptly, the riders steered their mounts to the right and disappeared into a dense stand of trees.

"Now that's interestin'," Farrell said softly.

Alistair agreed. "Perhaps they don't want to be seen. Shall we investigate?"

"Aye, sir."

He quickened the pace and motioned to Farrell to douse the torch. A pony whinnied in the distance, the soft thud of hoofs muffled on the damp earth. "Farrell." He kept his voice low. "There's a small clearing ahead, a few crofts on either side. When we reach it, I'll take the left, you go right. If you need to get out of sight, duck into the shadows near the cliff or behind the crofts."

The men stole forward, quietly pursuing their quarry. An owl hooted, breaking the silence, announcing that night was still at hand. The fine mist rising from the earth offered a measure of concealment. Alistair viewed the clearing. Good, it was empty. He nodded to Farrell, who slipped behind the scattered huts built under the overhanging cliffs.

He quickly assessed his surroundings before stealthily moving toward the left half of the village and disappearing into the shadows. Passing through, he emerged on the other side. Subdued voices and the steady shuffle of ponies greeted him. One of them, he felt certain, was a lass. When Farrell appeared at his right, he motioned to him to follow through the trees that paralleled the track. "Whoever they are, we'll head them off and see what this business is about."

"Might be a man and wife or daughter out to work."

"Maybe," he said, "but the fact they avoided meeting us 'tis odd." He shrugged. "If 'tis only a lass and her father, then we'll beg their pardon and be on our way. Let's go."

Step by step, they crept, careful not to rustle dry clumps of brambles. Thanks to the damp ground, the fallen leaves no longer crackled underfoot, further masking their approach. Drawing abreast of the riders, they heard the man whistling an old tune. The woman quietly urged her pony forward and unexpectedly, threw back her hood.

Startled, Alistair's breath caught in his throat. The McCallum lass, here on Skye and wandering about at an early hour—no doubt the girl was up to mischief. He recognized her attendant from the inn at Port Eilidh. Brows raised, he looked at Farrell who stared back at him in wonder. Pointing to a spot ahead, Alistair moved forward and Farrell joined him.

* * *

Kennis glanced about before she threw back the confining hood. "Daly," she said, uneasy. "How can you whistle at a time like this? 'Tis dangerous."

"Nay, lass," he said. "It passes the time, and I dinna think there's anyone to hear me out here."

"I wouldn't be so sure of that, lad," a rich voice returned from beneath the trees. Alistair stepped onto the track. "You should always be on your guard."

Kennis gasped. Shocked into silence, she stared at the man standing before her. Her eyes flew beyond him as Farrell joined his master. "What are you doing here?" she finally uttered.

"Seeing to it that you stay out of mischief, lass," he mocked. "It seems to be my current lot in life."

"What I do is none of your concern." She gathered in her reins and attempted to steer the pony past him on the narrow trail.

He stepped forward and caught the pony's bridle in his hand. "You're mistaken, as usual, so perhaps you'd care to explain to put my mind at ease."

Her heart skipped a beat as his dark eyes locked with hers. "You've no need to worry about me. Daly will take care of me, and so will the rest of my kinsmen."

His lifted both brows. "Kinsmen, here on Skye?" His eyes narrowed. Seeing her again convinced him that her real surname was McCallum. Her resemblance to young Rob and to Laird Robert was uncanny.

Her eyes flew to Daly. "I dinna think ye need to know our business, sir," he cut in warily. "We've an appointment to keep and ye're holdin' us back."

"With who? Maybe you'd rather explain to the McKinnon what you're doing here, if not to me."

"I've no need to explain anything to you," she hesitated, "or the McKinnon. He wouldn't be interested in my affairs."

"Nay?" Alistair scoffed. "But since I'm interested, you're going to explain them to me and to him." He pulled on the bridle and turned the pony around.

"Wait, what do you think you're doing?" she cried. "Let go of that bridle! You have no right to force me to go with you, to explain myself to you or anyone else." She turned around in the saddle. "Daly!" she entreated.

Daly moved his pony forward. "Here now, ye've no cause to upset the lass or give her orders since ye're nae her kinsman."

Alistair's eyes narrowed. "Is the McKinnon your master?"

190

"Nay." Daly answered. John Dhu was his laird without the Laird Robert or the lad Robbie present, but there was no way the confounded man standing before him should know. Looking into shrewd black eyes, he knew that a lie would prove to be his undoing.

"Then who is your master?"

"I dinna answer to anyone but the lass here, and her mother."

The corner of Alistair's lip curled into a half-smile. "Very wise. Where can I find her mother, then?"

At a stalemate, Daly looked at his mistress. "I canna say."

Kennis returned his stare, unable to help, not expecting him to provide evidence that would incriminate either of them. He'd not betray her but he also wouldn't cross swords with a laird except in the defense of her person.

"What does it matter to you?" she asked Alistair. "We're not related, in fact, I hardly know you, but you freely interfere in my affairs as if you had the right. I have urgent business that calls me away, and I must leave now." She appealed to what she hoped was his sense of justice. "I'm in good hands, not traveling unattended and up to mischief as you say, but you treat me like a naughty child who's running away from home."

"Aren't you?" Alistair murmured. "I have the impression that's exactly what you're doing and my instincts are never wrong."

"Never, sir?" She was irritated by his conceit. "You rate yourself far too high."

"Not usually," he said confidently. "I've made my decision. We go to the McKinnon now."

Kennis fought to control her temper. "Nay," she said one last time, restraining the pony. "You can't make me."

"I can and I will." He dismissed her protests. "And you," he said to Daly, "have other business to conclude tonight?"

Thinking of Fergus waiting in the cove, Daly acquiesced. "Aye, that I do, sir."

"I thought as much," he said, smug. "I'll take your mistress to the McKinnon and let him decide what to do with her, and you may join her at Castle Moil later. Is that understood?" His was the voice of authority and Daly was forced to obey.

"Aye, 'tis," Daly grumbled.

Kennis looked helplessly back at Daly as he rode off in the opposite direction. Left alone with Alistair and Farrell, she sat on the pony and stewed over her situation.

The ensuing silence added to her distress as they retraced their steps and climbed the hill toward the castle. Her grandfather and her mother would be seriously displeased by her behavior. Plus, she was certain that John Dhu wouldn't be amused at this escapade as he was by her adventure aboard the laird's galley.

At daybreak, the sun burst above their heads. The trio crested the hill by the postern gate and wound their way to the front of the castle. The hailing sentry ceased when he spied Kennis; the portcullis lifted and the great gates opened wide to admit them. She slid off the pony and handed the reins to a curious stable boy. She ignored him and started to run up the steps when Alistair gripped her arm.

"Not so fast, mistress." His stern tone brooked no argument. "You'll enter with me and speak to the McKinnon first." True to his word, he held her arm, keeping her close to his side, as they crossed the courtyard and walked up the broad steps.

Kennis squared her shoulders, bracing herself for the encounter. She hoped that by some miracle, her mother was late for breakfast and her grandfather had either slept in or disappeared by magick.

Farrell lifted the iron knocker, striking the wooden door three times in rapid succession. Slowly, it creaked open and Murdoch, John Dhu's henchman, stood gaping at them. "Mistress Kennis," he said. "What air ye doin' outside the gate this airly in the mornin'?" He dipped his chin to Alistair in greeting. "I see ye've brought company. Willna the Laird be surprised."

He sure will. Kennis smiled woodenly. "Where is he, Murdoch?" She pushed past him. "I must see him immediately."

"Takin' his breakfast in the wee dinin' hall."

"And my mother and sister?"

"Still abed, I reckon." Murdoch stood waiting for orders.

"Then I'll present our guest to him myself." She turned to Alistair. "You may come with me, and Farrell can go with Murdoch to the kitchen to find something to eat."

Alistair glanced at Farrell. He shrugged and stalked off, following Murdoch out of the room. "Wait," he ordered, gripping her arm again. "You'll not weasel out of this so easily. You're coming with me, not the other way around."

So it was that Kennis entered the small dining hall on Alistair's arm under her grandfather's careful scrutiny. The old laird rose from his place at the table and hobbled forward.

"Alistair, my lad!" He beamed at the younger man. "What a pleasure to see ye. And on the arm of my granddaughter, who I hear ye've already had the good fortune to meet. Just last evenin' I sat and wrote ye a letter to thank ye for takin' care of the lass. A real service to me, as well as to her mother. Now, come and break your fast with me, and we'll have a long visit."

* * *

Granddaughter, Alistair mused, startled by this turn of events. The lass's mother was the McKinnon's daughter. "I'd be happy to, sir, but not in all of this dirt." He smiled at the old gentleman. "'Tis a pleasure to see you, as always."

"Och, the slop-sink will do for your ablutions. No formalities wi'out the ladies present. Beggin' your pardon, lass," he said to Kennis, "but I know ye're used to my savage ways." He tottered over to the door and opened it.

"Murdoch," he called. "Murdoch!" After conveying his wants to the huffing servant, John Dhu returned to the table, satisfied.

"Grandad," Kennis said. "Will you please excuse me? I've been out riding and I need to refresh myself before Mam sees me like this at table."

John Dhu took note of her windblown appearance without comment. "Aye lassie, and inform your mother we have a guest, if she's up and about."

"I will, sir." She bobbed a curtsey and hurried out of the room. Shutting the door behind her, she ran to the Great Hall and up the staircase. Once in her room, she leaned back against her closed door and breathed out a long sigh of relief. *Phew.* She'd escaped for the moment. "My plans are ruined," she muttered aloud. "He would show up right now!"

Puzzled, she poured water into the basin and washed her hands. What was he doing on Skye, anyway, and how did her grandfather know he was the laird she'd spoken about? Pulling her riband from her hair, she considered her options. With each stroke of the brush on her tangled hair, it became clear what she must do. A new plan began to form in her mind and she determined to see Daly and Fergus as soon as possible. A light rap on the door interrupted her ruminations.

"Kenni, are you awake?" Mairi stood at her door. "Can I come in?"

Lud, now I'm caught in my own web! "Aye, love," she reluctantly called out.

The door squeaked opened and the child bounced into the room. She looked curiously at her big sister. "What have you been doing, Kenni?" She wrinkled her nose. "You smell like a horse."

Kennis grunted as she removed the offending garments. "I went out for an early ride so I suppose 'tisn't surprising."

"Since when are you an early riser?"

"Since I went away and worked for the Gilmores, that's when. Really Mairi, 'tisn't such an unusual occurrence."

Mairi snorted. "'Tis for you, but if you'll tell me what you're up to, I won't tell Mam."

"I'm not up to anything that you need to know about." A twinge of guilt pierced her conscience. "Nothing exciting ever happens here. Is Mam awake?"

"Aye, and she's ready to go down to breakfast and wanted to know if you were, too. What shall I tell her?"

She slipped off her muddy boots and unbuttoned her wrinkled old skirt. "Tell her I'll meet you both in her room in ten minutes and please don't tell her I've been out."

Mairi slipped off the stool. "Alright, I won't." She disappeared through the door, skipping down the hall.

While happy to be home, Kennis still felt a twinge of regret over her long absence. Time had marched on without her, strengthening her resolve to return to the mainland and find Robbie before all hope was lost. Hurrying, she slipped on one of her new dresses and ran a brush through her hair one last time before dashing to her mother's room. Skidding to a stop, she tapped softly and opened the door, popping her head into Alanna's chamber. Her mother and sister waited patiently.

"Good morning, Mam," she said brightly, trying to sound cheerful.

Alanna smiled, noting her daughter's rosy color. "Good morning, love. Mairi tells me you've been out riding."

She glanced at her little sister. So much for sisterly cooperation. The child silently mouthed *Sorry*, and Kennis discerned from her mother's tone that an explanation was required. "I decided to go for an early ride and oh, I almost forgot!" A rush of heat flooded her cheeks. "I met someone you're to come and greet. Grandad said to tell you that we have a guest."

"A guest at this hour of the morning and you forgot so soon?" She gazed at her daughter, amazed. "Who is it, or would you prefer not to say? We'd best not keep him waiting."

"How did you know it was a man?" she asked, surprised. "I'm sure I didn't say so."

"My dear, you blushed most prettily. I can't imagine a woman causing you to respond in such a fashion." Alanna glanced at her as they stepped from the room and walked toward the staircase. "I thought it might be Eavan but apparently not. Who is he?"

Flustered, Kennis slipped into a Highland brogue as she stewed on Alistair's behavior. "A mon I ne'er hope t' see agin in m' life, tha's who! He's a muckle interferin', bleck baist, awe tellin' me wha' I can an' canna do, as if he'd a right t' say anythin' aboot m' activ'ties or nae!"

Mairi giggled as she always did when Kennis sounded like Grandad. Her speech was almost unintelligible.

Alanna's lower lip quivered, amused by her lapse. "You're not making much sense, love." She arched a brow. "Kennis, is this the man whose galley you were aboard, the one who kept you from the pirates?"

"Pirates?" Mairi squealed. "What pirates?"

Alanna laid her hand on Mairi's raven-haired head. "Later, dearie, Kennis can tell you about her adventures." She returned her twinkling gaze to her eldest daughter, waiting for an answer.

Kennis groaned inwardly. Now she was in hotter water than before and she'd yet to tell her mother the truth about her morning jaunt. She took a deep breath. "I'm sorry, Mam. He is the man from the *Faioleag*. I went for an early ride and met him coming to the castle." At least this was a partial truth, she reminded herself with dissatisfaction. Deception wasn't her forte and gave her no pleasure. The beast. Look what she'd done now because of him and his interfering ways!

"I see. He was alone?"

"Nay, Farrell, his servant, was with him."

She surveyed her daughter with a sapient eye. "And why have they come?"

"I don't know," she admitted. "I escorted him to the small dining hall to see Grandad, and hurried away to change my clothes before breakfast."

Taking Kennis' and Mairi's arms, mother and daughters descended the broad staircase and crossed the great room to the opposite passage that led to the small dining hall. Murdoch waited outside the doors and opened them wide for his mistress and her daughters.

John Dhu rose and Alistair stepped forward to greet them. "May I present Alistair *McConacher* to ye, Alanna." He lightly emphasized Alistair's surname and Alanna blinked, wondering what her whimsical father was up to now. She knew the laird's name was MacDougall. "Alistair, my daughter, Lady Alanna McCallum. Ye're already acquainted with Kennis, and here's my youngest granddaughter, Mistress Mairi McCallum."

The three ladies curtseyed as Alistair bowed. Kennis avoided his eyes and began to sit at her usual place at table when John Dhu beckoned to her. "Come nearer, lassie, and sit by Alistair here. I dinna want ye so far down the table while we have conversation."

She obeyed, annoyed at Alistair's obvious amusement. At least this time she was properly dressed in a fine linen gown and much to her satisfaction, he noticed. She caught his unabashed look of admiration and was pleased that she'd selected the blue-green paisley that complemented both her coloring and her figure.

Her mother sat to her Grandfather's left and Mairi sat beside her. Protocol dictated that she sit to her mother's left but John Dhu, as usual, made his own rules. She sat opposite Mairi on Alistair's right.

The little dining hall was more informal than the Great Hall where the family sat at the dais. There the gentlemen would sit to their host's right and the ladies to his left, depending on the number and titles of the guests. Generally she enjoyed the cozy atmosphere of this room. Today she was disturbed by the proximity of the man who sat nearest her.

Mairi, unable to contain herself any longer, piped up. "Excuse me, sir," she said to Alistair. "Is it true that you rescued Kennis from pirates?" Her dark eyes sparkled, eager for a story.

He grinned. "Aye, lassie, would you like to hear the tale?" He glanced at Kennis, who sat unmoving at his side.

"Oh, aye!" She clapped her small hands together, excited to hear the tale.

Mortified, Kennis toyed with the food on her plate, forced to listen to his account of her adventure. Her cheeks grew hot with embarrassment.

The family groaned at his description of her appearance when he drew her from the crate. They grew silent when the poor enslaved men were cast on the sand in a sack and rescued by his men, and listened wide-eyed to his rendition of the wee battle.

When he finished, he leaned toward her, eyes dancing. "Well, mistress, what think you? Did I recount it well or not?"

She mistook the glint in his eyes for mockery and gave him an indignant look. "Well enough, I suppose." Her unruly heart fluttered. He was too near, his laughing gaze resting upon her. What he failed to mention was his high-handed behavior. I'm never going to hear the end of this, she fumed. Bletherin' blatherskate!

Her mother intervened. "For my part, I can only say thank you on behalf of our family for taking such good care of her. Indeed, I marvel at your forbearance."

"'Twas my pleasure, madam." Despite his serious tone, the twinkle in his eyes betrayed his amusement.

Kennis cringed at his obvious enjoyment of the situation. She stole a quick glance at his well-defined profile and discovered that he was smiling down at her in a friendly way. Suddenly, she noticed the pronounced laugh lines around his eyes. Odd, she'd not noticed the telltale sign of good humor before now. She covertly examined his countenance. Perhaps she'd been mistaken in him.

"I'm sure it was, lad," John Dhu said. "And now, before we talk business, Kennis can entertain ye for the rest of the mornin' while I see to a few pressin' matters."

"And Mairi," said Alanna, raising her brows at her wayward father's behavior.

"Nay, daughter, she'll just be in the way. She can help ye and keep ye company."

The party rose from the table, leaving Kennis, Alanna and Mairi displeased with the arrangement created by John Dhu for three very different reasons. Kennis dreaded being alone with him, Alanna disapproved of the impropriety of the proposed tête-a-téte, and Mairi was disappointed not to be included in the company.

Kennis cast her mother an imploring look as she exited the room. Alanna blankly returned her stare, offering no other form of rescue.

Amused by John Dhu's behavior, Alistair observed the exchange between the two women and waited for her to address him.

Resigned, she turned to him. "At my grandfather's request," she said, making an effort to be polite. "I am to see to your amusement this morning. Do you have a desire for a particular form of entertainment?"

"Since you've already been riding, mistress, I won't suggest it," he said smoothly. "However, I'd consider a walk along the battlements to be a pleasing way to pass the time."

Kennis stiffened at his words. "Very well. I need to fetch a wrap, and I'll meet you in the Great Hall in a few minutes."

"As you wish." He politely inclined his head.

His formal tone didn't escape her ears. "He's on his best behavior," she murmured as she ran up the steps to her room. Perhaps she could use this to her advantage. Thirty minutes later, Kennis ambled into the Great Hall.

Alistair leaned against the trestle table, arms crossed, appearing to be in deep contemplation of the floor. He continued to stare down at the flagstones as she approached. After she stood waiting for several minutes, he looked up and regarded her with a lazy eye. "Glad to see you could join me so soon."

A flush spread across her cheeks. She'd deliberately taken her time and he knew it. "I had an errand to run." The twinge of guilt that she always felt at the slightest deceit raised its irritating little head, reminding her of her duty.

"Of course you did," he said affably. "Now, you may escort me to the battlements to waste the rest of our morning." He gestured toward the steep, circular stair hidden behind the tapestry near the dais. "After you."

Kennis walked in the direction he indicated, wondering how he knew so much about Castle Moil. It appeared that he was on much better terms with her Grandfather than she realized.

He followed close on her heels, giving her little room to move ahead. The warmth of his hand penetrated through her shawl as it rested lightly in the hollow of her back, propelling her forward and supportive at the same time. In her haste to reach the narrow top step, she slipped and he steadied her.

"Thank you," she breathed.

He nodded, grasped her hand, intertwining her arm with his as he pulled her along the stone-paved walk of the parapet.

Surprised, she made no protest and walked with him, the wind whipping her skirts and hair until the loosed tendrils were a shimmering golden wave, blowing with the breeze.

He faced her, reached for a strand of her hair and coiled it slowly around his finger, staring deeply into her eyes, two green jewels made brilliant by the sun.

She couldn't move, mesmerized by his gaze and his presence.

Tempted, he lowered his head. Just one kiss.

Her heart pounded. He was going to kiss her again.

All of a sudden, the fire in his eyes died away and his expression altered. For no reason he pulled back, releasing his hold upon her arm.

She felt confused and wanted to cry out, "What have I done?" but didn't possess the courage.

He turned and leaned on the thick stone wall of the keep, gazing out to sea. "Where were you going this morning before I ruined your plans," he said abruptly. "To rendezvous with someone?"

"Nay," she said, perplexed. "I wasn't."

"Don't lie to me," he said coolly. "You're not out of trouble yet, despite the fact I didn't report to your grandfather where I found you and what you were doing."

"What I was doing!" she retorted, stung by his accusation. "You don't know anything of the circumstances which drew me out early this morning."

"On the contrary, I think I do."

"Then tell me, sir, just exactly what you think was going forward."

He scowled. "You were headed to the mainland, weren't you?"

"Aye, but how did you know?" she said, amazed at his perspicacity.

"I know a lot of things, and I'm usually in the right of it. So now," he deliberately changed the subject, "tell me what you know of Eavan Malcolmson's activities, and how you're involved with him."

She grew more bewildered by the moment. "Eavan?" she asked blankly. "I haven't seen him since he left here days ago after escorting me home from Port Eilidh. Why?"

"I have reason to believe you know more than you're telling." His expression turned to granite. "Do I have to tell John Dhu what his precious granddaughter was about to do or will you confess?"

"I will confess to nothing. I don't know what you're talking about and know nothing of Eavan's activities. I haven't had any connection with him since I was a child until recently." With sudden acuity, she was plunged into the past, recalling an afternoon that she and Robbie rescued a lad from cruel torment by an older boy.

Alistair misunderstood her changing expression. "You see, mistress, you shouldn't play at games with people who are bound to disappoint you through their deception." The sun stood high in the sky. "'Tis noon. I have business to conduct with your grandfather."

Irresistibly, he reached out one last time to savor the feel of her soft curls between his fingers. A mixture of emotions played on his face. "You little fool," he said finally, at war with himself. "I should've thrashed you when I had the opportunity." He dragged his hand away and strode off.

"No, wait!" she called. "I don't understand. You must explain to me what you think I've done. It's the only just way to end this."

He stopped mid-stride, facing her. "The only justice you'll receive, if 'tis justice and not sentimental nonsense on my part, is that I've no intention of telling your grandfather that you've plotted against him." His anger raging, he fought it back. "At least not yet."

Kennis was horrified. She, plot against her grandfather? How dare he make such an unwarranted accusation! In frustration, she ran at him and he caught her, gripping her shoulders.

"Who told you that I conspired against my own grandfather? I would never be so treacherous. What reason or proof can you possibly have to believe I'd betray my family? If you mean my connection to Eavan, sir, he is my family."

His hands tightened and she cried out. "You're hurting me, let go."

He dropped his hands. "Accept my humble apologies, I didn't intend it." He searched her face for several minutes. "Perhaps I've jumped to the wrong conclusion, perhaps not. Rest assured, time will tell all and if you're guilty, your sin will find you out." His boots clicked on the stone pavement, echoing in the dark night as he swiftly walked away.

After he'd gone, Kennis stood alone on the ramparts. Angry tears trickled down her face, betraying her disordered state of mind. The man moved her one minute with a tender display of affection and with the next breath, destroyed every thread of goodwill and camaraderie established between them.

Her tangled thoughts wandered to Eavan, and the uneasy feeling returned. The memory from her childhood was fresh in her mind. Perhaps this was the source of her conflict concerning him, not merely words spoken in anger by his obvious foe who, undoubtedly, thought ill of her in connection to him.

Alistair spoke harshly of Eavan, and believed that she was involved in some plot involving him and her grandfather. For her own part, she'd not judge Eavan or Alistair based on words alone. The truth deserved to be told; she must discover the justice or injustice of Alistair's declaration.

Until then, she'd lay fresh plans with Daly and Fergus to flee to Dunchalum at once. Her beloved home might be her only refuge and source of comfort for the present. She smiled through her tears. And maybe, just maybe, the news she sought concerning Robbie, or Robbie himself, might be on hand to settle her thoughts and bring her a long-awaited joy.

If she must leave Castle Moil under the watchful eye of Alistair McConacher, then she'd do so immediately. She could wait no longer; the delay was costly. Her fair brows knit together. If she planned her escape in broad daylight no one would suspect her subterfuge. She must send a note to Daly to make all of the arrangements. The boat was already prepared; no one would be the wiser until they were gone. A tiny smile played at the corner of her mouth. In the meantime, she'd be cordial to Alistair and treat him with the deference her family expected, and hope that her wily grandfather wouldn't thwart her plans.

Chapter 20

A Desperate Move

Kennis' patience and good behavior were rewarded by mid-afternoon.

She slipped out the postern gate and headed toward the cottages unnoticed. Her two comrades kept careful watch over Farrell and Alistair throughout the day. The kitchen walk near the gate was clear when Kennis arrived toting a basket filled with *manchet* loaves.

On her way to the cove, she called on several of the elderly and invalid villagers of Kilmoil to leave the much-needed bread. Although the visits provided her with an excuse to leave the castle, she genuinely enjoyed the errand and looked forward to helping more of the poor and needy in the future.

She trudged past more thatched cottages and drew near to a cluster of ancient rowans, planted to ward off evil in earlier times. To some of the local people, the grove was holy ground. Many clung to the auld ways, mixing Christian beliefs with mythology. A bird twittered above and a soft whistle trilled. She surveyed the barren track behind her then peered into the trees. "Come, Daly, 'tis clear."

He emerged from a thicket and the two trekked to the small cove where he and Fergus had hidden the sailboat. When they reached the cove, Kennis spied movement in the brush and out popped Fergus, startling birds nesting in the thicket.

"Where in heaven's name hae ye been? I thought for sure ye'd been caught." His voice softened on a kinder note to Kennis. "Or perhaps changed your mind."

She smiled tremulously. "I'm a wee bit uneasy but not afraid, Fergus. I was delayed in the village. Is everything ready?"

"Aye, lassie. I've been ready since early this mornin'."

"Well then," Daly cut in, "let's be on our way and stop the chatterin'. Where's the boat?"

"This way," he said. "Watch your step, lass."

He reached out and she placed her hand in his strong one. She'd lost count over how many times in the last fifteen years he'd done the same but she was no longer an eager five-year-old. She climbed into the boat, Daly followed and Fergus shoved off, scrambling in behind.

Her heart thumped with anticipation. In the end, the day proved uneventful and the weather fair. Near the Isle of Eigg, a fishing boat cruised past, the first vessel they encountered. When the coast of Mull came into view, the men tirelessly labored to row the boat in close to shore.

The McKinnons of Mull welcomed John Dhu's granddaughter and offered hospitality. After a friendly visit, the travelers resumed their journey. The cloudy sky above grew overcast and whitecaps formed on the sea, rocking the small craft. Daly caught Fergus' eye and glanced upward. The two mutely agreed that a storm was brewing, an omen boding their journey ill will. Daly pushed off, and the two men rowed away from the shore.

Before long, the unfurled sail caught the breeze along the coast of Mull opposite Morven and the vessel glided into the Firth of Lorne past the small island of Kerrera. In the distance, the huge white sails of a brigantine, cruising south, billowed out in the increasing wind.

Kennis shielded her eyes to get a better view. "Do you see that ship, Daly?"

"Aye, I do."

"What colors are they flyin'?" Fergus asked.

She took the spyglass he handed to her and peered through it. "I don't see any."

"That's queer. Every ship in these waters flies its colors."

"Perhaps not so much these days," Daly remarked.

She handed Fergus the glass. "Do you see anything?"

He shook his head in the negative.

"Do you think they're friendly or no?"

"I've no intention of findin' out," Daly said. "My guess is they're headin' out to sea and will leave us alone. If they've a reason for nae flyin' colors, then I'll wager they'll keep it to themselves. Liam mentioned some strange doings in the Firth."

"I hope you're right," Kennis said. "What else did Liam say?"

"Only that there've been more crossin's than usual," Fergus cut in, "and he dinna know the lads who came askin' too many questions. Dinna go over well with the locals."

"Why?" she asked.

Fergus' brow puckered. "They asked about men who were out in the '45, and are afraid the strangers are workin' for the *Sassenachs*."

"'Tis odd," she agreed. "I'd be suspicious, too. Do you think this ship has anything to do with them?"

"I dinna know." The wind shifted and the white sail puffed out, pushing the small craft forward.

She changed the subject since the ship appeared to be no immediate threat. "Fergus, I like your cousins. I felt quite at home."

He nodded. "Aye, they're true hearts. Liam and I grew up more like brothers, and Eileen was sweet on him since we were bairns." He chuckled at the thought. "That lass followed us everywhere and made a real nuisance out o' herself."

She laughed. "I guess she reached her objective."

"Aye, that she did." He joined in her laughter.

"But Fergus, what happened to you, was no lass sweet on you, like Eileen was on Liam?"

"Och, I willna say that," he said and shrugged. "I'm nae like Liam. Besides, 'twas about the time your mother wed the Laird, and I went with her to the mainland."

"I'm glad you did, only I hope you didn't leave behind a true love."

"Nay, dinna worry. I told ye before, I'm nae the marryin' kind."

At this, Daly broke in with a snort. "Nae the marryin' kind?"

"Now, dinna start that again!" Fergus exclaimed.

Amused, Kennis interrupted the ongoing debate. "Do you think we'll reach the mainland before dark? I'd love to see it in the day." She looked up at the changing sky.

"Mighty nice to see by daylight," Fergus said. "Question is, who'll see us? I wouldna like to take the chance."

"'Tis a chance we must take, lad," Daly said. "There're too many rocks, and I dinna like to think about bein' hung up on a shoal and smashed to pieces by the waves." Watching the cloudy sky, he added, "I hope we've good weather today."

"Do you think it's going to storm, Daly?" Kennis asked, worried, remembering the last tempest she endured on board the *Faioleag*. Alistair's image rose before her unbidden. The sting of his unjust accusation wounded her anew.

"Nay, lassie, dinna worry your bonnie head. We'll take care o' ye, Fergus and me, like we always done." His words comforted her but the events preparing to overtake them during the next few hours and days were greater than any other that they had faced together in the past.

Passing Kerrera, Daly steered toward a group of islets north of Scarba through clear waters to enter the Sound of Jura near Argyll. They three would remain there until dusk when they could go ashore unobserved. This was McCallum country and home, midway between the Campbell castle of Craignish to the south and the black McDougall's of Oban to the north. Her beloved Highlands and Dunchalum Castle on Lochangless drew near at last.

The sky darkened and the light breeze escalated into strong gusts, her worries realized with the sudden onslaught of the squall. A torrent of rain assailed the craft with ferocity, carrying it farther into the Firth of Lorne. Deluged, the little sailboat nearly capsized. Kennis gripped the side of the boat and desperately prayed. "Father, preserve us!" she cried.

When the fierce winds subsided and the white-capped water ceased to toss the little boat about like a toy, a new threat emerged. The thunderous roar of the Corrievrekan greeted their ears. Once described by a bard as "the roaring of a thousand chariots", the voice of the treacherous whirlpool between the islands of Scarba and Jura resonated for miles. Countless ships had met their doom in the deadly circle, pulled in by the strength of its swift rotation.

Since the sail and the oars were gone, the small craft continued to drift toward the gulf, propelled by the flow of the menacing vortex. "Look," Kennis cried out, pointing. "A castle! Do you recognize it?"

"Nay," Daly shouted in return. "The Corrievrekan's near Craignish, about four miles offshore."

The trio gazed at the grey structure, praying for someone to witness their plight.

"Ahoy!" a voice bellowed above the roar of the swirling water. "Look here, mates, I'll throw ye a rope." A longboat, manned by several men, bobbed in the rough waves behind the battered craft. One of the men threw a lifeline across the gap between the two vessels and Daly reached out to grab it.

He nearly missed. "That was close." He bound it to the severed masthead and the small boat jerked as the larger boat pulled ahead.

"Daly," Kennis said with misgiving. "I don't like the looks of this."

"Neither do I, lass." He stared at the men in the longboat. "They're nae towin' us to shore."

"Ship yonder," Fergus said, pointing ahead. "What do ye make o' it, Daly?"

"Hand me the glass."

He peered through the spyglass, examining the ship from bow to stern. "They're nae flyin' colors."

"Is it the same vessel we saw earlier, then?"

"Could be, I dinna know for sure." He passed the glass to Fergus.

Kennis' heart sunk as they neared the vessel. Her goal to reach the mainland of Scotland eluded her again. It seemed that some unseen force was at hand preventing her to reach her goal. Surely, Providence wasn't at work in her favor this day. She gazed at the coastline with longing; the rocky shoreline, the screaming gulls, and the distant heights of the snow-capped Highland mountains beckoned to her.

The longboat glided to a halt alongside the brigantine and the sailors scrambled to climb to the top of the bulwark.

Ahoy there," shouted the sailor who had thrown the rope. "Climb aboard, the Captain's expectin' ye."

"I'll go first," Daly said. "Lass, follow me, and Fergus, bring up the rear." The big man nodded.

Kennis tightly clung to the rungs of the ladder and climbed after Daly with great care. Her wet skirts tangled about her legs, making progress slow. When she neared the top, rough hands reached out to pull her aboard and drag her across the wooden deck.

"Wait here," a man said gruffly. Daly and Fergus, treated in like manner, stood at her side.

Encircled by the ill-favored crew, the three awaited the captain of the vessel.

"Cursed pirates," Daly muttered. "How'll we get out o' this one, I'd like to know?"

Kennis didn't reply, her gaze fixed upon the man who emerged from the Captain's quarters. "Oh God," she whispered in horror.

"Well, well, what've we gots here?" mocked a familiar voice. "A good day's work, lads." He leered at Kennis, the scar that ran down his face contorting hideously. "Ah, me bonnie lass, ye're a sight fer these sore eyes. Ain't she, lads?" The vile crew roared with bawdy laughter and Denoon's eyes narrowed into slits. "Lemme thinks, now where've I seen ye afore? Come here, me lass."

She backed away, but was thrust forward by unseen hands. The Captain grabbed her shoulders and drew her close. She turned her face away, grimacing in distaste. His sour breath stifled her. "Ye'll have to do better 'n that, lass, since ye're goin' to gets to knows me well." He stared hard at her, and the scar lining his cheek twitched as he started to laugh. "I has it. Seems your fate's to sojourn awhile with the likes of me, and nae with his blackness, the *fuil*." His greedy eyes narrowed into slits. "I wonder what he'll gives me fer ye?"

"Nothing," she retorted. "You'd best release me and my men. We're of no value to you."

"Gots sharp claws, eh? In spite of what ye say, his blackness'll pay me well for ye, he will," he gloated. He pinched her cheek and sighed. "'Tis a shame, but he'll nae pay fer damaged goods. I'll has to locks ye up. Take her away, lads."

"Wait," she cried, firmly planting her feet on the deck. "What about my men?"

"What about 'em? I've no use fer their likes just now. A fancy piece like ye will bring me enough profit." With a wave of his hand, he dismissed her. "Throw them two into Davy Jones' locker."

"You can't," she protested. "I'll pay you for them, willingly."

His beady eyes surveyed her trim form. "Will ye, now? If ye'll offer yourself willin'ly to me, then his blackness canna object."

"That's not what I meant," she said vehemently.

"Then into the brink they goes." He jerked his head toward the bulwark.

"Can we make 'em walk the plank, Cap'n?" a swarthy pirate asked eagerly.

He grinned. "Aye, lads, enjoy yourselfs."

She watched as the scurvy lot of pirates dragged Fergus and Daly to the long plank, jeering at their captives. She struggled in the grip of the man who held her, unable to break free from his tight grasp. Daly, prodded by the end of a sword, climbed onto the plank, hands tied behind his back.

He wobbled, walked to the end and met her eyes one last time. "I'm sorry, lass," he said soberly. "God speed."

"Jump, villain," shouted the pirates, "or does ye want some help?" Ugly laughter grated into the air as impatient hands jiggled the wooden board and prodded the prisoner with a pikestaff. Aghast, she stared as Daly lost his balance and plunged to the icy depths below. Fergus soon followed his comrade, his gaze sorrowful.

Numb, Kennis found herself hauled off to the brig in the hold of the vessel. A foul stench filled her nostrils as she descended the steps. The filthy cells bore witness to their recent human cargo. A few poor men remained, chained to the wall.

For the first time since her return to Scotland, she gave in to overwhelming despair and screamed as unseen vermin crept up her legs and under her skirts. She violently shook the bars of her small prison. "Let me out," she shouted. "I beg you!"

"Stop your screechin' if ye dinna want a beatin'," snarled the burly sailor who locked her in the barred cell. He turned and lumbered up the narrow stairs that led to the weather deck.

She retreated, seeking the least filthy spot in the cubicle. Finding none, she stood until her legs gave way in fatigue. "O God, preserve me," she prayed. "I can't bear this much longer. Forgive me for my impatience and disobedience that has caused the deaths of my dearest friends. God rest their souls." Tears welled over at the recollection of her two companions as events from their years of friendship and service flooded her mind.

Lost in her thoughts, she was unaware how much time had passed when a voice whispered from out of the darkness. "Mistress, I'm here to help ye."

"Who's there?" She rose, went to the door of the cell and reached through the bars, hungry for the touch of the kind soul to whom the voice belonged. A strong, rough hand clasped hers in comfort.

"Nae at the moment, ye'll have to be patient." He looked over his shoulder. "Ye're in this cage for good reason, mistress. Captain's orders or no, the men would ravish ye. He alone holds the keys, and 'tis for your protection. I hae to go."

"But—"

"I go by the name o' Tomas."

He left as quietly as he'd appeared. She wondered if he was real and caught her breath. Perhaps he was an angel sent by God to deliver her. Miraculous deliverances occurred in ancient times, why not now? God hadn't forgotten her or any of his people, ever. The righteous would never be forsaken.

Encouraged, she said a quick prayer of thanks and broke off a piece of the bread. She noticed a man next to her, chained to the wall. He was terribly thin and undernourished. He must be starving. She reached through the bars. "Here, take this. You've more need of it than I do." She tossed the crust within his reach.

He scrambled to gather every crumb. "Thank 'ee, miss," he said, grateful.

Giving in to her exhaustion, she gingerly sat down, trying to avoid the worst filth in the cell. She bowed her head and clasped her hands together, praying silently. *Father, I give myself into your hands and trust Your divine will for my life. Help me now to have hope, and to endure to the end.*

* * *

The wind ruffled Alistair's dark hair as he and Farrell hoisted the sail of their small vessel. A sudden, violent squall of short duration had delayed their return to Dunolly and driven them further down the coast toward Craignish. Now, the sky threatened to overflow once more. In the distance, the sails of a brigantine stood out, white against the graying horizon.

"Ship yonder, Laird," Farrell said.

"Aye, I see it," he said, reaching for the spyglass. "Can't make out who she is from this distance. Let's move in closer." The craft glided through the water, traveling south toward the brigantine. He continued to gaze through the glass, curious about the bulky vessel. "There's something afoot, I'll wager," he remarked. "A longboat's towing a wee sailboat to the ship. I can't make out the occupants."

"Do ye think someone's in trouble, sir?"

He frowned. "I don't know, but the ship seems strangely familiar. If I'm not mistaken, 'tis Denoon's, which means something wicked is brewing."

"We can't take on the whole crew by ourselves," Farrell observed. "How long before the longboat's at the ship?"

"Thirty minutes in this choppy sea."

"Enough time to go to Craignish for the galley."

"I agree, so let's be quick about it." The two men rowed vigorously, assisted by the wind and arriving in plenty of time to gather a crew to row the galley. Many of the villagers of Kilcreag were already at the shore watching the drama unfold. Swiftly, Alistair shouted orders and the waiting men boarded and rowed the vessel out to sea. Within minutes, they approached the creaking ship and watched a man splash into the icy water. Almost immediately following the first, another splashed into the freezing depths.

"Some poor devil's walked the plank."

"Aye," he said. "Here, we're almost there. Jocko, Rab, dive in and see if you can rescue those men. If Denoon's made them walk, they're probably good men. Farrell, make ready to come alongside and raise the white flag. The rest of you, draw your arms and be prepared for an unfriendly reception." He calmly waited for a response from the brigantine and prepared to board the vessel.

Jocko's head popped above the rolling blue-green water. "Help me, lads," he gasped. "Here's a heavy lad for ye." Several hands reached to pull the seemingly lifeless body and Jocko, aboard. Minutes later, Rab followed suit, and the men choked and sputtered as seawater emptied from their mouths.

Farrell sought Alistair in the bow of the galley. "Ye'd best come, Laird," he said in a grim tone. "Ye'll want to see these two lads."

Alistair cocked a brow and brushed past him; before him lay the henchmen of the McCallum lass. An ill feeling stole over him; the situation didn't bode well. Aware that she'd secretly departed Castle Moil, he promised the McKinnon that he would search her out. "Farrell," he said crisply, "it seems that the stakes are higher than I anticipated. What have we on board to bargain with?"

"Not much, sir."

His hand went to his pocket, feeling for its recently acquired contents. He'd have to replace the smooth pearls later. What irony. It should be enough to tempt the villain to give up the lass. The galley drew near the brigantine as a white flag fluttered on the mast. He nimbly climbed the rungs of the ladder on the ship's hull and jumped over the bulwark without incident. Farrell and several of his men followed behind. Awaiting him on deck, a smirk on his disfigured countenance, stood the villain Denoon.

Alistair bowed. "Your most humble servant, Denoon."

"Bah," he snorted. "Ye willna turn me up sweet, yer blackness. I knows ye better'n ye think. And methinks your favor's due me this time."

Alistair placed his hands on his hips. "How so, you villain? I only came aboard to see what treachery you're up to in my waters."

"They ain't your waters, 'tis free passage fer all who sails this way."

"Not now, they're not," Alistair said coolly. "I've come to exact a price and you'd best pay it."

"One thing I ain't is a *fuil*, your blackness. I've gots ye outmanned, I do, and ye can't tells me that this fee of yours ain't gots nothin' to do with them unfortunates ye just hauled aboard your vessel."

"Suppose you tell me exactly what you're referring to, Denoon?" Alistair said, eyes narrowing. "Are you hiding something from me?"

Hesitating, Denoon weighed his words. "Nay, but I gots some merchandise ye might be interested in."

Alistair's dark eyes grew blacker, certain now that the lass was on board. "Then let me see this merchandise before I agree to purchase."

He shrugged. "Ye'd best be ready to pays me well."

"You doubt me?" The white feather and sprig of cypress pinned to Alistair's sable bonnet blew wildly in the wind and he stood motionless, daring the pirate to thwart his authority.

Denoon wasn't impervious to his tone or expression. "Nay, I doubts ye've enough on your person to satisfies me needs. Tomas," he ordered. "Bring the wench to his blackness."

Kennis, wet and cold, leaned against the iron bars and shivered, wondering how long she'd be forced to live in the squalid cell. The man Tomas said he was a friend who would help her if he could. He had no time to explain more before Denoon called him on deck to do his bidding. And now, something was happening above; the hatch was thrown back and quick feet traipsed down the steps. She breathed out with a sigh of relief. It was Tomas.

"Ye're wanted above, mistress," he said.

Suddenly afraid, she said, "By whom?"

He smiled reassuringly. "I told ye all would be well soon, only I dinna expect this soon."

"How so?"

"Ye'll see, I canna explain now. Be still and dinna say another word." He roped her hands together. "I'm sorry about this, but orders are orders and if I dinna obey, my cover'll be blown."

She nodded, walking ahead of him, unaware of the scene playing out on the deck above. The late afternoon sun blinded her as she emerged from the belly of the ship. She hesitated and was gently nudged from behind. Tomas had been kind, and she was curious as to why such a man was in the midst of these vile pirates. Shading her eyes, she saw the villainous Denoon standing directly in her path and behind him— She drew in a sharp breath.

On cue, the slaver turned around. "Here she is, yer blackness, no harm's come to 'er though she's a little dirty." He guffawed. "Never stopped a man afore."

Intense relief and irritation flooded her soul as she spied Alistair standing on the deck. He was hardly an angel but she was glad to see him, thankful for his timely intervention on her behalf. After all she'd been through in the last several hours, she felt like crying and laughing all at once. Farrell and several of his men stood behind him, and she stood transfixed, unable to move an inch.

Alistair read the turmoil in her wide-eyed stare and his heart wrung. His anger rose toward Denoon. "You said you haven't mistreated her?" he growled. "By all that's holy, I should run you through right now."

"Ask 'er yourself," Denoon snarled. "When I says me goods ain't damaged, I means they ain't."

Kennis intervened. "I'm alright," she said, flushing. "They haven't hurt me."

Alistair's mouth was set in a hard line. "Tell me the truth, mistress."

She met his burning gaze. "I am telling you the truth. But they've murdered Daly and Fergus."

"I think you'll find they haven't, but that story is for later." He turned to Denoon. "By her own testimony, the lass says you've not harmed her and if I discover otherwise, you'll not live long."

"Then show me what ye've gots to pays fer the wench."

Alistair reached into his pocket and drew forth a pearl-studded brooch set in spun gold. Kennis gasped. He glanced at her, expressionless, and tossed it to Denoon.

"Very pretty," he said, greedy, "but a little more will complete the purchase. What else's in that pocket?"

Alistair drew out a pair of matching earbobs. "Only this, 'tis my final offer."

Denoon examined the pearls. "Ye sure ye dinna have anythin' more? I has a mind to looks in your pockets m'self."

"I wouldn't advise it," Alistair said icily.

"Then takes the wench and go, I'm tired of wranglin' with ye. If ye needs any more merchandise, ye knows where to find me. Be glad to do bus'ness with ye." He sauntered away, dismissing Alistair and Kennis with a wave of his hand.

Alistair walked to Kennis and removed the rope from her hands. "Well, lass," he smirked, "I hope you're ready to leave now that I've bought you. You'll find your henchmen in my galley."

"You may have purchased my freedom, sir," she said with spirit, the fight returning, "but you don't own me. And how do you have Daly and Fergus in your keeping?"

"We'll talk later." He gave her a gentle push. "Let's get off of this ship before that villain changes his mind and demands more ransom."

"Where are we going," she asked curiously as he hustled her along. "Do you have more pearls in your pocket?"

"Just like a woman. You should gratefully say, 'Thank you, kind sir, for rescuing me'," he mocked. "For now, being safe aboard my galley is enough for you to know."

She *was* grateful. How could he misunderstand her so? "Thank you, kind sir," she mimicked, "for so gallantly coming to my rescue." She curtseyed low, peeking at him through her lashes. "Aren't you going to tell me what you plan to do with me?"

His lurking smile awoke. "I've just bought you, don't you understand? You belong to me," he said firmly, taking hold of her elbow and propelling her toward the bulwark, "and I don't have to explain anything to my own property."

Annoyed, she opened her mouth to protest but he lifted her up and over the side of the ship, dropping her into the waiting arms of Daly and Fergus, who each greeted her with a warm hug. Later that evening, she rested, knowing that she was safe and secure in the company of friends.

* * *

Alistair gave his final orders. "You'll take the lass and her henchmen to Dunolly tomorrow morning. I have to be on my way to escort my mother and sister to Inveraray and can't delay. His grace awaits my arrival with great impatience." He looked thoughtful. "Don't let her out of your sight, Farrell, I have no doubt that she'll try to leave again."

"Perhaps nae, Laird," Farrell said, hoping for the best. "Maybe the lass learned a valuable lesson this time."

"I doubt it," he said in a dry tone. "She's determined to pursue her own course. If you must, post a guard to keep a careful watch over her and those inept kinsmen of hers."

"I will, sir."

Upon their arrival along the shores of Loch Craignish, Alistair briefly spoke to Kennis. "You will obey Farrell," he said sternly, "until I decide what's to be done with you. I'd better not receive an ill report upon my return."

"Or you'll do what?" She looked at him, a defiant spark of in her eye. "While I'm grateful for your assistance, sir, you have no real authority over me. My grandfather may tolerate your high-handed misdeeds, but he will expect you to behave honorably toward me."

He folded his arms, an indiscernible expression on his face. "To be sure, I may have performed my share of misdeeds as you say, but so have you." He smiled in gentle mockery. "I'm not in constant need of rescue nor do I allow myself to become booty for pirates. Which reminds me," a gleam lit his eyes, "since you are now my possession, you have the opportunity to grant me a most earnest desire."

She stared at him blankly. "I don't understand you."

On impulse, he reached out and caressed her cheek, his countenance softening. "Of course, I could simply take what's mine, but I prefer a willing lass to a reluctant one."

"Surely you jest, sir," she said faintly. "Am I to fall into the hands of another villain so soon after my release from Denoon? Faith, I'm amazed that you'd speak to me in such a manner. I hadn't thought this of you. My first estimation of your character must have been correct."

"By all that's holy, mistress," he scowled, jerking his hand away as if he'd been scalded. "What do you think I'm implying? Maybe I should have left you to the likes of Denoon. You seem to understand his motives better than you judge mine. You were willing enough at the inn in Port Eilidh, I'll wager, to return a small token of my affection. Or have you forgotten that pleasant interlude in favor of your inordinate preference for Eavan Malcolmson?" His dark eyes grew stormy. "Perhaps I'm forgetting all too easily that a lass who would betray her closest kin would prefer like company to an honest man's. I can see that I'm wasting my time." Disgusted, he turned on his heel and strode away.

Bewildered, she felt torn between the urge to rage at him or cry in frustration. If she didn't know better, she'd think he was jealous of Eavan. He still suffered the delusion that she'd betrayed her family, too. Why he distressed her so was a mystery; the sooner Alistair departed, the better for them both. She brushed back a curl with an unsteady hand. "I must be calm," she said, trying to settle her overwrought nerves, "and flee to the Highlands."

* * *

Kennis felt guilty about deceiving Farrell McConacher. She excused herself after supper, feigning weariness, and he fell for her deception. The man was by far too trusting and in future, he'd never believe in her again. Well, just like his master. She hoped Alistair's wrath would be short-lived for his sake. The two men possessed a deeper bond than servant and master; they were friends.

She bounced astride her pony on the bumpy track that led away from the Dunadd Road, caught in a daydream of many happy reunions, Dunchalum Castle and Robbie. They headed north, keeping out of sight of the village of Kilcreag.

Making camp that night, she worried that Farrell and the laird's men might catch up the following day. She tossed and turned on the hard ground, finally drifting off into a restless sleep. Loud whispers intruded into her dreams and she instantly awoke. The fire had dwindled and her heart started to pound, her fears confirmed.

Fergus Love sat upright and rubbed his eyes. What he'd mistaken for a shout was the voice of his comrade-at-arms, Daly McCallum, whispering into his ear. "Your whisper's like a donkey brayin', lad. Ye can be glad my sword wasna handy, Daly, else I'd have cut ye in two by now."

"Hush, man, somethin's movin' by the ponies. I dinna want to wake the lassie and worry her. Some devilry's brewin', I'll wager. Are ye awake yet?"

"Aye, I am now." Fergus stretched his arms over his head.

Daly ignored him. "Hold your tongue and follow me." He nodded at the clump of trees where he'd tied the ponies earlier in the evening. The animals fidgeted, disturbed by an unseen presence. He peered intently into the darkness. Goosebumps erupted on his skin. They weren't alone. A shout pierced the night air, shadowy figures loomed ahead in the dark and suddenly, the two men were besieged.

Kennis sat up and quickly threw a fistful of dirt onto the glowing embers of the campfire as Daly and Fergus crept off. Grabbing her pack, she ran for the thick underbrush. Her plain clothing blended well, offering her some protection. Caught between enemies and ponies, she crouched and sat quietly waiting, straining to see what occurred in the dim light under the trees.

Fergus wrestled with a man that pounced on him from behind. In the struggle, he reached for his *skean dhu* but was unable to grasp it before two more men overwhelmed him. A sudden blow knocked him senseless.

"Fergus!" Daly saw the big man go down under the weight of his attackers. Another large, black form running toward him in the dark diverted his attention. With a flying leap, the man was upon him. Daly struggled with all of his might to no avail. He couldn't shake the man off. Oof! He took a blow to his midsection. He fell to his knees in a daze, gasping for breath as his hands were roughly tied behind his back.

Aware that her friends had fallen, Kennis back-tracked the path they had followed earlier in the day until the sound of male voices following behind urged her on. Her attackers were gaining on her. A track, probably a deer path, veered off to her left under the near impenetrable trees and foliage. Caution aside, she ran on the rough, unfamiliar track until the voices at her back faded away, the path before her unseen in the dark night by the pursuing horse and rider.

At dawn, shadows on the footpath wavered as beams of light filtered through the leaves of the dense trees. The deer track twisted and turned until Kennis, exhausted, lost her sense of direction. The damp air indicated that a body of water lay nearby. *I hope I don't fall into a bog.* If she did, no one would find her or ever hear from her again. She would simply vanish.

A thick mist swirled upward and she shuddered, chilled, walking blind in the early morning fog. Struggling to see three feet in front of her, she tripped over a protruding root, lost her balance, and tumbled down a muddy bank. Rocks dug into her back and briars scratched her tender skin until Thump! She lay unmoving, stunned by her fall.

Chapter 21

The Phantom Keeps Watch

A *feminine hand.*

Alistair reread the note inscribed with the mysterious *KM* that Farrell discovered. Not wanting to believe the evidence of the lass' treachery, he awakened early from a troubled sleep, dreaming that she'd placed herself in serious danger. Again.

He grimaced. It was too late now to search for her, he couldn't delay his journey. He would do his duty to Argyll, deliver his mother and sister to Inveraray, and then find some reason to depart as quickly as possible. In the meantime, he and Farrell would keep watch for news of her exploits. She'd played her tricks on Farrell and escaped his protection. His scowl deepened. She'd not taken his word but was foolish enough to travel to the Highlands alone. Or, he gritted, with those two inept henchmen that doted on her, allowing her to have her way. So far, her attempts proved to be nothing short of disaster.

"Laird?" Farrell quietly entered the room. "Ye said to be sure ye were awake at dawn."

He threw aside the incriminating notes. "I did, and so I am," he growled. "Come in, McConacher."

Farrell hesitated. "Sleep well, sir?"

"Nay," he said. "I've done nothing but dream all night long."

"That's nae like ye," Farrell said, amused.

Alistair's mood was blacker than his dreams. "You have something on your mind, Farrell?" He rose, completed his morning ablutions and hastily dressed.

"I just wondered if ye found the lass. Also, the horses are ready, the men await your orders and my lady's bags."

Alistair scrutinized his longtime friend. "Found the lass?" he asked at last.

"In your dreams, sir."

He blinked, not surprised by Farrell's astuteness. If he were a mystic, he'd think the man possessed the Sight. "Nay, I didn't," he said flatly.

Farrell chuckled. "I thought nae."

Alistair tucked his *skean dhu* into his boot, choosing to ignore him. "Are the men ready, Farrell? Law or no law, we can't go about without the means to protect ourselves or the women." He referred to the law enacted by the English after the Battle of Culloden in 1746 that stated that no Highlander was permitted to bear arms or to have weapons of war in his possession.

"Aye, 'tis a foolish law, that."

"True, but we must be discreet nonetheless. Although we have my lord duke to cover for us, I don't care to advertise that we're well armed, only enough to give our enemies pause."

He strode out of the room, quickly descended the stairs and entered the breakfast parlor where his family was beginning to gather before their early departure. "Good morning, Ona. I'm glad to see you're prompt this morning."

"A good morning to you also, Alistair." A smile curved her full mouth upward. "Had you not expected to see me out of my bed so early?"

"Nay, lass, I've more faith in you than you know." He laid his hand on her shoulder. "Remember, I'm counting on your continued support in this wee battle in which we are about to engage. And, lass," he added as an afterthought, "don't be getting mixed up with any of those Campbells."

"But I am a Campbell!" She tossed her raven hair in pretended defiance, blue eyes sparkling. "I'll not say that I will or won't, nor will I promise you that I'll not embark upon a wee flirtation in the midst of your wee battle."

"If you do, you may find yourself in the same fix, especially if you look at the lads like you do when you're teasing." He smiled. "The lads at Inveraray might mistake your intent."

"Not if I can help it," she said confidently.

"Not if you can help what?" Duncan asked as he entered the room. "Are you two dawdlers ever going to be finished?"

"Aye, Duncan, but I'm surprised to see you so early," Alistair retorted. "I haven't seen Mother, either."

"You know she's an early riser. She's already breakfasted and has occupied the last hour giving last minute orders to the cook and housekeeper." He looked sheepish. "Me too, I might add, as if I were a wee laddie."

"Then I won't trouble you with more orders, just obey the ones I've already given you."

Duncan nodded, feeling guilty, knowing his plan was just the opposite. "Aye."

Rising, Alistair clasped him on the shoulder. "Good lad." He walked out of the room, and barked a few last minute instructions to the men in the courtyard. He turned to greet his Mother and help her into the saddle while Duncan assisted Ona. Finally, the riders were off at an easy pace, a cavalcade of men-at-arms, ladies and gentleman.

* * *

Duncan watched the feather in Alistair's bonnet bob up and down at the head of the line as the party rode through the gate. The men-at-arms brought up the rear, the women and baggage in between for protection. His thoughts returned to what had occupied his mind since he arrived home, the Great Stag of the McCallum's, but more importantly the McCallum's themselves. All that he needed to do now was to summon up the courage to go back to the village.

His plan was in direct disobedience to Alistair's command, and he'd given his word to remain at Dunolly. However, Farrell McConacher remained at the manor and he was a more than capable man. In fact, Duncan was forced to admit, a far more capable man than himself.

With that thought in mind, he made a final decision. He'd go for a day trip only—no more than two—and stay long enough to see how the McCallum's fared. With luck, he might discover the whereabouts of the Great Stag, so he must go into the hills while he had the opportunity. He'd speak to Jamie McConacher immediately. Duncan headed for the stables hoping he'd be inside. "Jamie?" he called. "Are you there, man?"

Jamie's head popped out from one of the stalls. "Aye, Master Duncan, I'm here. Do ye need me for somethin', sir?"

"I do," he replied. "I want you to gather supplies for a trek to the Highlands."

Astonished, Jamie was temporarily speechless.

"What's the matter, lad? Cat got your tongue?"

"Nay, sir, but the Laird gave ye strict orders, dinna he?"

"So he did, but he's planning to go to Inveraray and Craignish, so I've decided that I can't wait for him to return. I'm too impatient to be off, Jamie. Prepare for a two day outing, at the most."

"Two days, Master Duncan? Hardly enough time to be trackin' a beastie like that one." Jamie shook his head doubtfully. "'Tis a long ride, especially if ye plan to take some rations along for the villagers."

"We'll need to ride hard," Duncan said cheerfully. "But I'm not planning to go on a hunt this time. We go to help the McCallum's and to plan our assault on the Great Stag. Then, we shall return home to Dunolly and await Alistair." He faced Jamie squarely. "I'll be swearing each of you to silence about this journey, including that uncle of yours."

"I dunno about m' Uncle Farrell, Master Duncan." Jamie shook his head over Duncan's rash plan. "He's the Laird's man. There's no foolin' him or gettin' him to keep secrets from the Laird."

"Well, then, perhaps I'll have to bribe him."

"Bribe Uncle Farrell, sir?" Jamie was shocked. "The man's straight as an arrow. There'll be no bribin' him."

"I'll just have to take my chances with him, Jamie," he said firmly. "You be sure to have the men and horses ready, and I'll see to the stores I plan to take. We'll need a couple of ponies to pack up some food and other basic supplies for the villagers."

"Verra well, sir. And we'll be leavin' when?" Jamie glanced away from Duncan to the stall that he'd been cleaning.

"Dawn," he said, turning away. "Oh, and Jamie?"

Jamie waited obediently. "Master Duncan?"

"Don't fret over what your uncle or the Laird will do or say," he said. "I'm the one who is responsible, not you or anyone else."

Jamie nodded and went back to his work as Duncan strode away. A couple of hours later, Farrell came to him, shaking his head. "Jamie lad, I canna believe that the young master is so heedless of orders." He pursed his lips. "I'm countin' on ye to see he makes no mischief and ye get home all of a piece."

"Aye, Uncle, I will that. But I canna understand his obsession with yon Stag." He looked at Farrell expecting an explanation. "What say ye, sir?"

"I wouldna trouble o'er it, Jamie. The lad needs more work to occupy his time. Do what ye have to do and get him back here before the Laird returns or else," he grimaced, "there's goin' to be the verra de'il to pay on all our parts."

Jamie knew very well what he implied. There was going to be the devil to pay regardless. No one could succeed at keeping a secret from the laird. He had an uncanny way of mining the truth. Therefore, it was inevitable that the laird would find out about Duncan's exploits. Finishing his chores, he caught up with Duncan later in the kitchen to say that the men were prepared to leave at first light, and the supplies were packed and ready to be loaded onto the ponies.

The following morning, Duncan descended the steps of Dunolly House to the courtyard into a thick mist. It had rained during the night, dampening the countryside and his spirits. He felt some remorse in disobeying Alistair, realizing that Farrell and the four young men accompanying him also stood in danger of receiving Alistair's wrath. In the end, he hoped that he'd be the only one held responsible to pay for his misdeeds.

His boots clicked on the cobblestones as he approached Jamie, Big Coll, Andrew and Young Rab Colquhoun. The five of them had grown up together, close as brothers. The only separation they endured was the four years Duncan spent in Edinburgh at the university and during the '45. The four young men chose to remain in Lorne, guided by Alistair's decision. After news arrived of the tremendous loss at Culloden and in all of Scotland, the four friends were glad they stayed home. Otherwise, they might have ended like the poor McCallum's, dead, emigrated, enslaved or in the throes of abject poverty.

"Saddle up, men!" Duncan's voice rang out as he mounted. "Let's set a lively pace. You're all aware of the brigands roving about, so look sharp. Keep your eyes and ears open." He signaled to the gatekeeper to lift the bar from the gates, and two burly stable hands pushed them open wide. He trotted through under Farrell McConacher's disapproving gaze. "Your uncle's looking grim, Jamie, I think he'd stop us if he thought he could."

"No doubt." Jamie rode behind Duncan and led the first pony. Behind him rode Andrew and Young Rab, trailing shelties loaded with more goods. Big Coll McColl brought up the rear. Each pony carried a load of food and other necessities that Duncan deemed the most useful to take to the villagers.

The little cavalcade traveled at a steady pace for several hours until forced to slow down in a drizzling rain. Duncan pulled his bonnet low over his eyes and squeezed out his drooping feather. "It would rain."

A snort erupted behind him. "Perhaps 'tis a sign, Master Duncan."

"A sign portending what?" He turned in the saddle as the horses plodded along in the mud. "Being negative, are you, Jamie?"

"Nae I, sir." Jamie was the picture of innocence.

"Well, I think we'd best think about what we're going to do when we get to the village. This isn't the time for hindsight, we'll be there in a couple hours. After we break our fast, we'll deliver the supplies and have a talk with those bairns. I've a feeling Meggie's hiding something of import regarding that stag." He gazed ahead in anticipation. "And if so, I intend to find out exactly what."

"Aye, and the sooner the better if this mist continues to rise." Jamie surveyed the countryside. "'Tis gettin' thicker, if I'm nae mistaken. We may be forced to seek shelter for the night."

"I hope not, we don't need a delay. Here, isn't this the track we need to follow?" He pointed to the burnt-out shielings ahead. Stones tumbled upon one another and grass grew between the cracks. He reined in, took off his bonnet. "Remember the McCallum's and God rest their souls. We salute our brothers who gave their lives for a cause in which they believed."

"Amen," echoed his men in solemn agreement.

* * *

Hiding in the dense forest, a grey figure discreetly watched the group from a short distance. Well-disguised, It might have been another clump of drying bracken in the underbrush.

The phantom glided along the track behind the laden horses plodding up the track as Duncan and his men moved off. It flitted here and there, undetected, from tree to tree, covertly observing them from a short distance. In the end, It followed the riders to the village square and kept out of sight under the tall, coniferous trees.

* * *

"Before I go, I'd like to leave what I've brought for you and your people," Duncan informed Granny Jean. "It's not much, but will tide you over for a while. Can I bring it all in here?"

"Aye, the bairns'll see to it." Granny Jean bared a toothless grin. "Ye're a good lad, an' ye hae the look o' your bonnie mither. Greet her fer Granny Jean, will ye, laddie? S'been many years, many—" She nodded off in her rocker.

Duncan left the shieling with a sense of disquiet. He instructed Jamie and Young Rab to quietly take the packs into the shieling and not disturb the old woman. Tightening the girth on his horse, he prepared to mount, and then remembered that he'd forgotten to ask her which track led straight to Dunchalum.

Childish voices, raised in dispute, caught his attention. He chuckled. Meggie and Davy, followed by Young Gordie and a few other rascally looking older boys were soon upon him. He walked his horse toward them.

Meggie's shrill voice rose above the others. "I did too, Gordie Malcolm, an' ye dinna hae the right t' say isna true!"

Before the boy replied, he intervened. "Arguing with small lassies again, eh Gordie?"

Startled by the appearance of men on horseback, Gordie stuttered. "N-n-nay, s-sir, jus' gettin' her t' tell the truth." He raised a serious face to Duncan. "She's stretchin' it a wee bit."

The five men burst into laughter. "Aye, laddie, and you'd best take care now and get used to it. Lassies have a way of doing so, 'tis true."

Gordie gloated. "See thar, Meggie McCallum?"

"Laird, I thought ye were wi' me!" Meggie cried, disappointment in her face. "Ye've nae taken up now wi' the likes o' him, hae ye?"

"Nay, lassie," he assured. "I do apologize if it seems so to you. I was merely funning. I'm not getting into the middle of your argument again. You'll have to settle yourselves."

"Will ye stay an' hae tea wi' us? Mem will be along soon," begged Meggie and Davy. "Please?"

"I thank you kindly for the invitation, lass, but I've had a drop of ale with your Granny and must be on my way. The only thing I neglected to find out was the proper direction to Dunchalum."

"Oh, ye maun go beyond the shielings t' the fork. The right'll take ye straight t' the castle gate," piped up Gordie.

"But do you know a way around? There's no need for me to visit an empty castle." Duncan waited expectantly.

"Oh, 'tisn't—" He broke off as Meggie jabbed him in the ribs.

"Wha' he means t' say, Laird, is tha' ye take the north road," Meggie said quickly. "Ye canna miss it, looks doon on the castle."

Duncan regarded her with interest, wondering exactly what she prevented Gordie from saying. The girl Meggie was a shrewd little lassie, quick on her feet. Trouble might lie ahead.

"Well then, we'll be on our way. Any news of the Stag?" he asked wistfully. "I've not the time to hunt now though, I'm afraid."

She shook her head. "Nae seen him, Laird."

"Nae seen him," murmured the boys.

He tipped his bonnet. "A Good day to all of you."

"Will ye come again soon, Laird?" she pleaded.

"Perhaps, Meggie," he said. "Be sure to help your Mam and Granny with the few packs we left behind. And keep your eye out for that stag!" He spurred his horse forward, Jamie and the men close behind.

The children followed after the riders, madly waving good-bye. "Fare well!" they cried as the men spurred the horses on.

* * *

The grey figure peered at them from the tangled brush before moving toward the ridge. Which fork of the road would the cloaked figure take, the high or the low? Only the phantom knew. Without a sound, It floated through the still woods, an invisible shadow except to the most acute observer.

Watching the children return to the village, the phantom grinned broadly. After all, phantoms can be amused with the right provocation. Ghosts are merry at times and this was one of those times, especially since a long-awaited hour of revelation was nigh.

Chapter 22

Separation

"I'm so cold."

Daly struggled to awaken. Where was his plaid? He must have cast it aside in the night. Sunlight streamed through the leaves and branches, driving out the gloom in the foggy clearing. With sudden clarity, he remembered the night before as a frightening thought gripped him. What of Fergus? A chill spread through him as he crawled to the spot where Fergus lay sprawled in the dirt, unmoving. He placed his hand atop his leather jerkin. What relief, his heart was beating. So far, so good. The ponies were missing, too, and Oh God, what of his young mistress? He rubbed his wrists. Strange, the villains cut his bonds. Fergus and his own questions would have to wait awhile longer. He must find the lassie.

He couldn't imagine his mistress going easily. After careful examination of the clearing where they had pitched camp, he found no sign of a struggle. He scoured the ground until a glint in the brush caught his eye. With a groan, he returned to his friend.

"Daly," Fergus said, weak from the blow he'd received. "I thought ye were dead. Where's the lassie? Dinna tell me ye dinna know." He sat upright, resting his forehead upon his knee.

"I'll take a look at your hard head first," Daly said, gruff with emotion. "I woke before ye, and assured myself that your great heart was still beatin', and went to look for her. 'Tis almost like she got swept away by magick. Her pack's gone and in the bracken, I found this." He reached into his pocket and drew forth a circular silver buckle, a delicate piece inset with amethysts.

Fergus knew to whom that brooch belonged. "It seems our lassie spirited herself away. What do ye say, Daly, was she carried off or did she manage to flee the brutes?"

"I think she was awake all along, heard the ruckus and saw us go down. When we dinna return, she managed to escape, but lost or left the brooch behind. She's a *braw* lassie," he said proudly. "But it's still a guess, and we need to track her before the trail's too cold. She's got several hours head start." He eyed his friend. "Do ye think ye can travel on foot? We've no pony to bear us, curse the villains! I'm nae even sure if any supplies are left in camp, either. Come on lad, take my hand, and we'll go and see what's what." On this solemn note, he pulled Fergus from the ground and the two men went in search of a simple meal.

With heavy hearts the faithful henchmen trekked on, their worst fears realized. To experience such disaster almost immediately upon setting out on their journey—first the storm, then the capture by Denoon, and now this attack and separation from Kennis—was disheartening beyond measure.

* * *

The phantom watched Duncan and his men approach the fork in the road. "Shall we go to the Castle and see what's afoot, lads?" Duncan appealed to his comrades' sense of adventure. "What do you think?"

"I dinna see the need to, Master Duncan," Jamie said. "Perhaps we could see o'er the walls from yon ridge."

"You don't think we should go directly to the gate? There can be no danger. It's not occupied, although I wonder what Young Gordie was about to say when Meggie elbowed him."

Jamie shrugged. "Probably up to some mischief and dinna want ye to know."

"You may have the way of it, Jamie. Let's be off, then." He shifted impatiently in his saddle. "Are we agreed?" he asked the other three young men. "We head for the ridge, see what we can and head home."

The young men bobbed their heads in response, used to Duncan's rackety ways and general disregard for their opinions.

"And just what're we lookin' for?" Jamie asked.

"I wish I knew," he said. "It occurred to me that Eavan Malcolmson is probably up to some nasty business. Even if he didn't go out with Prince Charlie, there's still that cursed Jacobite connection. I also discovered from Granny Jean that my less than dear kinsman, Cameron Campbell, has been snooping around here."

"He's constable by Argyll's appointment?"

"He is, poor choice on Argyll's behalf, if you ask me. He would've been far better off choosing Alistair." Duncan was nonplussed over Granny's reference to his mother, wondering what story lay hidden, and if Argyll's decision not to appoint Alistair constable had anything to do with this unexpected revelation.

"A fair man, the Laird." Jamie had a lot of respect for Alistair; he was an honorable and just man to all. "That Cameron Campbell, he is what he is, a Campbell through and through, beggin' your pardon, sir."

"A man can't help his blood relatives, Jamie. But he can help what he does with himself." The truth of his own words struck him forcibly. "And speaking of Alistair, I hope he doesn't get wind of this expedition too soon or he'll be in a black rage, and come chasing after me."

"Use it as an excuse, more like."

"Excuse?" Duncan peered at the ground, hoping to see a cloven hoof print.

"Aye, sir, to escape Argyll's and the Lady Vanora's clutches," the keen-witted Scot remarked.

He laughed aloud. "How right you are, Jamie! In fact, I wonder how my dear brother fares at this very moment." The easy banter continued while the five men cantered up the hill track.

***

The phantom smiled, knowing that Duncan and his band paid little attention to their surroundings. It was obvious they didn't expect to meet a soul, and phantoms were created from stories meant to frighten babes-in-arms and old women. Slipping ahead of the train of horses, It covered the terrain in excellent time to fulfill Its sole purpose.

***

Duncan came to an abrupt halt. "I want to leave the horses here and walk to the ridge so we can't be seen. Andrew, you and Young Rab go southwest, Jamie and I will take the north road. Big Coll, see to the horses. And remember, lads, keep out of sight in case someone's about."

He glanced at his companions. "What now, Jamie?"

Jamie rarely hid his feelings. "We canna sneak up on anyone, sir, we've already announced our arrival," he said bluntly, "comin' up the track willy nilly."

"I don't think we're going to see anyone," Duncan retorted.

"And what if we do?"

"We'll have to deal with it then, not before. See you lads in twenty minutes. Let's go."

The men dispersed without comment. Standing guard, Big Coll drew the horses among the trees and tethered them, his hand on the butt end of the pistol tucked into his belt. Each carried a pistol and *skean dhu* tucked into their topboot within easy reach.

Hunching low, Duncan and Jamie scurried along the ridge, stopping at a sheltered crag overlooking the castle keep. To their surprise, there was a bevy of activity in the courtyard.

"What do you make of it?" Duncan whispered.

"Naught but I'm amazed. Surely they canna be Campbells."

"I don't think so either," he agreed. "They're a mighty shabby lot."

"Do ye suppose 'tis the same bunch we tracked by Dunolly?"

"Maybe. Smugglers, you think?"

Jamie grunted. "A well hidden spot, albeit a long way from shore."

Duncan peered through his spyglass. "Aye, the strange thing is that I don't see a tartan plaid among them, do you?"

"Nay, but wearin' a tartan's against the law, and these lads dinna want to attract undue attention, I'll wager."

"True," he said. The two watched as the men in the courtyard unloaded barrels and boxes of goods from a few rickety carts. "I wish we could get closer. Here, have a look." He handed his comrade his glass. "Do you suppose—"

Jamie cut him off short as he gazed at the scene below them. "Nay sir, 'twould be best to return to Dunolly, consult with m' Uncle Farrell, and let him send word to the Laird at Inveraray."

"Brilliant, Jamie, and let Alistair have all the fun again without us?" he said with asperity.

"'Tisn't about the fun, but about stoppin' these villains from doin' real harm."

"If they're running whiskey—" Duncan stopped in mid-sentence. "What if they're not just smugglers, Jamie," he said, excited. "What if they've set up an illegal distillery? 'Tis a perfect location."

"A bothy, sir?" Jamie wasn't convinced. "Nay, but it'd be a good spot to hide the spirits."

"Then we must find out what's happening, so let's go before we're discovered. No wonder the men are scarce around the village. Little Meggie was hiding something from us after all." Duncan pocketed his spyglass, and a low whistle sounded from beneath the trees. Andrew and Young Rab signaled their return from the south side of tree-lined glen. When he and Jamie neared the rendezvous, a horse whinnied.

"Master Duncan," Big Coll shouted. "The horses!"

Duncan and Jamie rushed to him. Too late! Seeing men flee to the woods beyond the tree line, they followed, only to be set upon themselves.

Duncan had no time to grab his knife or pistol. He gripped his attacker head-on in a bear hug, attempting to throw the man to the ground. The two locked arms in a desperate struggle for control. Duncan slid his foot around his assailant's ankle, pulled hard, falling to the ground. Fists flying, it was an all-out wrestling match. He reached for his *skean dhu* but had it kicked away by another of his attackers who appeared suddenly from out of nowhere. Overpowered, Duncan felt his senses dim from a sharp blow to his head. *Jamie.* The day turned to blackness.

He awoke lying on a pile of straw, staring at a thatched roof above. The cottage seemed snug and dry, and his hungry stomach growled at the aroma of food cooking on the hearth. His head throbbed and when he tried to sit up, the room started to spin.

"Don't try to sit up, Master Duncan," sounded a familiar voice. "Ye'll likely pass out again."

"Jamie!" God be praised, it was Jamie McConacher. "What the devil's going on here?" he demanded. "Where are we and what happened?"

"I dinna know where we are, but I can tell ye right enough what happened." He sighed. "Andrew and Young Rab whistled, and we went to meet the lads." Duncan nodded. "When we got there, we chased the men in the woods."

"What about Big Coll and the horses," he interrupted, "and the lads?"

"No sign of them."

Duncan turned his head sideways to look at Jamie. "You mean they're not here?"

"Nay, sir."

He groaned. "Go on."

"As I was sayin', we gave chase, and more villains jumped us. We fought but a short time. Ye were cudgeled and I was forced to give way."

"How did we get here?"

"Hooded my head, bound our hands, and threw us over a horse like a sack of meal and carried us here, that's how," he said, indignant. "'Twas a most humiliatin' experience."

"Your pride may be wounded, but I was sure glad to hear your voice when I came to," Duncan confessed. "Anything else?"

"Nay, I dinna know where the lads are or why they saw fit to abduct us."

"I can answer that," he said. "We've stumbled onto something that we weren't meant to see. I just hope the lads are alive, and well." Duncan felt a deep sense of remorse. Not only had he disregarded Alistair's direct orders but endangered his friends as well. The two of them were silent. Thinking was the only occupation left to them for the present.

Chapter 23

Malcolm House

Eavan paced the floor of his library in frustration. Blast the girl! Why could she not stay put where she belonged? He flung the letter onto the desk as a light rap sounded on the oaken library door.

"What is it?" he growled.

A blonde head poked into the room. "Cameron Campbell's here t' see ye, Laird," said Simon Malcolm, Eavan's henchman. A distant cousin of Eavan's, his family had close ties to the Malcolmson's. He was well acquainted with the activities of his lord, nefarious or otherwise.

"Move aside, man, I can announce myself," a piercing ill-tempered voice snapped. Cameron Campbell stood five-foot-six in his stocking feet and possessed a volatile temper, matching his high, shrill voice. His large nose was a byword among the villagers who laughed at the appropriateness of his name on two accounts—Cameron meant crook-nose and was well-coupled with his unsavory, villainous behavior. He wasn't a general favorite with commoner or laird.

"What brings you here, Campbell?" Eavan's mood was fierce.

"Weren't you expecting me?" Cameron glared back, watching Eavan with the diligence of a hawk. "I sent a man ahead with a message. Servants—can't trust anyone with anything of importance!"

He had ignored Cameron's recent message concerning his arrival. "I've only recently returned myself."

"And?" Cameron demanded. "What have you discovered? Any news about the movements of your ill-fated relatives?"

"I pursued the matter at hand as we agreed upon." He watched his words, giving nothing away. "The only news they've received was the letter you sent to them. It arrived promptly while I was in attendance there, as we'd planned."

Cameron narrowed his eyes. "I see. And the girl?"

"She arrived safely." He'd not offer more information to the villain.

"Bah! We must be rid of her. Another claimant to the property and title who stands in our way."

"You mean in my way."

Cameron waved his hand in dismissal. "Without me you would never be able to accomplish this goal."

Eavan's eyes flashed. Cameron must not discover the change of heart that he'd undergone or the change of plans forming in his mind. He'd not stand by and see Kennis harmed. It would be much more convenient and pleasant to marry the girl. He even felt a fondness for the auld laird; John Dhu amused him.

In addition, Kennis stood to inherit a goodly portion from her grandfather with her brother permanently out of the picture. "What about your kinsman who's supposed to assist us? Have you heard from him yet?"

"Magnus Campbell is a poor correspondent and an idiot to boot!" Cameron spat in contempt. "He'll do his part or I'll have his head on a platter. He's merely a pawn and will do my bidding. He operates the slave ships for me in his own name, and does it well. The man has no conscience or idea of what's going forward here," he said, smiling thinly. "If he was accused, I wouldn't be implicated in the business. Magnus alone will carry the blame."

He pulled a sheaf of papers from his leather satchel and turned to Eavan. "Here, take a look at these. This is the most recent batch of letters I've intercepted from Argyll. The auld fool thinks he's awake on every suit. Doesn't even know what's going on under his very nose," he gloated. "I've a notion to skewer that proud MacDougall at the same time as McKinnon for interfering with my plans." His hard eyes glinted with spite.

"What do you mean? He's thick with Argyll and kin besides."

Cameron's smile was cunning. "If I could prove he was a traitor to the Crown, Argyll would have no choice but to prosecute."

"And exactly how could you do that," Evan asked, "and for what reason?" The Campbell's notions for revenge were becoming far too grand. He'd skewer himself on his own spit if he weren't careful.

"That interfering MacDougall was the perpetrator of our problem, lad," Cameron replied. "'Tis he, not Argyll, who's acted upon the behalf of McKinnon to see the boy restored to his inheritance." He frowned. "I'm not sure if McKinnon has any knowledge of his actions but I'd like to think that they're in cahoots together. Moreover, I've discovered that his younger brother was involved at Culloden and fought for the rebels, and hasn't been prosecuted for his participation in the '45. That would be a sore blow, eh?" He rubbed his hands together with greedy anticipation.

"And how did you come by this information, Campbell?" Eavan sneered.

Cameron ignored him. The simpleton was already in too deep to escape these waters now. "I have my methods and everyone has their price," he said. "Remember that my lad, Everyone." Smug, he changed the subject and turned to Eavan with a knowing look. "Turned you up sweet, has she? Remember I'll be watching you, so you'd better stick to our agreement."

Eavan flushed with anger. This meeting wasn't going well. Fortunately, Campbell didn't know that Kennis was on her way to the mainland, accompanied by only two henchmen. Fergus and Daly were no match for Cameron Campbell's armed guard or the redcoats with whom he'd made an alliance. He must send his men out as soon as the man left the premises. The miserable wretch. Eavan felt trapped and wondered how he'd been so foolish as to become entangled in such a devious plot. He knew better than to become involved with a Greedy Campbell.

"So, have you anything more to say? I can see you're in the throes of doubt," Cameron observed. "You'll get over it, I'm sure, especially when you become Sir Eavan Malcolmson, Lord of Kilmartin and Dunchalum, eh? It will be more palatable to you then. Of course," he said, weighing the newest development in their plot that concerned Kennis, "if you want the girl that badly, perhaps we can arrange for you to have her. This is a messy business but if you take and school her, then I'll have one less problem on my hands."

Eavan said nothing, wishing that the little man would leave before he called to Simon to throw him out the front door. His own business for the remainder of the day was of a different nature. He must find Kennis as soon as possible. He and his men would scour the countryside until some sign of her appeared and before Cameron Campbell realized that he was withholding information.

Cameron stopped pacing in front of the fireplace. "I'll be on my way. We've no more to say to one another on this matter." He stuffed the sheaf of papers back into his satchel. "I'll contact you when I have further information concerning young Robert McCallum." He paused, aware of Eavan's bitter scrutiny, and raised his brows slightly. One last tidbit of information should stir his would-be accomplice to action.

"Didn't I tell you?" Cameron asked. "The last word I received was that the boy is being elusive and troublesome. He and that escaped band of criminals are raising hell for the plantation owners in Antigua. The sooner he is apprehended, the better." He turned to leave, his voice cold as he strode from the room. "Contact me with news, and don't cross me."

Angry, Eavan bid him no farewell. When the front squeaked shut, he called for his kinsman. "Simon. Simon!"

His henchman came running. "Ye called, Laird?" he asked.

"The moment Campbell is out of sight, have my horse brought round and send Niall to me."

When Simon had gone, Eavan ran his fingers through his sun-streaked hair. The light grey flecks in his eyes turned dark charcoal. A sharp knock at the door roused his attention. "Come in," he said.

Niall Malcolm, his first, quietly entered.

"Have the men saddle up and join me at the front gate in ten minutes," he said abruptly. "We're going on a search party, north and south along the coast from Sween to Oban, if necessary."

Startled, Niall inquired further. "But where do ye want to begin? That's a lot of coastline, Laird. Who're we searchin' for?"

"We're searching for the McCallum lass, Niall. The girl at the inn in Port Eilidh," he said. "If I have it right, she'll come ashore somewhere between Duntroon and Craignish, or maybe a bit farther north. I've received a letter from her grandfather that she's missing and he's requested my services." His eyes met Niall's. "Make it understood among the men that no one is to mention this to any other, understood?"

"I will, Laird," Niall said readily.

"Good." Eavan's irritability reflected back in his curt tone. "Whoever opens his mouth will be severely punished and shown no mercy. Am I making myself clear enough?"

Niall Malcolm understood. "Aye, sir," he said woodenly, retreating from the room. Any man who crossed the line risked a merciless flogging for his disobedience. Eavan appeared even-tempered, his behavior moderate. Nonetheless, his buried anger often welled up, overflowing in acts of cruelty.

Eavan perused the letter from John Dhu again. Based on the information he provided, Kennis, Daly and Fergus could easily be trekking along the coast or be in the woods at this very moment.

He'd divide his men into two search parties—one to head for the sea, the other to the open moor and forest. He must find them before one of Cameron Campbell's patrols spied them wandering about on the open road or a lonely track.

He folded the missive, sat down in his desk chair and took a small key from inside his jack. Fitting the key into the lock of a hidden compartment underneath the desk, he pulled open a narrow drawer where he kept his private papers. When his father was alive, the secret existed strictly between the two of them. Now, with no other close relative that he could trust, Niall Malcolm became the recipient of the knowledge of the compartment's existence.

He stuffed the letter in, and then pushed on the drawer until he heard a click. Once it was secure, he rose and went hastily into the hall, taking two steps at a time to the second floor. He quickly changed clothes, jerking on his riding boots and leather jack. Shoving his dirk into the top of his boots, he grabbed his pistol and strode hurriedly from the room. Running back down the stairs, he shouted orders to Simon.

"Aye, Laird," Simon said, closing the heavy front door behind him.

Outside, Niall and the men waited by the gate as he had ordered. Niall handed him the reins to his horse and he pulled himself into the saddle. He raised his hand and gave signal to ride. "Ride hard, men!" he bellowed. Once out of the gate, Eavan picked up the pace and galloped over the open moor. Reaching a fork in the road, he motioned for Niall to take the men north toward the forest while he led the rest of them toward the coast and the village of Kilcreag.

His thoughts were for Kennis alone. He could ill afford to have her fall into the hands of Cameron Campbell. She'd never understand what the villain would tell her about his dealings regarding her brother. She'd be lost to him forever.

It was past time to take this matter into his own hands and to pursue the happy conclusion that he desired for them both—to be Lord and Lady of Kilmartin and Dunchalum.

Chapter 24

Waylaid

"Shall we reach Inveraray tonight, Alistair?"

Astride a chestnut mare, Ona chatted to her brother on the road from Dunolly House.

The cool morning air was invigorating, the cloudy sky hinting at rain. "If the weather holds, lass, we'll arrive late this afternoon. If need be, we'll seek shelter at an inn."

"Surely our kinsman along the way would harbor us for one night."

"Aye, sure they would, but I don't want to encourage those particular connections," he said sardonically.

Ona laughed. "Oh, brother dear, you're droll today. In this mood, you'll either drive the Lady Vanora away or convince her more firmly that she must have you."

"You think I'm amusing, eh? 'Tisn't my intent." He glanced at her, smiling crookedly. "When we arrive upon the grounds of Inveraray my manner will undergo a severe change."

"I see. You'll be your most uncharming, black self. Correct?"

"I'm glad that you understand me so well."

"More than you comprehend," she said. "You know that I have my own plans for entertainment."

"You must be careful, Ona," he warned. "'Tis a good thing the Breadalbane family has no sons else you'd be a likely target for their matrimonial plans."

Ona shook her head sadly. "Of a truth, Alistair, how will I ever meet anyone worth having? There are no eligible young men in these parts."

"Ah, lassie, leave that to me."

"That's exactly what I'm afraid of," she said, making a face. "Leaving it to you."

"Don't you trust me, Ona?"

"It's not that I don't trust you, Alistair, but I would marry for love, not connections or to be auctioned off to the highest bidder." Her voice was taut. "You don't think Argyll will try to marry me off, do you?"

"Not while he has me to deal with, lass. Fear not," he assured, "should I lose my own battle, I'll not fail you."

"You won't lose, Alistair," she said, sympathetic. "We're going to see to it that you triumph."

A companionable silence ensued. The small cavalcade passed Dunstaffnage, the ancient seat of the MacDougalls, now a Campbell stronghold. The swift rush of water met their ears and Ona was in raptures. "Oh, how lovely! I wish we had such a sight near Dunolly."

"The Conell cascade?" he replied. "Aye, but you don't want to be caught there when the wind's blowing hard. I've seen boats tossed about like toys in those whirlpools. Look ahead, Ona," he gestured, "at the sight about to greet your eyes."

The majestic heights of Ben Cruachan loomed ahead, thickly clothed with a wood on one side and lofty precipices that rose from its foot near the rippling water opposite. As they passed Loch Etive, the famed peak appeared before them, rusty brown in the haze. Even from a distance, they could see the crags where streams dashed to join the River Awe. The forbidding sky rumbled, as if Cruachan dared the travelers to ascend his slopes.

Glancing overhead, Alistair decided it was best to shorten the journey by cutting through Glen Nant and to ferry across Loch Awe. From there, the company would bear north through the Highlands to the village of Cladich before turning south towards Glen Aray and ultimately, Inveraray Castle.

His thoughts shifted from the route taken to the McCallum lass, his uncertain feelings, and back again to the journey. Although his mother and sister were excellent horsewomen, traveling was difficult and the road dangerous. He'd not submit them to unnecessary discomforts.

The cloudy grey sky threatened the travelers as the morning progressed. The smell of rain filled the chill air. With the help of Providence, they might reach Loch Awe before the weather changed. Crossing the water in a storm was impossible; the ferry would be slippery and dangerous.

Consumed by his deliberations, the stirring in the brush at the side of the track nearly caught him unawares. "Watch out!" he shouted as a shot rang out. Ona's horse reared behind him and as he turned to grasp her bridle, another shot fired. Pain seared his forehead, he fell from his horse and lay unmoving.

Ona screamed. "Alistair!" Mac Tawesson and Jocko Dougall bolted into the woods in pursuit of a brown clad figure that jumped up out of hiding as the two men sped toward it. Within a matter of minutes, they returned, dragging the struggling man between them.

Lady Grear knelt on the ground beside Alistair, speaking softly to him. "Alistair, love, can you hear me? Speak to me, my son!"

Alistair groaned and blinked his eyes, his vision blurred as he sought to focus on the faces above him. He attempted to sit up and fell back against the hard, cold ground.

"Here now, love, take your time. There is no hurry."

"The shots, did anyone see who fired them—" he began.

"Mac and Jocko have a man in custody," Lady Grear soothed. "You need to rest a moment before you try to rise again."

Alistair lay still a moment longer before he forced himself up on his elbow, then to a sitting position. "There could be more," he gritted. "Where are Mac and Jocko? Bring the man to me!" He rose from the ground, dizzy from the effort. He fiercely gazed at the man who had dared to fire upon the party. "Who are you, and are there any others?" he barked.

The man said nothing and Alistair's temper flared. Grabbing him by the collar, he shook him hard. "I suggest you speak while you've breath left in you," he snarled. "I've no patience with cowards who fire on women." The man continued to glare at him, unresponsive. Alistair thrust him away.

"Tie him up, lads, and we'll take him to Inveraray and interrogate him there. I've no more time to squander on this villain."

Mac and Jocko obeyed and dragged him off.

"My dear," Lady Grear said. "We must bind your wound before we travel any farther. You're bleeding profusely."

He nodded and sat down again on a log nearby. Ona watched him, not daring to speak. "What is it, girl?" he asked roughly, still upset over the incident.

She hesitated, uncertain how to answer him. "Well, I've never seen you quite this black, Alistair."

"Hopefully you'll never have to see me so again."

"I wouldn't like to be the recipient of your wrath."

He laughed in self-derision. "There aren't many who would. Don't worry, lass, 'tisn't likely I'll ever aim such a blow at you," he said, sincere. "God forbid, but if ever I do, I will probably be the cause and not you."

Lady Grear began her ministrations and the conversation ceased. When she finished, Alistair directed the party to move on. His head ached and his temper was sore. He thanked God that no one was seriously hurt; his wits had gone begging. He'd pay closer attention to the road and press the riders a little harder than before.

The journey continued uneventfully and when noon arrived, he called a halt. The women walked and stretched, and Ona rubbed a particularly sore spot.

Seeing her, Alistair grinned. "Saddle weary already, lass?"

She turned toward him in exasperation. "Faith, I hope that I'm not such a weakling."

"Not weak perhaps, just aching a mite, eh?"

"Really, Alistair, must you make public my every move? I'm trying to be discreet." She glared at him. "If you must know, I'm aching in all the wrong places."

He grinned. "I can see that. Come, I'll escort you to luncheon, my lady." He doffed his bonnet and bowed. Rewarded with her laughter, he sauntered away to check on the men before returning to Ona.

"You shouldn't tease her so, my love," Lady Grear mildly reproved, "not in front of these men. You must try to remember, Alistair, Ona is not a little girl any longer."

"Perhaps not, but I don't think these fellows will concern themselves. Most of them have known her since childhood."

"True, but she is a young lady now, and they must learn to treat her with respect," she continued, "and so should you."

"Point taken, madam," he said, "and now I shall leave you briefly and escort my fair sister to our luncheon as I promised." He bowed, and she shook her head at his stubbornness.

Thick plaids covered the damp grass near a small fire. The women bundled up in additional tartans to stay warm. All enjoyed the small feast; the cold air had given each of them a hearty appetite. Soon, all were ready to move on, needing little persuasion from Alistair. Lady Grear rose while Ona leaned back and patted her stomach. "Now I'm ready for the next course."

"There won't be another course," said her mother, motioning to one of the men to come for the basket she had re-packed.

"I know, it's just nice to imagine," she said. "Do we have any sweets to follow our delicious repast?" she asked hopefully.

"I'm afraid not," Lady Grear replied.

Ona sighed. "I'll have to wait until we reach Inveraray, then. Surely the duke's kitchen will conjure up something fine." She directed her next barb at Alistair. "Wedding cakes, perhaps?"

He finished chewing a bite of cold meat. "I'll not take that bait, lass. Save your raillery for my lord duke and spar with him. I've more important things on my mind." His immediate thoughts persisted in returning to a lovely, fair-haired young woman but not the one eagerly awaiting their arrival at Inveraray Castle.

Alistair gave himself a mental shake. Why could he not get the girl out of his mind, was he bewitched? If he were a superstitious man, he might believe it to be true. Must be the talk of marriage or the fear of being forced into an unwanted one that made him dwell on the lass. Or, he grudgingly admitted, just one sweet, very sweet kiss that made him long for another.

His dark brows drew together. He was hard on her at Castle Moil but he needed to discover if she was involved in Eavan Malcolmson's despicable plot. Perhaps what he considered evidence was merely circumstance.

Had he jumped to false conclusions over her near relationship to his enemy—out of jealousy? The revelation shocked him and he quickly denied it.

"You're serious, brother."

"I've a lot on my mind, Ona," he acknowledged. "Soon we'll be at Inveraray."

She nodded. "And the war is on, then. Is this how you are before a battle, Alistair? I already think I know how you behave in a battle."

The corners of his mouth turned down. "I couldn't say, but a man has to deal with his feelings at such a time in a way that's best for him." He turned to her and attempted a smile. "But enough of this severe talk. You must have a merry time at Inveraray. I'm sure Argyll has invited more than one family as house guests, considering you'll be there."

"Families with young men he wants to marry me off to, you mean?" Ona countered, her tone frigid.

"More than likely." His eyes gleamed with good humor. "Isn't that what you wanted, to practice your wiles on some unwitting young men?"

"Not if Argyll has the choosing of them."

"You must give him more credit, lass," Alistair comforted. "I can't promise that he'll choose the most handsome, but surely the one with the most to offer."

"Just like he chose the girl with the most to offer for you?" She snorted in a most unladylike manner, turned toward her horse and waited expectantly. "Give me a hand, sir, if you will."

"Gladly, if you'll say Please."

"Please," she said ungraciously.

He heaved her upward. "Very good," he said, meeting her eyes. "I'll consider your other remark unsaid. 'Tis unwise to offend at such a time, Ona, or risk being overheard." He glanced around and she bobbed her chin in agreement. Alistair turned to Lady Grear and gently handed her into the saddle. Mounting his horse, he lifted his hand and gave the signal to ride. "Let's move out!"

* * *

Pouring rain descended on the company riding across the bridge at Cladich. The burn at the side of the road swelled, made violent by the rush of water that poured into its shallow depths. Between Loch Awe and Inveraray were many cataracts, a prospect of wild mountains and deep, dark glens covered with foamy torrents. Shelter was unavailable and the horses plodded on the now muddy road along the banks of the River Aray.

The narrow glen through which the group passed was sided with mountains and Alistair mulled over the fact that it always seemed to rain at Inveraray, adding to his already gloomy thoughts. Not soon enough, the rains ceased, and they picked their way slowly through the wooded hills to reach their destination by nightfall.

The damp, weary travelers were glad to see the embattled walls of Inveraray Castle with its varied outline of turrets, and clusters of square and round towers rising into the sky above steep roofs and decorated chimneys. A new castle foundation was being laid out, much grander than the edifice that stood before them.

Alistair wondered if all of Scotland was determined to forget its proud heritage by ridding itself of old structures and customs. For his own part, he arrived with a profound sense of determination to escape one ancient tradition, namely, betrothal and marriage. He'd not waste a moment to plot his escape; he must be on guard at all times.

The duke emerged from his library as the company entered the Great Hall. "Ah, you are here at last, Alistair." He bowed over Lady Grear's hand. "Welcome to Inveraray, my dear Lady MacDougall. It's been a great while since I've had the pleasure of receiving you here."

"Indeed, your grace, 'tis most kind of you to invite us, and may I introduce my daughter, Ona, to you? She was a mere child the last time we had the honor of receiving you at Dunolly, and has little recollection of you."

Ona bent low in a graceful curtsey.

Argyll swiftly appraised her, pleased with her general appearance. "I'm charmed, and most delighted to make your acquaintance, my dear. I hope that your stay here will be satisfactory."

"I'm sure, your grace," Ona said politely, not liking his scrutiny, "that my stay here will be more than agreeable. I've looked forward to this excursion since it was first disclosed to me."

"Good!" Argyll said, satisfied. "Not only have I been looking forward to your arrival but among the guests are several young people who are expecting you with equal pleasure." He turned to Alistair. "Lad, what's happened to your head?"

"We were set upon not far from Loch Awe," he said grimly. "We've captured one villain. He awaits our pleasure in your dungeon."

Argyll lifted his brows. "I see. We'll discuss this later, after you've rested from your journey. And now, Murdoch will show you to your rooms to refresh yourselves. Dinner is at eight, unless you prefer trays sent to your rooms after your long journey. I trust that you will be made comfortable and your requirements met."

"Thank you, your grace," Lady Grear said. "I'm sure that your preparations will be more than adequate to meet our needs. Now, if you'll excuse us. Ona, come my love."

Ona followed her mother and the servant up the staircase to the guest quarters on the floor above. Once they were out of earshot, the duke grasped Alistair's arm. "Once you have completed your ablutions, join me in my library. I have something of import to speak with you about."

"As you wish." Alistair bowed, preparing to follow the ladies.

"And Alistair," Argyll said, his light-colored eyes holding a curious expression.

He turned back to the duke. "Your grace?"

"Don't dawdle."

"Indeed not," he said curtly, his temper rising. The duke was already on the offense. Alistair mounted the steps, envisioning the battle before him. His stomach tightened, and his upper lip curled in self-derision. What a fool he'd been to miss Argyll's hints and ultimate intention. He should have known better, listened more closely to Argyll's conversation instead of relaxing his guard. Well, this time he was ready and wouldn't fail.

Ona peeped out from her room just as he reached the allotted guest wing of the castle. The MacDougalls were within easy reach of one another and she spied him striding down the corridor. "Alistair, what's happened? You look like a thundercloud."

"I find that I'm already on the defense, Ona. The duke orders me to attend him almost immediately upon our arrival to some urgent business."

The tightness in his jaw convinced Ona of his distress. She waited patiently for him to continue.

"What can it be other than the very subject that he opened to me upon my last visit?"

"Maybe you're reading more into it than you should," she said calmly.

He looked at her in surprise. "When did you grow to be so wise?"

"I'm glad you finally noticed," she said with a superior look. "I've grown up, you know. Until now, I didn't think you had."

"I suppose not, you'll always be my little sister." He pinched her cheek. "As for me, I'll do my lord duke's bidding on this occasion. He may reveal his plan if believes that he has the upper hand."

"Just so," she agreed. "He may also reveal that he simply enjoys the pleasure of your company and wishes to converse with you alone."

He parted from Ona and entered the room in which he usually resided when at Inveraray. It was a comfortable room, manly in its décor, with a magnificent view of the rising foothills beyond the castle walls. Alistair was capable of taking care of himself but he found that he missed Farrell's attention. He dug into his portmanteau for the appropriate garments to wear and set his other personal effects on the dressing table. There was a knock on the door. "Aye?" he answered, his head beginning to throb from his injury.

"I've water for your bath, Laird," a male voice returned.

"Come in, then," he ordered. The servant, Dermot, usually attended him when Farrell was unavailable. While Dermot and two lads poured the steaming water into the bath and stirred up the fire, he impatiently waited for them to be gone.

"Can I help ye with the bath or is there anythin' else I can get for ye, seein' how ye've naught a manservant along?"

"Nay, Dermot. I'll ring if I've need of you."

Dermot chased the two lads out of the room and bowed. "As ye wish, Laird."

He tested the water, gauging its warmth; it would chill fast. *Besides, I'm not supposed to dawdle.* He removed his jacket and tossed it on a chair. When he finally eased himself into the water, it was in danger of becoming tepid. He relaxed in its remaining warmth, becoming drowsy. No need to raise the duke's ire and yet, it would give him pleasure to do so. Perhaps this would help him to fight off the feeling of depression that descended on his spirits when he entered the castle.

He completed his bath and dressed in evening clothes. Despite the ban on the plaid kilt, he knew that here at Inveraray every gentleman would be so attired. The duke took liberties with the law to some degree as did every other Scot, not entirely adhering to English fashion. Leaving his room, he descended the stairs and made his way to the duke's library. Two more gentlemen were in the room with the duke and stood to make their bow.

"Ah, here you are at last, Alistair," Argyll said, pleased to see him. "I'd begun to think you would dally forever."

He smiled slightly. "You told me not to dawdle, your grace."

"So I did." Argyll was smug. "You're acquainted with Breadalbane," he said, extending a subtle challenge to Alistair, "and here is Sir Geoffrey Campbell, your kinsman, as well."

"Good evening, gentlemen." Alistair bowed, ignoring Argyll's challenge by disregarding the verbal gauntlet.

The Earl of Breadalbane responded in kind. "Good evening, Alistair. 'Tis a pleasure to meet with you on this occasion, is it not, Geoffrey?"

"Indeed," Sir Geoffrey replied. "A very timely moment for us to be gathered. It will save money I would need to expend, otherwise."

The duke cut in at that moment. "Alistair is unaware of what you speak, Geoffrey, I'll explain further. Perhaps it would be best if you read this." He handed him a parchment with a broken seal.

Alistair received it with some surprise. In a flourishing script, the letter read,

To my Lord Duke, His Grace of Argyll~

Let it be known that in my 'custody' is one Magnus Campbell, originally of Inveraray, Argyll, whom I would ransom for the sum of Ten Thousand Pounds and the following Terms:

1. Freedom, and 2. Safe passage for the former/indentured prisoners from the Uprising of the '45 and the Battle of Culloden, Specifically those of the counties of Argyll, Kintyre and Morven, and the islands of Mull and Skye who are in my employ.

How you lobby for their freedom is your choice. If you are desirous of receiving your miserable kinsman back into your fold in one piece, these terms and conditions will be strictly adhered to and finalized by the 31st day of October in the year of our Lord, 1750, at a location to be announced and in the fashion described herein. Any treachery will result in the termination of his worthless life.

Yours most sincerely,
Captain Aloysius Grahame

"When did you receive this, your grace?" he asked, his black brows furrowing.

"A fortnight ago. I've been endeavoring to discover the identity of this Captain Grahame, as he styles himself, but have had no success."

"Is he merely a profiteer, then, do you think?" Breadalbane queried.

"He's a rogue and a scoundrel," Argyll said, angry. "How dare he threaten me!"

"Must be a Jacobite, probably an exile," Sir Geoffrey observed. "Who else would be interested in the survivors of the '45?"

"Could be some cursed Frenchman taking advantage of the situation, for all I know," the duke retorted. "Opportunists!" He turned his eye upon Alistair. "You've been very quiet, sir. Come, tell us what you're thinking."

Alistair contemplated the missive as he stood near the crackling fire. Was this adventurer part of the group that he and his men sought a few short days ago or who attacked him on the road? This news, although by no means advantageous to the duke and of a most serious nature, was exactly the distraction he needed to escape Inveraray as soon as possible. He smirked, considering how he might profit by this turn of events. He might owe his marital freedom to the villain named in the letter.

"It appears to me that each of you may have surmised correctly as to the origin of this person, or the reason for his action," he said in response to the duke's question. "In fact, my men and I have been scouting the coast and the area surrounding Dunolly for a group of brigands over the past few weeks."

Argyll eyed his mocking expression. "And now you deign to inform me? Perhaps if you'd apprised me of the situation these scoundrels would already be apprehended, and you'd not have been attacked on the road."

"They've been no serious threat," he countered, "and I'm sorry to say they've disappeared without a trace. My men patrol regularly, and there's been no sign of them this last week. Besides, I've no proof these men are responsible for the ambush."

"I'll send a score of my men with you to Dunolly to double the search when this visit is concluded and you return home. In the meantime, we'll thoroughly interrogate your prisoner. I take it that he gave you no particulars?"

"No, he'd say nothing, curse his impudence," Alistair said darkly. His brow furrowed, contemplating these new events. Perhaps this Captain Grahame would become impatient and create another stir, causing enough of an uproar to make it impossible to remain at Inveraray in residence. In the meantime, he must face the inevitable confrontation with Argyll and possibly, the Earl of Breadalbane and his daughter.

Breadalbane raised an important question. "What else is to be done, then, about this ransom?"

"I've decided that Geoffrey will discover what can be done within the confines of the law. He is a member of the Baron's Court. We must see what feeling lies there," Argyll paused, considering, "and what assistance they may offer if it becomes necessary to address the rogue's demands before he's apprehended."

"I don't know if the court will be able to do much," Sir Geoffrey said. "Generally speaking, the men are sympathetic to the plight of all of our people here and abroad, but it is the King who dictates the fate of the rebels."

"Then I'll have to call in a few favors," Argyll said matter-of-factly. "I'm not without some power or connections in this world." He arose from his seat behind the broad cherry desk. "Well, gentlemen, enough business for the moment. Shall we join the ladies? I'm sure they eagerly await our attendance upon them before dinner."

Misgivings continued to fill Alistair's mind during the discussion. He must raise his guard to new heights. The duke was not easily distracted from his purpose.

Chapter 25

Of Things Hoped For

"Good morning, Uncle Ian."

A curly-headed lass of twelve summers skipped toward her great-uncle.

"Mornin' lassie," he greeted. "Why are ye out here at this wee hour? You'll be missed at the castle," he clucked his tongue, "and there'll be the de'il to pay if ye neglect your chores."

"Aunt Kate sent me to fetch herbs, so I am doing my chores," Cailan protested. "Did ye know the Laird's riding in soon with his lads?"

Ian McColl, constable at Craignish Castle, was surprised at the news. "Where did ye hear that tale, lass? I dinna know myself, and I'm the first person to know such things."

She grinned. "A gillie arrived same time I did. That's the other thing I'm supposed to tell ye. He's waiting for ye with a message from the Laird."

"Ah, a message." He nodded. "Dinna mean the Laird's comin' today. Gather what ye need for Kate and I'll wait for ye."

A rustle in the brambles, followed by a loud thump and a groan, interrupted his speech. "Some poor soul's taken a nasty fall on the other side of the *suidhe*. Run and see, Cailan." The great boulder blocked the view of the loch. Local villagers, lords and ladies alike sat upon it when the need for contemplative solitude arose.

Cailan rushed to the side of a lass lying on the ground in a heap.

Ian followed slowly after and knelt beside Kennis. "How are ye, lass? Ye've had a nasty spill." He shook his head. "Shouldna be comin' this way, a lass alone, but then ye're a stranger to these parts. Show me where ye hurt."

She touched her ankle, shivering from cold, as the damp early morning air penetrated her woolen skirts.

"Sit still a moment and I'll take a look. My name's Ian, and this is my great-niece, Cailan."

Winded, Kennis nodded her grateful consent. He seemed kind, old enough to be her father, and his companion was a girl about her sister Mairi's age. In her haste to escape the Campbells and their redcoat cohorts, she had gotten lost in the mist and tumbled down the hill where she'd lain, stunned, until a moment ago.

Ian carefully probed her ankle with his fingers.

"Where are ye from?" the girl asked, curious. "Nae the village or the castle. I work there now," she said proudly, "helping Aunt Kate in the kitchen."

"Hush now, Cailan, let her be," Ian admonished, smiling at Kennis. "Ye'll have to pardon her inquisitive nature, lass. We dinna see many strangers here about."

"I believe it." Kennis spoke for the first time. "Her curiosity is only natural. I've a young sister about her age. Thank you for your kindness in helping me, sir. Tell me," she said, weighing her options, "is the village of Kilmartin nearby or have I become quite lost? You wonder at my being alone, but I assure you that I wasn't until last night. I've been separated from my friends. Have you heard of them, by chance? Two men, traveling the Dunadd Road on shelties. They should have come through the village, and I must find them, if I'm to reach my destination tonight."

"I've nae heard of your friends nor would I advise ye to travel alone. 'Tis a wild country. Besides," he shook his head, "ye're nae goin' anywhere on that ankle today. My sister lives in the village and boards travelers. There's no inn." He paused, lifting his head to listen. "Go up the path a bit, Cailan, and see who's about. I thought I heard a noise on the ridge. Quick now, might be the lady's friends."

The girl sprinted up the path. Kennis studied her new benefactor while he bound her bruised ankle, judging it would be sore for a few days. She ached worse in other places.

After several minutes, Cailan returned, breathless from her labor and excitement. "Campbells and redcoats! They're coming this way."

Ian frowned and glanced at Kennis. "Is that so? We must hurry, then. Here lass, give me your hand and I'll help ye stand up. Cailan, bring the pack."

Firmly grasping Kennis' arm, he pulled her to her feet. He and Cailan half-dragged her further down the path. He drew her to the edge of the loch where a short drop led to the pebbled shore. He knelt down and pointed. "There's a wee opening down there, look behind the brambles. Hurry now, I'll hand ye over and ask questions later. They'll be here quick-like once they've made up their mind to come."

Even as he spoke, the sound of men's voices carried on the breeze. She slid over the embankment and Ian let go of her hands. She winced as her sore foot touched down, her full weight borne upon her injury.

He dropped her pack over the edge, and she slipped into a crevice behind a patch of dry berry brambles. After her vision adjusted to the blackness, she realized that she stood in a small cave. The smooth walls were hand hewn out of the rock, and the slightest noise resounded in the hollow place.

She stepped forward with care, one foot in front of the other, until she knew for certain that the floor was level. When she thought she'd gone far enough, she sat down to wait. After studying the cave in the dim light, she wondered what sort of creatures made their abode in the dark place. Weary to the bone, her head sank to her knees. "I mustn't fall asleep," she mumbled as her eyes grew heavy. "The Campbells might find me here."

Besides, how could she depend on a strange man and girl, and why would they help her in the first place? In spite of Highland hospitality, these were difficult times and anyone might be an enemy. Even as the cautionary thoughts crossed her mind, she went limp, falling fast into an exhausted sleep.

Why was someone shaking her? A child's voice interrupted her repose. It was the girl Cailan.

"Uncle Ian says ye can come out now. Wake up! Mistress?"

Kennis awoke with a start and suddenly remembered. The man, the girl—what had become of the Campbells?

"Help me to stand Cailan, and bring my pack, please." She stood to her feet as Cailan tugged on her arm. "Are the men gone?"

"Aye, Uncle Ian's above, waiting to pull ye up but we must hurry. Uncle Ian said so!" she said, adding the clincher to spur Kennis into action.

Kennis retraced her steps to the entrance of the little cave. Indeed, it was now broad daylight and the sunshine warmed her chilled body. She looked up and saw Ian's kind face. He beckoned, and she lifted her hands as he extended his own. Planting her good foot on the rocky wall, she climbed up and over the edge, landing on a patch of springy grass.

Ian pulled Cailan and the pack up after her. He pressed a finger to his lips and the child nodded. Explanations were for later.

Kennis wondered what she could possibly say to make her situation seem plausible. What had those men said to him? Campbells! But then, what should she expect? This was Campbell country and the Campbells were one of the most powerful clans in Scotland. No immediate answer to her dilemma presented itself but she'd have to think of something, and soon.

"Cailan," he said. "Say naught to your aunt or anyone else. Just go about your business at the castle, even if your Aunt Kate's in a dither. I'm countin' on ye, lass."

Cailan cast Kennis a conspiratorial grin and with a wave of her hand, marched off.

She smiled. Mairi would do the same, and a wave of homesickness washed over her. Although her mother didn't complain about their reduced circumstances, the desire for her home in the Highlands overwhelmed her.

She'd returned to Scotland with great hopes. But in the hope of what, empty and unfulfilled dreams? She glumly trudged after Ian along the rocky embankment. In her dreams, she searched for something unseen, the means to fulfill her heart's desire. Perhaps it was a fantasy after all. She had no father, her brother lived in exile and the family lands were forfeit to the English government. Weary tears threatened to overflow again. She still saw her beloved home in her mind's eye on the day that she lost everything and almost everyone important to her.

The normal bustle in the bailey outside of her tower window increased tenfold. She threw off the heavy quilt and wrapped herself in a warm plaid. Her hope chest sat in front of the stone casement, and she climbed on top to look outside. McCallum clansmen were everywhere; the bailey teemed with men and a few tearful women. Her heart thudded in sudden fear. No, it just couldn't be true! The pipers winded their bags and the men fell into line. A shadow of a smile crossed her face. A crooked line, but a small army nonetheless. They were going to war and many would not return.

Where were her father, and Robbie? Surely, he'd not go with the men. When his tawny head appeared on the front stoop, she drew in a sharp breath. He wore daggers criss-crossed over his chest and a broadsword strapped to his hip. In his hand, he lifted a studded leather targe bearing the McCallum emblem. She must stop him! Frantic, she dressed and rushed out of her bedchamber.

A new sense of urgency rose within her at the memory. She must return to Dunchalum, discover the needs of her clan and most important, how she could aid those few who remained. This journey might seem ridiculous to some but it was the only way for her to see her hopes and dreams fulfilled. Why could her friends and family not understand? Her heart would always be in the Highlands.

Ian's amiable chatter drew her back to the present on the short hike to the cliff summit. "Ye're safe now, lass, at least for the moment. I'll take ye to Kate's house and there'll be time enough for conversation then, but it'd be helpful to know what to call ye now."

Ouch, she winced, her manners had gone a-begging. She'd not told him her given name and couldn't reveal her surname. "I beg your pardon, sir. My name is Kennis Morrison." One more deception, she lamented. "Please call me Kennis."

"I'll do that." His pleasant tone and twinkling eyes gave her comfort but she still remained on guard. "So, Mistress Kennis, can ye walk on your ankle a bit more? I'd carry ye, but I'm afraid we'd both go sprawlin'. I'm not as young as I once was, see, but I can offer ye my arm."

"I'll be fine, sir, thank you again. I don't know how I can ever repay you for your kindness."

"'Tis of no account, lass, ye're welcome," he said good-naturedly. "We, at least some of us, hae no great love for the name of Campbell here. I'll inquire after your friends, and Kate and Siusan'll take good care of ye in the meantime."

Kennis and Ian grew silent, making a concentrated effort to navigate the winding path to Kilcreag. Birds twittered in the trees and green mosses lent color to the browning landscape. Under different circumstances, Kennis would have enjoyed the now sunny morning, but an unshakeable feeling of despondency crept over her. She longed for the end of her journey and for the fulfillment of her dreams. With each step, her heart grew heavier. Finally, she and Ian reached the mounded plateau and she sucked in a breath, reveling in the view. Oh my! The familiar aspect struck her with force.

Distant voices from the past and present called out from the heights, speaking her name. Reach further in, a breath of wind whispered. Encouraged, her spirit soared higher than the eagle circling above the pine trees.

A faint rustling in the bushes distracted her for a moment, perhaps some creature on the hunt, hoping even as she hoped that this search wasn't in vain. Again, the voices, nearer this time, urging her on, or maybe it was the echo of her wishing heart. She must hurry, it was almost midday and she must take hold of her vision, find her courage in the expectation set before her.

Her ankle throbbed by the time she and Ian reached the tiny picturesque village on the Bay of Craignish. Perhaps she'd find Daly and Fergus there, waiting. Perhaps not, she thought, regretting the danger that she'd placed them in, again. Determined to press on, she straightened her shoulders. This wasn't the moment to allow discouragement to lay hold of her when she was so close to reaching her goal.

She prayed that in the continuation of her journey, the enduring hope that drove her forward would arise stronger than ever before, to live powerfully within the reality of her long-awaited dreams.

From the lone shieling
on the Misty Island
Mountains divide us,
and a waste of seas
Yet still the blood is True,
The heart is Highland
and we, in dreams,
Behold the Hebrides....
–adapted from the Canadian Boat Song

Highland Dream

"...the evidence of things not seen."
Hebrews 11:1

Contents

Heart in the Highlands: *Highland Dream*
"...the evidence of things not seen." Hebrews 11:1

Chapter 1

In the Fox's Lair

Alistair MacDougall was born to be a leader of men.

Loyal to clan alliances, he was shrewd enough not to obligate himself or his family to those who might take advantage of his good will. A man of conscience, persuasive arguments failed to alter his convictions.

Lately, however, his usual canny wit had become disordered. Random thoughts intruded into his deliberations, vivid dreams plagued his sleep. What on earth was wrong with him? "Own up, lad," he snorted in self-derision, "you can think of little else but the lass."

His waking thoughts were of Mistress Kennis McCallum, proving his inner turmoil. She had disturbed his self-possession more than he cared to admit. The consequence? He'd allowed the Duke of Argyll to gain the upper hand. Plus, he could do naught for the lass while cornered at Inveraray.

Why she'd run away from Farrell, his first, and one of the finest men he'd ever known was beyond his comprehension. How could she not understand his intentions? He'd left her in Farrell's care for her protection, not to imprison her as she implied. "Females," he said, shaking his head from side to side.

The gloomy tenor of his thoughts blackened his mood even further. His temper was on a short leash, and he'd been on the defensive the moment he walked up the steps and into the Campbell stronghold.

From his point of view, the duke's house party was doomed from the outset. He lived with the hourly expectation of hearing dire news of the lass, and of having to ride once again to her rescue. If, of course, she didn't get herself captured by brigands or killed first.

"Alistair, my lad, you've been awful quiet this evening." Argyll's penetrating voice interrupted his dark musings. "Come, let us join the ladies in the saloon." He waited by the open door; most of the gentlemen had already passed through and were making their way above stairs.

"I've a lot on my mind, sir."

"I can see that," Argyll said. "Perhaps you're worrying needlessly about my, ahem," he cleared his throat, "recent proposal."

So, the duke was making a play in their match of wits. He'd not give Argyll the satisfaction of knowing how very disturbed he was or reveal his intentions. "Nay, just a small matter I must attend to soon." He rose obediently from his seat in the duke's library, following him out the door. If Argyll expected him to submit to marriage plans without consulting the would-be groom, namely himself, he'd best think again.

On the short trek upstairs, he rehearsed the events leading up to his rescue of Mistress McCallum aboard Denoon's slave ship, and the inevitable consequences. Her willful misunderstanding of his character bothered him most of all. She'd falsely accused him of outright villainy. His black brows met in a deep scowl. He would never dishonor a woman. Only scoundrels took advantage of women in the way that she implied. She believed that he was a ne'er-do-well. The corners of his mouth turned down as the hard truth bit into him.

All that he'd wanted was a single kiss. A deeper intimacy required a commitment, the very thing he was trying to avoid. Her foolish escapades had nearly landed them both into an unwanted marriage. His upper lip curled. She tried to pay him for his service to her on the ship, too, now that he recalled. Ha. Most lasses would be grateful, overflowing with gratitude for his gallant rescue. Not she.

Startled from his reverie, a shrill voice assaulted his ears, souring his temper even further. He looked up to see Lady Breadalbane approaching the duke. He glanced away, seeking refuge from her pretensions. His mother sat on a settee near the warm fire and he walked over to join her.

"My Lord Duke," Lady Breadalbane tittered, tapping his arm with her fan. "What's kept you from us for so long? Some urgent business has required your attention, I fancy." Effie Campbell, Lady Grear's cousin, acted as hostess for her kinsman, the Duke of Argyll, during Alistair's visit to Inveraray with his mother and sister.

"Let's not discuss business, my dear, when this visit is intended to give enjoyment to all." Argyll's brow lifted ever so slightly. "I hope you're planning to make the most of every available minute."

"Indeed, sir. The young people are definitely bent on pleasure, as you can see for yourself." She inclined her head toward the laughing group surrounding the pianoforte. "I believe our efforts will bring forth fruit," she said, lowering her voice. "This last half hour they've been busy planning amusements for the coming week."

"I hope Alistair will enter into your sentiments." Argyll was pleased by her general report but also well acquainted with Alistair's ways. Secretly, he liked him even more for his lack of deference to himself. "He can be uncommon stubborn."

She laughed. "What gentleman isn't when there is talk of betrothals and marriage settlements? Lud, I thought my own should never be finished!" She watched her comely daughter, the Lady Vanora Campbell, leave the circle that consisted of the younger members of the party and move toward them. "What is it, love?"

Every movement declared Vanora's petulance. "I can't seem to hold his interest. What shall I do, Mother?"

"Very simple, my dear," Argyll answered for Lady Breadalbane. "You force your attention upon him. There is no such thing as being subtle with Alistair."

"He attends his mother, and I don't wish to offend by interrupting their conversation."

"Nonsense," Lady Breadalbane said. "We're here for a house party. Stop pouting and make an effort to engage his interest or else he might ignore you for the whole evening."

Across the room, Alistair and Lady MacDougall were engaged in a similar conversation. "Well, I hope you're in the right of it, Mother," Alistair said. "The girl's been making eyes at me since I walked into this room. I must avoid her at all costs."

Concerned, her brow furrowed. "You should speak to her, at least. It would be rude to ignore her, and if I'm judging the situation correctly, unwise."

Since their arrival at Inveraray Castle a few days before, even Lady Grear's usual placid temper was ruffled. She'd known Effie Campbell for her entire life and recognized the woman's determination to snare Alistair into a declaration of marriage. It had happened before; the innocent words of an unwitting gentleman were deliberately misconstrued by a matchmaking mama or profiteering father, and the end result was a wedding. Fortunately, her eldest son was very aware of the scheme and his uncertain temper wouldn't endure further manipulation by her kinswoman or by the duke.

He smiled darkly. "Perhaps I should give her a disgust of me with my uncouth manners."

Tempted to laugh, Lady Grear hid behind her fan. "Very naughty. You need only be civil to her now and again." She smiled at him in an encouraging way. "For Ona's sake, my dear, more than anything. You know that the Duke's favor will influence her future prospects."

The corners of his mouth turned down. "I'll try to be polite for your sake, but if the trap begins to close I might depart suddenly. I won't be forced into something we'll both regret later."

"I hope the need won't arise. Besides, I may need your assistance with your sister." She glanced in Ona's direction where the girl sat flanked on either side by a gentleman, one young, and one considerably older. "I suggest you look to yourself for the moment, however."

Alistair followed her gaze. Like a sly cat on the prowl, Lady Vanora glided toward the two seated on the loveseat, ready to pounce at the first opportunity. He rose when she approached and politely offered his seat.

"Nay, don't bestir yourself on my account, my lord," she said demurely, peeping up at him through long lashes.

The pale face and calculating eyes of the ice maiden regarding him made Alistair shudder. In contrast, a vision of a wide-eyed oval face with sparkling green eyes materialized before him. He shook it off with an effort. The warmth of the McKinnon's granddaughter had captured his mind; the state of his heart, however, remained a mystery. Perhaps it was just as well. If he were constant in his sentiments, he'd fare better in this encounter. The young woman standing before him was determined to please and to catch him unawares. He wouldn't submit to her wiles now or at any time.

"On the contrary, please take my seat. My mother will be most glad of your company." He turned away but not before he saw a flash in the girl's eyes—anger, or frustration perhaps? This had been far too easy, if only every encounter would end thus summarily.

Alistair joined Sir Geoffrey near the fire. "Have you been properly introduced to my son Kyle, Alistair? It's been some years since we've had the pleasure of meeting."

"The recollection I have of Kyle 'tis of a grubby lad, not the young gentleman conversing with my sister." He glanced at Kyle and Ona, seated across the room at a table and playing chess. He'd taught her the game himself; she was quick-minded, and had become a fine strategist. Kyle would be hard-pressed to find a tougher opponent.

Sir Geoffrey's lips curved upward in a friendly smile. "Yes, I believe you're right. The two of them make a handsome pair, sitting there together. I'd be very pleased to see Kyle take an interest in your sister."

Alistair answered him coolly. "I must warn you that I'm not sure Ona is prepared to take a serious interest in any gentleman at this time. She's bent on pleasure."

"Perhaps so. But the alliance of our two families would strengthen our clans, would it not? Surely you can see the material advantages of such a match."

Alistair was unswerving in his devotion to his sister. "While I do see the benefits of such a union, I'm not interested in auctioning off my sister now or at any other time. I plan to allow her to speak for herself in the matter, within reason."

Sir Geoffrey eyed him speculatively. "Within reason, eh? I can't imagine a man of your caliber allowing a sister too much freedom in making such an important choice."

He looked Alistair directly in the eye. "I'll make free with you, Alistair. I'd hoped to converse with you on this subject during our stay. If Kyle develops a genuine interest in your sister, are you willing to discuss the possibility of coming to terms? Nothing final, of course, until we confer with the young people."

Inside, Alistair seethed. He detected the subtle hand of the duke at work, making pawns of them all. "I'll only say this, Geoffrey. If Ona develops a very real affection for Kyle, I'll give it my consideration at a future and appropriate time. For the present, knowing her disposition, I'll assume any fascination on her part to be the result of a first real flirtation."

"Very well," Sir Geoffrey said agreeably, "at least you didn't give me a flat No. I'll take that for the present."

Alistair held his tongue. The two men were of a similar understanding, sharing a mutual respect yet he knew that Sir Geoffrey Campbell would carry out the wishes of his Chief if it were within his power to do so. The old clan ways weren't entirely dead. Loyalties still ran strong and Argyll was powerful. The difference lay in the fact that Alistair was his own master, a clan chief in his own right. He'd not allow his family's future to be dictated by anyone, including the Duke of Argyll.

When Murdoch announced dinner, the duke entered first, escorting Lady MacDougall. The Earl of Breadalbane and his lady went in second, leaving Alistair little choice but to offer his arm to the Lady Vanora. Ona followed on Kyle's arm and Henry Campbell, the duke's cousin, escorted Grizel, the younger sister of Vanora christened "rabbit-tooth" by Duncan.

During dinner, Alistair watched Ona with some amusement; she was enjoying herself immensely. Kyle seemed quite taken with her but then, why should the young man not be? He must caution her even if she stubbornly resisted his advice. The sudden and unpleasant feel of cold fingers touching his hand interrupted his thoughts.

"Tell me, my lord, do you not yearn for a dance?" Vanora cooed. "Before you arrived, Grizel and I pressed the duke to provide musicians for an impromptu ball at the masquerade on All Saints Eve."

"Indeed, madam, I don't," Alistair said coldly, discouraging her pretensions.

"No?" she persisted. "I confess that I'm surprised. His grace assured me that you were most fond of dancing."

His frustration started to boil over. "I don't know how his grace would be in a position to know if I am or not."

Vanora laughed softly. "Ah, but his grace makes it his business to find out many things. Come now, we must ask him if he has spoken truly or not."

Before Alistair could stop her, she boldly addressed the duke, silent at the head of the table. When Argyll acknowledged her, she reminded him of his promise to consider a ball. "Did you not tell me, your grace, that all of the gentlemen present were fond of dancing? Yet my lord informs me that he's not, and you are in no position to have such knowledge."

"I did, my dear, and of course he is!" Argyll leveled a commanding stare at him. "Alistair, you must dance with the Lady Vanora at the masquerade I'm to give next week. You cannot refuse."

Alistair's eyes glinted dangerously. "I won't, sir," he said coolly, "but circumstances might draw me away, and I have no wish to raise the lady's expectations." He hoped that something would arise to grant him an opportunity to escape Inveraray, even if the duke resisted his efforts to leave. Perhaps the mysterious Captain Grahame would create a harmless stir and inadvertently rescue him from his difficulties. Argyll's next words confirmed Alistair's suspicions.

"I doubt that anything will arise to cause you to forego such a pleasure," Argyll said firmly. "We'll see to it for the sake of all the young people present."

"I'm so glad you've consented to this masquerade, your grace," Lady Breadalbane said. "We must begin planning immediately, and send out invitations to those who can be counted on to attend at such short notice. And you must help me, dear cousin," she said to Lady Grear. "Between the two of us and the girls, all should be easily accomplished."

Lady Grear agreed. "Ona and I will be most happy to assist."

"Aye, I'm delighted with the idea," Ona said with enthusiasm. "'Twill be most amusing."

"There, you see, Alistair?" Argyll pressed his point. "You must show more interest in this scheme since your family finds it delightful. In fact, you will send for Duncan. We mustn't exclude him from such an entertainment."

"I'll send for him, your grace," Lady Grear said, seeing the thundercloud that had descended on Alistair's face. "He'll come willingly."

"Very good, then." Argyll's countenance held a calculating look. He was obviously pleased with his efforts to unify his clan through marriage.

Satisfied, Lady Breadalbane rose from the table. "Ladies, let us take tea and leave the gentlemen to their own devices." For her own part and in spite of her silliness, she welcomed the idea of her daughters being betrothed to the MacDougall brothers since their mother, Lady Grear, had always been a favorite cousin. She counted on Argyll's support, and was pleased that he'd mentioned Duncan's absence at the family party. Now all was well; Grizel would be happily settled at the same time as her darling Vanora.

Argyll sat down, leaning back in his chair after the women had gone. "Well, it looks like we'll have a full house after all. I hope it will be worth the expense, especially at this time of year." The duke wasn't celebrated for his generosity and the other men were silent as Murdoch, the butler, poured each a glass of rich claret. "It can't be avoided now," he continued. "I'm compelled to follow through and I hope it's worth the effort." He looked directly at Alistair and Kyle, leaving the men little doubt as to his meaning.

Not wishing to pursue the topic, Alistair stared into his glass. He'd expected the duke to show his hand, and this move was innocuous enough compared to what he knew Argyll to be capable of plotting. He didn't like the inclusion of Duncan in the duke's schemes, but considering that the place would be teeming with Campbells, Argyll's plans could go amiss. New guests might interest Kyle, Vanora and Grizel far more than the MacDougall siblings.

Sir Geoffrey's voice interrupted his deliberations. "Your grace, are you not expecting a new steward soon?"

"Yes, I am. I have a very competent man in Peyton Gilmore." He rubbed his hands together with undisguised glee. "And compared to all of the Campbells who applied for the position, cheap beyond my expectation."

Sir Geoffrey frowned. "He has no family to support?"

"Why, yes, I believe he does."

"He has a wife and two daughters," Alistair put in, "and he's a fine man."

Surprised, Argyll raised his brows in question. "So, you're acquainted with the man, Alistair. Two daughters, eh?"

"Aye, a bonnie seven and ten-year-old," Alistair informed him with a smirk. "Very charming little girls."

"How do you know him?"

"He's related to a former neighbor." Alistair was careful not to mention Robert McCallum or his own recent sojourn to the coast of England. The less the duke knew of his activities, the better for all concerned.

"Former neighbor, you say?"

"Aye, on his wife's side, I believe."

"Then you must be referring to the McCallum's," Argyll said crisply. "Cursed Jacobites! Well, they've paid dearly for their misplaced loyalties."

"They have, sir," Alistair agreed, thinking of his mother's desire to help the simple, poor folk that remained. Perhaps this was the time to mention it to the duke. His mother could then pursue the subject with him without concern. "In fact," he continued, "it's been brought to my attention that the few people who remain at Dunchalum are extremely poor. If it weren't for the help of concerned neighbors, they'd starve."

"You expect me to do something about their situation, Alistair?" Argyll asked, incredulous.

"Nay, I don't. My mother expressed an interest in aiding them. She has former friends among their number, and is grieved by the reports that we've received."

"Of course, I see. Are you asking my permission?"

Alistair held his gaze with a steady regard. "I'm merely informing you that we have intentions to this end, and since you hold those lands in trust for the Crown, I've no wish to keep silent about our plans."

"Very well, tell your mother I don't object to her ministrations. In fact, you may make reports to me of your progress."

"It would please my mother if you'd tell her yourself."

"Then I will. Now, shall we join the ladies?"

The men arrived in time to overhear Lady Breadalbane's enthusiastic remarks to Lady Grear. "Oh, my dear, I'm so pleased you're to send for Duncan, such a charming young man! Grizel, I'm sure, is equally delighted."

"I wouldn't have him miss such a pleasure," Lady Grear replied, "yet I know that he's wanted at home with Alistair away."

"But do you not have a factor to look after Dunolly? Most advantageous kind of employee, I assure you."

Her air of superiority sickened Alistair. His own mother was a woman of sense and understanding. The idea of being contracted to Vanora Campbell was more repugnant than ever.

"We have no need to have such a person in our employ, especially with Duncan at home."

Lady Breadalbane sniffed. "Well, it seems to me to be an incredible waste of the young man's time."

The color rose in Lady Grear's cheeks, her patience severely taxed by her simpering cousin.

"Hardly a waste, madam." Alistair swiftly came to her rescue. "Duncan learns the way of the estate. A very useful occupation for a young man in his position."

She shrugged. "As long as he's able to attend, I won't complain."

"Generous," Alistair said sarcastically. "I assure you, pending a disaster, he'll be in attendance at the gathering. You've not only my word, but my mother's as well."

Argyll approached with Vanora on his arm. "Alistair, my lad, you look fierce. What's going on here? This is meant to be a happy occasion."

Lady Breadalbane, provoked by the duke's failure to intervene on Vanora's behalf, jumped into the fray. "A happy occasion, your grace?" She cast her eyes at Vanora and Alistair. "It will be an even happier occasion when *certain announcements* are made and this whole affair settled."

The duke laughed and Vanora smiled with satisfaction, tipping her nose in the air.

Alistair's eyes glittered dangerously at being so blatantly addressed.

Lady Grear directed him a quelling look. "Whatever can you mean, Effie?" she said, intervening again. "We've hardly begun to prepare for the festivities. With a masquerade included, 'tis quite an undertaking. Nothing is settled, and no announcements have been made at all."

Alistair silently applauded his mother as his grace roared with laughter. "Touché, madam! You've parried well, I commend you."

Lady Breadalbane was puzzled and said so. "I'm at a loss to know what's so very funny when I wasn't speaking of—"

Amused, Alistair watched Ona draw near and jump into the fray, unwittingly coming to the rescue. "Mother, Kyle and I have entered into the most grand scheme!"

"Have you, my dear?" she murmured, smiling at her and the young man.

"Aye." She then appealed to her for support. "We've decided to have a picnic tomorrow if the weather suits. I know 'tis not the most ideal time of year, but perhaps the sun will shine. Please Mother, do say yes."

Kyle gazed at her with open admiration. "The sun canna help but shine when you're present," he said gallantly, "and have called upon him to bless us with the warmth of his kiss."

Ona beamed at him, returning his gaze with warm appreciation. "Faith, what a delightful thing to say! Thank you, Kyle."

Alistair glanced at Lady Grear as Sir Geoffrey leaned toward her. "What a handsome couple they make. Do you not think so, my lady?"

"Indeed, sir." Turning to her daughter, Lady Grear deftly changed the subject. "I believe, Ona, you must apply to his grace for permission to picnic on his grounds."

Ona turned an eager face to the duke. "May we, your grace? It won't be inconveniencing you too much, I hope."

"Not at all, dear child," he said, agreeable to the scheme. "You may inconvenience the entire household, but you'll not bother me. There are servants aplenty to provide whatever you need."

She clapped her hands with enthusiasm. "Thank you, sir, very much."

He nodded and turned to Alistair. "And do you have a mind to picnic? I have some business to discuss with you in the morning before you are bent on pleasure for the day."

"I'm at your disposal, your grace." Alistair wondered what business would cause the duke to take him away from the proposed outing, not that he minded. The less he was obliged to be in the presence of the Lady Vanora, the better it would be for him.

"Good. After breakfast, then, in my library," he said, "and you may join the revelers when we are finished." The duke rose and politely bowed. "I believe I shall retire for the night. Good evening."

"I'll see you in the morning, sir. Good night." Taking advantage of the duke's departure, Alistair leisurely strode to the settee.

Lady Grear stood and extended her hand to Ona. "Come, my love, we must also retire." Turning to her kinsmen, she bid them good night. Alistair opened the door and the three stepped into the dim passage.

Ona pouted as the door closed behind them. "Well, that was unkind of you. I wanted to stay awhile longer."

"Of course you did," Lady Grear said.

Alistair glanced down at her. "You'll find yourself betrothed to Kyle Campbell if you continue to behave in the manner you did this evening."

"Nonsense," Ona protested. "I was merely entertaining myself. I must practice before I make my appearance at Court next year."

"Court! Whatever gave you such a notion?" He had a profound dislike for all of the pomp and circumstance associated to Court behavior. "Besides, without a Scottish king, there's no court in Edinburgh."

"But I meant London," Ona said.

"'Tis an unfriendly place for Scots right now."

"Oh come now, you two," Lady Grear admonished. "I'm afraid I'm to blame, Alistair. Of course she must go to Court. How else is she to meet a truly eligible young gentleman?"

Alistair groaned. "You know how I detest it."

"Then perhaps I'll take Duncan instead," Lady Grear said. "But you should go to present your sister, you know. It will be a momentous occasion."

"We can discuss it later. For now I, in fact, *we*," he said, looking at Ona, "must make it through this skirmish first."

"*We*, Alistair? What aren't you telling me now?"

They continued to walk slowly down the hall. "I've been approached by Sir Geoffrey about a match between you and Kyle."

Speechless, Ona's mouth dropped open in shock.

"You see, my dear, Argyll is one step ahead of you already. In fact, more than one, I'm sure."

They stopped at the door to Ona's chamber. "I told him you weren't in the market for a husband yet." He kissed her on the cheek. "Sleep well, Ona, and don't worry."

She made a face. "Good night, Alistair, Mother."

Lady Grear echoed her good night and continued down the hall with him. "What did Sir Geoffrey say to you?"

"Merely that they make a handsome couple, and would I consider coming to an agreement with him in the immediate future, if they conceived a genuine liking for one another."

"Oh no, I can hardly believe it! What did you say?"

"Only that Ona was too young to be married and that she was engaging in her first real flirtation."

Lady Grear laughed softly. "Don't tell her that. It will only cause her to flirt all the more."

"I have no intention of telling her. Good night, Mother, and sleep well."

She patted him on the shoulder. "Good night, my dear."

Chapter 2

New Friends

Kennis limped into the tiny village of Kilcreag under Ian's watchful eye.

He led her to the cottage of his sister Kate and their niece, Siusan McAllister, Cailan's mother. He rapped lightly on the door.

"Uncle Ian," Siusan said with some surprise, "'tis a pleasure to see ye, sir. Come in, come in!" She noticed Kennis standing behind him. "Have ye brought us a boarder? We've plenty of room today." Widowed after the battle of Culloden, she moved from Kintyre to live with her aunt and now helped to serve the occasional lodger in their available rooms.

Kennis surveyed the well-kept cottage. The thatch was in good repair and the newly white-washed shutters on the windows were shut tight against the wind and the rain. Beneath the windows, a few late-blooming herbs still volunteered their colors, creating a homey scene. Flowerbeds lined the short walk to the door and were clear of bracken, prepared for the winter months ahead.

Ian rapped on the door. "Uncle Ian," Siusan said with some surprise, "'tis a pleasure to see ye, sir. Come in, come in!" She gazed beyond him curiously. "Have ye brought us a boarder? We've plenty of room today."

"Aye, that I have, one who's in need of your healing skills."

She smiled. "I'm glad to help."

"Then let me introduce Mistress Kennis Morrison to ye." He drew her forward. "She's without her baggage, so perhaps ye can loan her a few things."

"I'll do what I can, ye can be sure of it." She turned to Kennis. "Please come in and sit down, mistress. I can see ye've had a rough time."

"Well, I'd best be off," Ian said. "I'll tell Kate ye've a guest, and be back for supper. Good day."

"Good day, Uncle," Siusan said pleasantly.

Weary, Kennis smiled at them both. "Thank you, Ian, and Good day to you."

He beamed. "Aye, ye're more than welcome, lass." Tipping his cap, he stepped out of the door and strode down the walk.

Siusan invited Kennis to be seated. "Well, let's have a look at that ankle." She unwound the tight cloth and gently prodded. After a few minutes, she looked up. "I think there's little damage done. I'm sorry if I've hurt ye, though."

Kennis smiled wanly, fatigue and pain finally overtaking her. "I thank you, Mistress McAllister."

She clucked her tongue. "Call me Siusan."

"Thank you, I will." Kennis glanced down at her muddied clothing. "I beg pardon for entering your home like this, I'm not fit for company."

"Dinna worry," Siusan said kindly, appraising her guest. "I'll bring a basin of water for ye to wash, and then make a pot of tea. Just sit back and rest now, I'll return shortly."

While Siusan busied herself in the kitchen, Kennis laid her head back and dozed. Dreams flooded her weary mind, she saw Daly and Fergus—had the soldiers left them for dead or were they held captive? Suddenly her eyes flew open and she bolted upright, heart pounding.

Just then, Siusan returned with the promised basin of water and a wash cloth. "I thought ye might be in a fever," she said, touching her forehead. "Ye've been asleep this last half hour."

Kennis raised a shaky hand to her brow. "I've been dreaming. My two companions were lost, attacked on the road. I saw them fall but couldn't stay to see if they were dead or alive."

"I'm sure things will turn out for the best. Uncle Ian will discover what's happened to your friends. He's Constable at Craignish, ye know, an important man in these parts."

Craignish! That meant nothing but Campbells, and Campbells were no friend to her and her kin.

"Ye've naught to fear from us," Siusan said quietly, noting her distress. "We'll do ye no harm, and ask no questions."

Her eyes met Siusan's for a brief moment. "Thank you. Perhaps I can tell you more in the future, but for now I must keep my own counsel. Still, I'd count it an honor to be your friend."

"Aye, it would give me pleasure, as well. I confess ye've aroused my curiosity." The teakettle whistled and she ran from the room, returning with a laden tray. A flowered china teapot, cups and saucers, and scones were nicely arranged on a silver plate. "'Twas my mother's," she said on a proud note. "I thought since 'tis a special occasion, we could enjoy it together and celebrate our new friendship. My Mam received it as a gift when she retired from service, and we use it here on a rare occasion. Sometimes the new Laird's mother and sister visit, and the lass comes by for tea."

"New Laird?" Kennis asked. Campbells didn't interest her over much.

"Aye, dinna ye know?"

"I've been away for some time."

Siusan gave her a sidelong glance. "He's a much younger man, and a *braw* one at that."

"Is that so?" She regarded her new friend with amusement. "And are you sweet on him, Siusan McAllister?"

"Aye, we all are," Siusan admitted, "young lassies and old grannies alike."

Kennis laughed. "He must be handsome, indeed, to set the whole village to swooning. Are you setting your cap at him?"

"Me, set my cap at the Laird!" Siusan was shocked. "He'll nae marry the likes of me, and I'll nae have a man without vows," she said on a decisive note. "I still have feelings for my poor dead Ranald. A woman dinna forget a true love easily." She looked sad for a moment, and then gave Kennis a sly look. "I'm thinkin' that if ye met him, ye'd be as *hinnie* on him as the rest of us. Only ye could marry him, too, which is more than I can say for the likes of anyone else in this village."

Horrified at the thought, her mouth dropped open. "Now what makes you think I could marry your Laird? I'm not looking to be married, especially to a Campbell!" She'd already had one near escape from a wedding since her return from America.

"The new Laird's no Campbell. Only half, I suppose, bein' a Campbell on his mother's side. He's the MacDougall of Dunolly. Do ye know the family?"

Uncomfortable with lies, even half-truths, Kennis squirmed. She did not, but remembered hearing her grandfather mention this very man. "Nay," she said with some reluctance, "I can't say that I do." Would the falsehoods she felt obliged to tell never end?

Siusan sat back, giving her a knowing look. "I'll nae pry, but ye canna hide from me ye're one of the gentles, Kennis Morrison. I shouldna think ye could hide it from anybody."

"I haven't told you anything about myself."

"Ye dinna need to," Siusan said simply. "'Tis written all over ye, mistress, the way ye carry yourself, and your fine speech. Plain clothes or no, anyone with an eye to see will ken who ye really are underneath."

Oh, dear. Siusan's observations confirmed her deep misgivings. She must leave this place as soon as possible. She couldn't wait for her ankle to completely heal. She'd rest today, and hopefully receive news of Daly and Fergus before she left on the morrow.

Siusan interrupted her musings. "Here, I've brought ye a cloth, soap and water. I've also made a poultice for your ankle. I'll run and fetch it now."

In her absence, Kennis bathed her face, neck and arms with the lavender scented soap and cool water. Refreshed, she sat deep in thought until Siusan returned with a small iron kettle that she set down on the floor.

Siusan drew a cloth, fragrant with herbs, from the steaming brew. "Raise your foot a bit, please? I'll wrap this around your ankle, and we'll let it set while we have a bite to eat and a cup of tea." She rose, wiped her hands clean on her apron and poured the tea. "Would ye care for a lump of sugar?"

She nodded, receiving the cup and scone with pleasure. "Will your Aunt Kate and Cailan be home soon?"

"Aye, and Uncle Ian with them for supper. Aunt Kate works at the castle during the week and Uncle Ian has a room there."

"Cailan told me that she works in the kitchen," she said. "She was very proud of the fact."

"Aye, 'tis a grand opportunity, if she desires to go into service."

Kennis thought of the brief time she had spent overseeing Jenny and Molly Gilmore. "Do you want for her to do so? Go into service, I mean."

"Sure, 'tis steady work for a young woman until she marries and has bairns of her own."

"Aren't you concerned about her being around the men at the castle?"

"Nay," Siusan shrugged, indifferent. "Uncle Ian and Aunt Kate are there, and the Laird's a respectable man."

Kennis changed the subject; enough talk about the Laird of MacDougall, even though she was curious about the paragon Siusan described. "Tell me about your husband, Siusan. Was he out in the '45?"

"Aye." She grew sorrowful again. "That he was, and dinna return."

Her face softened as she recalled an earlier day and time. "We met when we were bairns. I like to think 'twas love at first sight, if ye believe in such a thing. It makes me happy to remember him so. We married young, and Cailan was born when I was fifteen, so when word came that he was lost, I was thankful more than ever for my little Cailan."

Kennis' eyes misted. She wondered how she could help Siusan. Time was known to mend wounds, and she was well provided for by her aunt and uncle. Yet some wounds are so deep that even time is no healer. She hoped that she could offer the joy of having an intimate relationship with God to her new friends. He is the great healer of all of our troubles, those of the heart, mind and the body.

While Siusan completed her chores before her family arrived home for supper, Kennis spent a quiet afternoon. When the front door squeaked open, Kate McColl entered the sparse room like a small whirlwind.

Kennis gazed at her new acquaintance. She soon discovered that the bonnie redhead had a busy tongue. Before half of the evening was half over, Kennis became a reluctant participant in her gossip. All too soon, she was acquainted with the intimate details about every family in the village. She had the sudden urge to stuff her fingers into her ears. When Ian and Cailan entered a bit later, she breathed out in relief.

"Evenin', lass," Ian greeted, "glad to see ye lookin' so well."

"Thank you, sir, I was an untidy mess this morning, I fear."

"Ye sure were," Cailan piped up.

"Cailan, that's no way to talk to our guest. Now beg the lady's pardon."

The girl flushed to the roots of her curly hair and hastily bobbed a curtsey. "I beg your pardon, mistress."

Kennis laughed. "'Tis true, Cailan, I *was* in a mess until your mother took me under her wing. She's taken good care of me today and restored my sense of respectability."

The child returned her smile and skipped off to find her mother as Ian pulled up a wooden chair, turning it around to face her and propping up his arms on the straight back.

She raised her eyebrows in mute question.

"I've no news of your friends, lass," he began, "I'm sorry. When the Laird rides in, I'll present the matter to him. Ye were attacked on Craignish land, and we'll find out who's responsible. I sent out a search party this mornin', but they returned only with this." He held up a worn brown cap, similar to the one that Daly habitually wore. "Look familiar?"

"Aye, it does," she said, concerned. "Where did they find it?" She carefully examined the cap. Daly wore a similar plaid cap, dyed brown when the English outlawed tartans. She turned it over, looking for a colorful spot of plaid on the seam. He'd left it untouched, to remind himself that until he could wear the plaid again, he was not a free man. Loath to forget the tyranny of the English, he reasoned that the color peeking through would serve as a reminder of the necessity to gain freedom for Scotland.

"In a clearing northwest of Kilcreag, near the sea," he said. His casual tone indicated that he was seeking more information.

It was definitely Daly's cap. Kennis rubbed the nubby wool between her fingertips as a multitude of thoughts flitted through her mind. Ian was Constable, and would be loyal to his laird. Despite his kindness, he could prove to be a friend or foe, even though McColl was a McCallum *sept*. She decided that she could not risk revealing her purpose on the mainland. It became more imperative by the hour to leave this village. She shifted uncomfortably in her chair and glanced at Ian.

He waited patiently, his keen eyes watching every expression that passed over her face.

"Ian," Kate said, interrupting the telling moment, "would ye step into the kitchen?" Siusan and Cailan were busy setting the table for supper, and he winked at Kennis as he followed in his sister's wake.

She smiled at him in return. The woman had been kind but she was obviously distressed over the presence of her houseguest.

Once far enough from the front room to satisfy her purpose, Kate described in detail what she'd heard in the village market, fully enumerating on the ills of harboring a fugitive Jacobite.

"Ye call the lass an outlaw, Kate? Enough of the tittle-tattle, woman." Ian raised his hand. "Ye shouldna listen to everything ye hear in the square. There's more than meets the eye about this business."

"I agree," Kate said, very unhappy with the turn of events. "The gossip's worse than a hive of bees hummin', since everyone saw ye bring her right to my door. Look, the Campbell soldiers said if ye harbor the lass, trouble will knock at your door. Rumor has it that the Crown banished her kith and kin after the '45. I dinna know why she'd risk so much by comin' to the mainland, and I'm nae so sure I want to know. So keep that in mind when ye meddle in other folk's affairs and involve your own kin in their troubles."

"*Whissht*, Kate." He attempted to soothe her ruffled feathers. "I intend to lay the matter before the Laird first thing when he arrives."

"Well, I should hope so!" Dissatisfied, she swept from the room.

Ian had already decided to report these events to the laird upon his return. Right now, he could do little about Kennis' predicament, except make sure the lass stayed out of trouble. He must remind Cailan to hold her tongue and discover what she may have revealed about their guest at the castle. She was only twelve, to be sure, but the lass could keep her mouth closed. He would wait and see, stroll about the village this evening and have a smoke with friends. Whatever rumor was spreading among the people would make itself known. In the morning, he would keep his eyes and ears open, and tell young Cailan to do the same.

Chapter 3

Prisoners

Reclining on a bed of straw, Duncan examined his cozy surroundings.

Shadows danced on the walls of the woodland cottage as tongues of fire leapt gaily in the hearth. In the far corner stood a writing desk and a bookshelf, overflowing with leather bound volumes. A small fortune in itself. A parchment lay open upon the little desk as if the writer, interrupted in his work, had left his project in a hurry.

Puzzled, he studied the room, noting dried herbs and flowers hanging from beams in the loft. Small jars containing powders, leaves, stems and roots, all neatly labeled, sat in alphabetical order upon a dusty ledge. The enticing aroma from a stew bubbling in an iron pot on the hearth wafted through the room, making his empty stomach growl.

Hands tied, Jamie got up from his cot and peered into the pot. "Well, I hope 'tis as good as it hits the nostrils. I'd stir if I could find a spoon."

"Maybe it means that our captors don't mean to starve us."

Just then, the door squeaked open. "Nay, lad, but you've arrived at an uncanny time." The man pulled off his woolen cap and hung it on a peg. He slipped off his cape, eyeing Duncan with interest.

Duncan managed to sit up halfway, his head still throbbing from the blow he had received. "If you don't mean to do us harm, then why are we being held here? Surely there's no need to detain us any longer."

"Ah, but that's where you're wrong. We'll nae keep you any longer than we must, but the greater question is, what do we do with you? We've important business to attend to, and you lads are in the way." He ambled over to the bubbling pot. "Stew's finished cookin', I see. Are you hungry, lads?"

Jamie and Duncan nodded. "Aye, but we can't eat with our hands tied."

"If you think you can escape by havin' your bonds loosed, think again." He rapped on the door twice and the signal was soundly returned. "There are several men guardin' this cottage. So let's have a little talk while I take a look at your head. Then we'll eat," he said to Duncan. "Names first will do."

Duncan paused. If his captors were robbers, it would be foolish to give his real name. They might demand a ransom from his family. However, if he didn't and it was already known, they might think him a liar or worse. Opting for truth, he proudly raised his head and stared hard at the stranger. "My name is Duncan MacDougall of Dunolly and yon is my henchman, Jamie McConacher. Now, who are you?"

His eyes twinkled at Duncan's imperious behavior. "I am Conor Malcolm, and I'm right glad you told the truth about who you are. You'll be restored to your kin soon enough."

Duncan stared at him, incredulous. "You dare to retain us, then? Do you understand who I am?"

"Aye, you just told me, and that's the reason you're still breathin'," he said candidly.

"Don't you realize that I'll be missed, and the MacDougalls will come for me?"

"You brother will come, but by then you willna be in this location."

"And just exactly where do you plan to take us?" Duncan fished for information.

He shrugged. "I dinna know yet."

"And what about my other men, and the horses?"

"Dinna *fash* yourself, lad." He smiled at Duncan's persistence. "They're fine."

"Nearby?" Duncan said, impatient and concerned for his friends.

"I canna say, but you're deep in the forest where no man will find you that naught has the way of it." Conor finished dressing the bump on Duncan's head, then bent to unbind his hands. "Now dinna try anythin' foolish or you'll suffer the consequences."

"I won't," he scowled. Tired and hungry, his head ached and he was at the mercy of villains. In spite of his frustration, he was eager to discover the answer to his many questions.

After untying Jamie's hands, Conor placed a bucket of cold water at the end of the long table and handed him a rough cloth and bar of soap. Jamie and Duncan hesitated. "Get to it lads, the stew is ready now." He took a large ladle from a hook on the wall, dished out three generous portions of stew, and then set a loaf of dark bread on the rough wooden table.

What in the world is going on? Duncan wondered for the hundredth time as he dried his hands on the nubby cloth. He'd heard tales from the MacDougall bard of mortal enemies, who in times past, sat down to break bread together one evening and the next day resumed a long-standing feud. Conor Malcolm hardly seemed the type to be caught in the middle of a clan quarrel but then, appearances could be deceiving. He was a scholar, an educated man in pursuit of his studies. Duncan perused the parchments and book-lined shelves again.

Conor followed his glance. "Duncan MacDougall, how old're you?"

The man must be fey, hearing his thoughts. "I am two-and-twenty."

"You've been to the university at Edinburgh, then."

He gave little answer, suspicious of questions. "Aye."

"And how is your family?" Conor inquired. "I'm acquainted with your mother and your brother, lad. Tell me, how does the bonnie lass fare?"

Duncan was surprised at the reference to his mother. "She's well," he said more wary than before. "How do you know her, sir, and my brother?"

Conor looked thoughtful. "Your mother's story is her own to tell, but your brother Alistair visited these parts hunting the Great Stag Chalum when he was a lad. All he found for his trouble was a dull hermit in the woods. For that's who I am, the Hermit of Clan McCallum. I came here to dwell after the '15 when my family was lost, and I've stayed here ever since."

"Do you never leave these woods, then?"

"Aye, I go to market for supplies, but generally, no. So you see, I was dubbed the Hermit because of my unsocial behavior."

"And how did you meet Alistair?" Duncan felt like he had missed something important. "I know he came here upon one occasion, but nothing more. You said that he hunted the stag?"

"Aye, he did, and I've known him well in years past." Conor eyed Duncan keenly. "From all I've heard, he's grown to be a fine man, temper notwithstandin'."

Duncan grimaced. Soon enough, he would be the recipient of a verbal tongue-lashing, the result of Alistair's black temper. This time, however, he decided, a stern rebuke was well-deserved.

"And ties are close with Argyll?"

"He's a relative," he murmured, wary again.

"I'm aware of that, laddie," Conor said, amused. The lad might resemble his lady mother but had more than his fair share of the MacDougall disposition.

Duncan changed the subject. "What of the Great Stag? 'Tis the main reason I came here, you know."

He nodded. "I'm grateful to hear you came for a wee bit more than that, too. I would've known you for Grear Campbell's lad wherever I'd met up with you." A faraway look over-shadowed his brow. "You've a great look of her, but your brother, Alistair, now there's a MacDougall, if ever there was one."

A bang on the wooden door brought Conor to his feet, interrupting the moment. He stepped outside, and Jamie listened to the muffled voices. "I can't make it out," he grumbled, pressing his ear to the door.

Duncan closed his eyes and dozed off long before Conor returned. The consumption of a hearty meal, combined with the excitement of the day, had taken its toll on his weary body.

Finally, the door squeaked open. "You ride in the mornin'," Conor said as he struck the tinderbox and lit a candle, "to meet your present host."

Duncan opened his eyes wide. "You mean you're the one giving orders?"

"Nay, lad, why would you think so?" He seemed genuinely surprised. "Just be assured that what is about to happen here will be a good thing for the McCallum clan."

"I sincerely hope so. I'd hate to think you dragged these poor people into some trouble with the law by doing something illegal."

"Nay, you dinna understand." He clapped Duncan on the shoulder. "Someday, if all goes well, you'll know I've spoken the truth. And I hope in that hour, we'll call one another friend."

"As do I, Conor Malcolm," Duncan said gravely, meeting his steady gaze. The consequences of their meeting were serious, indeed, and he hoped for the best. The last thing the Highlands needed was another war between clans because of their abduction.

"Now lads, get some sleep. You've a long ride ahead of you come morning."

* * *

Alistair was dreaming again. The bonnie golden-haired lass wandered, lost in the mist, and he couldn't rescue her in time. Pounding, something was pounding. He awoke with a start, rolled over and groaned. Someone hammered the door. "Come," he said, groggy.

Dermot entered, apologizing. "I'm sorry to disturb ye so early, Laird, but his grace bid me wake ye before the other guests come down to break their fast. He wants to have private conversation with ye in the breakfast room. I've brought hot water for ye." He paused, watching Alistair's reaction. "Will ye be needin' anythin' else?"

"No, Dermot, you may go, and don't worry about waking me in the morning." He smiled darkly. "I promise I won't throw anything at you."

Dermot returned the smile. "Nay, Laird, I dinna think ye would."

Alistair lay still for a moment longer, arms pillowed beneath his head. What could Argyll want of him now? His eyes narrowed as he contemplated the message. Strange that the duke would send Dermot to wake him when he'd arranged the meeting the previous evening. He must need something else.

He threw the heavy quilted coverlet aside, swung his feet to the floor and rose from the bed. After dousing his head with cold water, he dressed slowly, his mind filled with thoughts pertaining to his goals and heart's desire. He possessed enough ambition for five men and marrying the right kind of woman would complement his life. Vanora Campbell struck him as the type of young woman who was more interested in her own consequence than in being a proper helpmate. Her cold manner, combined with self-preoccupation did not recommend her as a long-term companion

Running a comb through his hair, he stared at his own reflection. He was in the prime of his life, definitely not the time to allow himself to be deceived by a pretty face. Or by his vivid dreams. He couldn't shake thoughts of the McCallum lass from his mind. He envisioned her in his sleep and in his waking hours. What the devil was wrong with him? He turned from the mirror and strode from the room. Determined to forget her, he walked briskly down the remainder of the passage toward the breakfast parlor where he found the duke, reading a journal.

Argyll glanced up at him. "Ah, Alistair, here you are. I trust you've slept well?"

He nodded. "Indeed, I always sleep well when I'm at Inveraray."

"And so you should." Argyll was smug. "We're well protected within these walls."

He served himself from the assortment of dishes laid out on the side buffet and requested a mug of coffee. He decided to press the duke for information. "Well, your grace, what made you send Dermot to awaken me? Yesterday evening you impressed upon me the importance of meeting you this morning."

Argyll regarded him, wondering about his state of mind. "Apart from my desire for your company at breakfast, I'd not intended to have you disturbed, but we shouldn't discuss business here. Cameron Campbell arrived late last night with alarming news and although he's my kinsman and yours, I might add, somehow I always have this feeling that he's not to be trusted."

"Cameron Campbell is a conniver," he said bluntly. "You shouldn't trust him. His nose is always in some business where it doesn't belong."

"Strong words, Alistair," Argyll reproved, "but I agree. We'll have to see if his prophecy comes true, or not."

"Prophecy?"

Argyll waved his hand. "Just an expression. Anticipation, more like. Are you finished eating? Bring your coffee to the library, and I'll have Murdoch bring a fresh pot to refill your mug." The two men rose and retreated to the duke's library. Murdoch entered the room as they settled themselves in two armchairs before the fire, bearing a silver tray and coffee pot. He placed them within easy reach on a small table, and hesitated.

"What is it, Murdoch?" Argyll asked with a lift of his brow.

"Mr. Peyton Gilmore has called, your grace," he said with dignity. "Shall I send him to the estate office to await your pleasure?"

"No, no, have him wait on me here."

"Very well, your grace." Murdoch bowed and walked from the room in his stately manner.

"You don't object, do you, Alistair? He's only recently arrived and I must welcome him to Inveraray."

"I don't mind at all." He was relieved that the duke would have someone else to distract him from some undisclosed purpose that he might have in this meeting. Peyton Gilmore's arrival likewise interested him. Soft green eyes framed with thick lashes stared at him from a bonnie face. At this point, the girl was more than a distant memory that had captivated his imagination. Perhaps this was the opportunity to discover her true intentions and resolve the question in his mind. The duke interrupted his reverie.

"Alistair, did you not hear me? Come welcome my new factor to Inveraray." He continued with a brief introduction. "Alistair, Mr. Peyton Gilmore."

Smiling, he stepped forward. "A pleasure to see you again, Mr. Gilmore. How is your family? When we met last, your wife was a trifle seasick, I recall." The two men shook hands.

Peyton smiled. "She was indeed, but recovered quickly once we were on solid ground again."

"And your daughters and their companion?" he asked smoothly, not desiring to raise a question from the duke about the young woman.

"Well, all of them, and thank you for inquiring." Peyton was extremely pleased by the young man's polite interest.

Alistair's mind raced. *Perhaps I can speak with him later about the lass. Now isn't the time with Argyll present in the room.*

Murdoch reentered the room to pour the coffee and stood waiting for an opportunity to speak.

"What is it this time, Murdoch, more visitors?"

"Aye, your grace, but this time 'tis for Lord Alistair."

Alistair gazed at him, waiting expectantly.

"Your servant, Farrell McConacher is in the hall, sir, and requests your presence."

He rose quickly from his chair and started for the door.

"Nonsense," Argyll said, "have the man come into my library. We have no secrets here."

Alistair disagreed but kept his own counsel and awaited Farrell's arrival. The door opened, and Farrell tentatively entered the room.

"Come in, come in," Argyll said testily, "and close the door against the draft."

Alistair went to greet him, hoping for a word of private conversation. The duke did not interfere; Farrell wasn't his servant or responsibility. Instead, he engaged Peyton in conversation.

"Well, Farrell," he asked, curt, "what brings you to Inveraray when I left you to keep watch at Dunolly?"

"'Tis Master Duncan, Laird," Farrell said. "He's disappeared."

"Disappeared?" Alistair's dark brows lifted. "What did he do this time, evaporate into the mist?"

"He might as well have," Farrell said, braving Alistair's wrath. "He and four of the young 'uns left Dunolly the same mornin' ye did, day before yesterday. They promised to return by the next day at the latest but I've nae seen hide nor hair of 'em."

"Why didn't you stop them, Farrell? I gave Duncan strict orders to stay home," he said, infuriated. His eyes narrowed, considering. "You don't have to tell me. The Stag."

"Aye, in part," Farrell said, "but the young master was truly grieved by the condition of the McCallum's. He wanted to do somethin' for them sooner than later."

Alistair ran his hand through his hair. "Young fool. And so do I, but my greater concern at present is with Rob McCallum and others like him. This escapade will only serve to slow down the entire process." Risking Argyll's displeasure, he made a decision. "I'll come with you. We'll have to search the hills above Loch Awe, near Dunchalum. Did you bring any men with you?"

"Nay sir, I came m'self. I dinna figure to leave Dunolly unguarded, and ye had your tail with ye."

"Good. I'll ask Argyll for supplies. You see to my horse and the men. I'll meet you at the gate in twenty minutes."

"Aye, sir." Farrell exhaled, relieved to find him in a reasonable temper at the news. He bowed and exited the room.

"What is it, lad?" Argyll asked. "You look like a storm about to break."

Alistair met his eye. "'Tis Duncan. He's been missing since day before yesterday with four of our young men."

"Young men will be young men," Argyll said dryly.

"Not this time. He knew exactly where he was going and what he was getting himself into. If you recall, a band of men has been roaming the Highlands and the coast for a few weeks. I don't know for sure, but 'tis possible he could have run afoul."

"What are you planning to do?"

"I'm going to go after him, track him myself. I'll need supplies, your grace, enough for my men for a few days."

The duke nodded in approval. "Certainly, and do you plan to leave your mother and sister under my protection?"

"Aye, if that's acceptable." He hoped that Ona wouldn't get into trouble while he was gone. His mother must keep a close eye on her.

"I'll be delighted to have their company, and so will my guests. Moreover, I'd dislike tearing away the ladies at such a time. They're busy planning this masquerade, remember, and I expect you to be present."

Inside, Alistair was filled with glee at escaping Vanora Campbell's clutches. "I'll do my best, your grace, but I must find Duncan."

"Of course. Don't take any unnecessary chances, Alistair. I have more men-at-arms at my disposal than you."

"Thank you, and now I must be off." He turned back for a moment. "Will you also inform my mother of this circumstance?"

"I will, my lad," Argyll assured. "Leave everything to me."

Alistair bowed himself out of the room, ran down the hall and up the stairs to his chamber. He hastily stuffed a few items into his pack, pulled off his morning clothes and changed into his riding breeks. No time now to speak with his mother. He trusted her good sense to protect his sister and he must depend upon Argyll to tell her the reason for his sudden departure.

As he descended the steps, a door clicked open. Argyll appeared and spoke his name. "Alistair."

"Your grace?"

"One moment, please. I know you're in a hurry but you must hear what Cameron Campbell told me last night. I'll be brief, Alistair."

Alistair followed him into the now vacant library. "Well?" he said abruptly.

"He informed me that Robert McCallum's son has escaped the authorities in Jamaica and is wreaking havoc in the colonies. Somehow he's managed to obtain a ship, and turned to pirating."

"Buccaneering, your grace?" Alistair's mouth quivered in amusement at the duke's expression but not the topic of conversation. If Robbie McCallum broke the law, he'd be hard-pressed to succeed in his own quest to redeem the lad. The young fool.

"'Tis no laughing matter but a serious offense. Cameron seems to think that he and his cutthroats are headed to Scotland."

"For what purpose? They can't stay here without a pardon, although his grandfather was reprieved and restored to his home."

"Yes, yes, I know. The wily old devil," Argyll said in disgust. "I also am told a pardon is in process for this McCallum lad, that someone has filed legal documents with the Baron's Court in an attempt to seek his release."

Alistair's suspicion awakened. "And have you received a copy of these documents?"

"No, I haven't."

"Shouldn't you?"

"Not until a pardon is granted," Argyll said. "You think I should have, eh? The young man must also appear before me and swear fealty to England and the King, or go to London to do so." He paused, considering the implications. "Perhaps I'll look into the matter."

"I think that any information received from Cameron Campbell should be examined before a judgment's made. I'd like to know exactly what his objective is, what he stands to gain."

"I've made him Constable of Dunchalum, Alistair. Surely you know this?"

"No, I didn't." Alistair's eyes narrowed. "When was this?" He'd been away on his journey to track down the men he had rescued and hadn't had time to go through all of his letters at home.

"A month ago. I needed someone in close proximity and Breadalbane wasn't interested in the responsibility. You were away at the time, I recall." He observed Alistair's doubtful expression. "He's a capable man."

"Capable of feathering his own bonnet," he said grimly. "This isn't the kind of news I expected to receive."

"Cameron suspects that he may even now be in the area. Your brigands, Alistair?"

"'Tis possible, but I wouldn't be so hasty to assume his news is accurate or that the band currently roving the area are the one and the same."

"They must be apprehended and interrogated," Argyll insisted.

"Pirates or no, these men have wreaked no havoc in the area." He resented Cameron's interference in his own affairs as well as in the McCallum's.

"All the same," Argyll maintained, "we must find them. I have another idea concerning the matter."

"Aye, and what might that be, your grace?"

"You recall the ransom note I received from a Captain Grahame, curse the rascally fellow!"

Alistair nodded.

"Perhaps he and this McCallum lad are associates in crime."

"Rob McCallum is hardly a grown man, he's younger than Duncan."

"Hard circumstances make people grow up faster, Alistair."

"I still find it unlikely," he said, recalling the fair-headed boy with the big grin.

"Regardless, I intend to investigate this matter thoroughly." He shuffled some papers on his desk. "I also plan to interrogate your prisoner. Do you object?"

"Nay, your grace, do what you must." Alistair paced, impatient to leave. "But don't release him before I return. I must be off to search for Duncan."

"I won't," Argyll agreed. "Go, then, and don't hesitate to send for reinforcements if you encounter these fellows."

Alistair strode quickly from the room. His thoughts were racing. What devious plot had Cameron Campbell devised? Why had Argyll not received the documents that declared a pardon for Rob or at the least, notice that it was pending? Because of Duncan's disappearance, it would be several days before he could begin an investigation. He increased his pace as he walked across the cobblestones toward the rising portcullis. Farrell and his men were waiting. They would ride hard today to Dunchalum and try to discover Duncan's whereabouts.

* * *

Duncan awoke to the screeching of a hoot owl in the wee hours of the morning, troubled by the events of the previous day. Confounded bird. He rolled over and faced the wall. Time to rise. This day would have enough trouble of its own, so why worry about tomorrow? Maybe trouble makes each untroubled day special in itself.

He laughed at himself. If Alistair could hear him, he'd say that he sounded like a parson. And what of Alistair—what was happening at Inveraray, would he soon be caught in parson's mousetrap? Duncan drifted back to sleep until he felt himself being shaken.

"Wake up, Master Duncan," Jamie McConacher whispered, trying not to startle him. "Time for a morsel before we ride."

"Where's Conor Malcolm?" he asked sleepily.

"He went outside twenty minutes ago."

Duncan blinked as his eyes adjusted to the dim light in the cottage. "Still no chance at escape?"

"Nay, I've counted at least six men abroad this mornin', could be more."

"What do you make of this Conor Malcolm?"

"He's a right one, I'll be bound, but what the lot o' them are up to I canna think. I put my ear to the door but couldna hear a word."

"He has me in a puzzle," Duncan said. "Have you noticed the books and parchments in the corner, and the herbs and jars everywhere? I can't understand why he'd be involved with a ring of whiskey smugglers."

"Mayhap they're nae smugglers, or he hopes to gain somethin' in return. Folk are desperate these days." Jamie handed Duncan a bowl of porridge. "Better eat, Master Duncan, before he returns."

Duncan slowly spooned the hot porridge into his mouth. By evening, Farrell McConacher, Jamie's uncle, would wonder why the five young men hadn't returned to Dunolly. If they didn't appear by morning, he'd send word to Alistair at Inveraray.

Drat the man! Trouble was sure to find him in the form of Alistair, if not through Conor Malcolm's cohorts. At least Farrell's watchfulness would prove to be to their advantage in the end.

Conor entered the cottage, humming a tune. "'Tis a fine mornin', lads!" Seeing Duncan at breakfast, he added, "You have ten minutes before we're off, Master MacDougall. You'd best finish your porridge quick-like."

"I'm through, Conor, thanks all the same." He cleared his throat and tried to be nonchalant. "Now, where are we going?"

Conor laughed. "Ah, you canna expect me to tell you, lad. Good try, though, you're quick on your feet."

"Not quick enough for you," he retorted, "and considering that Alistair is my elder brother, I'd better be."

"True enough." The door swung open and a man poked his head into the room. "Conor, ready to ride?"

"Aye," he returned. "Let's go." He went out the door.

Four men awaited them, and Conor approached Jamie and Duncan, rope in hand. "Sorry about this, lads, it canna be helped."

Duncan gave him a sour look. They were to be bound and hooded. Jamie wore a black scowl as his hands were tied to the pommel of the saddle.

Duncan, prodded from behind, was urged to mount a horse. Then his hands were also roped down tight. How was he supposed to ride like this? It was ridiculous!

"It willna be so very bad," Conor sympathized. "The lads'll lead you well. I hope to see you again on more congenial terms."

"You aren't coming?" Duncan's dark brows lifted in surprise.

"Nay, I've my work to complete here. You'll be well taken care of, and soon you'll meet up with the other three members of your party." He smiled as they were hooded. "A Good day to you, lads. Fare well!"

Duncan grunted in response as his horse broke into a soft trot. *Fare well to you, Conor Malcolm.*

Chapter 4

The Search

Alistair and his men rode hard through the cool Highland morning.

The fog lifted, and as the sun rose higher in the autumn sky, the rumblings in his stomach induced him to briefly halt. Satisfied with the progress of their journey so far, he slowed the pace, calculating they would arrive at Dunchalum by early afternoon. "Farrell," he said, "now tell me again what inspired you to let Duncan go on this wild goose chase."

Farrell grimaced. "I dinna figure I could stop him, Laird," he said, "and I figured there'd be the de'il to pay one way or the other."

He snorted. "You know me well, man."

"Aye, too well, perhaps." Farrell said wryly. "What's your plan when we get to the Highlands?"

"We'll see who's about," he answered, "ask some questions. We may have to split up to track the lads, if the trail isn't too cold."

"And from there?"

Alistair had already considered his options. "I hope we don't have to ride much further. If necessary, you'll take a few of the lads back to Dunolly, search the coastline and stay there unless you hear aught of Duncan or the men we've been tracking. I'll take the rest of the tail with me to Craignish and search the southern coast. Look," he said, pointing, "yon is the track we must ride."

He turned his horse toward the Highland path that climbed into the upper regions of the mountains. It was slow work; the horses picked their way along the rocky slope as they ascended the misted hills. The overgrown track bore evidence that someone had passed through recently, visible in the beaten down underbrush. Silent, he grew absorbed by thoughts of the McCallum's who would never walk this way again, lost in a fruitless war against the English. His heart grieved over the lost men and for their families left behind.

The small village of Kilcalum sat nestled at the foot of Dunchalum Castle on the banks of Lochangless. A few ruined shielings were visible along the way. He signaled, hand upheld, and the men reined in close behind. "Farrell."

On cue, Farrell rode ahead to the little village of Kilcalum, and soon returned with solemn news. "It's as quiet as a churchyard," he said. "No one's about, but there's smoke risin' from the shielin's. 'Tis what Jamie reported to me when the lads returned after their first visit."

Alistair nodded. "We'll have to ride in then, and knock on a few doors. You come with me, Farrell, and the others can stand watch." Farrell passed the word along and the men urged their mounts to a trot along the well-used track. None of them witnessed a mysterious figure stealing through the trees, watching every movement the group made. A grey shadow, It flitted ahead and waited for the men to come into plain view in the tiny glen.

Alistair and Farrell dismounted, unknowingly following in the footsteps of Duncan and Jamie. Alistair rapped on the door, *skean dhu* drawn. Farrell stood on the other side, waiting.

The door slowly creaked open and a raspy voice greeted them. "G'day, Laird, wha' can I do fer ye? Come in noo, I canna stand in the cold an' the wind." Granny Jean's wizened face peered out from the smoky hut as she opened door wider, gesturing in welcome. Two children, a boy and a girl, stood behind her.

The men entered, ducking their heads under the low-hanging frame. Scanning the room and finding no threat, they sheathed their dirks.

The dim interior of the shieling was brightened by a small fire in the center of the room that provided a measure of warmth. Alistair surveyed the meager surroundings, hoping the old woman wouldn't offer him food. He didn't want to rob her of one single morsel.

"Good day," Alistair greeted. "Whom do I have the pleasure of meeting?"

"Ye can call me Granny Jean lik' ev'ryone else," she said. "The bairns air my grandchilders, Meggie and Davy."

Meggie bobbed a curtsey and Davy bowed. "'Tis a pleasure t' meet ye, Laird," Meggie said, her eyes bright.

Alistair smiled. "'Tis also mine, to meet you and Davy, Meggie."

"Who's your friend?" Meggie asked pertly.

"Pardon me, my manners are surely lacking." Amused, he stood with bonnet in hand as Farrell smothered a laugh behind him. "My name is Alistair MacDougall of Dunolly, and this is Farrell McConacher."

"Och, I would've known ye fer the MacDougall anywhar," Granny Jean said. "Ye've a great look o' yer father."

"But dinna ye think he looks like Master Duncan, too?" Meggie piped up.

Alistair stiffened. "Now what might you know of Master Duncan, Meggie?"

Meggie looked guilty and Granny Jean stared back, expressionless. "He," she stuttered, "he's been here a couple o' times searchin' fer the Stag. Last time he brought us sweets." She looked up at Alistair hopefully. "Ye wouldna happen t' hae sweets, would ye, Laird?"

"I'm afraid not," he said. "Do you have food to eat?"

"We've eno' fer a time," Granny Jean said. "An' speakin' o' food, would ye care fer a bite an' some ale?"

"Ale is most welcome," he said, taken aback by her offer, "but we don't need food."

Granny Jean sent Meggie for the ale and settled herself into her rocking chair. He received the ale Meggie brought to him, but his obvious surprise did not escape the old woman.

"Wonder whar I come by the ale, Laird?" She eyed him, taking his measure.

"Aye, madam, and I think I know who may have brought it."

"Och, can ye noo?" She gave him a toothless grin. "An' 'tis Granny t' ye, laddie," she reminded, "if it pleases ye."

He grinned back. "It pleases me greatly, Granny."

She nodded at him with approval. "Noo tell me, lad, whar I come by this ale."

"My best guess is that it came from Eavan Malcolmson, your kinsman."

"Hm, ye're close but nae tha' close," she murmured, rocking slowly back and forth. "The Laird comes by noo ' an' agin, but this ale comes by anither road."

Alistair wanted to question her further but she continued of her own volition. He sensed a tale coming and didn't have the heart to interrupt her.

"The road less travel'd 'tis the road fer the McCallum's, I'm afeart." Sorrow filled her voice. She leaned her bent shoulders forward and changed the subject. "Art worritsome o'er phantoms, lad?"

Alistair blinked. From ale to phantoms, a much less traveled road indeed. "Nay, Granny, I'm not afraid of phantoms nor am I superstitious, so you'll find little sympathy with me. Why?"

"Cause thar's a ghost in yon forest." Her old face took on a worried look. "I've seen it m'self, all grey an' lopin' cross the ground wi' nary a sound. 'Tis an omen."

"To what portent, Granny Jean?" Alistair was concerned. Was the old woman going daft? Many Scots believed in bogles and faeries but this could be a sign of some other serious trouble.

"Dinna be thinkin' tha' m' head's nae workin' proper, lad. I be fine noo," she sagaciously informed him. "When a departed soul appears he's merely callin' someone else t' join him in the afterlife."

"Are you thinking perhaps that he's calling you, Granny?" he asked gently.

"Nay, laddie, 'tis a sign like I said." She spoke like she would to Meggie or her little brother Davy. "Maun be a body from his ain clan if he appears."

"Eavan, then," said Alistair, his dark eyes growing blacker. *I'd like to help him to answer the phantom's call.*

"I canna say."

Alistair rose from his chair. "I thank you for the ale, Granny. Before I go, answer me this—has Eavan Malcolmson or any other stranger been here in recent days, or even weeks?"

"Aye. One Cameron Campbell, no less." Her old eyes glittered. "Tryin' t' get his hands on the young master's *siller*, he is. Poor laddie! Nae dead, but he might as well be. Sold off lik' a common thief, air Master Robbie."

She shuddered and pulled her worn shawl closer about her thin frame. "An' his poor dear Mem an' sweet sister chased from thar ain hame. The poor Laird's rollin' o'er in his grave, come fer vengeance on them tha' doon it. Tha's why he's a wanderin' yon forest, poor soul." She flung her apron over her head and wailed into it.

Alistair laid a strong hand on her shoulder in an effort to comfort her. "Come now, you mustn't think such things. My mother always says there's a future and a hope, and 'tis true for you and the rest of your clan, too."

"Ye're a guid lad." She wiped her eyes teary on her apron. "The seer Jeremiah said it t' be sae. *I know the plans I hae fer ye, fer welfare an' nae fer calam'ty, t' gie ye a future an' a hope.*" She rambled on. "A guid, sainted woman, yer mither. 'Twas a sad day fer the McCallum's when—but then I shouldna be tellin' a story wha's nae mine ain t' tell."

Taken aback, Alistair paused at her words. "My mother, you know my mother?"

"Noo, run along, laddie. This auld woman needs a wee nappie."

"Now just a minute, Granny Jean, you can't tell tales like that and not tell me what you mean."

"I surely can. 'Tis the only proper thing t' do."

He was dissatisfied with her answer. "Then I'll ask her myself when I return home, if you won't tell me."

"Aye, ye do tha', lad. 'Tis her ain story, nae one else's. I'm an auld woman," she said, "an' aboot t' fall asleep. I canna answer mair questions. Meggie'll answer fer me, she's a pert lass." Her chin dropped to her chest and within minutes, she lightly snored.

Meggie returned with a pitcher, and filled their mugs with more heather ale. "Are ye kin tae Master Duncan?"

He smiled at the child. "Aye, lassie, he's my brother."

"Wha' aboot Farrell?" she asked.

"He's my friend."

"Master Duncan hae a friend named Jamie wi' him," she offered.

"That would be Farrell's nephew," he acknowledged, wondering what the child knew.

She innocently gazed at him. "I'm supposin' ye're here t' hunt the Stag, too?"

"Nay, lassie, we're here searching for Duncan, Jamie and three other men who were here with them the day before yesterday."

Meggie's eyes grew round and her mouth formed a silent 'O'. "Ye mean they ne'er came home?" she cried.

"Nay," he said quietly. "Perhaps you can tell me all about the last time you saw them, what direction they were headed."

Davy came to stand by Meggie's side and spoke for the first time. "Tha's easy, Laird. We could show ye."

Finishing the contents of his mug, Alistair set it down on the small table. Rising, he glanced at Farrell, who immediately went out the door to notify the men. "That would be helpful, lad, if you could." He clapped him on the shoulder and Davy smiled.

The children followed Alistair out the door, closing it softly behind them in order not to wake Granny Jean. "Ye hae t' come this way." Meggie pointed toward a track that snaked upward at the other end of the village. "It rises, an' then forks. The left track heads north, and looks doon on the Castle. The right leads t' other way 'round."

Alistair tipped his bonnet. "Many thanks to you both, Davy and Meggie. Give our thanks to your Granny Jean for her hospitality. Fare well."

Meggie and Davy each lifted a hand. "Fare well, Laird, and we hope ye find Master Duncan soon."

The men turned and walked their horses toward the track Meggie and Davy had indicated. A childish voice called after them. "When ye see Master Duncan, ask him t' bring more sweets!"

The men guffawed as Alistair stopped and turned in his saddle. "I'll do better than that. Duncan and I will both bring you sweets. Will that do, Meggie?"

She jumped up and down. "Aye, Laird, come back quick-like!"

Amused, Alistair saluted, giving his horse the office.

Farrell sat astride his plodding horse, chuckling long after the children were out of sight. "That Meggie's a piece of work."

Alistair's shoulders shook with laughter. "She certainly is. Shrewd, too, unless I miss my guess. Those children and their Granny know something they're not telling."

"Aye, but I dinna have the feelin' somethin' wicked's afoot. I believe we'll find Master Duncan and the lads safe."

Alistair agreed. Somehow, he knew that Duncan and his men were alive and well, only time would tell. They continued to canter up the track and soon the fork that Meggie spoke of came into view. Farrell stopped to look at the ground.

"Trail's cold, Laird."

"Then I'll take the north road with half of the men, Farrell," he directed. "You take the rest to the south."

* * *

A grey figure watched the men divide into two groups and ride in opposite directions. Recognizing the visitors, It kept a low profile, certain that at least one in the party would observe Its form and pursue, given the opportunity. The phantom stopped to listen, and then slipped away to await the riders at the top of the ridge.

* * *

Alistair gazed down upon Dunchalum Castle, once home to the proud McCallum clan. The castle stood strong but its silence burdened him. Robert was dead, the lad Robbie banished. Lady McCallum had gone to live with relatives like other wives of chieftains who died at Culloden or who were banished from Scotland.

Robert was a popular chief; he'd met him when clan chiefs gathered at Inveraray from all over Argyll to discuss the actions of the English and their neighboring clans. He smiled, remembering Robbie McCallum's face when he rescued him from the Great Stag. In years past, Alistair spent many days in these very woods, sitting at the feet of Conor Malcolm, his friend and mentor. Those carefree days were gone with his youth.

Farrell interrupted his musings. "I canna see much on the ground, Laird. Back yonder 'twas a scuffle, I'll be bound. If anythin' did happen here, 'twas well covered."

Alistair's thoughts shifted to Conor Malcolm. He'd know if strange men were in the district and he might have knowledge of Duncan's whereabouts. *Hm, I wonder?* Conor knew how to cover tracks and make the ground appear undisturbed, too.

* * *

The phantom continued to watch, predicting Alistair's next move, recognizing the conflicting emotions upon his face. Pleased, It nodded in satisfaction, then turned and glided away, sure that Alistair McDougall would follow this very path.

* * *

Alistair ordered his men to return to the horses and await him under the trees. He removed his bonnet, stood for a moment in silence and bowed his head. *Lord,* he silently prayed, *help me to perform this work for the McCallum's that you have placed within my heart. Grant me favor with the Court to see Rob pardoned and returned to his family and clan. Help me to find Duncan and the other lads. Amen.*

Alistair seldom attended Kirk with his mother and sister yet he possessed a sincere, personal faith in God that grew deeper with each passing day. A man of action, he believed that God must be the same. Otherwise, what was the point? Sitting in a pew from week to week without acting upon what a man or woman knew to do in His kingdom was a senseless waste of time.

Rejoining Farrell, he mounted his horse and signaled to move out. He chose a track that led away from the castle and was clear of bracken. Conor, he assumed, probably used it to check on Dunchalum. He looked for familiar markings as they entered the heart of the wood. The landscape was as well-known to him as the region surrounding Dunolly. Taking shortcuts shown to him by Conor many years before, he entered a clearing in which stood a neat cottage.

He dismounted, walked to the door and rapped on it twice. No response. The latch gave way and he pushed open the unlocked door. Just like Conor. He poked his head into the room. "Hello?" Silence greeted him as he scanned the cottage.

The room had changed little. Conor's parchments, books, and herbs were still the focal point of his life and his entire occupation. He drank in the familiar scene and inhaled the aromatic scent of the drying herbs that permeated the air. He took one more cursory glance around and bid it farewell, disappointed. There was no help available here to find Duncan. It seemed that he and the other four young men had indeed evaporated into the grey mist.

Chapter 5

Discovery

Daly and Fergus pressed on, eager to reach the small village of Kilcreag in the hopes of eating a hot meal and take a much-needed rest before they resumed the search for their young mistress.

The blacksmith directed them to the McColl cottage and once there, Daly rapped on the freshly painted door.

"I'm comin', I'm comin'!" Kate McColl opened the creaky door, cheeks pink from the rush.

"We're seekin' a hot meal and a room, mistress, and were told ye can provide us with both." Daly reached to pull his cap from his head. Chagrined, he realized too late that it wasn't there.

"Aye, I can." She watched him feel his bare head and arched her brow. "'Tis for payin' customers only, and I'll have ye know that my brother's Constable at Craignish, and he willna stand for ye runnin' off and nae payin' your shot." She eyed him and Fergus up and down. "I suppose ye'll do. My name's Kate McColl. Well, my *muckle* man," she said to Fergus, eyeing him up and down. "Take your poke round to the back door, and my niece will let ye in. And ye," she ordered Daly, "come with me."

Fergus shrugged and obeyed. Next to finding the lass Kennis, a hot meal was his most urgent desire.

Entering the back door, he found Daly wearily listening to Kate, whose tongue ran on wheels with nary a breath between. Without pause, she introduced Siusan, and he nodded in greeting. She then led them down a passage to a small chamber and returned to the kitchen.

"Well, Fergus," Daly said, after she'd gone, "did ye ever hear such a noise? 'Tis a shame, a bonnie piece of baggage, too." He fingered the stubble on his chin. "I'll wager there's a good heart along o' that saucy tongue."

"I canna think of anythin' but supper, and what's become o' our poor lassie. Nae a word in the market," Fergus mourned. "How do ye ask outright when ye dinna want anyone to know what ye're about?"

Daly sighed, his thoughts echoing those of his friend. For the first time in his adult life, he uttered a sincere prayer. *If this prayer is answered,* he vowed to himself and to God, *then I'll go to Kirk regularly and become a new man.* He closed the door behind them before they strolled down the hall to the kitchen.

Kate poured ale into mugs as they sat down to table. "Enjoy the ale lads, but I'll no hae ye drunk in this house. Ye're welcome to all ye can hold otherwise."

"Many thanks for your hospitality, Mistress McColl, and also to Mistress McAllister." Daly sincerely appreciated their hospitality. "We've come a long way and 'tis welcome, indeed, to have our thirst and hunger quenched."

"Come a long way, have ye? Thought as much," she said, smug. "If ye dinna mind my askin'—"

"We do, fact o' the matter is," Fergus said with a near growl.

"Now, lad, I dinna think Mistress McColl means anythin'. Dinna get in a temper." The woman's prying ways irritated him too.

Kate McColl was a good woman despite her faults. She recognized their weariness and need for a hot meal. Her nerves were frayed, too, after the altercation in the square with the soldiers the previous day. "We've had trouble here the last day or so," she explained, mollified by Daly's attempt at peacemaking, "what with Campbells and redcoats searchin' for two lads just like ye." She watched the two men out of the corner of her eye. "Seems they took the villains for dead, went back, and the bodies just up and walked away! Fancy that, can ye imagine such a fey thing?" She refilled their empty mugs. "And please, call me plain Kate, always hae been, and will be."

"Aye, I can imagine it," Fergus said with a glimmer of a smile. "Forgive me then, plain Kate. I dinna intend to offend ye."

"Dinna *fash* yourself, luve," Kate gurgled. "'Twould take more fire than that to light this wick. I've a quick temper, so dinna try your luck once too often."

Amused by her aunt's flirtations, Siusan listened as she stirred the large steaming pot for supper, keeping her own counsel. "The colcannon's ready to serve, Aunt." She carried the hearty stew of buttered cabbage, turnips, carrots, and potatoes to the table. Kate fetched the bowls and spoons, and ladled out the salty, peppered dish in generous portions. Adding a platter of warm bannocks, Siusan joined the three for prayer.

"We thank thee, Lord, for this bounty," Kate began, "and for our guests. Bless this food, and kin all around. Amen."

Fergus dug into his supper under Kate's watchful eye.

Daly watched, amused by Kate's obvious interest in his friend, calling him love with such familiarity. True, it was his last name, a *sept* of the McKinnon clan, but he was shrewd enough to know that Kate was just the sort of woman to try to lead an unsuspecting man down the forbidden aisle. Fergus would never be taken in so easily, he was no *gowk*. Perhaps, Daly considered, her sudden infatuation with him would distract her attention away from their true purpose. Little did he know about Kate's reputation as the village harridan.

"Did Cailan have extra chores at the castle today?" Siusan asked Kate. "She's late, I hope she hasna gotten herself into any mischief."

"I'm sure she'll be home soon enough, lass," Kate assured her niece. "She started work late this mornin' and finished late too, especially since K—, I mean, the lass needed help to find the road."

"Lass, ye say?" Daly noted Kate's slip of the tongue, and Fergus looked up sharply.

"Ye've had other visitors, then? I shouldna think many folks'd come this way."

Kate watched them while she talked, shrewd enough to deduce the circumstances that brought them to her door. "We've a few, and a young woman passed through and left this mornin'," said she was searchin' for two companions."

Fergus stood, his large frame overshadowing them all. "Dinna play games with us, Kate McColl."

"Seems to me, I'm nae the one playin' games," she said sharply.

Fergus and Daly glanced at one another. "Ye said the lass left this mornin'." Daly rose from his chair. "What was she like and where was she headed?"

"I canna tell ye, when ye're both towerin' over me like two mountains," Kate snapped, "and I canna tell ye much of anythin' at all, because I simply canna!" She threw down her napkin and was about to leave the table altogether when twelve-year-old Cailan burst through the front door.

"Auntie Kate, Mam! They've got her, she's been captured by the soldiers!" The child burst into a flood of tears.

"There, there now, lassie," Kate soothed, always the first to respond. "Ye've told us. Now, who's captured her? Can ye tell us that, eh?"

"Aye," the child said, sniffling, "'tis the Laird."

"Which Laird, lassie?" Kate looked up at Siusan, concerned. "'Tis important."

"The new Laird of Craignish," Cailan wailed.

Daly groaned. "Craignish, that means Campbells."

"Well, no," Siusan said, "the new Laird 'tis the MacDougall. His mother's a Campbell by birth, and 'twas given Craignish by Argyll for nae going out in the '45. 'Twas an inheritance of a sort."

"Sounds more like a reward for nae followin' the Bonnie Prince," Fergus groused.

"What manner o' man is he," Daly demanded. "Will he harm our lassie?"

Three pairs of eyes stared at him. Fergus could hardly believe his ears. Daly seldom made such mistakes.

"Your lassie, eh? Thought as much." Kate stood up, arms akimbo. "Ye've some explainin' to do, Daly Morrison, if 'tis Morrison! I've been waitin' for ye to come clean with me since I heard your name. Ye're hidin' somethin' or my name isna Kate McColl." She waited for a reply, foot tapping. "Now, oot with it before I lose what little patience I've left!"

Daly looked sheepishly at Fergus, Kate and Siusan. There was nothing to do but to tell the truth or at least a partial one. He explained that the three had recently arrived in Argyll and were on their way north when set upon in the night. The two men were knocked unconscious, left for dead, ponies and supplies stolen. The lassie escaped. They hadn't known until now if she was safe or in the hands of those devilish Campbells. He and Fergus had just arrived in the village when they met Kate. Out of necessity, they concealed the details.

"Well, I'll accept that poor excuse of a tale for now," Kate said. "I intend to get the whole story out of ye before I'm through. The girl who stayed here was named Kennis Morrison, a bonnie lass with green eyes and straw-colored hair. I figured ye must be kin to her. Two Campbells and a handful of redcoats were searchin' for her and two lads yesterday. Too bad we dinna know sooner," she wagged her head, "she couldna been gone more than a few hours when ye arrived, and hobblin' to boot."

"Hobblin'," Daly repeated, anxious. "She's hurt?"

"Just a sprain," Siusan said. "Uncle Ian and Cailan found her by the loch yesterday morning after she'd taken a nasty tumble."

"Then we must be off, Daly." Fergus moved with surprising speed and agility for a man his size. He was back in a flash, carrying their meager possessions.

"Hold on a minute, luve," Kate called after him before turning back to her niece. "Cailan, child, how far were ye when it happened?"

"Near the shepherd's croft, the one that sits by the burn."

"Why, that's nae far at all!" Kate exclaimed. "Ye can reach that spot in a *twink*. How did ye manage to go so slowly, child?"

Cailan raised guilty eyes to her aunt's face. "I took the cart so she dinna have to walk. Uncle Ian wanted her to stay and wait for the Laird but she dinna want to. So, I told a wee fib at the castle, said I needed to fetch something for ye, and Gavin let me take it out the gate."

"But if ye had the cart, why did ye go no further than the shepherd's croft?" Siusan asked, sifting through the tale.

Her face crumpled. "The pony got away from me, and dumped us in the ditch. I felt so bad, the poor mistress already having a hurt foot and all. I told her to go into Gil's hut 'cause he wouldna mind. I came home quick as I could."

Siusan looked at her daughter in dismay as Kate began to scold.

"No time for that, woman," Fergus bellowed. "We need to go!"

"Here now," Kate said, "just a minute." She ran from the room and returned a moment later, extending a brown bundle to Daly. "Look familiar, sirrah?"

Daly flushed. "Confound it, woman, gie it o'er!" He reached for it impatiently.

She hid the cap behind her back, her eyes glinting with mirth. "Say please."

"Please, then," he said, exasperated, stuffing the brown woolen cap that Ian had shown Kennis earlier onto his head after she'd handed it to him. The two men scurried out the door, packs carelessly stuffed and all weariness forgotten. Within a matter of minutes, deep male laughter echoed in their ears.

* * *

Weary from his search for Duncan, Alistair found himself nearing Craignish at dusk. Farrell rode to Dunolly to await further orders and to oversee the estate in his absence. Tired and discouraged, he sent Mac Tawesson ahead to notify Ian McColl of his arrival.

At least he'd escaped Inveraray for the present. The duke, although occupied with new business concerning Rob McCallum, wouldn't forget the alliance he sought to make between Alistair and Vanora, strengthening Campbell ties to the MacDougall clan.

"Laird!" Mac Tawesson called, riding toward the string of men and horses on the narrow track.

Alistair reined in his black horse. "What is it, Mac?"

"There's a tumbled over cart up the track," he said, "and a lass hidin' in the shepherd's croft. Gil isna there, went off t' see his sick granny."

"You're sure of this?"

Mac nodded. "Aye, my cousin's been carin' for his flock while he's away."

"Well, there's no crime being in the hut, I suppose." He had no desire to be involved in local family disputes or secret love affairs. "Which of the village lassies is it? You can ride to Kilcreag and tell her father."

"That's it, Laird, never seen this one," he said, a bemused look on his face. "Wouldna forget her quick-like."

Alistair raised his eyebrows. "Is that so? Well then, we'll definitely investigate. You go on ahead and take my message to Ian McColl. I'd like a hot meal when we arrive, how about you, lads?"

Mac turned his horse around amidst a chorus of Ayes and trotted ahead. Alistair and the men followed, riding single file. When the shepherd's croft appeared, he reined in, dismounted and grinned. Surely, he was more than a match for one lass. Opening the door, he peered into the empty room.

He looked back at the waiting men and shook his head. Movement in the brambles nearby caught his attention as he put his foot in the stirrup. He tilted his head in that direction, and Jocko sped off into the wood in the hopes of flushing out who or what hid beneath the trees.

* * *

Kennis heard the soft neighing of horses and hushed voices in the distance. She peeped out the window of the tiny croft, hoping that Ian or Siusan had come to help her, and stared directly into the face of Mac Tawesson. A man on horseback could only mean trouble for her. Was he one of the men who attacked Daly and Fergus, and was now seeking her?

She rested her forehead against the sill in relief when he'd gone. Her ankle throbbed as she fled the sanctuary of the croft. The bare trees offered little cover but she managed to conceal herself and fortunately, her old brown frock blended well with the bracken.

Several minutes later, Mac returned and cantered past her hiding place. A group of mounted men trotting after him drew abreast of the croft. She silently watched one rider dismount and saunter to the door. She sucked in a breath. His tall figure seemed very familiar. The men laughed raucously when he returned empty-handed, and her stomach knotted. Since Culloden, she'd heard too many tragic stories of women raped and murdered by the redcoats all over the Highlands. But these men weren't redcoats and she feared that she'd discover their identity all too soon.

Without warning, a horseman appeared from behind and bore down on her. Crouching low to the ground, she quickly rose, pushing through the bracken onto the open track. She stumbled and fell in the dirt, enclosed in a ring of men and horses. Raising her head, she stared at the strong forelegs of a sable horse. Her gaze rose higher up to the rider sitting astride his mount and she suffered a shock.

He leaned over the pommel of his saddle.

There was no mistaking the raven hair or mocking eyes that slammed into hers. Her bosom swelled with indignation at the memory of their last meeting, his near kiss and outrageous accusations. "You!" she exclaimed, mixed emotions flooding her soul as her heart flip-flopped in betrayal. Dragging herself from the ground, she stood to her feet and backed away.

* * *

Slowing the pace, Daly and Fergus slipped off the track and carefully made their way through the trees. Peering through the brush, they saw a ring of horsemen surrounding a lone figure.

"What's afoot?" Fergus whispered to Daly.

"I dinna know," he replied, "'but 'tis our lassie alright.'"

"They'd better nae hurt a hair of her head," Fergus growled.

"I dinna think they mean to," he said. "Would ye look there now?" The leader walked his horse forward to speak to their lass. He gasped. "Him! By all that's holy, I should've known."

"Must be the MacDougall," Fergus said. "Got the looks o' them.

"Aye. The lass seems to be fine, though. We've no quarrel with the MacDougall. Shouldna we go ahead and talk to him? The McKinnon trusts the man, heard him say so." He paused. "Surely he willna keep her, do ye think? He canna keep her!"

* * *

Alistair's heart skipped a beat. A dream had entered his weary reality. This lass, who occupied his thoughts and dreams, stood before him less than an hour from his own castle. He walked his horse forward and reined in alongside.

"Good evening, mistress," he said lazily. "How may I assist you?"

"I'm not in need of your aid, sir," Kennis said firmly. "You may leave me to fend for myself with good conscience." She backed away, teetering on her injured ankle.

"On the contrary, as a gentleman that I can't do." He slowly surveyed her, head to foot, taking note of every detail.

Kennis flushed. She was at a serious disadvantage again, muddy and disheveled, and without the protection of her friends. Before she could protest, he reached down and easily scooped her up into his arms. "Put me down!" she said. "If you were truly a gentleman, you'd do as I say."

He laughed. "Ah, but as a gentleman, I can't leave an injured lass alone out here in the wood."

"You must." She wriggled in his embrace, trying to break free.

"We've met more than once, lass, you should know me better by now."

"I have friends coming for me. Let me go." Kennis wished he'd listen to reason. Were they fated to meet in such adverse circumstances? Her heart pounded as he held her close.

"What friends, Eavan Malcolmson?" His eyes hardened. "And I suppose you expect me to find him for you," he said bitterly. "Or perhaps your two inept kinsmen?" He turned abruptly in his saddle. "Jocko," he said curtly. "Go to Kilcreag and see what you can discover. If you find anyone, bring them to me."

"Aye, Laird." Jocko wheeled his horse and cantered away.

"I wasn't speaking of Eavan," Kennis denied, a lump rising in her throat. "Please, sir," she said, swallowing her pride, "don't force me to go with you. My friends are expecting me."

"If they're nearby, Jocko will find them," he said, unconcerned. "But before we move on, has no one ever taught you to wash your face properly?" He drew a clean linen handkerchief from his pocket, lifted her chin with his hand and carefully wiped off the splattered mud on her cheeks and brow.

"There, that's better," he said in approval. "Now you don't look as much like the forlorn, lost waif that you are."

She opened her mouth to protest again.

"Close your mouth, lass." The corner of his mouth lifted in a crooked half-smile. "Don't you know I'm teasing?"

Taken aback, Kennis was speechless. Confounded man. He always seemed to do the unexpected when she lowered her guard.

Without any more ado, he gave his horse the office, leading the way up the track toward Craignish.

* * *

"They're leavin', Daly," Fergus said. "We'd best follow. Dinna Kate say this track leads to Craignish?"

"Aye, she did. But what can we do, storm the castle, just the two o' us? We lost our chance, I think," he said, annoyed with his own failure to properly handle the situation.

The two men waited a few minutes, discreetly following the entourage. Closing the distance on foot would be difficult. Quickly losing sight of the swift horses, the pair grew discouraged. Among the McCallum's, the two men were reputed to be the finest trackers in the whole clan. If the Laird of the MacDougalls and his tail diverted from this path, they would uncover the trail.

The rain poured over Daly and Fergus, wearily trudging upon the winding track to Craignish Castle. The ground grew slippery and walking became treacherous. Soon it would be dark and the men desperately needed a rest. The feeling that Kennis was in danger nagged at both men as they pressed on. Plus, the warmth early in the day had brought out the midges. Maybe the cool evening air would discourage the pesky insects.

"Dratted creatures!" Fergus swatted his neck. "How's a man to be rid o' them?"

"The only way's t' get *away*, I'm sure. Fergus, have ye noticed the mist risin'? I dinna like it. We'd best pitch camp before it gets too thick, the *gloamin's* fallin' fast."

"'Tis a shame," he agreed, "when we're so close." Plodding along, they searched for shelter, hoping to find a dry patch to bed down for the night.

"I've a strange feelin' we passed this way before," Fergus said. "I feel like we're movin' in circles."

"Ye're scarin' me, lad," Daly said. "Ye dinna know how verra much." He sighed. "There's naught t' do now but get some sleep. We've a long day ahead o' us tomorrow. We'll roast that bird ye caught, and feel better after we've eaten a morsel. I'm fair near starved to death."

"Me too," Fergus said, smiling a little. "Take heart, ye'll nae faint while I'm with ye on the trail. A full stomach and ye'll sleep like a babe."

* * *

Safely tucked in the circle of Alistair's arm, Kennis found it hard to sit still. Pressed against his warmth, she was tempted to relax and enjoy the ride in cool night air. Suddenly, she stiffened, remembering their last meeting. He'd falsely accused her at Castle Moil. How could she possibly forget? And now he held her captive in his arms.

Tilting her head, she spoke to him over her shoulder. "I hope you're satisfied with yourself, sir. I've had plenty of time to think about you, Alistair McConacher, and how boorishly you behaved when you visited Castle Moil."

"So you've been thinking of me, eh?" He laughed, warm and low. "And to set the record straight, that's not my name. Alistair MacDougall at your service, mistress."

"Another deception," she said, disgusted, unable to think of a fitting remark to put him in his place. Could this situation get any worse?

"True, a minor one but not unforgivable, I hope. Is that all you have to say to your rescuer?"

"As long as your name's not Campbell, I've no complaint, except that I don't wish to go with you, wherever you're going," she said. "And if I thought of you at all," she added, warming to the occasion, "'twas not in a positive light. I've longed to report your villainous behavior to my grandfather."

"Your grandfather, mistress, had the bonnie idea to introduce me to you as a McConacher. And though my surname's not Campbell," he said humorously, "I'm afraid you've fallen into the, ah, arms of a Campbell. My mother's cousin to Argyll, and you're going to Craignish Castle."

"I suppose you can't help your vile antecedents," she said acidly as her stomach churned. Craignish Castle, home of Campells, and kinsman to the greedy duke himself! How could Grandad abide the man?

"Nor can you, since I know you have them," he retorted, "not mentioning any names. And now that you've examined my lineage and found it wanting," he said dryly, "I need to know what else you've not told me about your current escapade, and why you ran away from Skye. Farrell was very unhappy you chose to abandon his charge."

"'Tis no business of yours," she said tartly. "What did you do to Farrell, beat him?"

"Now that's where you're mistaken, my lass." His voice grew cool. "I found you on my property near my home. That fact alone makes it my business and," he said, his temper rising, "I did nothing to Farrell because your foolhardy behavior was to be expected. Him, I trust implicitly."

"I don't see why it should, and I'm not your lass."

"You will," he said gently, ignoring her rebuttal, "if I have to force it from you.

"You wouldn't dare!" She stiffened, glancing up at the hard line of his jaw.

"Don't defy me, mistress," he warned.

She shrugged. "If you must know, I'm seeking out a kinsman."

"I know that much, but who and why?"

Startled, she drew in her breath. "I told you on the galley that I was seeking someone who is close to me. You refused to help." Against her will, Kennis found that she didn't like for him to be upset with her. She'd have preferred to establish a good rapport and harmony between them.

"Not true," he reminded her with good grace. "I offered my services which you declined."

"I couldn't tell you all of my circumstances, sir." She softened a little, recalling his offer to help her.

"You might have trusted me," he said on a wishful note as his arm tightened about her waist.

"How could I have known you were an acquaintance of my grandfather? I can't spread my real name abroad." She sucked in a breath at the feel of his strong arms about her.

"No excuse. You're not fit to be wandering around Scotland on your own, putting your nose into the affairs of unscrupulous men."

She wriggled uncomfortably in his arms and he instinctively tightened the circle. "You're impossible, sir. If it weren't for an accident, my kinsmen would be with me even now."

"Accident, mistress?" he scoffed. "Like the accident you barely avoided by your foolish behavior on a ship named the *Faioleag* bound for Port Eilidh last spring? As I recall, a day or so before we docked there was a violent storm, and a young woman of my recent acquaintance who had no reason for being on deck was nearly washed overboard. If I hadn't been conveniently near, she most surely would've drowned."

He added kindling to the fire he was deliberately building. "Or the occasion you mentioned aboard my galley where a wellborn lady, also of my recent acquaintance, stowed away and made an utter nuisance of herself. Need I repeat the incident on Skye which," he said sourly, "I was obliged to repeat to your grandfather when you disappeared, and also the dire need to rescue you from a villain like Denoon?"

He continued to catalogue her misadventures. "I leave you with Farrell, a man whom I trust daily with my life to look after you for your own protection and you flee into the night. What am I to do with you, lass, what am I supposed to think?" he said, perplexed. "Now I find you injured and unattended near my own castle. I wonder, how can one lass possibly be the cause of so much trouble?"

Kennis flushed in embarrassment, forced to acknowledge the justice of his words. Fortunately, dusk had fallen and he couldn't see her red face. "You heaved me over your shoulder without a by-your-leave," she declared in her own defense. "It was intolerable, sir. I also told you why I was aboard your galley," she said disagreeably, "not that you believed me. I was forced to endure your insults and high-handed behavior."

"'Twas merely practical, lass." He ignored her ill temper. "I had to grip the bulwark and we'd have been swept overboard if I'd held you in both arms. I confess I was tempted, but 'twas not the moment to seek our pleasure," he taunted, his voice low in her ear. "In fact, you remind me of a forfeit that I must exact from you in payment for your audacity."

He was baiting her again! Miffed, she grew silent, not knowing or caring how she responded. If she denied his taunts, he'd persist and continue to twist the conversation to his advantage. Tired and in pain, she'd gladly have rested her head on his shoulder if only he wasn't such a scoundrel. Impossible man.

Fey, almost reading her mind, he spoke softly into her ear. "You might lean your head back, 'twould be more comfortable. I assure you I won't bite or tell tales."

She resisted a short while longer and finally, weariness overtook her as she gave in to his persuasions. The rhythmic beating of his heart combined with the gait of his horse, made her drowsy. *Forever*—the word appeared out of nowhere; she could remain here in the warmth of his embrace, his arm supporting her as her head lay on his shoulder, forever. Suddenly, she jerked out of her stupor. Such unpredictable feelings! What was it about this man that caused her to be so undecided?

Her thoughts flitted from one meeting to the next—their first encounter on the ship when he'd indecorously tossed her over his shoulder, the night on the galley, the inn at Port Eilidh, her rescue from Denoon and her recent flight from Farrell. Their brief acquaintance was a jumbled maze of adventure and mishap, and somehow he managed to intrude on her life as much as he occupied her thoughts. She sighed, encircled in the warmth of his arm, enjoying the sense of security and comfort his strength provided. *How fickle I am.*

* * *

Alistair heard the sigh and felt her relax against him. He closed the circle of his arm around her more securely, hoping that she was comfortable. If only she'd trust him. Perhaps this evening she'd converse with him over dinner.

Kennis, he mused, beautiful. She truly is a bonnie lass. The mystery attached to her was solved and as he'd suspected, she was a member of the gentry, her family impoverished after the '45.

John Dhu McKinnon confirmed that she was Robert McCallum's daughter. The amazing resemblance she bore to the lad Robbie and the Laird Robert was proof enough for him. A man couldn't deny his flesh and blood, and the family must have Morrison connections. *What Morrison do I know?* The images that rose before him bore little resemblance to this girl. It made sense that she adopted a family surname during her journey.

His brow furrowed and he wondered what interest the villain Eavan Malcolmson had in the McCallum's. The treacherous man wasn't given to benevolence without the expectation of a return. *I suppose I could give him grace and believe that he's genuinely concerned for their welfare.* He smirked. *On the other hand, 'tis more likely he's involved in some diabolical plot to make their lives more miserable once he'd gained their trust.*

His eyes glittered in the darkness. And what of the news he'd received about Cameron Campbell and Eavan Malcolmson's association, was it coincidental? He must have Farrell contact Conor for information about Eavan's relationship to the McCallum family, and especially to the lass. Some mischief was brewing, he felt it in his bones.

He continued to puzzle over Eavan's part in the riddle as Craignish came into view, lights twinkling in the near distance. A Campbell stronghold, it now belonged to him, courtesy of the Duke of Argyll. Ian McColl, his Constable, would be waiting with news. Business must wait, he must see to the lass' comfort first.

The sentries expected him and the gatekeeper hurried to admit the horsemen. Alistair called to one of the lads in the small courtyard as the horses' hooves clattered on the cobblestones. "Here, Rory, come take the reins. Where is Ian McColl?"

"I'm right here, Laird." Ian stood waiting on the steps leading to the main hall.

"Good. We have an unexpected guest," he said. "Is Kate still here, or any of the housemaids? We'll need a chamber and an extra bath prepared before dinner."

Ian spied Kennis in the laird's arms. "Is the lass hurt, sir?" he said, worried.

"Not too badly."

He felt her stir and tightened them for a moment. "Awake, lass?"

Kennis felt too comfortable within the ring of Alistair's arms. "Aye."

"Here Ian, take her while I dismount."

Ian obeyed, helping Kennis as she slid from the horse's back. She stumbled, stiff from dozing in the saddle. "'Tis all right now, lassie," he said softly. "I told you to stay put at the first."

She mutely gazed at him.

Alistair, overhearing this exchange, raised his eyebrows in question to Ian.

"When ye're ready, Laird, I'll attend to business and give ye an account of the last month."

"I look forward to our meeting," he said.

"Aye, sir," Ian said, noting the lifted brow. "And if ye'll pardon me, I'll see to a room for the lass."

He nodded and turned to Kennis. "Can you walk?"

"Of course I can," she said without hesitation.

He gestured toward the steps. "After you, then."

She gingerly stepped forward on her injured ankle, lightly placing her weight on her foot, limping ahead a step or two, and conscious of Alistair's scrutiny. The pain was excruciating.

He snorted. "If we continue to proceed in this manner, we may eat our dinner by tomorrow morning. Let me help you."

"Nay," she said, not wanting to be obligated to him. "I'm just stiff from riding, that's all."

"Is that so?" he mocked. "Strange, I rather thought that you couldn't walk." He moved toward her and she found herself in his arms again. Then, he carried her up the stairs and through the open doorway into a well-lit hall.

"Which room are you having prepared for her?"

"I dinna think 'tis ready yet, Laird," Ian said. "Just a few more minutes."

Alistair turned and set her down in an armchair near the fire. He lifted a crystal decanter from the table and poured a glass half-full of honeyed wine. "Here, drink this," he commanded, handing it to her.

She gratefully received it and took a sip. At present, it didn't matter if he told her what to do but in future, she'd make her will known. The warm fire in the grate and the sweet potion she consumed heated her all the way down to her toes.

A small figure appeared at her side. "Mistress Kennis," Cailan said. "I'm so glad to see ye safe." She curtseyed to Alistair. "Beg your pardon, Laird, but the chamber's ready."

Alistair set down his glass. So, there was more to this tale. He'd see Ian McColl later and hear it straight. Leaning over, he reached for Kennis, and lifted her into his arms. He followed Cailan across the Great Hall and up the turret stairs.

Chapter 6

Intercepted

Daly awoke with a start.

Opening his eyes, he stared straight at a pair of leather boots. A sword point pressed against his neck as he started to rise. "Be still, lad," a deep voice intoned, "if ye know what's good for ye." He couldn't see his assailant's face nor did he recognize the voice.

The soft neigh of approaching horses sounded in the glen and the captain signaled to one of his men. "Here," he said, "stay with this one while I fetch the Laird. Don't let him out of your sight." He stepped away and moved toward the muffled sound of hooves on damp earth. Peering through the trees, he stepped onto the track as the approaching men drew near. The leader lifted his hand and the men halted. He walked his horse forward. "So, what have you to report?"

"There are two men who fit your description in the glen. We've just now discovered them."

The laird dismounted, handing his reins to his henchman. "Here, I'll go see if it's who I'm looking for," he nodded to his captain. "You come with me."

The two men pushed aside the underbrush and strode into the clearing. It was a secluded spot, and he was surprised that his men had even discovered it. Two burly figures were held fast; one lay on the ground, the other had his head down on his knees. He went to the first man on the ground and smiled to himself.

"Well," he said, amused. "What have we got here?"

Daly's eyes grew wide. He tried to rise, and the sword point pressed harder against his neck. "Ye can tell this *gowk* to move that blade away before he draws blood."

"Here, Dugald, let the man be." Dugald removed the blade and sheathed it, and Eavan extended his hand. Daly gripped Eavan's extended hand and was pulled to his feet.

"Shall I let this one go too, Laird?" Eavan's henchman asked. He held Fergus by the hair, a dirk at his back.

"Aye, go ahead."

Daly grasped his liberator's arm. "Ye're a welcome sight, Eavan Malcolmson, and that's a fact."

"I'm glad to hear it."

Fergus brushed the dry leaves from his clothing before walking toward the two of them. "I'll second that, but what brings ye here?" he asked, quickly adding, "I'm right glad to see ye all the same."

Eavan studied the men. "Where's Kennis?" he asked abruptly. "She's not with you?" He looked from one to the other. "Never fear, I've had a letter from John Dhu requesting my assistance."

"Is that so?" Daly was skeptical.

He continued with a touch of impatience. "Devil take it, I know you two don't trust me, but you're going to have to this time. I received a letter yesterday morning. John Dhu requested that I keep my eyes open for you and Kennis. I immediately mounted a search and found nothing. Tonight I find you, and no Kennis. Where is she?"

"What's in it for ye?"

"Nothing, I say!" His anger flared. "I've been solicited, as I already said, to find Kennis and return her to her mother and grandfather at Castle Moil. And if you don't believe me, you'll have to return with me to Malcolm House to see the letter for yourself. Does that satisfy you?"

Fergus and Daly glanced at one another. "Very well, then, we'll tell ye all that we can. But first, speakin' plain, we're in dire need of sustenance," he said candidly. "What have ye got in your packs? Our resources are a mite limited."

Eavan's smile returned. "Niall," he said to his captain. "Find these men something to eat and have Dugald stir up that fire." He turned to Fergus and Daly and motioned to them to sit down. "Let's sit while you tell me your story and have something to eat."

Before long, Dugald had a cheery blaze going and Niall returned with ale, bread and cheese. He took out his *skean dhu*, sliced the bread, and pierced it along with the cheese before toasting it over the crackling fire. Soon enough, several slices of toasted cheese were ready for the men. He turned to Eavan first, who waved it aside. "Let these poor starved men have it, I'll wait." Niall then offered a slice to Daly and Fergus who received it gladly. Wiping his fingers on his breeches, Daly related their adventures.

At the end of Daly's recital, Eavan's eyes glittered. "Well, there's only one thing to do. We must go to Craignish and retrieve her."

"That's what we're planning to do. We couldna keep up with the horses, and night fell too soon for us to make our way there. Do ye have extra horses?"

He shook his head. "I'll have to send two of my men home on foot," he said, thinking aloud, "to prepare for our journey to Skye."

"I'm thinkin' our lassie willna return to Skye," Daly offered. "We've come this far, she'll want to travel to Dunchalum."

"Nay," he said firmly. "She must return to the McKinnon. 'Tisn't safe here."

Daly and Fergus eyed him with suspicion. "And why nae? She'll be safe enough with us."

"Safe with you?" he scoffed. "Look where you've got her, in the clutches of the Campbells."

"I thought the Laird of Craignish was the MacDougall chief."

"He is, but he's half Campbell and is thick with Argyll. I wouldn't trust him and neither should you."

Since Daly and Fergus knew that their laird, John Dhu McKinnon, favored the MacDougall, no immediate reply was forthcoming. In the present circumstance, they needed to accept Eavan's offer to recover Kennis, and let the lass decide where she would go afterward. Whether she chose the road to Dunchalum or to Skye, her faithful henchmen would stand by her decision.

"We'd best be off," Eavan said, rising. He called to his captain. "Niall, have two of the men put this fire out and return home on foot. They'll have to lend their horses to these men."

Chapter 7

Craignish Castle

Chilled, Kennis pressed on through the dense foliage.

A cloak of moisture penetrated her clothing, tangled, damp strands of hair clung to her forehead. Suddenly, she slipped and lost her foothold on the uneven ground. The path before her descended further into a heavy mist and unidentifiable voices urged her to march on. Wary, she stepped forward, a sense of joy sprouting within her as the voices became more distinct. A shadow loomed overhead and in a panic, she bolted upright, nearly knocking heads with Siusan McAllister.

"There now, mistress," Siusan comforted. "Ye must've fallen asleep, ye're that weary. I've only been away a few minutes, and the Laird's impatiently awaitin' your presence at supper."

Sleepy, she stared at Siusan, hearing her voice yet not comprehending what she said. At the words *the Laird*, it dawned on her in full force. The odious Alistair MacDougall was holding her captive at Craignish Castle. In addition, here was her new friend, Siusan, come to wait on her. "I don't want to have supper with him," she declared. "He is the vilest, most—" Words could not sufficiently describe him to her satisfaction.

"The most handsome man ye've seen of late?" Siusan teased.

She rolled her eyes. "Nay, Siusan. He's the most irritating man I've met of late, and more."

"Well, that opinion's of no account here and ye'd best keep it to yourself." Siusan turned away. "I've brought some fresh clothing for ye, left here by Mistress Ona. I'm sure ye'll find something to suit."

"Mistress Ona?" she asked.

"The Laird's sister, and a bonnie lass, she is."

She rose from the four-poster bed onto which Alistair had gently laid her and grimaced. Her ankle was little better.

"Here now, I'm to help ye as much as I can." Siusan moved a screen in front of her for privacy and continued to chatter, flinging items of clothing onto the bed and over the top of the screen. "When ye're ready, I'll call for the Laird and he'll carry you down to the little dining room."

"Can't I just have a tray sent here? I'd rather not have to endure his company."

Siusan grinned. "I'm afraid that's nae possible. The laird's already a step ahead of ye, and instructed me nae to let ye cajole me into doing any such thing."

"Did he?" She snorted. "And why does he think he can order me about? He may be your master but he's not mine!" The nerve of the man, up to his usual tricks.

"Faith, mistress, he's like any other man," she said sagely. "Men must have their own way in things, the wee ones as well as the larger. 'Tis like the Laird, always trying to get Master Duncan to do what he says without question."

"Master Duncan?" Kennis lifted an inquiring brow.

Siusan smiled. "His younger brother. I guess ye wouldna know. Are ye finished yet? I'll ring the bell."

"Oh, very well," she said peevishly. "I'm starving, so I guess I'll endure his insufferable company."

Siusan's contagious laughter filled the room and Kennis, caught up in her mirth, failed to hear the door open when Cailan peeked in and led Alistair into the room. He stood on the threshold, waiting, and she looked up to see him steadily regarding her. A tender smile lit his dark eyes.

Siusan immediately bobbed a curtsey and Kennis pushed herself up from the armchair in front of the hearth. He strode forward, Siusan winked at her from behind his back and Cailan giggled. When he swept her into his arms, she made a face at the mother and daughter choking back their laughter.

Alistair carried her to the dining room, an elegant little apartment well suited to a family party, and set her down at a round table set for two before the cheery fire. She looked about her with interest. It was a comfortable room, and clearly showed a woman's touch. She remembered that his mother and sister came here to visit, and was sure that the two women had a hand in the arrangement of the furnishings. He settled her in a chair and waited expectantly. Farrell entered the room followed by Kate McColl, Siusan's aunt.

"Why Kate," she blurted. "I didn't expect to see you here."

"And I dinna expect to see ye again so soon either, mistress."

"And do I have you to thank for this fine supper?" she inquired, observing the abundance of food spread before her.

"Aye, but with the Laird and his lads here, more's always expected."

Alistair laughed softly. Kennis glanced at him and at Farrell, who always seemed to have a twinkle in his eye.

"And you, Farrell, are well?"

He nodded. "Aye, lass, thank ye for askin'."

Alistair nodded his dismissal and the two left the room. He pulled out his chair and sat opposite her. "Would you join me in saying grace, lass?" He reached his hand toward her across the table.

Surprised, she extended her hand and laid it in his larger one. Kennis marveled as he prayed, giving thanks for the bounty set before them and for the blessings of God. The warmth from his strong hand spread through her. When he'd finished, she raised her head, and their eyes met and held. After an interminable moment, she turned away, swallowing hard, unsettled by the intimacy of the moment.

He carved the fowl and offered her a slice. They ate in silence for several minutes, each offering no gambit upon which to chew. The time flew by and she was astonished at the easy camaraderie they enjoyed. Perhaps he thought better of her now and regretted the rash words he'd spoken on the battlements at Moil.

The clock struck half past ten. She grew sleepy, more like a well-fed kitten than the outraged tigress she'd felt like earlier when confronted by Siusan's teasing. He sensed her mood; she was sure of it when next he spoke.

"You're content, mistress," he observed. "You approve of all?"

"Aye, though it's been a long day."

"For you or for me?" he asked, nonchalant.

She gazed at him, confused. "Why, for both of us, I imagine."

He smiled. "I don't mean to tease you, lass. I'd like to know what I'm to do with you."

"Do with me?" She blinked, more confused than before. "I believe it was you who decided, nay, insisted that I come here."

"I couldn't leave you in the forest alone," he said matter-of-factly.

She admitted that his statement was true. "Perhaps not, but I'm not without friends in these parts."

"Nay, you seem to make friends easily enough, I only hope that you can keep them."

His words pierced her afresh and she couldn't hide her feelings. "What do you mean by this new slur on my character? I'm not cruel, or an unfaithful friend."

"I didn't intend for my words to sound as they did, lass," he said with regret. He'd not intended to inflict a new wound upon her, damaging their new found amity. "What I mean is that the company you keep could send mixed signals to those who are genuinely concerned about your welfare."

Eavan, he means Eavan. "Perhaps you judge too harshly."

His eyes narrowed. "I think not. You know exactly who, and possibly what, I mean."

She didn't have the opportunity to respond. A firm rap on the door interrupted their conversation. Just as well. The subject didn't bode well and she loathed being the initiator of another dispute between them.

"Well?" Alistair said curtly as Farrell entered.

"Beg your pardon, Laird, we've unexpected company."

"Indeed?"

Farrell's expression gave way to his perturbation.

"Who, out with it."

"Eavan Malcolmson, and the lass's two kinsmen."

Kennis jumped up, wincing in pain. She dropped back into the dainty embroidered chair. "Fergus and Daly? Thank God."

He nodded. "What should I do with them, sir?"

"What do they want?" he said shortly.

"They're demandin' to see the lass, and I told them she was in no condition to be disturbed."

Alistair rose from his chair and walked over to the fire, put his boot on the grate and stood for several moments, deep in thought. Finally, he turned and addressed her. "What is your desire, mistress?"

"I must see them," she said. "We were set upon in the woods near here and they've been looking for me, which is why I didn't want to come to Craignish in the first place."

Alistair nodded to Farrell and stared back at the fire. "Bring them here."

"Aye, Laird." He departed the room, giving Kennis a searching look as he passed by her.

She didn't understand Alistair's response and apparent disinterest. Within a matter of minutes, the door burst open and Daly and Fergus tumbled in, followed by Eavan.

With joy, the two men crushed her in their arms. "Lass, I hope ye dinna scare us e'er again the way ye hae these last two days."

Weary, she smiled. "But Daly, it's turned out well after all. We're together again, and we can continue on our journey."

"I think not." Eavan interrupted the happy reunion and cast a wary look at Alistair as he entered the room.

Kennis followed his gaze. Alistair hadn't turned from the fire to greet the men. She was mystified over the relationship between him and Eavan. The two men detested one another and couldn't be in one another's presence without spewing mutual dislike. In fact, dislike was a mild word for their enmity. Returning to Eavan, she fixed her eyes on him.

"What do you mean, *you think not*, Eavan? Who are you to say where I go or don't go?"

He stood his ground. "I've a letter from your grandfather saying he desires for me, provided I found you, to return you to Skye at his bidding."

"To Skye!" she exclaimed, taken aback. "Where is this letter, Eavan? Show it to me."

"I don't have it here. 'Tis in Kilmartin, at Malcolm House."

She crossed her arms, suspicious at his tale. "Maybe there's no letter at all."

"Oh, there's a letter, alright," he said, an edge to his voice, "and you'd best heed my words."

One more hindrance to her plan had arisen. Although Eavan had proved a friend, she'd not permit him to divert her from her purpose nor would she submit to his demands. "Heed your words! I most certainly will not, and you can't make me. Daly, Fergus and I will proceed on as planned."

Eavan was astounded. "You'd go against your grandfather's wish?"

"If 'tis his command, then I need proof of it."

"You expect me to retrieve this letter," he repeated, incredulous, "and show it to you first before you'll come with me."

"Aye." The stubbornness that Daly and Fergus were well acquainted with reared its willful head. "I do."

"And in the meantime, what will you do?" His lip curled in a sneer, anger overruling his better judgment. "Sit tamely here at Craignish, currying his favor by offering yours?"

Kennis colored, furious at the implication in his words. Before she could reply, Alistair turned away from the fire and strode across the room. He grabbed Eavan's collar. "Apologize you," he gritted, "or I'll not be responsible for my actions."

"What if I don't?" Eavan choked out, gripping Alistair's forearms.

"You won't live long enough to regret it." Alistair tightened his hold and shook him. "Remember, you're on Campbell ground."

Campbell ground. She'd almost forgotten that he was half Campbell. Since her grandfather approved of him despite the connection, maybe she shouldn't object, either. Her presence of mind returned with Alistair's next statement.

"I've already decided what to do with the lass and I'll brook no argument." He thrust Eavan away and addressed the assembled company. "Tomorrow we ride for Inveraray." She started to protest but he raised his hand to silence her.

"I'm taking you there so that my mother can look after you. You'll not find the company unpleasant. My sister is there also, and more guests are coming to the entertainments that they have planned together with Argyll. I've every intention of sending a message to John Dhu to tell him of my plans and to bid him, your mother and sister to join us if they so desire, or I will take you to Moil myself as soon as possible, to see that you make no more mischief."

She couldn't believe her ears. Inveraray and a host of Campbells! He meant every word, and she would find it difficult to escape him.

Daly spoke up on her behalf. "I dinna think, sir, 'tis in the lass's best interest."

"Don't you?" Alistair glared at him. "You've bungled your responsibility toward her long enough, whatever your previous experience. Farrell will show you where to sleep, and get you something to eat in the kitchen."

Thus dismissed, Daly and Fergus vacated the room. Eavan remained behind and unwisely broached the subject once again concerning Kennis' departure from Craignish. "Lass," he attempted to soothe her feelings, "I'm sorry for my words."

She glared at him, livid at his insistence that she return to Skye and at his implications. Over the weeks since they had first met, her feelings toward him had undergone a significant change. His present behavior confirmed her former misgivings about him. "You have the audacity to insist that I travel with you after what you said and apologize as an afterthought? Nay, Eavan, not unless you show me that your letter is real."

"Very well. I'll leave tonight, and prove it to you on the morrow." He departed in a rage, slamming the door behind him.

A veil of silence fell over the chamber and the tranquil atmosphere vanished. The truce she and Alistair had established was now broken. Oh, how she desired to restore the brief harmony they'd so recently enjoyed. *Mercy me, I'm more confused than I knew.* Weary of body and soul, her shoulders sagged as she crossed her hands in her lap. The only prayer she could offer up was one for peace and understanding with the man who now stood distant across the room. Although it seemed impossible that the two would ever be united in thought or purpose, all things were possible with God. In Him, her very life depended upon hope for all good things concerning their future.

* * *

Alistair examined the papers brought to him by Ian McColl, constable of Craignish. Farrell sat in the chair recently occupied by Kennis throughout the evening, waiting to receive orders for the journey to Inveraray on the morrow.

"Well, Farrell," Alistair said, satisfied, "I believe we'll have a victory in court soon, according to this letter from Mathias Campbell. The information I provided was well received by the court, and it seems there's more willingness among the members of the government to grant pardons to members of the Scottish gentry, particularly the sons of deceased lairds. As to the property, a fine will be levied and if it can be paid, there's hope that it may be restored to its rightful owners. This is much better than I anticipated."

"'Twill mean a lot to the lass," Farrell observed.

"Provided we can find her brother," Alistair said thoughtfully, cupping his hands behind his head as he leaned back in his chair. "I was disappointed when none of the men we picked up from Denoon proved to be the lad."

"If it had, I'm thinkin' the lass would be mighty pleased with ye."

Alistair raised his eyes to Farrell's. "I take it you have some other obscure thought behind the statement that you just made?"

"Nay," Farrell said, "not obscure at all, sir. I just figured that since ye're taken with the lass, it might do ye good to have a way to bring her round to your way of thinkin', a little persuasion, like."

"You think I'm smitten with this girl, do you? I'm sorry to disappoint you," he said calmly. "Circumstance has brought us together and necessity bids me to assist her. I'm not taken with any lass, Farrell."

"We'll see," he said, wise to Alistair's moods. "I thought ye promised the McKinnon ye'd look out for the lass."

"I did. He asked me to do so and I couldn't refuse the favor as a gentleman, a Highlander or as a friend."

Farrell made no reply. He'd known Alistair since they were lads. Eventually the man would know his mind, recognize the truth and hear his heart speaking. Sometimes he just went the long way around to a short goal, took the high road instead of the low and made things just downright difficult.

Alistair tipped his chair forward, pushed back and the two men rose. "Good night and sleep well. To Inveraray tomorrow."

"Sweet dreams," Farrell returned, a humorous glint in his eye that wasn't lost upon Alistair who, in spite of his denials, would indeed dream of the winsome, bonnie lass asleep upstairs in Ona's bedchamber.

Chapter 8

The Road to Inveraray

Blast the man! Eavan hurried out of the heavy oaken doors of Malcolm House, down the steps and into the courtyard.

Late last night, he'd arrived home to find Niall Malcolm awaiting him with news. Cameron Campbell was up to his usual tricks, plotting more deceptions and intrigues than a man ought to have time to consider. He was a regular *blatherskate*.

He stuffed the letter from John Dhu McKinnon into his jack. Kennis would be forced to come with him when she read it. He doubted that even she would flout this missive from her grandfather. However, she was traveling to Inveraray today under the auspices of Alistair MacDougall. The man had no problem ignoring authority and a letter posed little threat.

Eavan believed that the best thing to do was bide his time. He berated himself for his behavior at Craignish; he might have persuaded her to come with him to Skye if he'd not lost his temper and insulted her. Instead, now he must travel to Inveraray with his own men and demand satisfaction based on the letter. Argyll would see the wisdom of following John Dhu's instructions and be glad to be rid of the girl and her kin.

Eavan suffered no illusions about the attitude of the Campbells of Inveraray towards the McCallum's. Kennis' family had served the Campbells as liege lords in the past but a bitter dispute caused all ties to be severed. The Malcolm branch of the family had stepped in, filling the void, and made their own fortunes.

Cameron Campbell was the one remaining Campbell closely associated to his family and Eavan wished he'd never had any connection with the man. Still, he was very close to achieving his goal and Cameron was the means to an end. He must silence Cameron over his intentions concerning her brother, Rob. It was best that she thought him gone forever and not know the contemptible part he'd played.

If their well-laid plans succeeded, she'd believe what he told her to be the truth. When they married, this was undoubtedly the best course of action, to put behind old sorrows and move on to live a new life together. He vowed to himself that he would make her happy.

*   *   *

Kennis' horse plodded along the Dunadd Road toward Kilmartin Glen. She hoped to get a glimpse of Malcolm House but figured that Alistair would circumvent it just to avoid Eavan. She admitted to herself that after the scene at Craignish the previous night, she felt safer with Alistair MacDougall and his men-at-arms than with Eavan, even though she might be going against her grandfather's command. And, she was uneasy about the notion of meeting his mother and staying at Inveraray. It would be difficult enough to be among so many Campbells and she a poor McCallum. At least, she thought glumly, to their way of thinking.

Her sad want of a decent wardrobe confirmed it. Her new dresses were at Castle Moil; she had no reason to bring them along. She sighed and looked down at her woolen skirt and scuffed up boots. She'd worn them to America and back again but Inveraray Castle wasn't a humble cottage in the Highlands or a three-storied townhouse on a narrow, cobbled street in America. She would be humiliated in front of everyone, including Alistair. He had absolutely no idea what she would suffer.

When they passed through Kilmartin, Daly pointed out the historical wonders that marked the beginnings of Scotland. She wished she had time to examine Dunadd hill, the rock carvings, the footprint and the wild boar, which were symbolic of the beginnings of the nation. Loch Awe and the glorious heights above it drew her gaze. Her beloved home lay in those misty blue hills. She was so very close yet so incredibly far away. It would be no easy task to escape Alistair MacDougall now. She'd best put it from her mind.

The journey would take them past Fincharn Castle before they left the main road to journey through the Highlands, approaching Inveraray from the south by taking a northern route along Loch Fyne.

At noon, the group halted to partake of a quick luncheon. Alistair drew near to Kennis and dismounted. He'd not spoken to her so far on the journey, except to bid her a gruff "Good morning". Disappointment nagged at her, lowering her spirits, and she hoped it wasn't evident. Daly and Fergus had kept watch over her, flanking her on either side throughout the ride.

"Ready to dismount, lass?" he asked. "There's a nice spot near the loch. You'll join me there." It was half request, half command. Kennis nodded and allowed him to clasp her by the waist and lift her from the saddle. She slid from the horse's back into his arms and her heart leapt. He didn't look down at her but turned and strode to a flat boulder, nodding to Daly and Fergus to come to her.

He departed briefly and returned, bringing a basket with him packed by Kate McColl. Daly and Fergus sat nearby, partaking of their own meal and keeping a careful watch on their mistress and the MacDougall.

She gazed out at the rippling water as he unpacked the lunch basket. The sun seemed to brighten overhead and she felt warmed by its rays. She turned to Alistair, noting the unruly lock of hair that constantly escaped his cueue. The sudden urge to grasp, to finger the silken strand consumed her. What was wrong with her?

When he glanced up and looked quickly away, her heart sank, her appetite diminishing when he frowned. Somehow, she'd disappointed him, lost the intimacy from the night before forever. She sighed and reached for a bannock, nibbling on it without enthusiasm.

* * *

Alistair glanced away from her, his mind in turmoil. Farrell's words rang in his ears. *Taken with the lass.* Her steady regard unnerved him. He was unable to maintain eye contact and wondered at his own sudden cowardice. He slowly chewed the cold meat he'd selected from the viands laid out on the cloth before him, and wondered what he should do or say next to set her at her ease. He'd obviously done something to overset her. She'd not eaten a thing, just toyed with the bannock.

"Is the food not to your liking, lass?" he asked. Fool.

She jumped, startled by his voice. "Oh, 'tis fine, I was just thinking about other things, that's all."

"What other things?" He was polite, hoping that she'd converse as easily with him as she had the night before.

Her face colored. "Of Robbie, and my father."

"I see." He could think of no word to comfort her, not desiring to impart false hopes. "You were close to your brother?"

She gazed at him, uncertain, wishing she could unburden her heart. "Aye, we're very close."

Her words to him on the galley concerning a man that she desperately sought became clear as the fog lifted from his brain. "He's the one for whom you've been searching."

"Aye," she said. "I went to the Americas with the Gilmores hoping that I'd discover some clue as to his whereabouts," she said, a little sad. "But I learned nothing of importance."

"How long were you away?" he asked, curious.

"Four years. I was sixteen when I left. It seemed a very long time."

The lass had courage, then. In truth, she'd demonstrated it on more than one occasion. And, he mused, the lad Rob must be nineteen or twenty by now, nearly the same age.

The sun stood high in the sky. "We need to be moving on. Are you finished eating, lass?"

She nodded. "I'll just take this for the road." She picked up another oatcake and stuffed it into her pocket.

Alistair rose, gave her his hand and pulled her to her feet. Before he lifted her from the flat surface of the rock, he gathered his courage and gazed into her eyes. What he saw reflected there terrified yet stirred the fire that already burned within him.

* * *

Kennis gazed at the edifice towering above her in the grey twilight and her heart sank. Inveraray Castle loomed ahead, a giant pile of stones and high towers tucked into the mountains of Argyll. No wonder the Campbells were so well protected. The fortress seemed impenetrable. She watched the iron yett rise and reluctantly urged her horse through the gates of the proud home of the Campbells. I'm a prisoner in the halls of my enemies, she thought with trepidation. Not only was the bailey full of Campbells but a company of redcoats had arrived just a few minutes before their party. She kept her eyes down, not wanting to attract unnecessary attention.

Alistair pulled her from the horse and gathered her into his arms. He mounted the granite steps and she tensed. He glanced down at her.

His confident look cheered her, giving her courage. The tall doors swung open, revealing a bevy of liveried servants assembled to see the Highland lass that the Laird of MacDougall had brought into Inveraray's hallowed halls.

Murdoch, the butler, was attentive and efficient as ever. Clearing his throat, he commanded them to return to their duties, ridding the new arrivals of his intrusive compatriots. "How may I serve you, my lord?" he inquired.

"You may serve me by announcing my arrival to his grace and by preparing a chamber for this lady who has come to stay as my guest," he said with an air of authority. "A room close to my mother and sister would be preferable."

"Yes, of course, my lord. His grace is in his library, and I am available to escort the young lady to her chambers."

Alistair was annoyed. "You can't escort her, Murdoch. You may escort *us* since the lady is injured and can't manage the stairs."

"And my lady's bags?"

Kennis squirmed in Alistair's arms and he tightened his hold on her. "My lady's bags," he said imperiously, "have been lost. Where are my mother and sister?"

"The Lady Ona is in the blue saloon with the other guests, and Lady MacDougall has retired to her room for the evening."

"Good, then I'll see her before I speak with his grace."

Murdoch cleared his throat as he led the way up the stairs to the guest chambers. "Shall I order baths for you and the lady, as well as have dinner served in your rooms?"

Alistair grinned. "How well you know me, Murdoch. That will do nicely."

The butler paused again as he opened the door to Kennis' chamber.

"Out with it, man," Alistair said, over-conscious of the girl he held in his arms.

"Begging your pardon, sir," he said, doing his duty. "I cannot call this young woman *the lady* every time I must make reference to her or answer her call to do her bidding."

Kennis, silent until now and enjoying the exchange between Alistair and the butler, giggled. He looked down at her and smiled. "You may call her either Lady Kennis or Mistress McCallum, whichever she prefers."

Murdoch's eyes grew wide. "Very well, sir." He entered the room and lit several candelabra, revealing a rose and moss décor that made Kennis feel like she'd entered a spring garden. "The servants will arrive shortly with your baths, sir, madam." He departed, leaving the door ajar, walking with his slow dignified gait, making Kennis want to laugh at his self-importance.

Alistair set her into an overstuffed chair by the hearth. He knelt to stir up the fire, adding a log and kindling. When he finished, he rose and stared down at her. She waited, patient, until he spoke. "I'll send my mother to attend to you, and I probably won't see you until tomorrow morning. If you have a need, pull this cord and a servant will come." He faced her, hesitating. "I'm down the hall, the third door on the left, if you have want of me." He took a step away from her.

"Wait," she said, starting to rise.

He came straightaway to her side. "What is it?" he said, concerned. "Are you in pain?"

Her smile wobbled. "Nay, I just wanted to say thank you, for everything."

Gazing into her upturned face, he bent nearer. *Just one kiss.* His breath caught, and he pulled back just in time.

Spellbound, she stared at him, not able to move. He was going to kiss her!

He backed away. "Good night, lass," he said, in a hurry to leave. Neither one could afford to be caught in a compromising situation here at Inveraray. They would find themselves standing in front of the minister of the Kirk in a heartbeat. His mother would see to that. Rueful, he glanced at the door. At least Murdoch had the sense to leave it open upon exiting the room.

"Good night, Alistair," Kennis whispered, slowly sinking into the chair after he'd gone. "Kennis McCallum, what did you expect?" He'd have nothing to do with her. Surely, some lass from his own clan would lay claim to him, not one who had no worldly goods to offer.

She surveyed the opulent room. The lovely tapestries on the walls, the Turkish rugs on the floor, even the velvet bed-hangings depressed her further. She thought of her mother and all that she'd lost. The adjoining solar and garderobes bespoke wealth, a life of ease. Alone with her musings, she awaited his mother. She nervously twisted her shawl, wondering if his mother was equally formidable. What would the woman think of her?

She despaired of her own appearance. She looked exactly like what she was, the fatherless daughter of an impoverished clan, existing off the charity of relatives. Maybe it was a good thing that she couldn't easily stand and look into the mirror. She didn't want to face what might await her there.

Chapter 9

An Unwelcome Guest

Alistair headed straight to his mother's door.

He tapped lightly and her serving woman opened it, bobbing a curtsey, admitting him into her mistress' presence.

Lady Grear smiled in welcome. "Alistair, my love, you're back. Did you bring Duncan with you?"

"Nay, Mother, I'm afraid not," he said in a calm voice when he saw the alarm on her face. "Don't fear. I believe he's safe, otherwise I wouldn't be here. However, I could find no other traces of him."

She stood to her feet, in a worry over her youngest son. "How can you be sure if you couldn't find him? He can't possibly vanish into thin air."

Alistair was confident. "Nay, 'tis a hunch."

"A hunch, my love?" She raised her brows in gentle mockery. Turning to her listening maid, she dismissed her and sat back down in her rocking chair by the fire. "Now we may talk more comfortably."

"You received my message from Argyll?"

She nodded.

"Then you know I planned to track him to the Highlands. I felt he was pursuing the stag again." He ran his hand through his dark hair, the unruly lock springing back over his forehead. "Troublesome lad. He disobeyed me after I reprimanded him about his last escapade."

"You said that you went to the Highlands."

"Yes, to Dunchalum, and the village there. "Mother," he asked, curious, "do you know an old woman by name of Granny Jean?"

She laughed softly. "Granny Jean is still living? She was ancient when I was a girl." She sat back in her chair, a faraway look in her dark eyes.

"Then you do know her."

"I did, very well. It was long ago and I've not had the pleasure of renewing our acquaintance." She glanced at his tall form. "What did she tell you?"

He shook his head. "Nothing. She said your story was your own to tell."

Lady Grear let out a gurgling laugh. "She would say so." She paused, considering. "Perhaps another time I'll tell you a tale about my youth, which for all intents and purposes seems to have been forgotten except by a few of us." Her face clouded over, saddened by a distant memory from her past.

In a rush for her to visit Kennis, Alistair continued without responding to her confidence, more than aware that Kennis awaited down the hall. "There is something else I must speak with you about, and for which I need your immediate assistance."

Surprised, Lady Grear said mildly, "Aye, what is it?"

"It concerns the McCallum's." He plunged into the story, giving her a condensed and unembellished version of how he'd met Kennis on the road to Craignish after having visited the McKinnon on Skye. "And I brought her here to Inveraray to you, knowing that you'd be the best person to look after her until she can be returned to her family. I couldn't take her there right away because I must continue to search for Duncan."

Lady Grear was astonished. "Good heavens! You brought the poor girl here so quickly, all the way from Craignish, today? She must be exhausted! And she's injured?"

"Just a sprain, nothing serious," he said in his own defense.

Rising, she pulled the bell cord. "Then you must take me to her right away." A furrow knit her brows. "She's been waiting all of this time we were talking? You should have waited to give me news of Duncan." Her maidservant entered the room and she directed the woman to gather various items from the kitchen, and to join her in Kennis' room.

"Well, yes, but I thought you would want to hear of Duncan first."

"Nonsense," she said as he opened the door. "I'm concerned for him, naturally, but this young woman must be my first priority. She mustn't think much of our hospitality."

He grunted. "I wouldn't worry about it. 'Tis Campbell hospitality she's loathe to accept."

Lady Grear stopped dead in her tracks, staring blindly. Of course," she muttered, "how could I forget such an obvious thing?"

Alistair eyed her, suspicious. "You aren't ill, are you?"

"No," she returned, moving on. "Let's go."

He placed his hand on her arm. "There's one more thing. She has no baggage or personal items in her possession."

"I see there's more to this tale than what you're telling me," Lady Grear said. "Well, Ona and I have more than enough between the two of us." She stopped before the door he indicated and softly knocked. When there was no response, she opened it slightly and peered around the edge.

* * *

A tawny-haired figure sat curled in the chair by the cozy fire. Lady Grear's heart beat faster as ghosts from her past sprang up before her unannounced. She beckoned to Alistair to follow her into the room. "I believe she's asleep. Come, you must wake her, I don't want to frighten the child."

She watched as Alistair walked over to the chair and knelt down, placing one hand upon Kennis' arm. When the girl stirred and he gently spoke her name, she watched and listened. Her practiced ears detected a verbal caress, unless her imaginations created what her ears, in reality, did not truly hear. A new thought concerning this affair entered her mind. She would mind the pair closely. Some mystery was attached to the matter and Alistair, although he didn't confide in her as he once did, couldn't hide his true feelings from his own mother.

* * *

Kennis awoke from her slumber at the sound of a familiar voice calling her name. Many voices seemed to surround her but this one was warm, a tender caress. She opened her eyes and stared into Alistair's face.

"Lass," he said quietly. "Here's my mother, Lady MacDougall come to greet you." He rose from his knee and moved out of her way as Lady Grear approached. Watching the two, he slipped from the room, satisfied with the outcome of his plan to bring Kennis to his mother at Inveraray.

Half asleep, she stared at her visitor. The raven-haired lady was dark-eyed like her son yet her countenance didn't bear much resemblance to his.

"What a pleasure to meet you, my dear," a kind voice said. "I do hope that your stay will be of sufficient duration so that we can become better acquainted. For now, I would like to attend to your ankle, isn't it?" She smiled. "You may call me Lady Grear, since it's much more informal. My maid will be bringing some clothing for you and a hot bath has been ordered, as well."

She struggled to take in the courtesies that the woman uttered. She replied incoherently and managed to say a small thank you.

Lady Grear laughed softly. "Poor dear, you *are* tired. Did he compel you to ride all the way here with no rest? It wouldn't surprise me in the least. I'm his mother, you know," she said, in an effort to win Kennis' confidence, "and I know all of his tricks."

"Nay, madam," she managed at last. "He was most considerate, and we did stop for luncheon. The journey was long but I believe if it weren't for my ankle, I'd have fared better. And please, my lady," she added. "Call me Kennis."

"Of course," she said as a loud knock interrupted their exchange. The door opened and the maidservant entered the room, carrying an armful of clothing. Behind her, two footmen carried a bath, set it by the fire and filled it with hot water before promptly departing.

Lady Grear and Sybil, her maid, assisted Kennis as much as possible, maintaining an easy conversation while she bathed. She was thankful for the screen that hid her from view; she was therefore not obliged to keep up with the stream of chatter. Finally clothed in one of Lady Grear's bed gowns, she emerged from behind the screen and climbed with some assistance into the large bed. The embroidered coverlet was very pretty, soft to the touch, and the scent of roses from her bathwater now filled the room. A weary sense of contentment washed over her.

"Well, my dear, you must be wishing us gone. If you are in need of anything, please don't hesitate to pull the bell. Sleep well," she said, "and Good night."

The door clicked shut before Kennis had time to respond in kind. The events of the day whirled past her and her mind flitted from one incident to the next. She was amazed that she, a daughter of McCallum's, would be so welcome in this Campbell stronghold. Of course, she'd not confronted the rest of the household but tomorrow would be soon enough. The Duke of Argyll, of whom she'd heard little good, was the most imposing figure of all.

She yawned, gazed up at the canopy and counted the roses and knots of violets. Her eyes grew heavy and she drifted off to sleep, lost in the deep comfort of the feathered mattress and downy pillows.

* * *

Alistair stood before the duke, eyes ablaze. While he'd anticipated Argyll's displeasure with his news, he'd not believed that the duke would react with violence.

"What do you mean by it, sir?" Argyll continued his tirade. "I've labored on your behalf to bring about this marriage with the Lady Vanora, and you've gone behind my back on more than one occasion to thwart it. Now, you bring a young woman to Inveraray of all places," he said, exasperated, "who happens to be the child of one of my oldest enemies, a nemesis that I was glad to be rid of in the '45. I ask you again, what do you propose?"

"I propose nothing," Alistair said coldly.

"What is she to you, a lover, perhaps? And you have the audacity to bring her here to consort with decent women?"

Alistair, his color heightened in his fury, struggled to control his temper. "How dare you speak of her with such contempt? She's done nothing to deserve your censure. I will not tolerate it, your grace," he growled. "Take back your insults."

Nonplussed, the duke issued a command instead. "You will tolerate it, Alistair, and listen to everything I have to say concerning the matter. Perhaps I was hasty in my judgment of her character. But you will remove her from this household as soon as possible, do you understand? I expect my wishes to be obeyed."

"I can't remove her tonight, your grace, and I have brought her into my mother's care." His eyes glinted with a sudden sense of victory as a new thought occurred to him. "I must continue my search for Duncan. However, if you're so bothered by her presence, I'll remove her and my mother and sister to Dunolly tomorrow. Would that suit you?"

Angry, Argyll slammed his fist onto his desk. "No, you know that it will not!" he barked. "Do you take me for a fool? This is none of my affair and I'll play no part in it. You will write a letter to the McKinnon and tell him to come and collect his grandchild and send one of your men to deliver it, for I'll send none of mine. Cursed Jacobites, and he's one of the worst offenders yet you expect me to pour out my hospitality upon this girl and her henchmen. Three more mouths to feed, my lad, and winter approaches."

"Then I'll escort Mistress McCallum and my family to Dunolly on the morrow so that your stores and your purse won't be emptied by their intrusion."

Argyll paced the length of the library, his hand upon his brow. "No, you won't. I won't allow this to upset the plans the ladies have made for this week. You do realize that I will have a houseful of guests by mid-week, and I can't cancel the entertainments." Disgusted, he added, "More food would be wasted."

The sound of triumph resounded in the air. "Then I'll leave tomorrow in pursuit of Duncan," Alistair said firmly, "and when I return, I'll escort the lass to Skye myself."

"No, I say, you will not," Argyll said, his color rising.

Alistair protested emphatically and the lengthy debate continued.

Chapter 10

Schemes and Stratagems

Cameron Campbell kicked his heels at Inveraray for a week enjoying the fruits of his kinsman's hospitality.

A busy man, he grew impatient. He'd sent a message to the whelp Malcolmson with instructions to secure the McCallum girl and in turn, his future, which included the title and the land. For his own part, he'd rather have the gold that he could obtain for such a fine wench on the slave market. Men like Denoon would do what they pleased with her and then take their share of the booty. *Eavan Malcolmson is a sentimental fool.*

After dinner that evening, he avoided the company assembled in the blue saloon for tea, a maudlin drink that he despised, and sought the duke's library. He sat in Argyll's comfortable leather chair, smoking his pipe and drinking his grace's whiskey, a very fine brew, until the sound of arrivals in the Great Hall stirred his curiosity.

To his surprise, Alistair MacDougall strolled in with the McCallum lass. Gleefully, he returned to the library to consider his options until Argyll himself entered the well-apportioned room.

After a brief conversation, Cameron departed, lingering in the hall until he heard the click of heeled boots approach from behind. Hiding behind a suit of armor, he watched Alistair enter the library. He waited until Murdoch, the butler, exited the room and strode toward the servant's quarters.

Creeping to the door, he listened at the keyhole. Ha, the fool's caught now, he gloated, failing to hear the whisper of a lady's gown upon the slate floor.

Lady Vanora Campbell followed Alistair to the duke's library, hoping to waylay him before he entered. Since he departed Inveraray so abruptly a few days before, she failed to secure time alone with him. Frustrated and tired of the game he played, she decided that a direct approach was necessary.

If it meant compromising herself and trapping him dishonorably into marriage, she would do it, as long as he married her. She believed that her father would support her as long as she accomplished the goal. Her mother must never know the sordid details. The duke would compel him to marry her when the deed was done.

She shuddered. For her own part, the idea of having a husband to lord it over her in place of her father was as unappealing as the marriage bond. For a young woman of her breeding, matrimony was the only way to escape her family and be her own mistress. Once married and an heir conceived, she could freely seek her pleasure elsewhere. She must tempt him to come to her late in the evening. Her nervousness abated when she perceived the vile Cameron Campbell crouched at the keyhole of the library door.

"So," she scoffed as she drew near, "the great little man is also a sneak. You're a poltroon, sir."

"Sh-h, lass," Cameron hissed. "If you know what's good for you, be still and listen."

Out of curiosity, she leaned toward him, attempting to understand the voices within the chamber. "I hear nothing," she complained.

He rose and straightened, eyes glittering. "You should make a practice of listening at keyholes if you hope to sink your talons into Alistair MacDougall. Followed him here, didn't you, hoping to get him to come to your bed," he sneered. "Don't deny it, lass, I can see it in your eyes. You've the soul of a harlot although you appear as cold as an icicle. I know your kind, hidden behind the facade."

"How dare you insult me! I am no such woman," she said angrily, denying her recent thoughts and turning to leave his foul presence.

"Don't go now, my lady," he said, "not when an idea has occurred to me that would suit you and me very well. Believe me, you'll never get the man with your plan, so why don't you listen to mine? It will benefit us both and you'll be rid of an unexpected adversary."

"Adversary," she repeated. "What do you mean?"

He'd gained her complete attention. He took her hand and pulled it through the crook of his arm in a companionable way. "Come, walk with me back to the saloon where you belong before you're missed, and I'll tell you something of import."

* * *

Lady Grear summoned Ona to her bedchamber late the following morning. She desired to acquaint her daughter with the evening's newest development before she heard of it from servant's gossip or other guests.

Ona waltzed into the room, humming an old ballad. She leaned over and kissed her mother on the cheek before she settled in the opposite chair by the fire.

"Did you enjoy the rest of the evening, my love?" Lady Grear said, amused.

"Aye, immensely," she replied. "I believe that I'm growing to be an accomplished flirt."

"That is *not* an accomplishment," her mother reproved. "You'll make more enemies than friends among your peers if you continue in such a manner. Young ladies aren't fond of others who endeavor to hold the attention of all the gentlemen."

Ona laughed. "I don't think I could do that even if I tried. Very well," she conceded wih a naughty grin. "I won't try to conquer all of their hearts, just a few."

Lady Grear sighed, hoping that one problem, at least, was on its way to being resolved. "I'm glad to hear it but I didn't send for you to read you a sermon. While you were flirting," she said, "a new visitor arrived."

"Oh," she asked, excited. "Male or female?"

"Most assuredly female and quite lovely," Lady Grear said.

"Lud, more competition! Not that I consider Vanora's paltry fair looks to be a serious threat."

"Enough, Ona. You're too bold to say so, and vain besides."

"I'm sorry, Mother," she said, instantly penitent.

"In any case," Lady Grear said, "I believe this young lady already has an admirer. I'm not sure how ardent a lover he is yet, or if he's even aware of his own feelings."

Ona puzzled over her statement. "But who do you mean?"

"Alistair," Lady Grear crowed, triumphant.

"Alistair?" Ona said in disbelief. "Surely you jest."

"No, I don't. You must help me, and the two of them to discover the truth for themselves."

"But how is this possible?" she said, astonished. "Who is this girl?"

Lady Grear hesitated. "She's the daughter of an old acquaintance, a gentleman I once knew well." She shook her head in wonder, transported to another time and place. "It amazes me how very much like him she is, there can be no doubt that she is indeed his daughter."

Ona gazed at her mother, thoughtful. "Was he very handsome, Mother?"

"Aye, extremely handsome. But getting back to Kennis—"

"She must be suited to her name, then."

"Aye, she is indeed comely." She smiled at the crushed expression on Ona's face. "But she won't outshine you, my love. The two of you will deal together admirably, I believe. She's fair and you're dark, perfect foils for one another's beauty."

"Is she more appealing than Vanora?" Ona asked curiously.

"Aye, but I think it's in her expression, something more than mere beauty." She paused, working out a strategy. "We must make her comfortable here. I expect you to do your best to include her in your activities. I assure you it will be little trouble. She has a sprain, you see, and can't get about easily."

Lady Grear warmed to her plan. "The end result, Ona," she said impishly, "is that your brother has carried her up and down stairs, to breakfast and dinner, and even to her bedchamber last night. It appears they've been thrown together often but I don't know the whole tale. I hope she'll confide more readily in you."

"You want me to spy for you?" Ona asked, incredulous. "I'd love to! It will be the greatest fun, and I'll tease Alistair mercilessly." She gloated at the thought of her eldest brother's discomfort. "Wait till Duncan hears the news."

"Duncan," Lady Grear said, worried, "is still missing, I'm afraid. Alistair found no trace of him, and plans to resume his search immediately. He brought Kennis and her two servants here to leave her in my care until she can be returned to her family on Skye."

"Skye?" Ona was amazed. "Who do we know that lives there?"

"No one, perhaps, but apparently Alistair is well acquainted with the McKinnon."

"McKinnons!" she exclaimed. "But they're rebels, well, at least they were. Is she a McKinnon?"

"No, she's a McCallum, and I expect you to befriend her for that reason alone. His grace won't be happy to have her in our midst. I'm sure he'll ignore her for the most part." She paused, weighing her options. "In addition, we must keep Vanora away from her as much as possible. In light of the mode of her arrival, I have no doubt the other guests will also be suspicious, and keep a careful eye on her and Alistair. Perhaps 'tis best that he departs soon."

Ona tapped her fingers on the arm of her chair. "This may be harder than I anticipated. Why does he have to fall in love with a McCallum? Of all the clans in Scotland from which to choose a girl. No wonder Argyll 'tis overset."

"Aye, but the heart isn't a predictable object, Ona," she said, too aware of her own emotions. "Loving another person cannot be foretold. Love is simply not that tame."

Chapter 11

In the House of Campbell

Kennis slipped into the busy Great Hall of Inveraray Castle and gazed in wonder at her surroundings.

Bright tapestries woven of silken threads adorned the grey walls. Not unlike the Dunchalum of her youth, in that respect. She affectionately recalled the comfort of her childhood home and the transformation wrought by Alanna McCallum on the cold and rough interior of the castle. Here at Inveraray, rich patterned carpets warmed the cold floors in the guest apartments and in the blue saloon. She stared at the many trestle tables covered with white linens. Only the wealthy could afford such luxuries, including the silver candelabra lighting the expansive room.

Her thoughts darkened. She remembered the blood that had been shed in order for the Campbells to obtain such wealth. Campbell gold, at least to her way of thinking, was blood money. Her surroundings owed their richness to years of bloodshed, the pursuit of influence and power among ruthless men. The McCallum family had suffered at the hands of such as the Campbells of Argyll as had other lesser clans in the Western Highlands of Scotland. Nevertheless, she was currently beholden to their hospitality and willing in the naiveté and hope of youth, to be an ambassador for her people and work toward a better future.

Adjacent to her sat Ona MacDougall, Alistair's sister, whom she'd met that morning. Kyle Campbell, son of Sir Geoffrey, and Vanora and Grizel Campbell, daughters of the notorious Earl of Breadalbane, surrounded her like a veritable horde. And, she'd been informed, more Campbells were coming.

Daly and Fergus stood a short distance behind her, grim in the midst of their enemies, disliking the company and wishing to be anywhere but in the hall of the Campbells. Earlier in the day, she laughed at them as they moaned about their imprisonment. They were convinced that at the first opportunity the duke would have them thrown into the dungeon to rot if they weren't executed outright. She might not understand the violence of the hatred between their two clans but her two henchmen did, and hoped to avoid further entanglement at any cost.

She glanced toward head table where the Duke of Argyll sat, flanked by the Earl and his lady, Sir Geoffrey, Lady Grear and Alistair, and one Cameron Campbell of Fraoch Eilean. An English officer sat at his side. Not surprising, since Argyll had allied his clan to the English. She sighed. More enemies to avoid.

Alistair lifted his head and his dark eyes met hers across the hall. She looked away, not desiring to draw attention to herself and caught Ona's eye upon her instead.

The pretty, dark-haired girl smiled in a friendly way. "Mistress Kennis, 'tis a pleasure to have you with us. We're planning festivities for All Saints week, and you'll make a welcome addition to our number."

"Thank you, mistress," she murmured in response. "Of a truth, I don't think I'll be able to participate but am more likely to be in the way in my condition."

Ona was determined not to let her off so easily. "Of course you will," the girl said cheerfully. "Mother says that by the end of the week you should be well enough for some light dancing, and the masquerade will be such fun! I'm most eager for it. Kyle, you must help me and implore this lady to join us." He readily added his entreaties and a half hour of easy banter followed.

Kennis found the Lady Vanora Campbell's eye upon her on more than one occasion. Why the girl was looking at her was more than she could imagine; her cold manner made Kennis ill-at-ease. Vanora's sister, Grizel, was polite but seemed to be under the negative influence of her elder sister.

At the conclusion of the meal, the guests were free to pursue their own amusements. She waited for Daly and Fergus to assist her to the blue saloon when luncheon was over. She'd been invited to join the ladies and felt obliged to fulfill their wishes. The duke nodded curtly to her as he withdrew and the other gentlemen bowed. Alistair remained behind and stood behind her chair. She rose and he caught her as she steadied herself.

"I must speak with you before you join the other ladies." He commanded Daly and Fergus to wait in the passage and drew her to the fire, a light hold about her waist as she slowly limped toward the warm hearth.

"You're better today," he said, pleased.

"Aye, and well rested."

He nodded. "Good. I'll be leaving Inveraray today to continue my search for my brother. You'll be well cared for by my mother while I'm away."

A twinge of disappointment passed over her. "I don't doubt it, she's very kind. But what of your brother, he's missing?"

"Of course, you wouldn't know. I'd just returned to Craignish from the Highlands above Loch Awe when I encountered you."

"So your search was interrupted because of me," she said, frowning, "and you were hurt, sir?" She longed to reach out and touch the thin scar on his forehead.

"We were attacked on the road to Inveraray." A smile awoke in his eyes at her concern. "It's only a graze."

"You should have left me in the village with Siusan and Kate, so that you could continue your search. I told you that my friends were nearby."

His expression darkened. "Nay, there are other circumstances of which you know nothing that persuaded me to bring you here. 'Tisn't safe for you to be abroad. Besides, you have friends here, too."

"An army of Campbells?" Her brow wrinkled in dismay.

He smiled crookedly. "Nay, aside from the two outside the door, you have relatives right here at Inveraray." He gazed into the depths of her sea green eyes, finding it hard to believe that the lass had betrayed her family. If he discovered the rumor to be true, he'd have none of her. "Your guardians for four years, lass, and you can't remember their names?" His dark eyes gleamed with amusement as undeniable longing coursed through him. The becoming willow green morning gown that she wore only added to her allure. He shook it off, disturbed by the tenor of his thoughts.

Kennis grew warm under his deliberate gaze. Bemused, she forced herself to snap out of the foolish dream that she had fallen into when he smiled at her. "Oh, Mr. and Mrs. Gilmore and the girls!" She pressed her hand to her cheek. "I'd forgotten. I never dreamed I'd see them so soon, although they gave me an open invitation to visit."

He raised his brows in mock disbelief. "And were you planning to visit Inveraray of all places, surrounded by the Campbells?"

She pursed her lips, and shrugged. "Of course I was, Campbells notwithstanding."

He swallowed hard, her every expression moved him. He'd best keep his distance, master his emotions. In spite of the troubling fact of Duncan's disappearance, perhaps it was a good thing he was leaving today.

A liveried servant entered the room and bowed, interrupting their conversation.

"His grace requests your presence in his library, Laird. A gentleman has called and demands your presence and," he said nervously, "that of Mistress McCallum."

Alistair's eyes narrowed. "A gentleman? You don't know his name?"

"Nay sir, only that ye're to come now, and the lady is to wait with my Lady MacDougall in the blue saloon until she's needed."

"What does this man look like, Red Alan?"

His eyes darted to Kennis. "Fair, like this lady."

"Very well." Alistair's voice was grim. "You may go."

The footman backed away. "So," he said coolly, "your fine kinsman is here."

"I didn't ask for him to come," she said, dismayed. "In fact, I'm amazed he's done so. It must be the letter he claims to have from my grandfather."

"Is that all it is, lass?" he said quietly, searching her face. "What interest does he have in you?"

Kennis flushed. "Interest in me? I barely know the man, really."

"Yet he spent time on Skye with you," he said evenly, "and he came for you in Port Eilidh. Do you have an understanding with him, unknown to your family?"

"Nay," Kennis hotly denied. "I wouldn't enter into such an arrangement."

"You wouldn't be the first." Alistair's voice remained chilly.

"That's beside the point. I accepted his escort at the request of my family and entertained him as I would any guest of my grandfather's. I've told you this before, why do you not believe me?"

He looked down at her, uncertainty written on his face. "I'm not sure what to believe about you. What happens if your brother never returns to claim his rights to the title?"

Kennis was astounded. "Was there ever any hope to reclaim what rightfully belongs to the McCallum's? Look around you, sir," she spat, "the gold that supports this luxury exists only because of the greed of those more powerful than the weak, and at the expense of the poor. 'Tis the obligation of men who have wealth to see to the needs of those less fortunate. What hope does Robbie have, or any other unfortunate man in his position, for his own to be restored?"

"I don't disagree with you on that head. For men like Rob, very little hope exists, especially when there are those who plot to gain by the misfortunes of others."

Horrified, she stared up at him. "What are you implying, sir? You made reference to this on Skye, accused me of unthinkable treachery. How could you? You can have no evidence against me to give you such ideas, if such ideas exist."

"What if I did have evidence?" His eyes were hard. "And such ideas do exist." The messages Farrell had intercepted proved that a devilish plot was afoot. The mysterious 'KM' assigned to the notes led Alistair to believe it was an abbreviation for Kennis' name. Furthermore, he was unaware of her existence until recently. Her sudden appearance, and Eavan Malcolmson's involvement with her, nearly convinced him that she'd deliberately hidden herself to conceal the awful truth about her intentions. "I'll get to the bottom of this mystery and God help you, mistress, if you've had a hand in betraying your own brother."

Kennis clenched her fists at her side. Odious man. He strode away, leaving her no opportunity for rebuttal. Fergus and Daly entered the hall and escorted her to the saloon. In no mood for polite company, she was silent, anticipating a summons at Eavan's request to the council of men in the duke's library.

* * *

Lady Grear observed Kennis' arrival in the blue saloon and was disturbed by the expression on her face. Obviously, Alistair had upset the girl but the question remained as to why he'd done so. Determined to set her at ease, she joined her on the settee by the hearth. "I'm looking forward to knowing you better, my dear," she said, taking Kennis' cold hands into her warm ones. "There was a time in my life when I was acquainted with your family." She squeezed her hands in encouragement.

"Indeed, my lady," Kennis returned, a bitter edge to her voice, "but how could you, being a Campbell?" She pulled her hands away. "Campbells and McCallum's have no use for each other."

Lady Grear was compassionate. "Aye, but there was a time in my youth when I had the opportunity to set aside family feuds and pursue a cordial relationship with the McCallum's. I'm not your enemy."

She stared at the woman, wondering how such a connection had been possible. "But where would a Campbell lass such as you, come in contact with my family?"

"The court at Edinburgh was once a merry place," Lady Grear remembered fondly. "We were all obliged to set aside our differences and revel for days on end. It was a grand time, and I'm sorry 'tis lost to you young people." She became serious. "Many alliances grew out of those meetings and sadly, feuds were either added to or happily resolved."

"Who," Kennis asked, curious, "did you know from my family? I never knew my grandparents. They were both dead before I was born. My brother and I have only known our maternal relations well."

"Your mother is a McKinnon."

"Aye, and her mother a Morrison."

"That would account for my not knowing her. She must be considerably younger than me, so I wouldn't have met her at court." She smiled at Kennis' questioning look. "I was married and having children, and didn't travel abroad much. Plus, I've had little connection with the wives of the Islemen, although my late husband held frequent councils with the Lords of the Isles. As to whom I knew," she drew in her breath, "I knew your father best. He was a very good dancer, and was often partnered with me."

Kennis warmed to Lady Grear. "He was also very handsome, was he not?"

"Indeed, he was," she said, a sudden pang in her heart. "And you're very much like him."

"As is Robbie. People say that he's the image of my father."

This portrait of Robert McCallum's son increased the desire within her to meet him. She would do everything with her power and circle of influence to help this girl in her quest.

"I miss Father very much," Kennis said, sad and homesick. "Unlike most daughters, I spent a lot of time with him. And now, my brother is gone, too, and I had such hopes that he'd return from Culloden." Her eyes welled with tears. "I've been abroad for four years," she confided, "and I confess my hopes have been dashed to the ground. I'd hoped—" She stopped, unable to tell Alistair's mother that she'd hoped he would help her and was indeed the answer to her prayers.

Lady Grear waited, patient. "What did he say to you," she prodded gently, "to upset you so? I could see it in your face when you entered the room."

Kennis, annoyed with her own lack of discretion, was still tempted to pour out the whole. "'Tis nothing," she finally said. "I'm merely distressed over recent events, and I can't accept the very real likelihood that Robbie is dead."

"You have reason to believe your brother is alive?" Lady Grear was genuinely sympathetic.

"Only hope, Lady Grear, a profound feeling," she said. "You see, we've always been very close, connected in a special way. I know that he's alive somewhere, and I feel he's nearby but I don't know where or how to find him."

"I see." Lady Grear considered the situation. "And can Alistair help you to find him?"

Kennis froze. "Nay, I don't think so." He wouldn't help her, just accuse her of betraying her beloved brother.

"Have you asked him to do so?" She watched the conflicting emotions flit across Kennis' face.

"He won't help me, my lady," Kennis said firmly. "*That* has already been settled."

What has already been settled? Lady Grear wanted to cry out. Before Alistair departed, she must have a serious talk with him. He was as obstinate as his father, and she had no doubt that he was at fault in the disruption of Kennis' peace of mind.

Chapter 12

Conspiracy

The Duke of Argyll leaned back in his red leather chair at his mahogany desk and pressed his fingertips together, a self-satisfied smile on his face.

He couldn't hide the fact that he was pleased with Eavan Malcolmson's timely arrival; his demands would most assuredly be satisfied. The letter he bore from John Dhu McKinnon lent credence to his claim and the request of the girl's grandfather would be honored. It was the perfect way to resolve a fractious situation. Now, waiting for Alistair to arrive, he could prove his point without argument.

"When do you wish to escort the young woman to Skye, Malcolmson?" Argyll asked Eavan. "I realize that you must be eager to be off, but there is the slight matter of her injury. I cannot overlook this fact and beg you to consider before you hastily begin your journey."

Alistair quietly entered the library. Hearing the duke's speech, he knew that his present benevolence didn't arise from a genuine concern for Kennis. Rather, the duke was using it as a means to his own end. He considered his options. It might be best to be on the offense from the beginning instead of waiting for the duke or Malcolmson to make the first move and then have to counter a loss. Eavan turned as he approached and stiffly bowed. Alistair returned the gesture, more for the duke's sake than for his own.

Argyll spoke first, a challenge in his eyes. "Well, Alistair, we have a most interesting visitor. You're acquainted with Eavan Malcolmson, Laird of Kilmartin."

The two men measured one another with a hostile eye. "I am," he said calmly, "and I'm aware of his purpose here."

The duke's blue eyes glittered. "Are you, indeed?" He'd frozen lesser men with his haughty stare. "And how is this possible when the man has only just arrived."

Alistair returned the icy look with a cool one of his own. "He came to Craignish first seeking the lass but she chose to come here to Inveraray instead."

"With you, and a host of Campbells at your beck and call? An unlikely story!" He studied Alistair, suddenly aware that his kinsman was about to disclose information that would upset his own plans. "Out with it, lad, what are you about and what is the girl to you?"

"Other than the fact that she's currently under my protection, nothing," he said, unperturbed. "But there's a gentleman here at Inveraray who has more of a claim upon her than Eavan Malcolmson does, letter or no letter from the McKinnon. I'm sure that if the McKinnon could have foreseen the lass would end at Inveraray, then he'd have requested her nearer kinsman to claim her."

Argyll frowned and sat up straight. "Of whom are you speaking? We have no McCallum's or McKinnons here."

"Nay, perhaps not," Alistair said. "But you do have your new factor, Peyton Gilmore, a much more worthy individual than Malcolmson to see to the care of the young woman."

"What!" Argyll exclaimed. "And how is he related to the girl?"

"Through her mother, I believe," he said, smug. "Furthermore, his wife and his two young daughters accompany him, and the lass only recently returned to Scotland after a journey to the Americas with this family. In other words, your grace, her family entrusted her to the Gilmores for four years, and you're going to counter that trust by giving her over into the custody of this man, known abroad for his villainy?"

Ready to take charge of Kennis and depart Inveraray, Eavan impatiently listened to the exchange between the duke and Alistair. "The letter from the McKinnon can't be discounted. You have no reason to distrust me in this matter. What is Peyton Gilmore to me? I have a personal request from no less a personage than her grandfather, the McKinnon of McKinnon. I'm therefore responsible for the lass, there's no other alternative."

"There is only one thing to be done." Argyll turned to Alistair and at the same time pulled the bell cord. "I'll summon Gilmore now. He should be here within an hour or so and we'll settle this then."

One way or the other the girl would be leaving the premises; he really didn't care with whom. His objective was to see her removed from Inveraray and from Alistair, who he must corner into a proposal to the Lady Vanora. This wasn't the time for a beautiful upstart to stand in the way of his plans.

If Alistair wanted the girl, he could have her, but not until the knot was safely tied to the Campbell lass. "In the meantime, Alistair, you and I have unfinished business and I'll offer Malcolmson an opportunity to refresh himself before supper. Ah, here is Murdoch."

This summarily dismissed, Eavan strode out of the room, throwing Alistair an angry look as he passed. Alistair held his ground, determined not to let the wretched man win this battle.

* * *

"It appears that you're left to your own devices, Mistress McCallum," Ona said sweetly. "Would you care to join us?" She gestured to the group at the other end of the room. "We're planning what we'll wear to the masquerade, and the duke has promised that we may have anything from the basement of Inveraray to use for costumes. I think that I should like to dress as a gypsy." She chattered on as Kennis rose from her seat. "Here, let me help you." She reached for Kennis' arm.

"I'm able to stand, mistress," Kennis said. "'Tis really not necessary to include me in your planning. I don't think that I'll be here to attend the festivities."

"Oh, but you must," Ona protested, "and please, call me Ona. May I call you Kennis?"

"Aye." She smiled at the younger girl's enthusiasm, and wondered at herself. There was a time when she would have been in alt over the idea of such grand entertainments. The worries of the past several years had affected her far more deeply than she'd realized. Perhaps the merry company would help to mend her heart and spirit a little. Her mind wandered to the meeting downstairs in the duke's library. She might be on the road to Skye soon although it was contrary to her purpose. Eavan surely misunderstood her resistance to his escort. She must send Daly or Fergus to arrange a meeting with him.

The door to the saloon opened and to her surprise, Eavan entered. She looked up, met his gaze and smiled with more enthusiasm than she'd intended. At least his was a friendly face and his surname bore no relation to that of Campbell.

She excused herself from the group and hobbled to meet him, extending her hand. "Eavan, 'tis a pleasure to see you here."

"Is it, lass?" he said, angry over his frustrated plans. "The last time we met you seemed to prefer the company of another gentleman over mine."

She shook her head. "You don't understand. I simply don't want to go back to Skye with you or anyone. I came to the mainland for a purpose, to go to the Highlands to see my people and—"

"To search for your brother? Isn't that why you went to the Americas," he said abruptly, "and did you find him? Nay, and you won't. You have to face the reality that you never will, that he's gone like so many others who fought at Culloden and who'll never return."

She searched his face for some clue to his harsh words. "How can you say this with such certainty, have you heard news of Robbie?" She gripped his arm. "Tell me, Eavan, at once, if you do. I beg of you!"

His heart lurched at his own duplicity. It was too late to turn back now. "I know only this, 'tisn't safe for you to be abroad, and if your brother's alive somewhere and returns to Scotland then he won't be alive much longer."

Her lovely face paled. "Of what are you speaking," she demanded, "tell me!"

"Lower your voice, lass," he said, curt. "I can't speak of it here."

"Then when?"

He glanced around the room. No one seemed to be paying them any attention. "Later, we'll have to meet when no one's around."

Distressed, Kennis failed to see Alistair as he entered the room. He approached from behind, startling her.

"What's going on here, Malcolmson." His voice was gruff. "What have you said to upset her?"

"Nothing," Eavan gritted. "Our conversation is none of your business."

Vanora had followed Alistair to where Kennis and Eavan stood conversing. "Come now, sirs, 'tisn't the time for bitter words," she said smoothly. "Supper's served in the dining hall and we're expected. We mustn't keep his grace waiting." She curtseyed to Eavan. "If you will, mistress, kindly introduce your kinsman to the assembled company and then allow him to escort you to the hall." Dismissing Kennis as an unworthy opponent, she took possession of Alistair's arm. "Good sir," she said, fluttering her eyelashes, "lend me your arm." A look of triumph crossed her white face as he was caught in her web of platitudes.

Alistair scowled and glanced at Kennis, his eyes hard, obligated to endure Vanora's machinations. Kennis laid her hand on Eavan's arm and waited for the rest of the party to exit the room before they slowly followed.

* * *

Peyton Gilmore promptly answered the summons of his employer. Awaiting the duke in his library, he wistfully reviewed the numerous leather-bound volumes. How grand it would be to own a tenth of what lay upon the shelves in obvious disuse. Caught up in his reverie, he failed to notice Argyll enter the room until he heard voices. He turned around, viewed the small cavalcade that followed in the duke's wake and blinked. Among them was one who he was amazed to see and joyfully welcome.

"Why, Kennis lass," he said, "what brings you to Inveraray?" His eyes twinkled. "Not more adventures, I hope."

"Adventure is hardly an appropriate word," Alistair said acidly, in a foul mood from having endured Vanora's company for over an hour. "Trouble follows her every step."

He chuckled. "Well, lassie, what have you to say for yourself?"

"I hardly know what to say, sir, except that I'm very glad to see you," Kennis said happily, ignoring Alistair. "I look forward to visiting Mrs. Gilmore and the girls. They're well?"

"Aye, they are," he said, noticing her limp and shrewdly adding, "but you seem to be in a hobble. I suppose I'll have to wait for the full tale."

"You'll have your tale, Gilmore, soon enough," Argyll said crisply, "but for now we have an issue to resolve and I believe that you're the man for the job."

"I'll do my best, your grace. How may I be of service?"

Argyll stated the facts of the case as Peyton listened, attentive to his employer. He read John Dhu's letter, a deep frown on his brow. "You're in a pickle again, lass. How came you to be in the middle of this?"

She swallowed hard and looked down, shame-faced. "I left home, sir, for a reason that I don't care to discuss in the presence of these gentlemen. In my defense, I came in the presence of Daly and Fergus." A snort erupted from the window seat. She met Alistair's mocking gaze coldly, then ignored him. "I'll be glad to tell you all, and only beg that you don't send me to Skye until you hear me out. It would be much more comfortable to be in Mrs. Gilmore's presence, since I'm here."

He slipped his thumbs into his vest pockets. "Now there's the difficulty, lass. Ailis and the girls are away visiting and won't be home before Sunday. But I agree with Alistair, that you should be kept with the womenfolk, and not be sent off in the company of men, distant kin or no."

Eavan stepped forward. "You must admit, sir, that I've been entrusted with her care once before when I escorted her to Skye, and Daly and Fergus are here also to accompany us. There's no difference in this instance."

Peyton read the plea in Kennis' eyes. Stubbornly, he refused to acknowledge Eavan's claim. "All the same, I'm her nearer kinsman and since I'm present and have been called upon to settle this matter, I believe 'tis in the lass's best interest to remain here at Inveraray until Mrs. Gilmore returns, and I can take her home with me. That is," he said, turning to the duke, "as long as she's welcome."

Eavan began to protest again and was silenced by his upraised hand. "You forget, sir, that up until a few short months ago I was guardian to the lass, acting in the place of her grandfather. Therefore I shall assume responsibility for her now."

Kennis breathed a sigh of relief.

Furious, Eavan stomped from the room, slamming the door behind him.

"Well," Argyll said, dissatisfied, watching him leave, "it's settled. And now, Gilmore, if you will escort your kinswoman to join the other ladies, or wherever she desires to go, Alistair and I have much to discuss."

Peyton bowed. "Aye, sir, with pleasure." Taking Kennis' arm, he slowly pulled her along. "You've some real explaining to do, lassie," he said softly as the footman opened the double doors. "I hope the tale's a good one."

* * *

In the passage, Cameron Campbell awaited the outcome of the meeting. When Eavan emerged, he stole from the shadows and apprehended him. "Well," he demanded, "what's the verdict?"

Eavan glared at him. "'Tis all your fault, Campbell! I've a good mind to pull out and leave you to the vultures."

"Do that, my lad, and you'll be hanging with me," he said viciously, "I assure you. Don't fret over the girl, we'll win out in the end. I've other plans and a new accomplice."

"Who have you deceived now with false promises," Eavan sneered, "one of the serving maids?"

Cameron snickered. "Nay, lad. That's your problem, see. You think small. I've managed to secure the aid of one of the jealous ladies of the house." He paused and let it sink into Eavan's mind. "Aye, and so far her information has been invaluable. In the end, I may make plans for her, too, which will suit me very well. A fine piece of baggage, she is."

"Then what am I to do now?" he said, sullen, his feet knocked out from underneath him again.

Cameron unveiled the next segment of his masterful plan. Eavan listened, the vision of increased wealth and lands causing the picture of Kennis' golden loveliness to grow dim in his mind. In his heart, he had room for only one true love, and no woman could hope to compete with the love of money and power. He departed Inveraray, joining Niall Malcolm and the rest of his tail at the appointed rendezvous. When he returned next to Inveraray, his dreams would almost be fulfilled.

Chapter 13

Between the Devil and the Deep Blue Sea

The nubby cloth from the makeshift hood tickled Duncan's cheek.

Irritated, he tried to shake off the discomfort but only succeeded in frustrating himself further. In any case, he could see the ground through its open bottom and fortunately, the air circulated just enough to make breathing easy. The tight rope that secured his wrists to the pommel of his saddle cut and burned, and he wondered if Andrew, Young Rab and Big Coll fared the same as he and Jamie.

"I've done it this time," he grumbled to nobody in particular. "The fat is in the fire, and I'll be roasted when Alistair gets wind of this." He knew that Farrell would quickly report the news to Alistair that he and his friends were missing. A new thought occurred to him. At least Vanora Campbell wouldn't have much opportunity to ply her wiles on Alistair. In fact, his dear brother would use the opportunity to escape Inveraray. His musings were interrupted by the sound of cantering horses.

"Ho, Donal!" a voice rang out.

"Aye, all here and accounted for, Cori."

"Then let's be off, we're to rendezvous by noon." The men quickened the pace and Duncan held on tightly, gripping the sides of the horse beneath him with his knees. He wondered for the tenth time how they expected him to stay in the saddle.

"Hold on, lad," Donal said with perspicacity, "and ye'll make it. Ye've a good seat, and a steady animal under ye."

He snorted in disgust and Donal, riding abreast of him, laughed low. Strange enough, Duncan found his captor's presence comforting since his deep voice resembled Farrell's. From the uneven gait of his horse, he pictured his surroundings, savoring the smell of the fresh autumn air, the damp leaves on the ground wet from a recent drenching. The trees were probably bare of leaf, and must line the rocky track that wound its way through the dripping forest.

Just then, he heard a trickling sound, and cold water splashed onto his boots and thighs as the riders crossed a burn. Still disoriented inside the dark hood, he decided it must be almost noon by now since his stomach rumbled, usually a fair indicator of the hour. Suddenly, the horses picked up the pace and he nearly fell off the saddle.

His silent companion once again offered a low chuckle. "We've a wee hill to climb, lad. Hang on tight or ye'll take a tumble."

A bird squawked loudly overhead and he jumped. "I could've sworn that was a gull."

"Aye," said his companion, "we're near water."

"The coast?" Duncan asked, hoping to catch the man off guard.

"Now lad, I canna tell ye that. Learn to use your senses, there's more to seein' than lookin' with your eyes."

Duncan sniffed the air; a tangy smell drifted on the breeze. Aha, the sea must be near.

The horses continued to pick their way down the rocky embankment and he gripped the pommel of the saddle with both hands. The ground leveled out and the animal beneath him ceased to sway. He heard the tide gently lapping against the shore and the scream of gulls fighting over a morsel of food. Certain now that the sea was at hand, he wondered what was next in store for him, Jamie, and the other three young men.

In answer to his unspoken question, a voice shouted in the distance. "Ahoy!"

The sound of boats scraping bottom against the sandy beach told him all that he needed to know.

"Well, lads," Donal said, untying the ropes from Duncan's wrists, "time to move on."

Duncan, rubbing his wrists, peered through the weave of the thick cloth.

"Master Duncan!" a familiar voice said.

"Andrew!" Duncan cried. "Are Young Rab and Big Coll with you?" He blindly reached out for his friend. "Where have you been?"

"We've been here all along, ridin' in the tail."

"And you're well, lads?" he said, anxious.

"Aye," Young Rab replied. "We spent the night in a shielin', and the rascals kept us tied up, even t' eat a bite o' supper and—"

"Wouldna give any news of ye till this mornin'," Big Coll finished. "We met up wi' ye awhile back."

"They could've told us earlier," Jamie said dourly. "We asked about ye and naught one o' them villains said a peep."

"Villain's a harsh word, lad," Donal inserted. "Methinks ye dinna know a villain from a friend."

Jamie growled. "A friend willna bind a man to a horse, exceptin' he's dead."

"Well, ye're nae dead, so get movin'." He gave Jamie a light push from behind. "There now, laddie, get into the boat!" Jamie tumbled in as the rest of the smugglers roared with laughter and tossed in the other young men.

When all were safely aboard, they shoved off. The boat glided smoothly through the open waters, propelled by a brisk wind. The smell of the sea all about him, Duncan wished he could remove the blasted hood and enjoy the sunshine that warmed his shoulders. Before long, he and the others would be at some nameless destination, held captive against their will and surrounded by desperate men. With more than deep regret, he wished for the hundredth time that he'd heeded Alistair's command and kept his promise.

"Jamie," he ventured.

"Aye, Master Duncan," he said.

Relieved, he asked about the others. "In the other boat, I'm the only one back here."

Duncan lost all track of time, lulled to sleep by the rhythm of the boat gliding through the water. The vessel came to a grinding halt, and he awakened with a start. The five young men were promptly cast ashore.

"Wait here, lads," Donal said. His boots crunched on the stones as he walked ahead. "Ahoy! You up there, ahoy!" From a considerable height above, a booming voice returned the call. "Ahoy lads, and Welcome!"

"Ye'd best take the hoods off, Donal," another of their captors remarked. "They canna climb up like that, else we may lose one."

"Lose one?" Duncan didn't like what he heard.

"Nay, lad, I willna lose ye," Donal assured, "but I canna take the hood off just yet. Mind you, the ground's rocky and the steps broken, so be careful."

Steps? He wondered. Where on earth are we? The hoods had performed their office well; he couldn't determine in what direction they traveled. Something in his bones told him that he was in a familiar spot. He looked forward to consulting with his friends to hear their ideas about the location. The five hooded men stumbled over broken steps and uneven ground in the slow ascent. Twice, Duncan faltered and a strong hand steadied him.

Reaching the summit, Donal called for a halt. He rapped the butt of his pistol upon solid rock. "*Deus refugeum nostrum,*" a muffled voice intoned.

Donal's gruff voice resonated above the wind, Duncan thought, with pride. "*In ardua petit.*" He heard the creaking of ancient hinges and was fascinated with the mystery of it all— their present location and captors' identity, and the biggest question of all, why? Surely, these men were Scots born and bred, and the war was over. Smuggling whiskey seemed the only logical answer to his questions.

Following the climb, they descended several steps and were shoved through a door. Relieved of the hoods, the men were left alone in the gloom. The chamber appeared to be a storeroom of sorts, hewn of stone and patched to seal the crevices and keep out unwanted elements. It was definitely a ruin, and Duncan knew that he'd been in this very room before.

"Well, lads, what think you of our adventure so far?" he asked. "'Tis hardly what we expected, but I'm right glad to see you all safe."

"Do ye think we're goin' t' be released then, sir?" Andrew asked.

"Aye, at some point. The greater question is when, so we must keep our eyes and ears open."

"Especially our ears," Jamie said dismally, "as we canna see much of anythin'. The villains could've left us a torch. I've been worried that perhaps they're slavers, not smugglers."

Duncan laughed and the sound cheered them all. "Oh, Jamie, what would I do without your positive remarks? Conor Malcolm's no slaver. He gave me his word no harm would come to us if we didn't resist. Come on, lads, let's put our heads together and figure out where we are now."

"I think we're somewhere between Craignish and Loch Etive," Jamie said.

"Me, too." Duncan stewed over the password Donal had spoken with pride. "What thought you of the passwords spoken to gain entrance to this place?"

The men wagged their heads, except for Jamie. "I'm nae skilled but I'd swear 'twas Latin."

"Aye, Jamie, and it sounded like something I've heard before." He leaned forward on his elbow, chin in hand. "I've been trying to make it out. I believe the first phrase means something like *God is our refuge*."

"What about the other part?"

"Well, it means *He has attempted difficult things*, more or less." He tapped his cheek with his forefinger. "Has a familiar ring, I think." The four men waited expectantly. "It's a clan motto, don't you see?" He sat up straight. "If we knew which clan, we'd know who our captors are and maybe figure out what ruin we're in." His brows drew together into a deep furrow as he considered the motto.

The silence grew as the men sat on the crates, mulling over the puzzle. Outside the door, feet shuffled and voices murmured. The old iron hinges of the door creaked as it slowly grated open. "Stand back!" a clear, firm voice commanded as a torch was thrust into the chamber. "Well, lads," the voice continued, "what unlucky pigeons have roosted here, anything useful?" He swaggered across the threshold.

Duncan's heart pounded in anticipation as the door creaked open, and his breath caught as he met the newcomer's familiar gaze. His jaw dropped open in surprise. Never known for his lack of words, Duncan was speechless for the first time in his life.

Hands on hips, the tall, lean man standing before them oozed confidence. His long, ragged sun-bleached hair hung about his shoulders atop an ornately trimmed scarlet coat. Across his chest, he wore a gold-studded leather sling, the pearly butt ends of pistols hanging on either side, ready to be drawn at will. A dirk peeped from the tops of both boots and a sharp rapier dangled at his side.

"You!" Duncan cried in disbelief. "Well, if this don't beat being between the devil and the deep blue sea!"

The man's eyes gleamed with unholy amusement. "Welcome to my humble abode, Duncan MacDougall of Dunolly," he intoned with mock seriousness as he removed his plumed hat and swept a cavalier bow.

The absurdity of the situation struck Duncan forcibly. He threw back his head and hooted, his mirth causing him to choke and gasp for breath between guffaws. Jamie stood, arms crossed as he, Andrew, Young Rab and Big Coll eyed their friend with mixed emotions, ranging from wonder to annoyance and finally, to disgust.

Chapter 14

Many Meetings

"We think Mr. Gilmore will send ye home, lass, nae to the Highlands. Perhaps 'tis for the best."

Kennis led Daly and Fergus down the winding garden paths of Inveraray Castle, glad to be outdoors and escaping the stifling hall of the Campbells. Green-leafed rhododendron lined the gravel walks, mosses clung to the nearly bare trees. A cool breeze tumbled leaves about the courtyard as a hawk soared in the autumn drafts overhead. The fresh air cleared her mind and she pondered how her simple plan to sail from Skye with her two friends had gone awry from the start. Providence, or mayhap improvidence, intervened and landed her at Inveraray instead. By Friday, the castle would be teeming with Campbells and Campbell allies.

Eager to be on her way, she wondered if Mr. Gilmore would grant her permission to adhere to her original plan. Surely, her grandfather understood her need to get to Dunchalum. She was now heir to the dignities that remained to the McCallum clan unless, of course, Robbie was alive and well somewhere on Scottish or American shores. Eavan must be wrong; the feeling that Robbie was nearby had increased, not decreased since her arrival on the mainland.

"Is that what Mr. Gilmore said when you spoke with him earlier, that he was sending me back to Skye?"

"Implied it, he did," Daly said.

"But we're so close, Daly, we must go on," she said, anxious. "I can't let this stop me now. Won't you and Fergus go with me?" She looked the big man straight in the eye. "I thought you wanted to fly from here as much as I do."

The two men glanced at one another. Dunchalum and the tiny village of Kilcalum were ravaged after the uprising by marauders. Their young mistress would be shocked by the condition of her beloved home.

Kennis understood their reluctance. "I know what you're thinking, that I'm going to be overwhelmed by what I see when I finally return there." She paused, uncertain how to continue. "When I was away, I met many Scots who told me of the horrors they'd endured since the '45. 'Tis one of the reasons I must go home. I have to do something for our people. If I can give hope to one village or even one family, then all of my labors won't have been in vain. Please, will you go with me," she said, desperate, "or must I steal a horse and go myself?"

"Aye, we'll go with ye, lass, there's nothin' we'd like better," Daly said. "But how do ye propose to escape this vast pile o' stones and sneak by a host o' Campbells? And redcoats?" His face blanched. "We've spied out the place, 'tis sealed up tight."

"I have a plan but I need your help to refine it." She eagerly described the planned festivities for the upcoming weekend. Among the assembled company would be many comings and goings as well as new arrivals, providing the perfect opportunity to make their escape. "All we have to do is steal out in a hay cart or," she grinned, her eyes dancing with mischief, "borrow a couple of his grace's ponies. Reivers and rebels, that's what we are, we McCallum's."

"McKinnons, too," Fergus added, grinning.

Daly pushed his cap back on his sandy head and grunted. "I like it, lass, we'll do it," he said decisively.

"You'll do what, make more mischief?" Alistair's authoritative voice interrupted as he approached, his firm step crunching the stones beneath his boots. He was dressed for riding. "Leave us, I want a word with your mistress. I'll see her back to the castle."

The two reluctantly ambled away. "No need to hurry, lads," he said, sarcastic, "I have all day." They picked up the pace, grumbling as they strolled toward the gate.

Kennis glared at him, the green of her eyes alight with gold sparks, meeting his dark gaze. "You don't need to be so rude," she said. "They'll do what you tell them unless, of course, I command them otherwise."

"Not here, they won't," he said loftily. "My word's weightier than yours." He planted his foot on the bench beside her, rested one elbow on his knee and leaned forward. "So, what are you plotting now, lass? You've created enough havoc already. If only I'd known you'd continue to be so much trouble to me, maybe I'd have let Denoon have you for a fair price and not wasted the pearls."

Kennis smoldered. Audacious man. "If that's what you believe, then I'm sure it could be arranged if you had a mind to do it. You're a villain."

He laughed mirthlessly. "Ah, but then I wouldn't have the pleasure of annoying you, would I?"

"What do you want from me?" she flashed. "I've nothing to say to you and no more to do with you since Mr. Gilmore is to take charge of me." With an effort, she managed to control her rising temper.

"Ungrateful lass," he chided. "Who do you think is responsible for seeing to it that Peyton Gilmore became involved in the matter? Eavan Malcolmson?"

"Why don't you leave Eavan out of this? My affairs are none of your business." She smoothed a wrinkle in her skirt and clasped her hands tightly together.

His eyes glittered with a dangerous light. "You've managed to interfere enough in my plans to make them my business, and you eagerly rise to his defense."

"Nay, I haven't, it was purely mischance that our paths have crossed." Her chin rose in defiance. "And as to Eavan, sir, I know no evil of him."

"You know nothing at all," he said, bitter. "Mischance! 'Tis your ridiculous penchant for running off whenever you've a mind to, without considering the effect of your actions on anyone else that's brought you, unfortunately, into my path. And Malcolmson's the real villain, not me. Perhaps you should've left with him. He eagerly awaits you to fall into his arms like a ripe apple, and to fulfill his greatest desire."

His black eyes burned into hers. "Then what will happen, eh? The land, the title, and the gold will be his," he said gruffly, "and yours, to live happily ever after upon. Unless, of course, you recall how you came to be the recipient of it." The harsh note he ended on served to kindle her anger further.

She stood to her feet, enraged. "Ye dinna know wha' exists in my dreams." In her frustration, the Highland words just popped out. "Keep your foul ideas t' yoursel'." Outrageous, interfering man! Always bringing out the worst in her. What was his purpose in doing so? Shaking, she clenched her hands at her sides.

Glowering, he looked down at her from his towering height. The golden flecks in her eyes reflected the warm sunlight and his anger died away. Once again he found himself sinking into the sea green depths, a now familiar emotion tugging at his heart. He dropped his gaze to her cheeks, rosy in the chill air, her soft lips, inviting him to— Alistair struggled to control his feelings as the memory of a single kiss consumed him.

He let out a ragged breath. One kiss had shaken him to the core. Just one kiss, he admitted, and her openness, what he thought was a lack of guile until Farrell brought him the confounded note that condemned her. So far, nothing had appeared to prove her innocence yet he still found it hard to believe that she'd betray her brother. Everything about her seemed contrary to the notion.

Feeling the tide of his passion, she lowered her defenses and the angry words died on her lips.

Without warning, a cheerful voice abruptly intruded into the moment, dissolving the sudden tension between them.

Alistair snapped to attention as Ona approached on Kyle's arm. "Oh, Alistair, you're still here," she said. "I thought you'd gone to search for Duncan." She turned to Kennis eagerly. "I'm glad you'll be here for the festivities, mistress. You will, won't you," she said hopefully, "stay for the entire time?" She glanced at her brother. "You must entreat her to remain longer."

"I don't know. 'Tis entirely up to Mr. Gilmore," Kennis said evasively, looking away, "and Mrs. Gilmore when she arrives." *So, he's leaving again.*

Alistair glowered at his sister. "You'll have to find someone whose advice she's willing to follow. I'm hardly the one to persuade her."

"The Gilmores are invited to come, too," Ona reassured, eyeing her brother with interest. "We'll be observing some of the All Saint's customs, you know, though not all. The Kirk doesn't think highly of the pagan traditions although I particularly enjoy ducking for apples. In our family, Duncan has always been the most successful." Her face fell as she recalled his absence. "You'll find him, Alistair, won't you?"

"I'll do my best, lass," he assured her. "I need to go. Escort Mistress McCallum to the castle for me, Kyle, I can't delay any longer." He nodded to Kennis and strode away before any of them could answer.

* * *

"Take as many of my men as you need, Alistair," Argyll instructed. "I want you to find that boy and bring him home. This is very disturbing, and I don't want it to cloud the festivities this week."

"I will, your grace."

"Perhaps I can be of service, your grace." Cameron Campbell, standing near the fire, had waited patiently for an entry into the conversation. This was the opportunity he needed to insinuate himself into the duke's affairs.

"How so, Cameron?" Argyll was skeptical. "You've been here for two weeks and not offered to lift a finger in any direction. What do you have in mind?"

"Only this. I've been in the Highlands where the young man seems to have disappeared several times in recent weeks, and my men keep a regular watch on the region. I can return to Fraoch Eilean and demand an account of their activities, and news of whatever they've discovered."

"We could send a gillie, Cameron, just as easily," Argyll said. "There's no need for you to ride out."

"Unnecessary," Alistair interrupted, not wishing to be beholden to Cameron Campbell. "I've gathered enough of my own intelligence."

"Nevertheless, there may be something to be discovered," Argyll said. "We'll send a gillie, and if you're not satisfied with his report, Alistair, then Cameron may go on. For the moment, I prefer that he remain here so that our arriving guests aren't aware of the problem. If you both leave Inveraray, they'll know something is afoot."

* * *

Vanora sneaked from her bedchamber and scurried down the hall, glancing over her shoulder. Good, no one saw her. She opened a narrow door and stepped inside, gently closing it behind her. Halfway down the circular stair on the narrow landing below, Cameron awaited, tapping his foot.

"Well, my lass, this had better be worth the effort I've put into escaping my erstwhile kinsmen and meeting you here tonight."

"'Tis, good sir." A willowy blonde, Vanora stood nearly a head taller than Cameron Campbell, who was only half a man as far as she was concerned, compared to the tall and darkly attractive Alistair.

"Good sir, is it? Bah," he snorted. "You might change your mind about that epithet before this is all over."

Vanora stiffened. "How so?" she hissed. "You'd better deliver on your part of this bargain."

"As long as what I've bargained for pays off for me, I'll keep my word. 'Tisn't within my power to make the man adore you. You'll have to use your own wiles for that feat," he said snidely. "You'd best be creative, lass, you have serious competition."

"Do you want the information I have or not, you vile creature." She sniffed in disdain. "I sent my maid on an errand that I'm supposed to be performing, and I'll be missed if I don't return soon."

"That's more like you," he approved. "What have you discovered?"

She related the conversation that she overheard between Kennis and her henchmen earlier in the garden. After luncheon, she'd remained in the dining room with her mother, hoping to gain Alistair's attention. When he left, thinking that he'd saddled up and departed Inveraray, she followed Kyle and Ona outside. Once there, she drifted away from them and hearing voices, positioned herself near Kennis and her companions.

"She's planning to leave Inveraray on Friday evening during the festivities," she crowed, exultant. "I'll be glad to be rid of her!"

"I'm sure that you will, my lass," he said, a devilish smile upon his face. Eavan Malcolmson would intercept the girl and bring her to Fraoch Eilean. If pursued, he'd take the McCallum lass to Dunchalum instead and then he, Cameron, would spring his trap upon erstwhile followers. She trusted Eavan enough to offer little resistance. He must make good his departure when the gillie returned. This definitely changed things—the report to Argyll must be unsatisfactory, so that he could easily depart Inveraray.

Vanora didn't mention the details of the meeting between Alistair and Kennis. If Cameron didn't intervene soon, she must take the matter into her own hands. It was obvious that the man was infatuated with the wretched girl. To think he'd prefer a McCallum to a Campbell was unthinkable.

Fortunately for her, either he wasn't fully aware of his attraction or stubbornly wouldn't admit the fact. His obstinacy, in this instance, was an unlooked for boon and Grizel must assist her in laying the perfect trap. She'd draw him into her net and he'd not be able to refuse to marry her when the deed was done. Men weren't as superior as they believed themselves to be—more than one had become entrapped in a clever woman's snare.

Chapter 15

Reflections

All Saint's Eve dawned crisp and bright.

The entire household awakened early to prepare for the daylong festivities. A huge bonfire was laid for sunset since the people had gathered nuts and apples to divine their future in spite of the beliefs of the Kirk. The duke would grace the annual hunt with his falconers and hunting birds, and as many of his guests who chose to ride with him. When the hunting party returned late in the afternoon, the guests would rest before dressing for dinner and the masquerade.

Kennis bided her time in a small antechamber adjacent to the Great Hall. The Duke of Argyll had little desire for her company and her mending ankle was excuse enough to decline her participation in the hunt. Throughout the week, the duke ignored her. Just as well. She had no desire to converse with him, either.

However, she'd been pleasantly surprised to meet several Chieftains and their families who inquired after her family. Apparently not all Scotland believed her father to be a rebel. Indeed, Jacobite sympathizers seemed to be in abundance at this particular gathering. Relief washed over her, knowing she'd not be completely snubbed.

The Lady Vanora watched her more than she liked and her younger sister, Grizel, wavered in confusion between friendliness and hostility. Kennis thought that if Grizel had a more decided opinion and wasn't so easily persuaded by others, she'd be quite pleasant. Her pretty heart-shaped face lit like a candle when she smiled and a light sprinkling of freckles dusted the tip of her straight little nose. Her hair was light red and curly, unlike her sister Vanora whose pale coloring gave her a ghost-like appearance.

The previous afternoon, the four girls rummaged through several old trunks for costumes for the masquerade. Ona insisted that Kennis don a vibrant gold and green embroidered bodice and full satin skirt with large panniers for the evening, in addition to the traditional painted domino.

"You must wear this, Kennis," Ona insisted. "The green makes your eyes shine like emeralds and your hair as spun honey." She giggled and gave her mother a sly look. "I should think the gentlemen will find it most pleasing, don't you, Mother?"

Lady Grear sat upon the settee, observing their antics. "Indeed, my dear, 'tis quite lovely although a trifle bold."

Ona, in high spirits, refused to be cast down, undeterred from her purpose. "If only the gentlemen were here, we could ask their opinion. Kyle is out hunting with his father, and Alistair has gone to search for Duncan. *He* is fond of green and gold, I'm sure." She giggled at her own wit.

Kennis ignored the conspiratorial look Ona threw to her mother. The sly hint that Alistair would like the color wasn't lost upon her. "But, Ona," she protested, "the bodice is extremely low cut. I'd be uncomfortable, and am not eager to don the garment."

"Lud, you needn't worry over such a trifle." In high spirits, Ona dismissed the thought. "Look at this royal velvet. I shall wear it, 'tis similar to your emerald. We'll take the company by storm! What do you think, Vanora, Grizel?" The sisters ceased their rummaging to respond to Ona's question.

"It doesn't matter to me," Vanora said in her usual bored manner. "I can't wear such colors. Are there no light blues or roses?"

Embarrassed by her sister's lack of interest in the other girls, Grizel pulled a cerulean blue dress, trimmed with embroidered silver and lace from a trunk. "Oh, I'll wear this. It looks like a fairy princess! And I think," she hesitated, her eyes darting to her sister, "'tis most becoming to you, Mistress Kennis." She smiled, her generous mouth turning up at the corners.

Kennis continued to poke through the old garments. In the end, she decided on the green and gold satin. The rest of the gowns paled in contrast to her favorite colors and she admitted the truth to herself, Ona's words concerning her eldest brother.

Later in the afternoon as she sat in the antechamber awaiting Lady Grear, she heard the clatter of horses in the courtyard. More Campell arrivals. The place absolutely crawled with Campbells. Just then, high child-like voices echoed in the cavernous Great Hall and Kennis arose from the window seat where she sat embroidering to peep out the door. A familiar voice greeted her ears.

"Jennie!" she called with delight as she stepped from the room. The child ran to greet her, embracing her fully. Little Molly toddled after her and Mrs. Gilmore followed. "How happy I am to see you, Mrs. Gilmore."

A gentle smile lit Ailis' pleasant face. "Aye, and you, Kennis, though 'twas such a surprise to hear from Peyton. We came home early to be here for you."

"You needn't have," she said in dismay. "I'm well provided for here and have been kindly treated."

Ailis laughed. "In the halls of the Campbells? You surprise me, Kennis love. I thought you'd be eager to depart."

"I'm impatient to be off," she admitted, "but I'm pleased to have the opportunity to visit with you."

Jennie tugged on her skirts, eyes sparkling. "Guess who I saw, Kennis?" She was eager to pour out her story. "Do you remember the Highlander on board the ship? Sometimes he comes and has dinner with us when he visits the Duke, and he's here right now."

So, Alistair had returned. Her heart fluttered. He must have just arrived; she'd been downstairs most of the morning and the front doors remained closed. All of a sudden, soft laughter echoed behind her.

Lady Grear laid her hand upon Jennie's bright head. "It appears my son has an admirer," she said with a welcoming smile

"Indeed," Mrs. Gilmore replied. "She talks of nothing else when he's come to Inveraray."

"Tell me, child," she said, "how did you meet? It seems you're well acquainted with Alistair."

Jennie chattered non-stop for several minutes, long enough for Lady Grear to understand the gist of the story, providing the details she'd not been able to wheedle from Kennis or Alistair. Now, this delightful child revealed all in a matter of minutes. The look on Kennis' face confirmed it; she obviously wanted to silence the girl.

The click of boots echoed on the stone floor as Alistair strode down the passage toward them. He politely bowed to the ladies.

Rising from her curtsey, Kennis marked the weariness in his face, the shadow beard on his chin and his mud-spattered clothes. He'd ridden long and hard to be at Inveraray tonight and hadn't found his brother. Jennie's antics made him grin and his laughter resonated in the hall.

Kennis' heart soared with his and she wanted to join in his delight. She'd not heard him laugh since their journey aboard the *Faoileag* when he laughed at her on deck. *What a long time ago.* A sudden twinge of regret surprised her. How nice it would be to enjoy his good humor and not be constantly fighting a battle of wills.

The broad smile she wore faded as he swept Jennie and Molly up into his arms and swung them in a circle. He knew the Gilmores well, it seemed, and reserved his good opinion for those he deemed worthy. She stared down at the floor, thoughtful. What made her desire his good opinion, anyway? He'd done nothing but accuse her from the beginning of their acquaintance. A slight frown creased her forehead.

From the moment he'd drawn her into his arms on the heaving deck of the *Faoileag,* she'd believed there was something extraordinary about him, something that transcended the obvious. *Like his ruggedly handsome face.* She had the sudden urge to reach out to touch him, stroke his stubbly beard with her fingers. Where had that come from? Her face grew warm as she gazed at him, an unspoken question in her eyes.

Alistair watched Kennis out of the corner of his eye as he twirled Jennie and Molly around for the second time. Her cheeks were red; she looked self-conscious and uncertain. No wonder, considering all of the provocative things he'd said to her in the past few days. His happy laughter died as he set the little girls on their feet again. He glanced at Kennis, a new light in his dark eyes.

Kennis blinked in surprise. Had she just seen a flicker of warmth in those coffee eyes? She looked quickly away. She must be mistaken.

"My love," Lady Grear said to Alistair, keenly aware of the tacit exchange between the two, "you had best see to yourself. Please come to me later."

He inclined his head. "I will, madam." Alistair turned away from her, his dark brows furrowed as he strode out the door. *What a complete fool I've been.*

* * *

Dressed for the masquerade, Kennis stared at her reflection in the looking glass. A painted stranger returned her gaze. Her coal blackened lashes and the low, ornately embroidered bodice of the costume made her feel like a vulgar woman. She'd allowed Ona to persuade her to wear the gaudy ensemble because of one word. Alistair. She couldn't deny her true feelings any longer. She sighed. Too late to change her attire now. She'd not miss this opportunity for the world. *Perhaps he'll invite me to dance,* she thought wistfully, *though I've no reason to believe that he will now or ever.* If only he would trust her. His perception of her involvement with Eavan was mistaken; he was convinced that she was a despicable traitress. Yet when he'd arrived earlier in the day she could have sworn—nay, it simply couldn't be true.

A knock sounded on the door, startling her out of her reverie. The Gilmores summoned her to join them for dinner. She picked up her fan from the dressing table and rose to her feet. She cast one more look at her reflection and groaned. Good heavens, what would Mrs. Gilmore say?

Chapter 16

Masquerade

"How lovely you are this evening, Kennis."

Ailis cast a practiced eye over Kennis' costume. "The gentlemen will surely throng about you. Are you able to dance?"

"A little, perhaps, but I don't think I'm up to anything vigorous. And I'm sure there are other young ladies who are eager to dance, too."

"Well, love," Ailis teased, "it only takes one man to make a marriage."

"I should hope so." Her eyes sparkled with mischief. "I think one husband 'twould be more than enough for any woman, don't you?"

Ailis' tinkling laugh floated down the staircase causing several of the partiers to glance upward.

Kennis scanned the crowd and suddenly her breath caught. Alistair was resplendent in a crimson doublet trimmed with black piping, the white of his linen shirt bright against the crimson. Her gaze collided with his and their eyes held, each unaware that Ailis was not the only observer to note their mutual fascination.

Vanora Campbell was swift to respond. She bore down on Alistair with purpose. The black look he turned on her convinced Kennis that he'd formed no attachment for the girl. She'd heard rumors that they were to be betrothed soon. Argyll desired the match and his command was to be obeyed. It pleased her enormously that he'd not buckled to such a powerful chief's dictum.

Dinner passed slowly for Kennis, sitting on a hard bench at the long, trestle tables at the foot of the dais. Close relatives and allies occupied the duke's table. Tonight Argyll broke with tradition and permitted the women and men to intermingle at the head table. Without a doubt, he was promoting the match between Vanora and Alistair.

She cast a fleeting look at Alistair and their eyes locked again. Seated at Argyll's right between the Earl of Breadalbane and his daughter, a scowl covered his handsome face as he endured her continual advances. Vanora's eyes darted to Kennis and her expression altered. She glared at her rival, turning away only when the gentleman on her right demanded her attention.

The evening wore on, and course after course tempted the palates of Argyll's guests. Finally, the skirl of the bagpipes resonated in the hall, sending a thrill through her that set her pulse racing. Kennis rose to participate in the circle dance and fastened a green domino to her hair.

Crushed in the midst of the throng, she inched her way forward until she came face to face with a tall man in a strange costume. A gold earring dangled from his ear, reminding her of Denoon's pirates. He sported a black vest, a red silk shirt and black knee breeches that billowed when he moved. He cocked his head inquisitively, like a bird, and held out his hand. "Good evenin', lass," he lisped behind a black domino. "Will ye honor me wi' a dance?"

She laughed at his odd manner. "I must forewarn you, sir, I'm recovering from a sprain and must be careful."

"Of a truth, fair lady," he lisped again. "'Tis of no consequence."

He bowed with exaggerated grace, his comical behavior making her laugh again. Convinced that his costume was a disguise, she curtseyed and played his game. The strong hand holding hers was rough to the touch and deeply bronzed. Although he passed for a pirate, she decided that he was simply an audacious clansman mingling with his betters. *And I'm fair game since I'm not a Campbell.*

The pirate easily twirled her about in his strong arms. After she danced with him twice, he bowed. "I thank ye kindly." Without further ado, he disappeared into the crowd. Amused, she watched him stroll away.

"Who's your admirer, lass?"

Kennis jumped as Alistair's deep whisper resonated in her ear. "Must you always sneak up on me?" She pressed her hand over her thudding heart. "Faith, you gave me a scare."

Bereft of a domino, Alistair stood close, his hand lightly clasping her elbow. His eyes raked over her appreciatively, taking in every detail of her attire. "Did I?" He dropped her elbow and slid his hand possessively along her arm. "You're most becomingly garbed tonight."

Kennis' fears about her attire now haunted her from an unexpected quarter. "If you must know, your precious little sister insisted that I wear this delightful costume. If you disapprove, sir, perhaps you should mention it to her."

"Oh, I don't disapprove. But more than one gentleman here tonight has remarked upon your, er," he stumbled, "attributes." With a firm resolve, he kept his eyes upon her face. What a blustering idiot he'd become over a mere lass.

"As long as they keep their comments to themselves," she said, turning away from him and consequently bumping his chin, "I don't care."

The sudden movement of her silky curls brushing against his cheek nearly overpowered him. He sucked in a breath to steady himself. "That may not be all they have in mind," he warned. "You should be more worried about them behaving like gentlemen."

Including me. Her smooth golden locks were piled high on top of her head and soft ringlets fell down her back in a honeyed wave. Alistair swallowed hard. It was becoming increasingly difficult for him to govern his emotions. He'd determined to stay away from her tonight yet here he stood behaving like a fool, jealousy stealing over him when the tall pirate whirled her around the floor. Her happy laughter made him wish he could share in her joy. "Dance with me," he murmured, drawing her close and propelling her to the center of the Great Hall.

Kennis' heart hammered in her chest. "I should sit," she said, in a quandary over what to say and do, "but you leave me little choice." She'd waited so long for this moment, why did she resist now?

"You don't think I can twirl you around like your pirate friend?" A familiar glint lightened his dark eyes. "You do me a severe injustice, lass."

"Nay, I truly don't." When he drew her into his arms, she wondered if she'd regret her weakness. She sighed, abandoning herself to the movement of the dance and in the security of his arms. She raised her eyes to meet his and the music faded into the background. They were alone on the floor.

The warm coffee of his eyes deepened, he tightened his arm around her waist. Enveloped in a dream, they failed to notice the growing interest of the guests watching their performance. She carefully executed a portion of the intricate footwork; he lifted her into the air and spun her easily around. In one accord, they gracefully repeated the sequence in a perfect rhythm.

"Are you enjoying your stay at Inveraray?" he asked suddenly. "I hope you've been comfortable while I was away."

She looked up at him, surprised. "Aye, most have been kind. Have you news of your brother?"

His face clouded. "Nay, let's not speak of it tonight."

He pulled her so close that her feet barely touched the floor. The music played on, the strings and the pipes sweetly blended, creating a magical moment that belonged to them alone. When the tune changed, they paused in the middle of the floor and she gazed up at him in wonder. He lowered his head, unable to resist any longer. Just one kiss. She caught her breath, spellbound.

Oof! Pushed hard from behind, Kennis was thrust against Alistair's chest.

"Pardon us, mistress," Ona called gaily from within the circle of Kyle's arms. "We didn't mean to *interrupt*." She laughed at Alistair and Kennis, brows aloft in mock horror.

Recalled to her senses, Kennis appreciated Ona's intervention. Lud, what had she been about to do? She looked fleetingly up at Alistair and felt her face grow hot.

Alistair smiled at her blushes as the pair whirled away. "Well, lass, what say you?" he said, his eyes warm.

* * *

Lady Grear watched with pleasure from the dais, amused when the two stopped dancing, wrapped in each other's arms in the middle of the hall. She laughed aloud when Ona and Kyle bumped into them on purpose. It was just as well. The gossip mill already had plenty of meal to grind. She'd hoped that Alistair might swallow his stubborn pride and dance with Kennis. Ona, the little minx, was right after all.

Later, when Ona came to her and whispered in her ear, the two shared their little joke. Perhaps someday Kennis would share in it with them. Next to having Robert himself, Lady Grear would gladly welcome his daughter into her immediate family. The only thing that spoiled her pleasure was the malice she saw on Vanora Campbell's white face as the young woman watched the pair with displeasure equal to her delight.

* * *

The music ceased and Kennis stood with Alistair arms in the center of the great room. "Come," he said quietly, taking her by the hand, leading her from the floor through the press of people. He led her to a small door, opened it, and stepped inside. A narrow winding stair stood before them.

"What's this?" she asked.

He grinned. "A little used stair to the battlements. We can be alone there."

Alone, he wants to be alone with me? "Do you know every hidden stair in all of the castles of Scotland, sir?" she said, remembering Castle Moil.

"Not all," he laughed low in her ear, "most."

"I can't climb those stairs."

"I'll carry you."

Before she could protest, he swept her into his strong arms and carried her up the long flight of steps. Kennis looked down and gasped. There was no handrail and the drop was considerable. "Be careful," she said, wrapping her arms around his neck.

"Afraid I'll drop you, lass?

"No, more afraid we'll both tumble into that chasm."

His arms tightened about her. "Never fear me."

She frowned. What did he mean by that? She had no reason to fear him, even if he did aggravate her at times.

Finally, they reached the top landing. A small door appeared and he set her down, undid the latch and pushed it open. He took her hand and drew her through, leaving the door ajar. The moon shone bright overhead in the clear night sky and Kennis shivered in the cool, autumn air. He guided her to the stone parapet and together they gazed out over the darkened glen. Lights twinkled in the distance where some of the villagers left lanterns ablaze, prepared for their late arrival home following the festivities.

From the height of the battlements, they watched the mist swirl upward, slowly winding its way through the dense trees. She could almost feel it, cold and moist, dampening her hair and clothing. She shivered again and he slipped his arms around her, encircling her from behind in his warmth. The stars above reflected on the loch, a diamond collar spread unclasped upon the inky water. Oh my! The scene resembled her dream, the one she'd had often, where something extremely desirable was just beyond her reach.

Closing her eyes, she envisioned the dream sequence again. She descended a wooded hillside in the mist. The dark waters of a rippling loch stood at her feet as the dawn prepared to break. Urgent voices surrounded her, compelling her onward to something unreachable, maybe to her heart's desire.

What, she wondered, do dreams and visions have to do with the inner workings of the heart and mind? Perhaps it was God speaking, a revelation about the past, present, or future events. Lately her dreams had taken on new meanings.

Alistair murmured into her hair. "Something on your mind, lass?"

Kennis considered her answer. She didn't know her own heart on the matter. If dreams were a portent of an event to come, what did her dream signify? Curious to hear what Alistair might say, she took the plunge and asked his opinion. "What do you think of dreams, sir, are they from God or are our imaginations working in an untimely manner?"

"Either that," he said with good humor, "or you've had a wee bit too much supper before you sleep."

She laughed with him. "I'm serious. Sometimes when I dream," she chose her words with care, "the events come to pass."

"You've the Sight?" he asked, surprised.

"Nay," she said. "I don't always understand what a dream may portend until parts of it begin to happen, and then, in a rush, it all comes together." Kennis' heart pounded, concerned that she'd revealed too much. What would he think of her?

Alistair considered her question. He believed in God and studied His truths. He'd spent many hours with Conor Malcolm in his cottage in the woods above Dunchalum in his youth. Somehow, dreams never entered their discussions. "I'd not considered it, since I don't dream often. I believe God speaks in many ways if we're willing to hear Him." He wouldn't admit to her that he'd dreamed of her often in recent weeks. It was true, though, that up until now he seldom dreamed of anything.

"You believe God speaks to each of us, then."

Alistair tightened his arms about her. "Aye, I do."

She breathed out in relief at his response. "I confess that I'm glad to hear it. Not many people think as you do."

"'Tis unfortunate that men are unwilling to know God, lass. He has more to offer than most realize, and people settle for much less than He intended." He fell silent for a long moment. "I've an admission to make," he said abruptly, changing the subject. "I can't tell you the details now, but I've accused you wrongly. I apologize for implying you had betrayed your brother, and for my words concerning your involvement with Eavan Malcolmson." He tightened his arms about her, pulling her closer.

Relief flooded through her as she relaxed against him. "You have no idea, sir, how glad I am." How very glad indeed. "How came you to this conclusion?" Her voice quivered as he planted a tender kiss below her ear.

"In my search for Duncan," he murmured into her hair, "I've uncovered several unpleasant circumstances of which I was unaware."

"Such as?" Her heart pounded in her chest, he must feel it.

"I'll tell you later, lass," he murmured, "we've more important details to occupy us now."

Kennis stood quietly, relieved of her burden, as joy washed over her. She gazed out into the night with a renewed hope, content in her present circumstances. He slid his hands to her shoulders and gently turned her around to face him. She lifted her eyes to meet his, captivated by the yearning that mirrored her own.

* * *

Late for the masquerade, Eavan jumped from his horse and threw the reins to a waiting groom. He hoped he'd not missed Kennis' departure, feeling certain that she'd not attempt to leave early in the evening since she must put in her appearance at the ball. He crossed the threshold of the hallowed halls of Inveraray and stepped into a crush of humanity.

Vanora watched him enter and pushed through the crowd. Shoved from behind, she smacked hard into his back.

"Watch where you're walking," he barked at the culprit who had nearly sent him sprawling. Seeing her, he immediately apologized. "Begging your pardon, my lady."

"Never mind me," she retorted. "I know why you're here. I need your help."

"So you're the lady traitor," he said in contempt. "What's your game? Somehow gold doesn't seem to be the proper motivation for the likes of you." He held her gaze, considering her motive. "I think I know." His deep rumbling laughter rolled over her. "You won't win playing foul, however." His eyes gleamed with mischief. "I'll do my best to assist you."

Vanora was indignant at his scorn. "Speak of playing foul, you're no gentleman either, Eavan Malcolmson. Crooknose told me enough to know that you're equally deceitful and vile."

"Name calling won't win your prize, lass, so I suggest you pay attention and do what I tell you." He studied the crowd, his height giving him the advantage over her. "Where's our quarry? I don't see them in this room."

"I don't know," she said, annoyed. "They slipped away."

"And he didn't dance with you, did he?" Eavan said knowingly. "Trust me, mistress, he won't come near you. You will undoubtedly have to pursue him using every means at your disposal."

"Do you think I'd be spying for a creature such as Cameron Campbell if I didn't know that already?" she snapped. "I'm not a fool."

"For your sake, I hope not." He observed the curious faces in the crowd watching them. "Here, dance with me. 'Tisn't wise to hold counsel together for so long, someone is bound to notice." He extended his arm and led her onto the floor. "Just remember, I'm in this for myself. You're no concern of mine, so if you get caught nosing around or found out in your treachery, I'll not stand the nonsense and swear I'd nothing to do with you."

* * *

"Here, lass, let me take a look at you," Alistair teased. He tucked in the few strands of hair that escaped her coiffure and smoothed the tawny fall of hair down her back. She shivered at the warm touch of his fingers on her cool skin.

"Ready?" he asked, taking in her slightly disheveled appearance one last time with pleasure. She nodded, certain that the stain of color upon her cheeks would betray her. They strolled into the Great Hall in perfect harmony, having enjoyed a pleasant half-hour together.

She felt overwhelmed and amazed by his change of heart. Though God answered her prayers, rekindling her hope at the same time, misgivings invaded her heart. This night seemed too good to be true. When Eavan and Vanora advanced toward them, her heart sank.

"Good evening, Eavan," she said lightly, trying not to pay him too much attention. She nodded at Vanora.

"Alistair," Vanora cooed, ignoring Kennis, "you've been missed. Where have you been for so long?" She sidled up to him, playing the coquette. "You're warm, mistress?" She stared intently at Kennis' flushed countenance. "Strange, since the evening air 'tis most cool."

Alistair held Kennis' hand within the crook of his arm and possessively placed his other hand on top of hers. "Mind your own business, mistress."

Eavan eyed him with hostility. "I'd like to know the answer to that question myself, being her kinsman."

"That ploy is becoming old, Malcolmson," he said tersely. "State your business so that we may be on our way to Mrs. Gilmore."

Eavan wore a grim smile. "Don't interfere in how I conduct my affairs with my kinswoman." Seeing the distressed look on Kennis' face, he ceased the attack. "I merely came to request a dance since I've not yet had that pleasure."

Vanora cut in, taking advantage of the moment. "Nor I with you, sir." She tapped Alistair's forearm with her fan. "Come, sir, 'tis his grace's command, and you're obliged to fulfill my wishes."

Alistair glowered at them both.

Kennis searched his face. She withdrew her hand from the comfort of his strong grasp. "It would be rude of me not to dance with my own cousin." His face darkened and she instinctively laid her hand on his arm. "'Tis best not to create a scene with so many interested onlookers."

He scowled. "As you wish."

"I do not, sir," she said bluntly. "But I believe it to be the best solution. We're being watched." She glanced around again, noting the duke's cold expression.

The foursome separated for the dance and Vanora's triumph was significantly lessened by Kennis' intervention. Eavan gazed at her over the top of Kennis' head, mockery in his face. She ignored him, her attention on Alistair.

Several minutes later, a loud shout erupted and the music ceased. "The horses, Laird, the horses!" A servant pushed through the crowd.

Alistair was the first to reach him. "What is it, Brand?"

"They're stealing the horses, sir," he cried.

"Who is?"

"I dinna know."

The duke, stepping down from the dais, intervened. "It's probably a prank, and they'll return them tomorrow after the race. I see no reason for alarm."

"On the contrary, your grace," Alistair said. "The brigands we've been searching for could be the instigators of this raid."

Incredulity lit Argyll's face. "You think that they would dare to invade Inveraray? That would be a bold move."

"These are desperate times," he insisted, "and desperate men make bold moves."

"Then take several of the men and see if you can track them down." Argyll shrugged. "I still think 'tis a hoax." He walked away, ordering the musicians to strike up the music before approaching Lady Grear.

Alistair was torn between leaving Kennis and Inveraray, or pursuing the thieves. The last thing he needed was another wild goose chase into the Highlands. His sense of duty won out and he strode briskly from the room, disappearing into the moonlit night.

By this time, Eavan and Kennis completed their turn on the floor. "Do me the honor again, cousin."

In need of a rest, she declined. "I'm afraid I must excuse myself, Eavan. You know I twisted my ankle and though 'tis much better, I must sit down for a while. Please escort me to Mrs. Gilmore and Lady Grear."

"As long as you say that I may join you. I must speak with you."

"Certainly, Eavan, 'tis some time since we had pleasant conversation together."

"Aye," he said in a serious tone. "We never did take that walk in the garden at Castle Moil."

She grew wary at his sudden interest. "I think 'tis fortuitous we did not."

"Do you?" he said. "What makes you so certain?"

"The events of the last month, to be sure," she said, careful to weigh her words. "I was shocked, sir, by your behavior at Craignish. Do you care to explain yourself?"

"I was overwrought, lass," he said with a pleading look. "I received the letter from John Dhu, found your inept henchman in the woods, and found you'd disappeared. I'd been searching for you for a couple of days, and was frantic. Don't you see why I behaved as I did?"

Kennis acknowledged the sense of his claim but stubbornly resisted. "But you should have explained yourself more thoroughly and not insulted me."

"Explained myself!" he exclaimed, holding his temper in check. It would do no good to be angry; she'd never consider accepting his escort from Inveraray. "I tried to, but you were hardly receptive to my news. If I didn't know better," he said, sullen, "I'd believe you had feelings for that rogue."

She looked down at her hands, neatly folded in her lap. *I do have feelings for him, and he's not a rogue.* She smiled to herself. *Well, maybe he is, a little.* "Why do you hate him so, Eavan? I've been mystified as to why you despise one another."

Eavan, careful to check his temper again, hesitated. "It goes back a long way, lass. We were lads, and I don't care to recount the details."

Kennis frowned. Whatever happened between the two must have been dreadful. "Well, then, I'm sorry for it but I can only offer to help you to reconcile your differences. Unforgiveness is a bitter root in a person's heart. You must let it go."

"More of your God talk, Kennis?" he retorted. "I already told you that I'm a God-fearing man. What more do you want from me?"

"I think 'tis more than fortunate that we had no opportunity to further our relationship, Eavan. We don't suit." She rose from the bench upon which they were sitting. "I think I'll retire early. I bid you good night."

He rose, keenly aware that she was about to make her escape. He took a desperate leap of faith. "Come away with me tonight," he said in earnest. "I can take you to Dunchalum since you want to go there so badly. Do you really think that Peyton Gilmore or any of these Campbells here, including Alistair MacDougall, is going to allow you to tramp about the Highlands unattended? Allow me, at least, to offer you my services. Make use of me, mistress."

Startled by his offer, Kennis wondered if he'd somehow discovered their new plans. It was impossible; he'd left Inveraray the very day that she and her two henchmen had discussed them. Uncertain as to whether or not she should trust him, she hesitated. It was eleven o'clock. Rising, she made her excuses and bid him await her return from her rendezvous with Daly and Fergus.

Pleased with his efforts, Eavan waited, believing that his patience would pay off in the end. While he didn't enjoy the role of deceiver, the forthcoming result would be well worth his tireless efforts. Soon all of his dreams would come true, and the bonnie lass and all that she was entitled to inherit would be his own possession.

Chapter 17

Horse Thieves and Intrigues

"They're on our heels, Cap," Patrick declared, shifting uncomfortably in his saddle. "Ye know I'm no landlubber. Ye shoulda left me on the ship where I b'long."

The Captain grunted as he carefully guided the horse along the steep track. "Nonsense, lad, you've a good horse beneath you, one of his grace's bloods. There's no reason to complain." Listening, the rest of the men murmured, not wanting to be hung as horse thieves. "Be quiet lads, I'll wager we'll have a host of Campbells on our tail before long. In fact," he mused, "I'll wager Alistair MacDougall will lead the pack."

"Do the lads back on Kerrera belong to him?"

He grinned. "You could say that."

"Then why are we keepin' them, if the man's comin' after us now?"

The Captain was smug. "Have you no imagination, Patrick? He won't find us this time, and we can use their assistance. In fact, the MacDougall will be persuaded by his brother's presence later when we'll need his influence the most." He halted and turned in his saddle, addressing the men who lagged behind. "Be sure you leave a visible trail back there."

"What good'll that do?"

"What a naysayer you are, Patrick. Mayhap I should've left you behind, even if you're the finest horse thief I've ever known."

"More like the only one ye've ever known. An' Cap," he asked, curious, "why did ye risk goin' into the Duke's hall? Ye picked one fine wench to dance wi', but how'd ye persuade her?"

"Ah, you forget my inestimable charm, lad."

The men laughed again and the Captain shushed them, even though he believed that the searching company he'd eluded would never discover their whereabouts. He'd taken a winding route, and felt confident that they would ride in circles for hours.

* * *

Eleven o'clock. Kennis was late for her tryst with Daly and Fergus. After slipping out of the Great Hall, she stole down the passage, descending the steps to the *entresol*. Much to her relief, the two men awaited. Worried, she quickly related her conversation with Eavan. "Do you think that Eavan knows we planned to leave tonight?"

Daly picked at his stubbly beard. "How can he, lass? If ye're plannin' to leave, now's the time with half the Campbells and the MacDougall gone. Why?"

"Since Eavan wants to go with us and offered to escort us to Dunchalum," she said in earnest, "we're less likely to be waylaid by marauders."

"'Tis true, but do ye trust him?"

Her shoulders heaved in uncertainty. "Aye, and nay. If he knows we're planning to leave, he may follow us anyway."

He shrugged. "Then I guess he might as well come along."

"I thought you were suspicious of him."

"I am, but so far he's done no harm and has been of service to us."

"I'll accept his escort then. I must get back before I'm missed. We'll meet as planned at midnight." She turned and climbed the narrow stone steps slowly, in pain from the evening's exertions.

Eavan waited in the passage outside the double doors that opened into the Great Hall and stepped forward when he saw her approach. When the toe of her dancing slipper caught on the stone floor, she tripped. He rushed forward, catching her in his arms.

"Oh," she gasped. "Thank you."

He gazed into her eyes for a brief moment, caught by her sweetness. With a pang he released her, knowing that it was too late to turn back the clock and begin anew. He was involved in this plot for good or ill but if Cameron expected him to do harm to the lass, he bargained for serious trouble.

* * *

"Grizel, you must do as I say," Vanora insisted. "Meet Cameron Campbell in the garden and pretend to be me. I must go and see what Eavan Malcolmson and that girl are doing. I won't be long, I promise. Here, take my cloak. He'll never know the difference unless he sees you without it. Everyone says our speech is similar, and we're about the same height."

"I can't do this, Vanora," Grizel whined. "I'm not clever like you. I'm just going to get into trouble and Father will take the rod to me, you know he will, because I'm always stupid."

"Do what I say or I'll tell Father that you wouldn't help me when I needed you the most," she hissed. "You know what I mean, now get going." She hurried away, eager to find Eavan and to see if their plan was proceeding smoothly.

Feeling caught in Vanora's trap, Grizel looked back and forth helplessly, skittering away like a frightened rabbit. She stole down the passage to the arch that Vanora indicated and prayed a simple prayer. *Help me, God.*

A lone figure emerged from the shadows as she opened the door a crack. She gasped as Cameron Campbell jerked it open.

"Finally here, eh?" He lifted a brow at her silence. "What, lost your nerve?"

She didn't answer and pulled the cloak even closer around her delicate frame.

He clutched her arm, his fingers bruising her skin. "Come on, then."

"Where are we going?" she whispered. Vanora hadn't said that she was to go with the man, only meet him. "I thought you had instructions for me."

"I've changed the plans, now move along. Be a good lass and you won't get hurt. Watch these steps, that's it, careful now." He led her across the grass to a grove of leafless trees. A tethered horse waited patiently for its master.

"Nay," she cried. "I'm not going anywhere with you!" She tore loose from him and her hood fell about her shoulders as she ran back to the safety of the castle.

Cameron cursed. "Don't try that again," he said, catching up to her. He grabbed a fistful of her hair and pulled back her head. "I should've known," he muttered. "You're coming with me anyway, girl."

He dragged her along. "You think I'm a little weasel of a man and you're right, but I'm stronger than you and if I have to," he said in a nasty tone, "I'll break you in before I give you over to—never mind, you'll find out soon enough."

"Please, don't do this," she whimpered as he threw her onto his horse. Ignoring her plea, he jumped behind her onto the saddle and raced through the opening gates of Inveraray, the Campbell stronghold.

Vanora waited in vain for her sister to return from her errand. After seeking her in the garden and the kitchens, she stole out to the stables. There was no sign of Grizel anywhere.

Dismayed, she retired to her bedchamber and paced, not knowing what to do and afraid to confront her father. She sent her maidservant to perform a task before dismissing her for the night.

Soon she'd not be able to conceal the awful truth. The maid would report to her mother that the Lady Grizel wasn't in her bedchamber. Vanora, dreading the inevitable confrontation, wrung her hands and waited for the storm to break.

* * *

Kennis and her companions joined Eavan's men at the appointed rendezvous outside the castle walls where mounts were provided for each of them. *He must have been sure of my cooperation,* she thought. Having agreed to his escort, she knew that he'd tolerate no argumentation if she reversed her decision. Moreover, the three of them were outnumbered by Eavan's men.

With misgivings in her heart, she gave her horse the office and silently rode in the midst of her distant Malcolm kinsmen. Daly rode in front of her and Fergus brought up the rear. Incredibly, her dream of returning to her beloved Highlands was about to be fulfilled. She'd finally be able to see her clan and perform the work that she had set out to do in the beginning of her journey.

Her courage rose and she eagerly pressed on, one objective in her mind, unaware that more than one player in this game planned a different future for her than what she imagined. What had begun as a simple plan to aid the needy had grown into a plot to overthrow every good intention she possessed.

Throughout the night, the riders sped on toward Dunchalum. Splashing through a burn in their haste, the horses scrambled up the bank to climb a scree-laden hillside. Branches slapped at their faces and suddenly, Eavan came to an abrupt halt. His horse reared as strange horsemen threatened, appearing directly in his path. Gaining control of the animal, he peered into the darkness. "Who are you?" he barked.

"Like you don't know." Cameron Campbell's shrill voice pierced the stillness of the night. "You'll join me and my lads for this portion of your journey."

Eavan was furious. "How dare you interfere with me, Campbell!"

"I dare to interfere because I don't trust you," he retorted. "You've been reluctant to cooperate with me recently. So I decided that I'd best meet you and escort you to Fraoch Eilean."

"Fraoch Eilean!" Eavan gritted. "Nay, we ride for Dunchalum as agreed."

"That's where you err, sir. Remember who is in charge here."

"Over my dead body." An uncomfortable silence fell over the company. No one dared to interfere lest unwanted violence break out.

"Precisely," Cameron said, unruffled. "Look into the trees, Malcolmson, you're surrounded." He drew his sword and all heard the metallic whisper, joined by a multitude of drawn swords. "Oh yes, my lad, I will kill you if you attempt to thwart me now."

Kennis gripped her reins tight. Her worst fears were about to be realized. She'd fallen into the hands of her Campbell enemy and her own kinsman was his accomplice. Alistair was right about Eavan after all. Daly and Fergus sidled closer to her in the event the meeting came to blows, prepared to defend her to the death.

Cameron spoke again. "I hope you've decided to come peaceably. Where is the McCallum lass?"

"She stays with me." Eavan stood his ground. "That was the bargain."

"I don't want her at present." He motioned to one of his men. "Bring the wretched girl." The man dragged Grizel to the forefront of the company. "Let her ride with you. I've had enough of her sniveling."

Outraged, Kennis deeply felt Eavan's duplicity. Cameron Campbell had perfected his scheme until his web of intrigue embroiled them all. Her thoughts flew back to Alistair. By the time he discovered her absence and the evidence of her departure, it would be too late. He'd think that his first opinion of her was correct, that she truly had betrayed them all—her brother and family, the Campbells who provided her with Highland hospitality and worst of all, himself. He'd never forgive her.

"Fergus, bring that poor girl to me," she commanded. The girl lay on the ground in a heap, sobbing. "Grizel," she said, astonished when she saw her face. "Whatever are you doing here? What have you to do with that odious Cameron Campbell?"

"'Tisn't my fault," she sobbed. "I was tricked into it, and I didn't mean to do anything wicked."

Kennis' heart wrung with compassion. "Here Fergus, put her behind me."

"Are ye sure, lass? I can take her with me."

"Nay!" Grizel cried out pitifully, clinging to her.

"I'll be fine."

The cavalcade reordered itself and traveled on toward Loch Awe. Grizel finally ceased to quiver and the progress of the company, traveling single file on the narrow track, was slow. Kennis foresaw that the night would be long; surely, the party would ferry across the black water in the morning. Dawn not only drew out the ferrymen and the rising sun, but would also bring a rescue party.

***

Alistair directed the search party with Farrell McConacher at his side. He was convinced that the horses were stolen, not borrowed on a whim to be ridden at tomorrow's festivities. The minutes grew to an hour and no clue was forthcoming. The trail was visible in the beginning but the thieves knew their business well. On the plus side, he'd escaped Vanora Campbell's clutches for the moment. The deflated expression on her face when he departed was his present reward.

A sudden longing for more of the too brief moments he'd spent on the battlements with Kennis consumed him. Impossible. He couldn't be falling in love. He'd sworn off to deeper emotions long ago. Perhaps it was fortunate he was forced to leave her tonight. His thoughts clouded as he remembered that he'd left her unguarded, open to the devices of Eavan Malcolmson. He must hurry back to protect the lass from the man's deceit.

The long night passed and dawn approached, yet still they were no closer to finding his grace's stock. "Well Farrell, shall we head for Inveraray?" he said, frustrated. "Confound it, I feel like we've been going in circles."

"We have, sir," Farrell replied. "I've marked that rock at least four times. I canna figure it out. I've naught seen the likes of it."

"Nor I," Alistair grumbled. "If we head back now, we'll be there in time to break our fast. What say you?"

"Ye'll get no argument from me."

"Good," he said, raising his arm to halt the men. "Lads," he called. "We ride for Inveraray!" With nary a rustle, the riders expertly wheeled the horses about and trotted down the track in the opposite direction. Several hours later the weary, hungry searchers clattered into the court of Inveraray as the sun broke over the horizon.

Chapter 18

The Fun Begins

"Do what ye like, daughter, but I'm goin' to Inveraray," John Dhu McKinnon declared.

"Cursed Campbells! If they harm one hair of the lass' head, I'll have Argyll's noggin on his own platter, and dinna ye try to stop me. The murderous and filthy dogs," he ranted, "who do they think they're dealin' with, some poor old decrepit chief who canna hold a sword in his hand? Murdoch," he bellowed, yanking on the bell cord. "Murdoch!"

The man threw open the double doors, running toward his master.

"See to it that two dozen of the lads prepare for a journey to the mainland. And be sure to bring plenty o' shot and powder."

"Aye, Laird," he said, bowing, "and when are we leavin'?"

"Tomorrow mornin', first light, and you're stayin' with the Lady Alanna and Mistress Mairi."

Murdoch's face fell in disappointment. He longed to hold a sword in his hand and fight the Campbell dastards who had taken the young mistress captive.

"I'm coming with you, Father," Alanna said calmly. "There's no need to fight, I'm sure there is a reasonable explanation. And Mairi will ride also, I'll not leave her behind."

Murdoch's face brightened at her declaration.

"'Tis no place for a woman, daughter," the McKinnon said, "but all the same, it'll do the lass good to have ye near. Pack your things, and we'll be on our way early. Ye'd best get to bed soon as ye can, we've a bit of a journey ahead of us."

* * *

Alistair, weary from the night's pursuit, entered Inveraray to the resounding din of a screaming banshee. The noise of bedlam echoing from the duke's library was unheard of at the castle. The duke valued the solitude of his personal retreat and none dared to invade his personal space without permission. The footman, an arrested look on his face, opened the door for Alistair. He nodded and entered, astonished by the scene that greeted him.

John Dhu MacKinnon stood nose to nose with the duke. Each red-faced combatant argued at the top of his voice. "What do ye mean, ye dinna know where the lass is? Wasna she here yestereve? Ye took her in and abused her trust. I'll have your head for this, ye filthy Campbell!"

"I'm not personally responsible for your misfortunes, McKinnon! She was here, I say, and if she's not here now 'tis not my doing." Argyll's volume rose. "The girl's a nuisance, running here and there with two aimless servants that do nothing but add to the trouble!" Disgusted, the duke threw his hands in the air. "Three extra mouths to feed, and winter coming, sir. Pretty soon you will expect me to house and feed all the McKinnons too!"

"Ye greedy man! Is that all ye think about, your gold?" John Dhu raised his voice a notch to match Argyll's, not to be outdone. "Aye, ye can house me and m' daughter and her bairn, too, and spend some more of your *bluid* money. At least I'll be receivin' a return on some of m' own!"

Alistair leaned back against the closed doors, enjoying the contest between the McKinnon and Argyll, an amused gleam in his dark eyes. His keen gaze shifted to the Earl of Breadalbane and his family.

The Earl shook the Lady Vanora by the shoulders so hard that her teeth rattled.

"I meant no harm, Father," she wailed. "'Tis not my fault. She wasn't supposed to go with him."

Lady Breadalbane circled them, wringing her hands. "Oh dear! Don't hurt her, William!"

"Hurt her!" he roared. "Of all the deceitful wretches to have for a daughter. You've spoiled her, madam. The girl has no sense of honor or maidenly decorum. I've a good mind to disown her!"

"Father, please," Vanora sobbed.

"Don't beg me for any favors, my lass," he said, grim. "If we receive ill news of your sister, you'll rue the day you were born. I'll have no deceivers in my household." He crossed his arms as he stared down at her. "Ha, and you expected a man like Alistair MacDougall to be taken in by your wiles? Saw through you, did he? The man is rid of a bad bargain." He walked away in disgust and rested his forehead against the wall. "You've shamed me, girl," he muttered, "disgraced your honorable name and that of your family."

Alistair felt little compassion for Vanora. She would receive her punishment and the reward for her deceit soon enough. Lady Alanna McCallum and Mairi stood near his mother, Lady Grear. Neither lady made conversation with the other but stood watching the disorderly scene before them. He vacated his spot by the door and moved toward the two women. "Lady McCallum," he greeted, "Mother. I see that I've arrived in the midst of a small war. I take it I've missed something important?"

Lady Grear smiled, relieved. "I'm glad you've arrived, Alistair. Perhaps you can calm them all down. Argyll and the McKinnon have been shouting at one another this half hour. At least William seems to have quieted down. He is more in control of himself now."

"But what's happened?" he asked. "I've not been gone twenty-four hours and all Hades breaks loose. I take it that Mistress McCallum is gone missing again?"

She nodded. "I don't know all but apparently she stole away with her henchmen, and Vanora claims, with Eavan Malcolmson."

His brows snapped together. "What!" A spark of anger lit a fire within him.

She placed her hand on his arm. "Before you jump to conclusions, you must know the rest. He promised to escort her to Dunchalum, and I believe you already know 'tis her heart's desire. Vanora knew of the plan because somehow Cameron Campbell is involved in all of this, which is why Grizel is missing."

"Grizel?" he said, his expression vacant.

"Aye," she said, "the earl's other daughter."

Understanding dawned on him. "Ah, the rabbit-toothed one."

"Fie on you, Alistair," she remonstrated. "This is no joking matter. And speaking of Duncan, have you any news at all?"

"Nay," he said, a worried note creeping into his voice. "He seems to have vanished."

A firm hand clapped him on the shoulder. "Alistair, lad, 'tis good to see ye. Mayhap ye can persuade this *fuil* of a Campbell to offer us hospitality and the information we seek." John Dhu McKinnon's eyes twinkled into his, captivating him as always. The man fascinated and amused him; if only Argyll possessed a tenth of his magnetism.

A smile appeared as the corners of his mouth tilted upward. "I promise I'll do my best, sir, in fact, I'll be so bold as to offer hospitality on his behalf as a near kinsman. Will that satisfy you?"

"No need to be polite on my account," Argyll cut in. "Do you think I wouldn't offer him and his family a simple courtesy? Have I not housed his ungrateful whelp of a grandchild for a week or more? You do me an injustice, Alistair."

At his words, Alistair observed Lady McCallum stiffen. Although he didn't know her well, the martial look in her eye gave him the feeling that behind that calm exterior and given the provocation, lay the same feisty temper that her father openly displayed. Unlike her father, she did not vent her feelings in public.

"I believe, your grace, that if I were you," he hinted, "I would apologize to your guests."

"Apologize?" Argyll said, exasperated. "After I've been insulted in my own home?"

"Aye, since you're the host. I don't believe this lady appreciates her daughter being referred to as a whelp."

"Well, I never—" he began, gazing at Lady McCallum. Seeing the hostile light in her eye, he very wisely begged her pardon.

She bowed her head in acknowledgement. "Certainly, your grace."

Argyll summoned his butler. "Now that we are finished arguing," he said, giving John Dhu a quelling look, "I should like to extend the hospitality of Inveraray to you as long as you have need. Murdoch will see you to your rooms and I will order refreshments. In the meantime, Alistair, Breadalbane and I will determine what is to be done about this business."

"Murdoch, eh?" John Dhu said acutely. "Canna escape the name. I'll be glad of a respite, Argyll, and I'll join ye in a wee bittie to hear what ye've determined and," he added, "to tell ye if your plan's sound or nae." He directed his sharp gaze first at Argyll, then at Lady McCallum. "Come, Alanna."

Alistair chuckled and the duke glared at him. When the McKinnon and his daughter had retired from the room, Argyll said testily, "At times, Alistair, I wonder where your loyalties lie."

He grinned. "I canna help m'self, sir," he said, lapsing into broad Scots. "Th' mon amuises m' somethin' uncommon-lik'." Giving in to weariness and to the hilarity he'd controlled, he howled with laughter. Frowning, the duke and the earl impatiently waited for his mirth to cease.

Now," he said, wiping his eyes, "what the devil is this about, and what's your daughter to do with it, Breadalbane?"

The earl related the tale as he understood it from Vanora. Alistair rose to his feet and paced the room. The wretched girl had knowingly sent Kennis into a trap and caused her sister to be kidnapped.

Cameron Campbell was a villain. He must have planned to take his revenge on his chief through Vanora, preventing the supposed marriage to him and using the girl to gather information for his own purposes. In addition, he would eliminate her as witness to his plans. Unfortunately for him, this part of his plan had gone awry; he'd inadvertently taken the wrong sister. The poor girl deserved a better fate.

"I must go after them immediately, there's no time to waste."

"I'll go with you," Breadalbane said quickly.

Alistair nodded. The powerful chief would be a valuable asset in his own right. He commanded his own small army and possessed innumerable resources.

After a brief respite and a quick meal, Alistair ran lightly down the steps from his bedchamber, his boots clicking on the stone floor as he strode down the corridor. The footman opened the doors and he joined the earl in the courtyard.

Preparing to mount his horse, Alistair's thoughts drifted to Kennis. She'd accepted Eavan Malcolmson's escort to Dunchalum, and he found that he wasn't disturbed or surprised. He'd never encountered a lass more determined than he was to pursue her own course. He smiled at the thought. He still had his doubts as to her heart and wondered how far he should go in an attempt to discover her true feelings.

Once again, the still, small voice that he'd learned to trust over the years whispered to his mind, telling him not to fear the outcome. He'd fought a desperate battle within himself, and won. His pride persuaded him that he didn't need a woman in his life, that he was self-sufficient and his own master. Now the very emotion he'd scorned engulfed him. He would do everything in his power to win the intended object of that emotion. Dare he call it love, or was he afraid to admit to weakness?

Love, he decided, is not weak. It's a raging fire, a passion that cannot be quenched and as strong as death itself. He would find her, and together they would discover exactly how strong of a love they possessed.

Chapter 19

In Hot Pursuit

The wooden ferry crossed the smooth waters of Loch Awe without mishap and unloaded its passengers upon the shores of Fraoch Eilean.

Strangely enough, the Heather Isle lacked the flowering plant common to the Highlands for which it received its lovely, though erroneous, name.

Cameron Campbell had wheedled the ruined castle and property from the McNaughton clan for a bag of gold and a service he'd rendered the clan. He believed that the island would be easy to defend from attackers and had built an addition to the original structure in the form of a snug tower house, imagining his small domain to be a kingdom.

Aside from loyal Campbells, a small contingent of redcoats, led by a disgruntled lieutenant, camped on the grounds. They herded the prisoners toward the tower house and up the wooden steps into the hall. Kennis noted the subtleties of wealth in the richly appointed chamber. Apparently, the miser Cameron Campbell not only had grand ideas but had managed to amass riches. "A greedy Campbell trait," she muttered under her breath.

"Welcome to Fraoch Eilean," Cameron said with a smirk. "I offer to you the hospitality of my dungeon. Guards! Take those four miscreants below." He pointed to Kennis, Grizel, Fergus and Daly. "I'll deal with them later."

Eavan leapt forward, grabbed him by the collar and pressed his dirk to the base of his throat. "That's not our agreement, Campbell! I should finish you now, but I'm no murderer. I'm leaving, and taking Kennis with me."

"Are you?" Cameron choked out. "Not with my men stationed at every door. I suggest you let go of me before you all die. I don't need any of you to see this through to the end."

"Release her into my custody now."

"Not unless you promise to do something for me first."

Eavan pressed the point of the dirk harder against his skin. "You're hardly in the position to bargain, Campbell. No more promises, and tell your men to lay down their arms." He loosened his grip enough for Cameron to give the order.

"You can have her shortly, Malcolmson," he snarled. "Don't you see, fool, that the opportunity to rid ourselves of some very powerful enemies has arrived? They'll *all* be here soon, and we'll be ready for them. I've gathered men who aren't fond of Argyll's Campbells from Fraoch Eilean to Dunchalum, and they're ready and waiting for my command. I've formed many alliances with other disgruntled clans, too, and the Lieutenant here." He nodded at Grimsby.

Giving in to his persuasions, Eavan thrust him away.

"You won't regret it," Cameron assured him, straightening his collar. "By tomorrow evening, you'll have everything you desire."

Eavan followed Cameron's men to the dungeon. "Wait," he said to the guard, who thrust Kennis inside a cell. "I wish to have a word with her." The guard stepped aside and she gave Eavan a searching look. "Here, take this," he mouthed silently. In the palm of his hand, he held a miniature dirk. She understood. It for self-defense, if the need arose. "I'll be back, I promise," he said. "I'm sorry about this, lass. Nothing has gone today the way I planned."

"And just what *did* you plan, Eavan?" she said coldly.

He touched her cheek and smiled reassuringly. "To be far away from here, for certain. But for the present, there's nothing I can do, short of abducting you myself."

"Then why don't you?" She crossed her arms and waited for his reply.

Eavan was surprised. Perhaps he'd been mistaken in her after all. "We'll talk later, the guards won't refuse me entrance." He left and the guard slammed the door shut.

She was alone in the dark cell. Beams of light filtered through the iron bars at the top of the door and a rickety bench leaned against the wall. The cell was dank and cold, and she shivered. To make matters worse, the foul smelling straw piled in the corner was moving of its own accord. Grimacing, Kennis jumped back. Rats or mice, maybe. Knowing that her three companions suffered the same fate offered little comfort. She tucked the dirk into her bodice and to pass the time, reflected over the last several days.

She knew that Alistair would come, hopefully out of love for her and not a sense of duty. The events of the previous evening had led her to hope beyond all hope. He was reconciled to the fact she'd not betrayed her brother and seemed convinced of her innocence. The short time they spent on the ramparts had settled her mind and won her heart. Her feelings for him were real, and she would cherish the memory forever. An understanding of sorts had developed between them and she heaved a sigh, wishing for a happy conclusion to their uncertain relationship.

Eavan, however, was a mystery. She told him at the masquerade that they wouldn't suit. Surely, he wasn't planning to ask her to marry him or worse, force her into an unwanted marriage. He implied an intimacy that didn't exist. Over the past weeks, her feelings for him had developed into a sisterly affection. He must have overcome, in fact abandoned, any tender feelings he felt for her since he was in league with the villain Campbell. His betrayal hurt her deeply; she must discover what Grizel knew of the scoundrel's plan, otherwise, why was she abducted?

The sound of leather brogues shuffling on the wooden stairs indicated that the guards had gone upstairs to begin their vigil. Jumping up from the bench, she dragged it to the door. She stepped up onto it and peeked out through the bars. "Daly, Fergus, Grizel, can anyone hear me?" she called.

"Aye, lass," Daly replied. "Fergus is in the cell next to me, and the lass is two doors down from ye."

Sobs echoed down the hall. "I wish I could do something for her," Kennis said, "and get out of this nasty cell!" She rattled the bars in frustration.

"There's nothin' ye can do for her, lass. We need to put our heads together, and devise a plan. I wish I'd somethin' to pick the lock or carve out the masonry."

"Daly," she said, excited. "Eavan gave me a dirk. How can I get it to you?"

"Ye canna, but I'll tell ye what to do while those villains are away. We'll have to pay attention in case they come back."

Kennis proceeded to follow his instructions. It was slow work, but at least her body warmed as she labored and the mindless activity occupied the time. Plus, she was glad to have a reason not to think about her current troubles.

* * *

Eavan returned to the hall and found Cameron awaiting him. "You know, Campbell, I should kill you for this treachery."

"We've already discussed this, lad. If you even attempt to kill me, then you'll be dead along with me." He handed him a glass of whiskey. "Don't sulk, soon this will be over and you'll be a Laird of some significance as long as you keep your part of our agreement."

"You expect me to sit tamely by while you perform more misdeeds concerning the lass?" Eavan received the glass and his hand shook slightly.

"Nay, I promised that you could have her since you want her so badly," Cameron said, calculating, "but I've a proposition for you to consider. She'll bring an excellent price on the block, a much better use of her beauty and of the time and effort it took to bring her here."

"I'm not the dastard you are, Campbell." Eavan downed the potent contents of his glass, in need of its narcotic effect. "I am, at least, still enough of a gentleman to abhor your suggestion, and was brought up to be one which is more than I can say for you."

He set the empty glass down on the table and filled it with more of the amber liquid. "And what about the other lass? What do you intend to do with her?"

"A mistake, a vital error on my part," he said, frustrated. "She masqueraded for her sister and was caught in my trap. Perhaps," he said, a new idea occurring to him, "this will be even more punishment for the fair Vanora than if I'd brought her here instead. Breadalbane may disown her and she'll be disgraced. I hadn't thought of it before— What a delightful end to her nauseous pursuit of Alistair MacDougall."

Appalled by Cameron's delight in the ruin of others, Eavan determined to intervene on Kennis' and Grizel's behalf. The affair became uglier as each day passed. Cameron Campbell was more than evil; he was in league with the devil himself. He must get Kennis away from here and the other lass as well, if possible. Alistair MacDougall would arrive before long with a host of Campbells and to gain his trust, he must carefully lay his plans.

* * *

Alistair stood on the shores of Loch Awe considering how to approach the small isle of Fraoch Eilean. Cameron Campbell might not be a formidable chief but he was wily and determined. He wondered how long this plan had been in motion, and when he'd recruited Eavan Malcolmson. The messages Farrell intercepted and the various aspects of the plot began to make more sense now.

The prisoner in Argyll's dungeon provided invaluable information and confirmed, when forcibly persuaded, that Kennis wasn't a traitor. He regretted his treatment of her but privately thought that she stood up well to his mercurial temper. Faintly smiling, he recalled their first meeting. Growing serious again, he determined that their time together at Inveraray wouldn't be their last, but the beginning of what he hoped was an enduring relationship.

"Farrell, are the ferrymen here yet?" he demanded. "We haven't got all day. I'm sure Cameron's lying in wait for us but I don't want to give him more preparation time. Surprise may yet be an element in our favor."

"He's here, and a few boatmen besides. They've agreed to give us the use of the boats for a fair price, and stay with the horses."

"I want a few of our men to stand guard as well."

Farrell nodded. "'Tis already done."

"Good. Then let's position ourselves and move out. I'll not make a frontal attack but leave that to Breadalbane. You and I, and a dozen of the men will circle around and attempt to gain entrance from the postern gate. He'll have most of his men focused on the front gate." He wore a determined expression. "Much is at stake here. Are you ready?"

"Aye, sir," Farrell said, inscrutable. The stakes for Alistair in this quest were higher than most.

"Then let's move out." He raised his hand and gestured in a forward motion. Men piled onto the ferry and into long boats, manning the oars. The small army of boats glided through the dark waters of the loch toward the Heather Isle. A mist arose, providing a measure of cover. Alistair was pleased; it seemed that Providence had chosen their side, and he was confident that soon he would rescue his lass.

* * *

Cameron's sentry sounded the alarm. The men rushed to their positions, awaiting the onslaught of soldiers and orders from their chief. Seeing the small armada, they braced themselves for battle as the ferry drew in offshore.

Alistair's men splashed into the water, the long boats beached and a cry of *Cruachan, Cruachan!* arose, the ancient battle cry of the Campbell host as the men thronged onto the shore. From atop the battlements, the cry was returned, echoing that of their kinsmen rushing toward them. It was a sad moment as one clan prepared to fight the other, brother to brother, spilling the blood of distant cousins upon the ground.

At the tree line, Alistair and his men picked their way quietly through the foliage, skirting the crackly underbrush as they neared the postern gate on the rise of the mound. The original structure served as an outer curtain wall to the newer tower house within. He was appreciative of the clever construction blending the new and the old buildings into one.

Surprising the Campbell soldiers at the gate, they managed to break through and overtake their opponents. Gaining the front doors, he burst into the Great Hall. Finding no one there, the men stole through the passages, seeking the stairway to the rooms in the tower. "Farrell," Alistair whispered, "take half the men, and go up yonder. I've a notion to check out the dungeon first."

Farrell nodded and motioned to half of the men to follow him. He disappeared around a bend and Alistair moved forward. The lower door stood ajar before him and the sound of angry voices greeted his ears. A deadly light shone in his eyes as he recognized his quarry, Cameron Campbell and Eavan Malcolmson.

He signaled to his men to be quiet and on guard as he crept down the stairs. His heart pounded in anticipation, hoping that his lass was safe. He clenched his teeth when her cry echoed in the chamber below, gripping the hilt of his broadsword in readiness as the clank of iron upon iron resounded in the hollow place. Finally, he reached the bottom step.

Eavan saw him arrive and Cameron, taking advantage of his distraction, drove his sword into Eavan's shoulder. Alistair jumped forward with a shout as previously unseen Campbell swordsmen converged upon the newcomers. His sword rose and fell, piercing his opponents as he and his men pushed Cameron and his guard deeper into the blackness of the dungeon. Suddenly overwhelmed, he slammed against the wall. At the last moment, he grabbed his dirk from his boot and thrust it upward. Their last adversary fell and he leapt to action, searching the cells. He found Daly and Fergus safe in their cells but no sign of Kennis and Grizel.

"Where are they?" he demanded. "I heard Kennis only minutes ago, I know I did." He grabbed the front of Daly's shirt. "Do you know nothing, man?" He let go and Daly fell back.

"Cameron took them." Eavan gasped for breath from the doorway. "To Dunchalum." The blood from his wound flowed freely.

"But how could he escape? We had the only door covered. Out with it, Malcolmson," he growled, clenching his fists, "before I run you through."

"Bind up my wound and take me with you," Eavan said, "and I'll show you his secret escape route."

Alistair was livid. "Go to the devil."

"Take me or I may do just that, and you'll never find the lass in time.

After scouting the upper chambers, Farrell hurried to the lower regions of the tower house. Entering the dungeon, he awaited Alistair's orders as the men dug out the stones Eavan indicated, revealing a hidden tunnel that led to the shore.

Upstairs, Breadalbane burst through the door into the hall. He rushed to find Alistair, and when given the news about the two girls, looked crushed. The battle was over but Kennis and Grizel were still missing. The men consulted and agreed to pursue their Campbell kinsman to Dunchalum. The earl appointed a small company to hold the castle at Fraoch Eilean while he joined Alistair and Eavan. The tunnel surfaced at a short distance from the tower but Cameron had disappeared. Disappointed, the men returned to the beachhead where the rest of the host awaited.

Alistair frowned. "We're losing valuable time on this chase. I fear we may need to break up into two parties. We must return to the horses, yet there are too many to ferry across at once. I'll take a handful of men and go ahead, Breadalbane. You must go round and meet us at Dunchalum, and I'll post a man to keep watch for you."

"Very well, Alistair, God speed." His voice shook with emotion. "Find the lassies."

Alistair laid his hand on his shoulder. "I will, sir, don't fear."

* * *

"Cease your babbling, girl," Cameron growled. Grizel's tears had abated but her fear translated itself into nervous chatter.

Despite his cruel behavior, Kennis agreed. Grizel was young but not a child. She needed to control her emotions and brace herself, since there was little hope of escape. Armed men surrounded them and their hands were securely bound. Even if they managed to run during a respite, the two girls wouldn't get far.

At Fraoch Eilean, Alistair had come as she'd foreseen. Eavan had fallen and though she didn't think that he'd been killed, he was wounded, perhaps mortally. She felt saddened over his misguided conduct and wondered again at his lack of faith in God. The thought that he might die or that any of these men who had no relationship with God might not live out the day, deeply troubled her. She prayed for their souls as they rode in silence. *God help us all.*

The hours dragged on and the terrain became more familiar. Sighting a familiar *burn* and crossing over it, she knew that they were nearing Lochangless and Dunchalum Castle. The scattered shielings on the track to the castle weren't far from here. Soon they would pass the *clach dion* where she and Robbie had spent so many hours at play as children. Kennis heaved a sigh. This wasn't the homecoming that she imagined.

* * *

A silent grey-hooded figure watched the Campbells approach from behind the trees. In stealth and haste, It loped ahead, weaving in and out of the dense foliage possessed of wings instead of mortal feet. The grey form studied the trussed young women plodding along on the horses with concern. He'd not foreseen this development.

The phantom decided that he must quickly send word to his comrades with a request for reinforcements. He would then double back, discover their direction and await the entourage of Inveraray Campbells. There was no doubt that Alistair MacDougall must be in hot pursuit.

Chapter 20

The Enemy of My Enemy

"I'm that worrit about the lass, Alanna."

The McKinnon and his daughter, Alanna McCallum, stood together in the small dining hall of Inveraray Castle in serious conversation. "No word after all this time," he said, tweaking his beard. "Canna be a good sign."

"I agree with you, sir." Peyton Gilmore entered the room, a grave note in his voice. "I've been with his grace, and the gillie had little to report. However, there's been a new development which I'm commanded to present to you, and his grace requests your presence in the library." He proceeded to tell them the latest news, wrested from Alistair's attacker, who currently made his abode in the dungeons of Inveraray.

"Good heavens," Alanna exclaimed when he'd finished speaking, "what's to be done? Is the duke planning to send a messenger or additional troops?"

"As to that, madam, I canna say," he said, "but 'tis the reason he requests the McKinnon's presence immediately."

"Then I'm coming, too," she declared.

John Dhu didn't argue with his daughter. He had raised her to defend her family and the clan in the event he or Charlie could not. She'd sat in many councils at his side.

Robert McCallum, fifteen years older than she, found it amusing that a chief of the McKinnon's caliber considered his daughter equal to a son until he sat on councils where she was present. He fell captive to her beauty, her wisdom and indomitable spirit. John Dhu gave his consent to the marriage and it had been a happy one. The sharp pain in Alanna's heart at his death was slowly ebbing away but she would always love her late husband.

The Duke of Argyll sat at his desk in the library, his hands before him, fingers interlaced. Deep in contemplation, he failed to hear John Dhu and Alanna enter until Murdoch announced them. "I'm glad you're here," he said, looking up. "We have a serious problem which I hope we can speedily resolve."

John Dhu and Alanna waited to hear the updated account.

"I'm sorry I have nothing good to report concerning your daughter, madam. It appears that all of our people are run afoul. They won the day at Fraoch Eilean, and have pursued Cameron Campbell to, of all places," he shook his head in disbelief, "Dunchalum. My kinsman has betrayed my trust on several fronts. I have no way of knowing at this time if Alistair and the earl have reached Dunchalum, or if the entire company has been ambushed and massacred. I've discovered that my own destruction as well as that of Alistair, the McCallum clan and," he locked eyes with John Dhu, "even yourself, McKinnon, was planned by the villain."

His shoulders straightened. "Since Alistair is unaware that he's riding into a trap, I've decided to go in pursuit of them myself and call to arms every Campbell within fifty miles, if necessary. I've already sent running gillies out, and expect a reasonable turnout by tonight. You, sir, are welcome to join us, if you so desire. Sir Geoffrey and his son, Kyle, plan to ride with me as well as several others who remain at Inveraray." He exhaled deeply and ran his hand through his thinning hair. "After all of the fighting amongst us in recent years, this is a sore blow. I'd hoped we were headed to a long term peace."

"On that score I agree, your grace," John Dhu said amiably. "And I'll ride with ye, and the few McKinnons with me, in the mornin'. This'll be the first time in eons that a McKinnon has ridden with a Campbell instead of against one."

"Then let a new era begin, McKinnon," Argyll said with sincerity. Difficult times often called forth the best from men, even mortal enemies. "Shall our hands meet as gentlemen on it?"

"Aye, and as fellow Scots," John Dhu agreed, reaching forth his hand.

"As fellow Scots," Argyll concurred and having shaken hands, the three drank a toast, sealing their newfound amity.

* * *

Kennis' eyes misted as she rode through the proud gates of Dunchalum Castle, ancient seat of the McCallum's. The emptiness gripped her, and she wanted to weep in grief. Her father was dead, her brother banished and now she was a prisoner in her own home. Sliding down from the saddle, she stood on the cobblestones and stared at the neglected castle. Someday she'd awaken from this four year nightmare. The snide voice of Cameron Campbell intruded upon her meditation.

"Ah, observing the state of this poor example of architecture, are you?" He rubbed his hands together. "This shall be the last you look upon it, lass. Don't think that Eavan Malcolmson or the MacDougall will come for you. Soon they'll be as dead as your father and," he added with glee, "your brother, once I finally get my hands on him."

Kennis stared at him in dismay. "What do you mean, villain? Do you know where he is?"

"Aye, that I do, and he won't live for long. You see, mistress, I've been plotting for a long time to have this property and gold," he said, "and you and your erstwhile brother and kinsman are going to deliver it up to me."

Her brow furrowed. "Eavan, how?"

"He didn't tell you, of course. He planned to leave your brother to my, er, ministrations, marry you and declare himself the legal heir to all that concerns you. And after that," he said, an evil glint in his beady eyes, "the fool Malcolmson will receive his just desserts at my hand."

Appalled, she fell silent. For all of Eavan's faults, she'd never suspected such treachery. He'd hinted at this once before, she believed, trying to warn her away. In fact, he'd sent numerous mixed signals and she felt sure that if possible, he'd have reversed his role in the scheme. Eavan must be unaware of Cameron Campbell's foul plans for him.

Pushed along by the Campbell soldiers, she entered the Great Hall and appraised its denuded state in silence. The bare chamber was forlorn and unwelcoming, robbed of tapestries, family heirlooms and the McCallum's that gave it life. Doubtless, English marauders and the conniving Cameron Campbell were here before her arrival.

Kennis recalled the happier days of her childhood, the gay banquets and proud McCallum's, the banners gracing graced the dais which now stood in disrepair. There was little time for reflection, however, since she and Grizel were forced from the hall and led down the passage to an antechamber now used for storage.

Once the soldiers left, her first order of business was to free herself from the tight leather thongs binding her wrists. She pulled on the knot with her teeth, attempting to work it loose. After some time it gave way and the knot fell slack. Finally, her hands were free. She tossed the leather strips aside.

"Here, Grizel," she whispered to the girl. "Come and I'll remove your bonds."

She worked to free Grizel's hands, rubbing her wrists to restore the circulation. "When they come," Kennis said, "we must pretend that our hands are still tied. I have a plan." She knew the castle better than Cameron Campbell. Obnoxious little man. She wondered if he'd discovered the hidden passages that led to important chambers in every wing. Indeed, one door was in this very room. She must locate the lever in order for them to escape unseen. She probed the carvings around the small fireplace, engaging Grizel in light conversation and bidding her to keep watch. Hoping to keep the girl focused on pleasant topics, she asked if any young men at home had come courting.

"Nay, but I hope that someday one gentleman will," the girl murmured, dreamy-eyed. "I think he's the most handsome young man I've ever laid eyes on."

Kennis stopped and looked up at her, smiling. "Who's this Adonis," she teased, "or is it a secret?"

Grizel shrugged. "'Tis no secret, Kennis. He's a kinsman of mine, Duncan MacDougall by name."

"The Laird's younger brother?" she asked, surprised. While Alistair was ruggedly handsome, he didn't fit the description that Grizel provided of his younger brother. Duncan must be a handsome devil, she concluded. "I've never met him. He's been missing since I became acquainted with the family."

"I know," Grizel said, worried. "I'm amazed that no one can seem to find him, not even Alistair and he's a canny one, Father says."

"Aye, I suppose he is," Kennis laughed. "How well do you know Alistair, Grizel? Like you said, you're close relatives." She sneaked a quick peek at the other girl.

"Oh, not well at all. He frightens me, and Duncan doesn't like me," she said, chagrined. "He called me a little brown rabbit because I'm shy and talk too much when I'm nervous. Kennis," she asked suddenly, her forehead creasing, "do you think I'm homely?"

Her heart touched, Kennis ceased from searching and knelt by Grizel, placing her arm around her shoulders.

"Nay, I think you are one of the loveliest girls I've had the good fortune to meet."

"Thank you." Grizel's eyes were bright with tears. "I wish you were my sister instead of Vanora. She's so cruel to me and my younger sisters."

"Don't worry about that now," Kennis said, rising. "We need to escape as quickly as we can. This is my old home, you know, and I think I know it much better than that nasty Cameron Campbell." Her fingers resumed probing the scrolled masonry. "And, once Alistair finds your Duncan, we must persuade him to think very differently of you."

"We?" Grizel perked up at the word. "You'll help me to be as beautiful as you are?"

"Nay, love," she laughed again. "To be as beautiful as only you can be, the way that God made you. Oh, I think I've found it at last!" She pressed a miniature shield. The lock released and the secret door grated open as cold, stale air penetrated the room.

"Kennis," Grizel cried. "Someone's coming!"

She pressed the knob again and the door slid into place. The two girls curled up on a pile of empty sacks, rewrapped their wrists in the leather thongs and pretended to be asleep as their captors entered the chamber.

Their gaolers were talking as if the girls weren't present in the chamber. "Git that sack there, Wee Willie, and take it t' the kitchen. The chief'll have his dinner tonight." Spying the girls fast asleep, he lowered his voice. "Did ye hear what he's plannin' t' do wi' these two wenches?"

"I canna say I did," Willie replied.

"Ye know that foul man who came by last month, that Denoon," he began. Willie nodded. "He's plannin' t' give 'em t' him t' sell down Bristol way. Git a fine price for the two o' them, dinna ye think?" A leer spread over his face. "Mayhap we should break 'em in. No one'll e'er know 'twas us."

Kennis longed to reach for the dirk that she'd hidden in her laces but didn't dare, afraid that the men would see that she was awake. Much to her relief, the man called Wee Willie demurred.

"I dinna think so, lad," he said without hesitation. "I dinna want no lass who isna willin'. Let's go."

She watched the men through barely closed eyelids. Wee Willie strode out of the room but his companion cast a last greedy look in their direction before he exited the chamber. Waiting until they were gone, she tossed the leather bands and sat up. Grizel did likewise, and they sat quietly for some time, conscious that they had barely escaped a depraved act.

"What are they going to do with us?" Grizel asked. "I don't understand."

"Denoon is a wicked man, Grizel. He's a slaver, and a vile one at that. There's a very large slave trade in Bristol." The two girls grew silent and Kennis considered her options. "As soon as the fighting starts," she finally said, "we must make our escape. 'Tis even more imperative now, since we know what will happen to us if we don't get away."

She stood up. "Let's explore the passage behind the door. We may not have much time before someone returns. I'm fairly sure this one leads to the courtyard and if there's a lot of activity, I think we could make it to the postern gate. The only problem is, I don't have the key. I hope the second key is still in its hiding place in the wall." She pressed the tiny shield, shivering in anticipation of what lay ahead as cold air poured out of the musty passage, chilling her to the bone.

Chapter 21

Of Phantoms, Bogles and Lost Men

Alistair followed the familiar track to Dunchalum. If only he'd been more circumspect, he berated himself.

He might have discovered what was afoot in a timely manner. Now he was at a disadvantage, and being on the defensive instead of the offensive gave him no pleasure. He'd been careless. Not only was Duncan missing, the two lasses were now in jeopardy. Out of nowhere, a piercing wail cut through the air, disrupting his thoughts. His horse pawed at the air, and he fought to gain control.

"What the devil was that?" he exclaimed. Unknown to him, it was the same howl that Duncan, Jamie and the lads from Dunolly heard the day that they disappeared.

Farrell covered his ears. "Screamin' like a banshee," he said uncomfortably. "Perhaps the auld woman was right."

"Nonsense, that's a lot of foolish superstition."

The bloodcurdling scream erupted again and a brilliant white light flashed under the dim canopy of trees. Alistair glanced at the men following behind and muttering about bogles and banshees. He must maintain order. He slid off his horse and strode to a pair of flat rocks jutting out over the loch, stepped up, and started to encourage the men to take heart when a noise exploded beneath him.

Motioning to Farrell, he pointed to the ledge below. A grey form darted out from the mouth of the *clach dion* and ran up the hillside. An audible murmur passed through the group. Alistair jumped on his horse. "Follow him!" he bellowed.

Instead of running off into the woods, the phantom stopped and beckoned to them with ghostly arms.

"'Tis a trap," Alistair said, wary of the invitation.

The figure shook its head and beckoned again.

"It wants us to follow," Farrell said.

The phantom vigorously shook its head again, up and down, and gestured toward the track before moving forward in haste.

"Then we'll follow." Alistair hoped that his discernment hadn't led him astray in pursuit of this would-be phantom. "That's your banshee, Farrell," he said as they rode up the track, "and Granny Jean's phantom. What do you make of it?"

"It dinna move like a man," he replied, "and It dinna speak. I'd swear that howl was nae of this world." He watched the grey figure speed along.

"Well, I think 'tis a clever man in a grey cloak who knows how to play upon the fears and minds of men."

"Beggin' your pardon, sir, but how do ye account for the trail of mist?"

Alistair frowned. "A man of science might have a notion. Reminds me of a trick Conor Malcolm might play. We'll see."

They continued to follow the gliding figure, marveling at the ease with which it sped across the ground. To the uneducated eye, it appeared to be a phantom but Alistair was convinced it was a mortal man, sent either to aid or to distract their company.

To his astonishment, a group of riders trotted toward them and a cheery voice called out in welcome. "Hallo Alistair, well met! I'm glad you could join in the fun. We've had quite a merry time of it."

Alistair, weary from the journey and worry of the last several days, stopped short and vented his frustration. "Fun, Duncan?" he roared. "You have the audacity to sit there and tell me you've been enjoying yourself, as if you were on a holiday? Do you know what I've been through searching all over Western Scotland for you, tramping every God forsaken, overgrown Highland path, enduring foul weather and having to return to Inveraray days on end and tell our mother and sister I've not found you, or had word of you—fun's not the word I'd choose! It's been a living Hades." He ranted on and Conor Malcolm, sitting astride his horse at Duncan's right hand, chuckled.

"Aye, the man's got a temper alright," he commented to nobody in particular, enjoying Alistair's discomfiture. "God help the lass he finally marries someday."

Duncan, Jamie and the other young men from Dunolly laughed merrily.

Conor walked his horse over to Alistair. "'Tis good to see you, lad." He stretched out his hand in greeting.

Alistair gripped Conor's arm up to the elbow. "I should pull you off that horse and toss you in the mud." His laugh held a self-derisive quality as he shook Conor's arm. "It's been a long time, Conor, and you're a welcome sight, in spite of the fact you've encouraged that scapegrace brother of mine. So, tell me, how are you involved in this, and who's yon pretender? I swore it must be you."

The phantom waved and disappeared again into the trees. "I canna tell you, lad. You'll see soon enough but for now, we've a battle to fight if I'm nae mistaken." He consulted with Alistair about Dunchalum, what their spies had reported and Cameron Campbell's activities. Alistair gathered from his information that Cameron possessed a much larger army than he'd anticipated. Now he was forced to wait to attack until the Earl of Breadalbane arrived. In the meantime, he must bide his time and send a gillie to await the earl and lead him to the camp. Duncan could give an account of his adventure later. At present, Alistair was relieved to have found him or rather, to be found by him.

Evening fell before the earl arrived with the Campbell host. If the morning dawned fair, Providence would again shine down upon them in their quest.

Alistair dreamed of Kennis and it was sweet. He awoke in the night, her winsome face before him and knew that tomorrow he'd fight not only for her freedom but for her heart.

Eavan Malcolmson was wounded and Alistair knew fear for the first time in his life. Nothing was settled between him and the lass. If she genuinely preferred the man to him, he'd not stand in her way but do everything in his power to assure her happiness.

And, he thought bitterly, I'll make sure the villain lives up to his part of the contract.

Chapter 22

To the Rescue

The Earl of Breadalbane greeted Alistair at dawn.

He arrived in the night, leading a host of Campbell allies. Over breakfast, the two men finalized the plan of attack and again, the earl would head the frontal assault while Alistair attempted to discover an alternate route into the castle.

The knowledge Daly and Fergus provided about the Highland region proved invaluable. Alistair consulted with them about the lay of the land and the floor plans of the castle. With their help, he positioned archers above the courtyard in the heights. The shooting distance seemed excessive but he had confidence in the strength and ability of his men to use their longbows.

On the march to Dunchalum, he contemplated his plan to enter by the postern gate. Daly informed him that a thick stand of trees covered the hillside and the sortie would have little difficulty remaining hidden. Concealed doors also existed but one must know the lock combinations. A previous McCallum laird had installed the intricate mechanisms for added security. Daly knew one combination and the family members were privy to the rest. Intrigued, Alistair wanted to examine the devices but there was a rescue to implement and a small battle to wage.

* * *

The morning sun peeped through the arched glass window of the antechamber, awakening Kennis. Suddenly alert, her skin tingled; someone other than Grizel was in the room. Kennis nudged her and she softly moaned. "Grizel," she whispered. "Wake up."

Grizel opened her sleepy eyes, trying to focus. Kennis placed her finger on her lips, bidding her to be quiet. She drew the dirk from her bodice and hunched behind a barrel. To her astonishment, the door of the hidden passage slid open and a grey-cloaked figure crept out.

The phantom surveyed the room left to right, and she didn't dare reveal herself. Grizel crouched next to her, wide-eyed and mouth open in amazement.

"What is It?" she asked.

"A man, I'm sure, but I don't know if he's a friend or foe. Let's wait and see what he does."

The grey figure swept through the room on a whisper. It slipped behind a granite monument in the passage, one that she and Robbie had hidden behind when at play as children. Now, the large stone served as a shield from real enemies.

Footsteps sounded in the hall. A Campbell soldier strode down the passage toward them, two bowls of gruel on a tray.

The two girls scrambled to their makeshift pallet, pretending to have just arisen.

"Thank you very much, sir," Kennis said sweetly. "Forsooth, might we also have an urn of water and a basin?" She patted her hair. "To wash, you see."

The man grunted as he slapped down the tray. "Ye can be glad for this muck, lassie, but I'll see what I can do for ye."

The grey figure stole behind him, arm upraised, and struck a hard blow to the man's head. He crumpled to the floor and the phantom pulled the body behind the crates and barrels, hiding it from all seers. Emerging from behind the stock, he beckoned to them to follow as he slipped through the arched doorway and quietly trod down the hall.

He seemed familiar, and Kennis recalled the funny pirate who had engaged her for two dances at Inveraray on All Saint's Eve.

The din of battle greeted them as they neared the Great Hall, the cry of *Cruachan!* echoing outside the walls of the once grand McCallum stronghold. Her heart leapt. She never imagined that hearing a Campbell war cry outside the gates of her beloved home would stir her as it did, or that she could be utterly thankful to a host of Campbells.

* * *

The Earl of Breadalbane, astride his powerful grey steed, watched the ongoing battle as he prepared to reenter the fight. He'd received a light wound in his thigh and pulled back for a short moment to bind it tight. Gazing upon the combating forces, he realized that more and more of their adversaries poured from the surrounding hills. He hoped Alistair would win the gates in time. This was no ordinary battle, it was an ambush.

The small band that fought with them, Conor Malcolm's friend Patrick and his men, was simply not enough of an addition to the Campbell host to prevent them from being overwhelmed in the onslaught of a second wave of enemies. If he were to meet his Maker this day, then it would be with the ancient cry of his forefathers upon his lips.

"*Cruachan!*" he cried as he sped forward on his horse, raising his broadsword one last time. He heard Duncan shout, "*Buaidh no bas, Victory or Death!*" as his sword locked with that of an opponent.

* * *

Alistair crept through the brush with his sortie of men toward the postern gate. To his surprise, it appeared unguarded and he whistled, signaling the archers above to shoot at need. His heart beat in anticipation of the fight. He heard the shout of the MacDougall battle cry far off in the distance. *It must be Duncan.* His blood pulsed through his veins, singing with the rush of battle. He gained the trees by the gate and miraculously, it swung open in greeting. Surprised, he pulled back as a grey figure stepped through in welcome, giving him pause.

"How in Hades did he get in there?" he muttered, remembering the secret doors Daly had mentioned.

Farrell, close behind him, grunted. "Must be a phantom."

"'Tis no phantom, I tell you," he said, certain of himself. "When this is over, I plan to learn the man's tricks." He ran lightly forward and warily stepped inside, waving at his men to follow. As he slipped into the shadows, a most welcome sight greeted his eyes. Kennis and Grizel stood pressed to the wall. A wave of relief washed over him. "Lass," he said, the words a verbal caress.

The phantom turned and paused for a moment, listening. A Campbell jumped at him from behind and the fight was on. Alistair wheeled to engage his enemies, drawn into the battle. He parried and drew first blood, leaping after the man in his fury. When he was driven off in pursuit of his quarry and surrounded by more attackers, Kennis lost sight of him in the fray.

Outside the walls of Dunchalum, the Campbell host suffered heavy losses. Duncan and Patrick fought desperately side-by-side, Highlander and pirate of the high seas, attempting to hold the high ground upon which they stood. A new hum erupted in the hills surrounding them as they neared the heavy gates. The mist slowly dissipated and the skirl of bagpipes resounded through the Highland tors and glens. *The Campbells are coming,* the pipes loudly sang.

Argyll, it must be Argyll, if only he is not too late! Renewed hope caused strength to flow through Alistair's body. He dodged musket fire and rejoined the fight with enthusiasm.

* * *

"I only hope we're not too late!" Argyll voiced his concern aloud.

"We canna be," the McKinnon said firmly. "We should make a charge of it now. The poor lads are overwhelmed."

Argyll nodded and his Captain sounded the alarm. *Cruachan!* The low pitch of the battle cry surged to a crescendo as the first wave of combined Campbell forces inundated the Highlands surrounding Dunchalum Castle. Rushing through the trees, down the tracks and through open spaces in the brush they charged, battleaxes, broadswords and ancient claymores raised high, a shout of war upon their lips.

Alistair sprinted for the great gates of Dunchalum as the men broke through to the curtain wall. He climbed into the tower, slew the gatekeeper and drove the point of his sword into the wooden floor with purpose. He cranked the windlass, connected by pulleys, ropes and chains to the portcullis, and slowly raised the iron grill.

Below, his men struggled to gain the gates and lift the heavy wooden bar that held them fast against outside forces. At last, the portcullis began to rise. Farrell, Daly, and the big man Fergus lifted the bar before pulling open the thick, iron-clad gates. Duncan and Patrick led the charge into the teeming bailey as the gates swung inward.

Eavan Malcolmson, his wound opened from fighting and profusely bleeding, followed behind. He had two thoughts alone; the first was for Kennis' safety and the other, to kill Cameron Campbell. The coward was probably hiding somewhere, confident that he'd win the day.

Eavan's dreams were over; he was sorry for his misdeeds. Never a hero, he resolved to leave this world avenged of his real enemy. He dashed to the entrance of the Great Hall and finding no one there, sought his quarry in the former library. He found Cameron, stuffing a sack with a few of his precious possessions.

"Well, Campbell," he snarled, "I've found you at last. Prepare to meet your death."

"You always did have too much of a flair for the dramatic," Cameron said, an edge to his voice. "Don't underestimate me, Malcolmson, I'm not a novice." His beady eyes glittered. "Swords, or pistols?"

In answer, Eavan raised his unsheathed broadsword. The heavy swords clashed and the men careened under the blows. Eavan grasped the hilt with two hands, weak from his injury, and brought his sword down upon the villain's blade. His height gave him the advantage but he was rapidly losing blood.

Cameron's eyes gleamed with a murderous light. Eavan backed Cameron into a table and as it flipped over, nearly lost his balance. Cameron shied away, threw a lantern at him to block his path and ran for the door, hoping to gain an advantage on the steps outside. Eavan leapt after him and the two men crashed through the double doors of the Great Hall, tumbling down the steps onto the hard stone of the flagged courtyard. Eavan lay on the ground severely weakened, struggling to stand up and fight.

Kennis and Grizel, hidden in the shadows against the castle wall, awaited their opportunity to dash out of the open postern gate and into the wooded hillside. Kennis closely watched the fighting and lost sight of Alistair as he raced into the bailey where the men thronged and the battle raged. The phantom, too, had disappeared along with most of the sortie who accompanied Alistair. She intently searched the sea of men for Alistair's dark head. Suddenly, the shrill gloating voice of Cameron Campbell, raised high above the clamor, pierced the air.

"And now, Malcolmson," he avowed, "you'll meet your end. You should have listened to me, lad, and not become attached to the girl."

Kennis' heart wrenched at Eavan's anguished groan. On impulse, she rushed around the corner into the courtyard and arrived in time to see the Campbell jerk his sword from Eavan's chest. "Nay!" she cried, running toward the two men.

Alistair and the phantom each heard her outcry. Engaged in battle, neither was free to hasten to her side. Cameron crept toward her, menacing, and grabbed her by the wrist. She fought him, clawing, twisting out of his grasp. He overpowered her, dragging her to where Grizel waited, cowering in the shade. "Come with me, girl," he commanded.

"I'll kill you first." Kennis glared at him, reaching for the dirk Eavan had given her.

"I think not, mistress," he hissed. "'Tis unfortunate I can't take both of you right now. I'll take her instead, the little coward, although your spunk and beauty would benefit me more."

"You won't take her anywhere, you monster!" She seized Grizel's arm and pulled. "Fight him, Grizel, we can do this together."

Cameron smirked, raised his dirk and pierced Kennis' shoulder. "There," he snarled, "let that teach you, wench."

Grizel screamed. Kennis collapsed in excruciating pain, breathing hard, groaning before a dark shadow clouded her mind and she knew no more. When she awoke, she lay in the Great Hall on a pallet, an anxious John Dhu keeping watch. "Grandad?" she whispered faintly.

He patted her hand in an effort to comfort her and pressed a cool cloth to her brow. "Ye gave me a terrible fright, lassie. When the duke and I saw ye lyin' there in the midst o' the *glee glashin'*—" He choked on the words.

She gave him a tremulous smile. "You should've known that I wouldn't go easily, sir. I'm half McKinnon, remember?"

Tears misted over his eyes. "Aye, lass, that ye are. Can ye sit up a little? Slowly, so ye'll nae faint." He slipped his hand behind her back and raised her to lean against the wall for support.

"Grandad," she asked. "How did we fare?" She shifted, uncomfortable and in pain.

"'Tis a long story, lass, but I think I can safely say that all them that matter to ye the most are well." He smiled at her look of relief.

"And Eavan?" she said weakly.

"I was about to tell ye. He's askin' to see ye, lass, 'tis why I wanted to see if ye could raise your head."

"I don't think I can walk."

"Naught a problem." He nodded to a man standing nearby that she hadn't previously noticed. Alistair kept watch over her as she spoke with John Dhu. Silent, he leaned over and carefully swept her into his arms. His face was streaked with dirt and sweat, his clothing torn and bloodied.

"Are you hurt?" She gazed with concern into the haggard face of the man she loved.

"Nay, lass," he said in a quiet voice. "'Tis the blood of other men."

He set her gently down by Eavan's still form. His breathing was ragged, an untimely death near. "Eavan," she said, endeavoring to recall him for a moment. "Can you hear me?"

She drew closer to him and pleaded to Alistair to give her assistance. He knelt beside her and lifted Eavan's head onto her lap. "Eavan," she said quietly, "I want you to know that in spite of all that's happened, I've already forgiven you." She tried to hold back the tears but a few escaped and ran down her cheek. "I hope you remember what I've told you about God, you must think of Him right now. He loves you no matter what you've done and," her breath caught on a small sob, "I love you, too."

He spoke so softly in return that she leaned over further to hear his final words. "It's time I took the low road, Kennis, dinna grieve for me. The high road 'tis yours, promise me you'll live, and love hard. I just dinna see it right before, the things that really matter." He coughed weakly, struggling to speak, a rivulet of blood trickling from the corner of his mouth. "I'm glad I've a chance to tell you how sorry I am, lass, sorry for all of this." He trembled. "I, I—" he gasped, growing inordinately still, "told Him, too. See Him soon, I hope."

He stared, unseeing, reaching for her with his once strong hand. She clasped it, intertwining her fingers with his blood-soaked ones. "You must...talk...to Niall. Key—" He drew in one last shuddering breath as his body relaxed into death. His hand fell limp within hers and Kennis, weary from the events that had brought her to this place, wept unashamedly. Tears coursed down her cheeks in grief at the loss of a friend, a man who she had embraced as a brother. His repentance moved her deeply and all treacherous acts were forgiven.

Alistair gently pried her away and returned her to John Dhu, then strode out of the room, his face expressionless. Unbidden, his question was answered and his greatest fear realized.

"Grandad," Kennis sniffed, drying her eyes. "Why did Alistair leave just now? I needed him to stay with me."

"At a time like this, lass, there's little a man can do," he said simply. "What did ye say to him?"

"Very little," she said. "I asked if he was hurt and he said no, and then I sat with Eavan." The tears welled up in her eyes again. "Oh, Grandad, I can't believe that he's dead." She threw her arms around his neck and sobbed.

"There, there now, dinna worrit, lassie," he comforted. "Everythin' will work out for the best, ye'll see. Get some rest now. There's to be a meetin' later after supper."

* * *

Alistair drew a bucket of water, his dark brow clouded, brooding over Kennis' words to Eavan. Perhaps in time she would forget him. She was young, and time was known to heal wounds of the heart as well as the body. As for him, he didn't think that he'd ever love another woman and in spite of his earlier resolve, he couldn't forgive her for this final betrayal.

Duncan interrupted his dark thoughts. "You're serious, brother, and here I thought you were glad to see me."

"I am glad to see you, scapegrace," he said soberly. "But it doesn't mean I want your company just now."

"I see," Duncan said. "If you want to talk about it, I'm available."

"Not this time." Alistair found an unoccupied spot in the busy courtyard to sit and meditate before the evening meeting. He wetted his face with cool water and washed dried blood and dirt from his hands. The realities of battle weighed heavily upon him. He would do everything in his power in future to ensure peace and to prevent brothers from killing one another. Tonight's meeting would prove interesting. He must rest and think no further about the lass. *Impossible.*

Chapter 23

Revelations

Kennis waited impatiently for the evening meeting to begin, reclining on cushions that Argyll's Campbells discovered lying about the castle.

She recognized each embroidered pillow with a heavy heart. The cross-stitched sage came from her own bedchamber and the russet floral from her mother's solar. Tears formed in her eyes. Amazing how emotional she became over a few lost pillows. Her former life was gone forever, and now more important things weighed on her mind—Alistair, for one.

She knew that he was weary from battle yet he'd not spoken a word to her since he returned to the hall for supper. She felt hurt and neglected; he'd not even inquired after her health. The second person that weighed heavily upon her heart was Grizel. She'd let the cruel man abduct the poor girl. I'm such a failure, she thought bitterly.

The Duke of Argyll rose to address the large group assembled in the once grand McCallum Great Hall. "As you all know, we've put down the villain Cameron Campbell, our former kinsman who will soon be legally disinherited to all rights and claims of the Campbells. But we have only accomplished a portion of our task. The Lady Grizel Campbell is still missing, we assume taken by him as hostage. Does anyone have any information concerning her disappearance?"

"Grandad," Kennis exclaimed, holding her hand to her forehead. "I forgot to tell you!"

John Dhu turned his gaze upon his granddaughter. "Eh, lass?"

"Grizel," she said. "I know what the villain will do with her."

"Easy now, ye've had a terrible shock. Tell me what ye know."

"But I've known all along he was going to sell us as slaves. 'Twas supposed to be Vanora, not Grizel. Denoon was his contact. You remember, I told you about him when I—" She frowned, detesting the reminder of her own foolishness.

"Aye, go on."

"He's got a ship, sailing up the coast to pick up new cargo. That's all I know."

"I'll tell his grace." The old chief rose from his chair and hobbled forward to give the duke the information. Upon hearing the news, Grizel's father, the Earl of Breadalbane, slumped back in his chair.

Alistair and Duncan both offered to ride to the coast with him to mount a search near Oban. The earl thankfully accepted the offer. They would ride immediately following the meeting with the notorious Captain Grahame, who had sent the Duke of Argyll the infamous ransom note at Inveraray.

"Now for the second area of business," Argyll said crisply. "Earlier this month, I received a letter from one Captain Aloysius Grahame demanding a large sum of money in exchange for one of our kinsman. He's bringing Magnus Campbell here tonight as per my request, and demands a ransom of ten thousand pounds to be paid upon his return as well as pardons for various participants of the '45."

A disapproving murmur spread through the crowd. "The man's a villain, why should we want him back, or them rebels?" a Campbell cried out.

In answer, a grey-cloaked figure floated into the room, surrounded by the pirates who had escorted Duncan and fought in the battle. Bloodstains spotted the phantom's cloak, his own as well as that of the men he'd slain. His clear voice reverberated in the hall. "You should want him back to try him for his infamy, to give justice to his victims."

Alistair poked Farrell. "You see, Farrell, I told you that your phantom was mere flesh and blood."

Farrell looked sheepish. "He was most persuasive, you'll have t' agree."

Alistair nodded and listened, intent upon the would-be phantom and his cohorts.

Kennis sat up higher and gave the stranger her full attention. She was grateful for his aid. He'd taken her and Grizel from the castle to the postern gate in safety.

"You are, I presume," the duke said with hauteur, "the author of this outrageous missive?"

He dramatically swirled the folds of his cloak. "I am."

"Then you are Captain Aloysius Grahame."

"To some." A smile lit his clear voice.

"Nonsense, you are or you're not, sir," Argyll said, impatient to get to the bottom of the mystery. "Enough of this insolence! I demand an answer."

The phantom chuckled. "You agree to abide by the rules of parlay, as we do upon the high seas, giving quarter to mortal enemies and villains alike?"

The duke was astounded. "You dare to barter with me?"

"Indeed, your grace, I do, for not only am I in need of your consideration but so are the gentlemen who accompany me. In addition," he said, "we humbly thank you for the loan of your horses."

A few scattered guffaws echoed around the room.

"I see." Argyll scowled and waved his hand in acquiescence. "Very well, I grant you what's due for your activity on behalf of my kinsman. Now, enough of the play acting."

"'Tisn't acting, sir, I've come to claim what's rightfully mine." He threw back his hood, dropped the stained cloak to the ground and stood with both hands on hips. "Sir Robert McCallum, at your service, your grace. And these men are my shipmates, fellow Scots who insist that you accede to our demands in exchange for this human filth, Magnus Campbell, your kinsman." He pushed the bound man to his knees.

Kennis was speechless. Her own brother Robbie for whom she'd mourned, longed for and mounted a search of her own was the phantom. She sat, frustrated, unable to rise to her feet and run to him.

Knowing her thoughts, he turned and faced her in the long hall and grinned. "Excuse me, your grace." He strode to where she lounged on the floor and gently gathered her into his arms. The tears that ran down his face mingled with hers as the two were lost in happy reunion.

"I thought I'd never see you again," Kennis murmured.

"Nor I, but we must talk later." He studied her face keenly. "Mam and Mairi are well?"

"Aye, but you must go to Inveraray to see them, not Skye or Lewis."

He blinked. "Inveraray, how's this?"

She giggled, echoing his words. "We must talk later, 'tis a long story."

He released her and turned to his grandfather. "Och, lad, ye had me fooled!" The old chief clapped his arms around him. "Ye went away a boy and came back a man."

Rob laughed and hugged him before pulling away and returning to the duke.

Argyll gave him a hard stare. "A remarkable resemblance, young McCallum, not only to your sister but to your father. You're equally audacious."

"Am I? I'm delighted to know that, sir." A boyish grin spread across his tanned face. He turned to his first mate. "My irresistible charm, Patrick, didn't I tell you?"

"Aye, ye did, Cap."

"And how exactly did you return to Scotland in the company of these reb-, er, companions of yours?"

"By ship, how else?" Rob was unapologetic. "'Twas the only way, to commandeer the very ship that had taken us there against our will in the first place."

"You've stolen it, then," Argyll said cryptically.

"Not at all, your grace," he insisted. "Consider it borrowed. The vessel was used for villainous acts and became an open target for the honest man."

"Your grace," Alistair interrupted. "Don't you think we'd best settle this at a later time, when we've found the Lady Grizel or discovered her whereabouts? We lose valuable time bantering."

"What do you suggest, Alistair?"

"That we adjourn this discussion to a future date and in the meantime, offer pardon to this young man and his followers for their participation in the confrontation today."

"Ah." Argyll tiredly passed his hand over his eyes. "A very good notion." He rose and hammered the table in front of him. "Now hear this, all present. I, Archibald Campbell, Duke of Argyll, declare Robert McCallum and his followers a temporary pardon until this issue can be resolved."

Rob frowned and stiffened. "Temporary, your grace?"

"You must understand that even I can't grant you a full pardon, lad. Only the Baron's Court and the King himself have the power to do so. However, I can stay any hand in the West of Scotland from moving against you for the present."

"Very well, then," he said with reluctance. "I'll go with you to the coast to search for the young woman. We'll sail from here to Bristol and north, if necessary, seeking word of her if that will suit."

"Do you desire this rogue's assistance, Breadalbane?" Argyll asked his kinsman.

"Indeed, I'm grateful for his offer and accept with goodwill."

"Then let us depart," Alistair said, "within a half hour." He bowed to the duke and strode out of the hall.

Kennis watched him go, disappointed by his neglect. He didn't even glance in her direction.

Rob came to her in parting. "Greet our mother and wee Mairi for me, Kennis. I'm eager to see them," he said, winking, "but I think I must assist these poor helpless Campbells."

She held onto his hands tightly. "We have so much to talk about, Robbie. Hurry, and return to us."

"At Inveraray?" he quizzed her again. "That must be a tale."

"Aye," she said, blushing. "'Tis your fault, really."

He arched a fair brow. "My fault," he retorted, "how so?"

"For being gone so long and never once contacting me, or letting us know that you were alive and well."

"'Twas more difficult than you know." He gave her hands a parting squeeze. "Fare well, lass."

"Fare well," she whispered. Two of the most important men in her life had walked out of it, again.

Chapter 24

Consultations

No trace of Grizel could be found.

Alistair and the Earl of Breadalbane searched the coast between Dunolly and Craignish, making careful inquiry along the way. Later that night, Farrell, who had scouted south of Craignish, brought similar tidings. The men retired early for the night; the earl, suffering from mental and physical exhaustion, slept incredibly sound. Rob and Duncan would arrive from their journey along the southern coast by morning.

Struggling between exhaustion and bitterness of spirit, Alistair couldn't make up his mind about Kennis. Joy and relief welled up within him when he saw her at the postern gate of Dunchalum, she must have seen it. His heart nearly stopped when the Campbell soldier carried her limp body into the hall. He'd waited hours for her to stir, not leaving her side until she awakened. Then, he thought bitterly, he'd carried her to see Eavan Malcolmson on his deathbed and she'd uttered the precious words that he longed to hear upon her lips, *I love you*, to the villain.

If it weren't true, she'd not have said it. Or would she, to appease a dying man? Maybe it was his own fault for not declaring himself sooner. His dark brows drew together in a straight line. She seemed sincere in her affection. Restless, he tossed and turned, an endless tangle of emotion knotting his breast. When the sun finally streamed through his window early the next morning, his mood was darker than the night. *God help me to find the truth.*

* * *

The journey from Dunchalum to Inveraray seemed inordinately long to Kennis. Random thoughts, from Kilcalum to Robbie and to Alistair, flitted through her mind. Her dream of home had evaporated with the morning mist. She'd been unable to visit the clan in the village, at least the few who remained. When Robbie came back, if he ever came back, she thought sadly, the two of them would return to the Highlands. Her shoulders drooped. Alistair's behavior mystified her and she didn't know what she'd done to offend him. She exhaled in frustration.

"Alright, lass?" Daly asked.

"Nay, Daly, I'm not," she said, rueful. "I ache and hurt and there's nothing for it, I have to go on."

He was sympathetic. "We could pull a litter, give ye a powder to ease the pain. Ye might be more comfortable."

She shook her head. "Mam will think I'm half dead if you carry me to Inveraray like that. She'll cosset me for a year, and then I'll become nothing but a cross old maid for sure."

He chuckled. "I hear ye, lass, but one look at your face and the mistress'll know ye're nae up to snuff."

The words he prophesied came true. Lady McCallum, hearing of their arrival, ran to the Great Hall to greet her daughter and father. "Kennis, love, you're ill," she said upon seeing Kennis' chalky face.

"Not sick, Mam," she smiled wanly. "I was hurt in a little scuffle."

"A little scuffle, eh," John Dhu said, walking behind her. "That murderous Cameron Campbell stabbed our lass in the shoulder with a dirk, he did. Ye'd best hae a look at that wound and get the girl to bed, Alanna. I tended it myself but we've had a long journey. Here, we need a footman to carry the lass up those stairs."

Alarmed, Alanna scurried about and ordered hot water and linens. By the time Kennis' wound was dressed and she was laid upon her bed, she fell fast asleep from exhaustion. Alanna spent the night in her room upon a couch and Lady Grear and Ona visited to inquire after her health.

"I'll sit with her, Lady McCallum," Ona offered, "when you need a rest."

"Thank you, Ona, that is very kind of you, perhaps later when she's better and seeking a companion to entertain her."

Ona curtseyed and excused herself. Lady Grear also offered her services which Alanna gratefully received but declined.

* * *

When Duncan and Rob arrived at Craignish the next morning, Alistair was as sociable as a bear. For once, Duncan refrained from teasing his elder brother as the four men made plans to travel to Inveraray on the following day. Occupied with thoughts of Kennis on the entire journey, Alistair's mood grew blacker by the time they reached the castle, his steely composure severely off balance.

"Alistair," Lady Grear said, concerned. "Are you ill?"

"Nay, Mother, I'm not." The scowl on his face would have intimidated anyone but his mother.

Lady Grear pressed her case. "What is the matter with you? I've naught seen you like this since you were a child and couldn't have your way."

His laugh was harsh. "A spoiled child, am I, well that's something wonderful. Next you'll say I've been—" He stopped. He'd nearly revealed his feelings in his distressed state of mind.

Lady Grear regarded him thoughtfully. Since Kennis was ill, he must confess the truth. "You were going to say disappointed in love," she said, testing the waters, "were you not, my son? I might be able to help you," she encouraged. "I'm not Duncan or Ona, I won't tease."

Alistair felt tempted. It was true, she was the one person who genuinely had his best interests at heart.

She gently touched his arm. "I'm not blind, Alistair, to your feelings for Kennis. I think you've been the last to discover them yourself. It's not weak to love or for others to see it in you."

He gazed at her blankly before walking to the door. "Perhaps not in most cases like this, Mother," he paused, hand on the latch. "But not when the one for whom you have deep feelings doesn't return your affection and has declared her love for someone else." He pulled open the door. "I'm returning to Dunolly tomorrow, and will travel to Craignish from there in a couple of days. When you're prepared to depart Inveraray, send a gillie to me with a message."

"You shouldn't go with this issue unresolved."

"'Tis resolved," he said stiffly, reminding her of his late father. "I've nothing more to say on the subject." He strode out of the room to the stairs and paused at Kennis' door. He should inquire after the lass. He'd felt her distress when he ignored her at Dunchalum, saw the pain etched in her face.

He reached out to knock and withdrew his hand, cursing himself for his foolhardiness and all women for their fickle behavior. Entering the duke's library minutes later, he discovered all of the men gathered there in the midst of a heated discussion.

Duncan jumped up at sight of him. "Alistair," he said, excited. "I've decided to go to Jamaica with Rob and the earl, that is, if I have your permission."

"What's the girl to you?" he said roughly.

Duncan frowned at him. "I'm going to help search for her, that's all."

"Somehow," Alistair said, sarcastic, "I rather thought you were more interested in the adventure."

"Of course he is, Alistair," Argyll interrupted. "What lad isn't? He'll be good company to Breadalbane."

"Aye, and to me, too," Rob chimed in.

"What's in this for you, Rob McCallum, eh? You've just now returned to Scotland from all of your meanderings, and you're eager to be off sailing the seas again?" he mocked. "You may have some explaining to do concerning your activities."

"You'll not intimidate me, Alistair MacDougall," he said cheerfully. "When I was a lad I stood in awe of you, like the older brother I never had, but now I'm my own master."

"Och," said John Dhu, "they're roastin' ye, Alistair lad. Our Rob here's come by some important news, and we're all goin' to the dungeon to see if there be truth to it."

Alistair was skeptical. "I've no interest in my prisoner. Do what you want with him."

"I will," Argyll said. "But we're talking about Magnus Campbell, not the other rogue. See here, Alistair," he said, tapping his fingers impatiently upon his desk, "you've gone to an enormous amount of trouble to help the McCallum's." He held up his hand to silence Alistair's protest. "And I intend to get to the bottom of this matter."

"What matter are you speaking of, your grace?" he asked, confused.

Argyll was smug. "You see, you don't know everything. Rumor has it, according to Master McCallum here, that his father is alive somewhere in the Caribbean."

Alistair was astounded. "But the papers stating his death were verified."

"I know, by Kenneth Malcolm."

Kenneth Malcolm was the mysterious *KM* that Alistair assumed was Kennis when he mistakenly accused her of being involved in a conspiracy to betray her brother. He should have known better than to suspect her of such a despicable act. His thoughts wandered to her, lying abed upstairs, and his pulse quickened.

"Your wits are gone a begging, Alistair," Argyll said. "He was Cameron Campbell's accessory on the Baron's Court. We're sure that he falsified the records, and shipped Robert off to Jamaica when a full pardon was granted, due to the influence of several lairds who insisted that his case be reexamined. Sir Geoffrey, who wasn't a member of the court at the time, has discovered that Robert McCallum was exonerated and required to pay a fine to have his title and estate restored. This is a very serious affair, and I'm attending to it personally."

"And I want to go with Rob and the Earl," Duncan added, hopeful, "to search for Laird Robert and Mistress Grizel. Say yes, Alistair."

"If he won't, Duncan, I will," Argyll said matter-of-factly.

"I see my authority over my family is easily overruled," he said, a touch of coldness in his voice. "It seems everyone delights in flouting it these days." He shrugged. "Do what you wish, Duncan. I'm headed for Dunolly tomorrow," he said, rising to his feet. "Keep me informed, I'd like to know of such news concerning Robert McCallum. I expect you to join me at Craignish before you leave. Where is your ship, Rob?"

"Gylen Castle, off the Isle of Kerrera."

"That's where Duncan was so well hidden."

"Aye," he said, grinning.

"Very clever. Good night, gentlemen." He stood and bowed. "I have a long journey tomorrow." He departed, his countenance bleak, not caring what any of the men assembled in the room might think of him.

* * *

Kennis' wound was healing fast but her spirits were low. She tried to concentrate on the game of chess she played with Robbie but was easily distracted and stared into the fire, detached. He tried to cheer her, imitating the pirate he'd played at the masquerade and succeeded in making her laugh for a short while.

"What ails you, Kennis," he said, concerned, laying his hand over hers in comfort. "It pains me to see your sorrow. Won't you tell me, lass?"

"I can't, Robbie," she said, embarrassed. "If you think I'm sad, what must the rest of the household believe? Perhaps we'd best go home."

His face darkened. "To Skye? We have no home, Kennis, and you know it. It could take a long time for the court to prove anything and restore our lands. Besides, I thought you wanted to return to Kilcalum, to see our people before I leave with Duncan and the earl."

"I do, I'm just so tired right now."

Rob eyed her, speculating. "I could talk to him for you," he ventured. "I've known him these ten years, or more."

Suddenly shy, Kennis stared with guarded eyes into the bright green ones so like her own. "Who exactly do you mean, sir?"

"Don't play games with me, Kennis." He leaned back in the chair and returned her coy gaze. "If you won't admit it, I won't say. I've heard the whole story in bits and pieces, and put one and two together myself. And I might add, dear sister, that Alistair's behavior at Dunolly was worse than yours before we came here. I never saw such a black humor. Kennis," he teased, changing his mode of attack. "What have you done to Alistair MacDougall? The man has the coolest head I've ever seen. If this is what falling in love does to a man," he declared, "I swear that I never will!"

"I think he hates me," she said in a small voice. "He's ignored me completely since Dunchalum."

Rob's ears perked up. "I doubt it. Were you on good terms before that?"

"We were," she hesitated, "getting on a better footing, I think. You remember the masquerade?" He nodded. "After you danced with me, he asked me to dance and we spent the most pleasant half hour together. And he seemed glad to see me—"

He nodded in agreement. "By the postern gate at the castle. I noticed it, too, before that Campbell jumped me. But you said he stopped speaking to you at Dunchalum. Think, Kennis, you must've done something."

"But I didn't," she said, frustrated. "I woke up after I was stabbed and Grandad was with me."

"Aye, and so was Alistair for half the day," he said matter-of-factly. "If that doesn't tell you something, then I don't know what will convince you."

"Faith, I confess that I'm amazed," she marveled. "I didn't know. Grandad helped me to sit up so that I could go to see Eavan before he died. Alistair carried me to him."

Rob leaned forward, an idea forming in his brain. "Kennis, were you friendly with Eavan, too friendly, perhaps?"

"I thought he assumed too much concerning me." She folded her hands neatly in her lap. "It became obvious he loved power and gold more than he ever cared for me."

"But what did you say to him on his deathbed. Did Alistair hear?"

"He couldn't help but hear, he was kneeling right there, supporting me. Robbie," she said, her lethargy disappearing, "do you know something that I don't?"

"Think hard, lass," he said, exasperated. "What did you say?"

She passed her hand over her eyes. "'Tis such a blur, I was hurting and so exhausted, I barely remember."

"Think Kennis," he said more kindly, trying another tack. "Your future happiness may depend upon it."

She stared hard at the floor, brows knit. "Eavan didn't speak at first," she said slowly. "I didn't know what to say or if he could hear me. I told him that in spite of everything I forgave him, and that God loved Him no matter what he'd done. And I said," she breathed, her eyes opening wide as she recalled her words, "I love you, too."

Rob groaned and burst out laughing. "Oh Kennis, he thought you meant it! I never thought I'd feel sorry for Alistair MacDougall, and of all things over a lass. My own sister, no less." He hooted for several more minutes.

"It's not funny, Robbie McCallum," she said, smarting. "I did love Eavan, like a brother. I'd say the same to you, or Daly and Fergus."

"He thought you meant you loved Eavan and not him." He gazed at his sister in amazement. "Do you love him?" he asked curiously. "You've never said you did. 'Tis no small feat to engage the feelings of such a man."

"Are you making fun of me again?"

"Nay, I'm not," he said seriously. "You need to tell him the truth."

"You don't understand, Robbie," Kennis declared. "Since I've met him, I'm constantly explaining myself to him. I know I've acted rashly but he always makes me feel stupid, like every misfortune that follows me, or him, 'tis my fault. At the masquerade, I thought we'd moved beyond suspicion. Now this happens, something for which there's a simple explanation, and he believes the worst of me. How can men be so dim-witted and unfeeling?"

She burst into angry tears, overwhelmed by the events of the last few weeks. "You have no idea what I've been through. I simply can't take any more of this nonsense."

He slipped his arms around her to comfort her, giving her a brotherly squeeze. "We'll fix this, lass, I have an idea."

"How?" she asked hopefully, dabbing at her eyes with a handkerchief.

"We'll discuss it later but for now, I'd like to know a few other things." They talked about her sojourn in the Americas. "You know," he said, remembering, "I saw a girl on the quay before we left Cape Hatteras and thought it was you. She gave a poor child something to eat."

"It could have been me. We left for Scotland about the same time you did, and I spent a lot of time searching the docks for you. I kept hoping that a sailor might have seen you somewhere."

"I had a dream on the night I saw the girl." He stared past her at nothing in particular. "Kennis, have you been dreaming that you're lost in the mist, and you'd give anything to see all of your hopes and dreams fulfilled?"

"Aye, I've had a similar dream but it's been changing recently. I've seen bits and pieces unfold, like something grand is going to be revealed."

He nodded in understanding. "By the way, have you told them about us here? Our people have always known we're different, but these folks just stare at us like we're an exhibition at the fair."

"Nay, I never have. I thought it was best for the Campbells to know as little as possible about us."

Kennis and Rob spent another hour in conversation, comparing notes about their travels, realizing that for at least the last month of Kennis' journey, they were in the same town and walked the same streets but had never connected.

It seemed that Providence intervened and sent Kennis, instead of to Robbie, straight into Alistair's path and into his arms. She hoped that Robbie's current plan to unite her with Alistair would succeed and accomplish the same goal.

Chapter 25

Hope Deferred

The rain drizzled over the string of riders as the horses plodded down the soggy track.

The village of Kilcreag appeared in the distance and the riders separated. Three of the riders trotted down a separate path; soon the gloaming would envelop them all in its damp grey cloak.

One young lad sniffed the hazy air, drinking in the familiar smell of the loch nearby. Wisps of tawny hair, curling in the moist air, escaped his green hood. He eagerly anticipated yet dreaded what tomorrow might bring, and was prepared to thrust himself upon the laird's sense of justice and mercy, if necessary.

The Captain of the party sent a rider ahead to the laird with news of the travelers' arrival and a request for hospitality. He bade the men to pick up the pace. The long journey was overshadowed by rain and cloudy skies, and the thought of a hot meal and a warm bed spurred him onward.

Alistair greeted his guests on a cordial note, bidding them to enter with goodwill. Rob's resemblance to his sister conjured images of Kennis in his mind, which remained in a disordered state. His disappointment heightened his natural reserve; persons unacquainted with him might think him haughty and disagreeable.

Rob watched his host with a keen eye, sensing the raw state of his nerves and didn't plague him with his usual light conversation. Tomorrow would be surprise enough, provided he and Duncan were able to make Alistair cooperate. If all else failed, he'd kidnap him and sail away on a brief voyage.

Forced to spend time with Kennis, he might open his heart to the lass. Alistair was uncommon stubborn, it could take a lengthy time to breach the wall he'd built around his heart.

He smiled. Kennis would have her hands full with Alistair MacDougall but for his own part, he couldn't have chosen a finer man to be her husband. Then again, his younger sister was like quicksilver, impulsive, not always thinking about her actions and landing in trouble, which was exactly how she and Alistair were thrown together in the first place.

He laughed again at the thought of the tale his grandfather related, pleased that he had one axe to hold over Alistair's head. The man was probably squirming even now, wondering if his own net had entangled him. Surely, Alistair comprehended enough of the McKinnon's character to know that the auld chief wouldn't forget a declaration of intent, even if it was a bit irregular. He hoped that they didn't have to serve papers; it would do the relationship little good.

Rob prayed that this matter would be resolved peaceably and take its natural course. In two days, John Dhu and Alanna would arrive at Craignish on their journey home to Skye. In the meantime, he hoped that the lovers would come together of their own accord. Lovers' quarrels were of little interest to him. Women became too emotional and men lost their sense of reason. If it weren't for Kennis' sake, he'd not become involved.

* * *

The lad and his companions rapped on the wooden door of the neat cottage in Kilcreag. Siusan McAllister wiped her hands dry on her apron and walked into the front room to open the door.

When the door opened, the delight upon her face filled the lad with warmth. "Mistress Kennis," she cried. "'Tis a pleasure to see ye, come in, come in." She pulled the door wide to admit the three of them. "And your henchmen, as well. To what do we owe the honor? Cailan, child, come and see who's arrived."

She embraced Kennis. "But why are ye dressed like a lad? I sense another tale's to be had. Ye sure are one to be havin' adventures." She chattered on, and soon Cailan and Aunt Kate entered, followed by Ian McColl.

Kennis enjoyed their company. "You can't tell anyone I'm here. Tomorrow I have a secret meeting," she said, eyes sparkling, "and I came to you because I knew I could trust you. In fact," she told Ian, "you can't tell your Laird either."

"I've no wish to tell him more than needed at present," Ian informed her. "He's been in the blackest mood I've seen in many a day. I do what I must and get out of the man's way." He eyed her with lifted brow. "Ye wouldna happen to know why he's so black, would ye, mistress? I heard a rumor t' other day."

Kennis grinned as her face turned pink. "I *canna* say. But I do have other exciting news that I'm eager to share."

"Good," Siusan said. "Now I'll take ye to your room to refresh yourself, and we'll have a bite to eat and a hot cup of tea."

"And a wee bit of gossip," Kate added with a twinkle.

Laughing, Kennis gladly followed Siusan and reappeared dressed as a young lady. She reserved her suit of lad's clothing for her short journey on the morrow.

* * *

Rob requested a private interview with Alistair after breakfast. Duncan crossed his fingers as the two men left the room. Rob wasn't hopeful; he feared that Alistair would be uncooperative. His second course of action would anger Alistair and he personally felt that it would seem like nothing more than trickery which totally went against his personal code of honor. Still, a verbal declaration of intent was as good as a written one in Scotland. Alistair's pride, as well as his heart, was obviously wounded.

Alistair sat on the edge of his desk, arms crossed, and waiting for Rob to speak. He was unsure of the case Rob would present but knew that the young man would defend his sister.

"I don't know where to begin, Alistair," Rob said, taking care with his words, "but a matter has come to my attention that I must address. I've come to believe that you've made advances to my sister, convincing her of your affection. Is this true?"

Alistair stared at him in amazement. He'd expected a different topic of conversation, another tactic altogether. "Advances?" he said, incredulous. "Tell me what you think these advances consist of, my charming manner, for instance?"

Rob frowned. "Only you and she know what's between you, Alistair. I do know that you hovered over her at Dunchalum for hours when she was wounded. I saw your face, and heard the caress in your voice when you spied her by the gate at Dunchalum. What do you want me to do, resolve this lovers' quarrel for you by describing every detail? I don't know every detail, I haven't been here, if you recall. I do know that you aren't being honest with her or with yourself, and that you've mistaken her intent."

Alistair was on the defensive. "And just what do you think her intent is, lad?"

"'Tis generally a man's responsibility to declare his intent first, you know that. And from what I've gathered, you've done nothing but confuse the lass, browbeating her one minute and making love to her the next."

"Is that so?" he said, sarcastic. "And you think this is all my doing, that she's an innocent and hasn't been playing her own little games?"

"I don't believe she has," Rob replied. "You've mistaken her nature."

Alistair's eyes narrowed. "Have I?"

"Indeed. Of a truth, we've always had a special bond. I can almost feel what she feels *and*," he emphasized, "you judge her wrongly."

"I wonder about this *special bond* between the two of you," he mocked. "It seems unnatural."

"What do you mean by those words, sir?" Rob said, angered by the implication. "Explain yourself."

"Nay." Alistair's mood was fragile and his temper rose. "I won't, neither will I tolerate any more impudence from you, Rob McCallum."

Rob, alias Captain Grahame, was no longer the tow-headed lad that Alistair rescued from the Great Stag Chalum. He'd grown accustomed at the advanced age of twenty-one to obedience without question by his followers. He drew himself up to his full height and played his ace. "Well then, since you won't see reason and admit that you love the girl, I insist on reminding you of your pledge."

"Do you indeed?" Alistair's brows drew together and a slow, angry flush spread over his face. "Of what pledge do you speak that you insist I honor?"

"It wasn't made to me but to my grandfather, and you know exactly of what I'm speaking."

"You mistake the matter, lad."

"Do I?" Rob said with hauteur. "I wouldn't ask for a lass' hand in marriage from her nearest kinsman without the intention of honoring my vow."

Alistair was furious. Caught in his own net, he still refused to yield. "I made no formal promise. You dare to threaten me?"

"Not I," Rob said calmly. "The McKinnon. He'll demand that you marry her, honoring the verbal pledge you made to him on Skye. If you don't cooperate, he'll serve you papers for breach of promise or go to Argyll and demand satisfaction."

Alistair's eyes hardened. "I believe you, knowing the McKinnon, but that hasn't changed my mind as of yet. There's no breach of promise. What of you?"

Rob decided to be honest. "You can argue that point with my grandfather when he arrives. I'll enforce any decision he makes. For my own part, I don't wish to see Kennis made unhappy and if you don't love her, I wouldn't force the match." He held Alistair's eye. "I'm disappointed, Alistair, and inclined to believe that she's rid of a bad bargain by not marrying you under any condition. At any rate, you should talk with her. This whole situation is the result of a misunderstanding."

He consulted his timepiece. "She's prepared to talk to you to resolve this issue. You have ten minutes in which to meet her by the loch. If you don't go, then the opportunity to resolve this issue amicably is over. I'll leave it in the McKinnon's hands." Rob shook his head in wonder at Alistair's attitude. "Aren't you even curious to hear what she has to say?"

Caught between his pride and his desire, Alistair submitted. "I'll go," he growled. "It would seem I have little choice."

"Before you leave there's something else you should know."

His eyes narrowed. "What, more secrets?"

"Not at all," Rob said pleasantly. "To set the record straight, the special bond Kennis and I share, and you openly sneered at, is only this—we're twins. Sometimes I feel what she feels and dream what she dreams, and vice versa." He shrugged. "That's all there is to it, can't be helped."

"Hmph," Alistair grunted and strode from the room, his face grim.

Duncan loitered in the hall and apprehended Rob for news when Alistair had gone. "Well?"

"It doesn't bode well. I fear for her, Duncan." He clenched his fists. "If he treats her roughly, I'll—"

Duncan placed a comforting hand upon his shoulder. The two men entered the silent library and awaited the outcome of the fated meeting.

* * *

Kennis paced by the loch of Craignish in trepidation. Five more minutes and she'd leave, devastated. She hoped Robbie was right in thinking that Alistair would be sensible enough to converse with her. She climbed onto the *suidhe* and wondered how many ladies in a similar situation had sat in this very spot, thinking of the men they loved, hoping against all hope that issues of the heart would be resolved.

Someone was coming, a quick firm stride that she intuitively recognized. She sat down and swung her legs over the side of the *suidhe*, prepared to jump down. The lad's breeches were comfortable; she decided that she liked them and would wear them more often when she was out by herself on errands or roaming the woods.

* * *

Alistair saw the lad plop down on the flat stone, merrily swinging his legs. He wondered if Kennis had gone or if she'd actually had the nerve to come to talk to him. His heart was heavy; it was better if he didn't see the lass now. He would honor his word to the McKinnon rather than drag the lass' name through the mire but the arrangement wouldn't offer the pleasure that he'd anticipated. He felt trapped, and his anger rose to the surface.

His intention was to seek an alternative to an engagement to Vanora Campbell, and the McKinnon knew this to be true. The lass pleased him from the first and he'd already decided to pursue her acquaintance before his involvement in her many difficulties. To be forced into a marriage, whether he desired the lass or not, only served to arouse his wrath. His manner was stiff and cold as he neared the lad to inquire if he'd seen a golden-haired lady.

"Tell me, lad," he called. "Has a fair lady been here in the last ten minutes or so?" He began his descent down the steep path.

A deep mischievous gurgle answered his inquiry. "Nay, sir," Kennis attempted to mask her voice, "only we lads are out early this mornin'."

Alistair smiled a little in spite of his ill humor. "You can't fool me, lass. I've been the brunt of your tricks too many times." He studied her from head to foot, amused and enticed by the slim look of the lass in a lad's clothing.

Kennis grinned, relief flooding her soul. "I'm glad you've come, Alistair," she said, addressing him by his given name.

His heart skipped a beat, hearing his name upon her rosy lips. "Why?"

Taken aback, she stared at him. "Didn't Robbie explain, I mean, that I wanted to speak with you about," she hesitated, and then took a bold step, "our misunderstanding?"

His eyes hardened. "There's been no misunderstanding. I'll marry you, even if 'tis under duress." He bowed formally. "I'll make you a proper husband, mistress, I promise."

She immediately disliked his words and tone of voice. "What do you mean, *Marry me under duress and make me a proper husband?*" She jumped down from the *suidhe* and stood facing him.

"Don't play games with me." A fierce light burned in his eyes. "You, your brother, and your wily grandfather have succeeded in your objective."

Smoldering, Kennis crossed her arms and planted her feet apart. "What objective is that, sir?"

He smirked and drew near to her. "One of your own devising, apparently. Soon you'll be mine and you'll have no say in the matter." His mocking eyes raked over her, taking in every detail. He stroked her soft cheek with his finger.

She quivered at his touch. "That's not what Robbie and I discussed."

"Nay? Then perhaps you should speak to the McKinnon, he'll come to the point more readily."

She stamped her foot in frustration. "I still don't understand what you mean. Will you please not speak in riddles?"

He slid his arm around her shoulders and pulled her close. Irresistibly, he bent his head to hers. *Just one kiss.* After all, she belonged to him now. "If an arranged marriage is what you wish, lass," his voice was husky, "then here I am, ready and willing."

Suddenly breathless and filled with her own desire, Kennis melted into his embrace. She tilted her head back to meet his kiss and suddenly realized that it was wrong. "Nay, let me go." She'd done nothing to earn his disdain and wanted his genuine affection. He must need her, love her, not just want her. She would have him no other way.

"How dare you insult me?" She struggled to be free of his tight embrace. "I came here of my own free will to speak with you and this is the treatment that I deserve?" Trembling, her worn emotions flew out of control. "I hate ye," she said, her Highland temper raging. "I ne'er want t' see ye agin!"

He frowned. So, the truth was before him. She did love Eavan Malcolmson. His full-fledged anger poured forth in a torrent. "You hate me, and this is the gratitude I receive for honoring my word. 'Tis what you planned from the beginning, and you've involved not only your own family in your deceit but mine as well. You wretched girl," he said resentfully, "you're bound to me whether you want me or not." He gripped her shoulders tightly and pressed his lips to hers, hard and demanding. "Your clever grandfather has manipulated us both into this confounded engagement."

"I'm nae betrothed t' ye and I ne'er will be, Alistair MacDougall." Kennis tried to break free again. "I'd rather be daid!" She pummeled his chest.

"I can arrange that," he gritted, "and you can join your despicable lover, Eavan Malcolmson, the cursed traitor. You're no better than he was, a deceiver."

"He was nae m' lover," she retorted, "and why do ye keep blamin' Grandad? I've ne'er discussed marriage t' anyone wi' him. He'd consult me first."

Alistair barked his laughter. "You simpleton, don't you know anything?"

"Simpleton!" she fumed.

He ignored her. "Nay, you don't because you were fool enough to fall into Malcolmson's web. Why do you think I stand here and insist that I will honor my vow? I made a promise to the McKinnon that I would wed you."

Kennis was horrified. This was not what she'd expected. Had Robbie known this to be true? How *dare* he, Grandad and Alistair meddle with her future so cavalierly!

He mistook her expression. "I begin to comprehend your feelings only too fully. Your grandfather, mistress, bade me do what I wished with you when I visited Skye."

"He wouldna dare."

479

"He did, for better or for worse," Alistair said dourly. "And he intends to see that I honor my part of the bargain."

* * *

She succeeded in wrenching herself away from him. They had all betrayed her; the men that she'd depended on to love and protect her, had mortally wounded her heart. Her grandfather, Robbie, and even her father betrayed her in his death by fighting for a lost cause and heaping a bitter inheritance upon the family. Now, Alistair betrayed her by falsely accusing her once again.

Her face ashen, she backed away from him. Her head ached, her shoulder throbbed, and she wheeled away from him and ran. She heard him call after her but she ran like the wind. His heavy footsteps pounded after her but her feet sprouted wings as she ran for her very life.

Her horse must be nearby; she reached the spot where she'd tied the animal. Thrusting the reins over the mare's head, she leapt halfway onto her back and jerked on the reins before she was secure in the saddle. She heard Alistair come crashing through the underbrush, loudly calling her name.

She must get away and never look back. There was nothing to return to, her hopes and dreams were shattered. Robbie must take her with him to search for Grizel. She would not submit to her grandfather's will but only to her own. *God, You've deserted me.*

* * *

Winded, Alistair couldn't compete with the horse. Indeed, he barely caught up to Kennis, swift in her desperation to flee from him. Her parting expression pierced his soul; he was undone. She was right. He must be mistaken, something about his understanding was faulty. He must set all to rights before he lost her forever.

Trudging back to Craignish, he turned his anger upon himself for his ill treatment of her. It wasn't only unjust but also unkind. He'd make the devil of a husband. She'd be well rid of him, if the McKinnon would only see it his way. *God forgive me, I must make amends with Kennis even if,* he took a breath, *she does hate me.*

When he arrived at Craignish, he sought the library and locked the door, a heretofore unknown depression creeping over him. When Duncan pounded on the door calling his name, he wouldn't answer.

Duncan and Rob stared at one another in dismay. Alarmed, Rob said, "I'd best go see Kennis. Meet me at the ship in an hour if he won't talk to you."

Alistair was convinced that he'd been at fault. He, who prided himself on his understanding, had misunderstood. His own double-mindedness appalled him. He reviewed their conversation, meditating on each word, every statement. Coming to no immediate conclusion, he thought back further to the masquerade. He and Kennis were in perfect harmony that evening. She was breathtaking and charming.

He'd not seen her since Dunchalum when she stood hiding in the shadows of the castle. His heart leapt for joy at the mere sight of her. His dark brows drew together. She'd said *I love you* to Eavan Malcolmson and he'd fallen apart, become bitter instead of loving her enough not to doubt her heart.

Several questions needed answered such as, did she really love Eavan and if so, how and why had he not seen it earlier? Love has many facets and expressions. 'Twas possible that he'd mistaken her affection for a dying man, nay, a friend and kinsman, regardless of his opinion of the man, for more than what was intended.

She wasn't ashamed to declare her love in front of him. Rob stated that he'd misunderstood her intent. He pounded his fist onto the desk. His pride wounded, he'd become blinded by jealousy. A still, small voice spoke his name. *Alistair,* the voice said. *You can still ask her forgiveness.* He must be mad. *Do it,* the voice repeated. *You'll deeply regret it if you don't.* The small voice spoke the truth. He already had too many regrets. Rising with determination, he strode toward the door, unlocked it, and stepped into the passage. "Farrell," he bellowed. "Farrell! Where are you, man?"

Chapter 26

Matters of the Heart

Kennis stood on the deck of the *Teosairg*[22] with Rob at her side.

The cool wind tossed wisps of hair about her face and except for her wounded heart, she felt more content than she had in a long time. It was a beautiful autumn morning, and she was journeying with him to the Caribbean to search for Grizel. The ship sailed along the coast toward Port Eilidh, bringing memories of happier times to the forefront of her mind.

Her berth on the vessel was comfortable. Rob built a temporary partition in his large cabin and taken the half that contained his charts, documents, and navigational instruments for himself. Lord Breadalbane was kind and Duncan, whose dark coloring and manner reminded her too much of his brother, was cheerful. Alistair must resemble his late father for Duncan undoubtedly looked like his mother.

Crushed by the events of the last twenty-four hours, she watched the activity on the deck in silence. Rob stood at the helm, guiding the vessel through the currents and shoals. Yesterday's events continued to haunt her and she longed to forget the discouraging conclusion to her brief love affair.

---

[22] *Deliver, restore. Restoration.*

A one-sided love, she thought mutely, staring at the choppy sea. How could he behave toward her the way he had at the masquerade and then treat her so abominably? It just didn't make sense. It seemed, at least at the time, to be more than a mere flirtation. She racked her brain, trying to understand all of the things he'd said.

The beginning of their acquaintance was mortifying. She'd been stubborn, even rude to him. She flushed, embarrassed by her poor behavior. Mam was right, she owed him her thanks and an apology. To make things worse, he thought she was trying to trick him into marriage. He believed that she'd actually plotted with her family against him! She grew cold, shivering in the heat of the day. The thought was too horrible.

"Well, lass," Rob said, interrupting her mournful thoughts. "Soon we'll be leaving Scotland behind us. Are you sure you want to do this? It may be a year before we return."

"I'm sure," she said with certainty. Right now, the first and last place that she wanted to be was Scotland. It seemed the country itself had rejected her. She had returned to Scotland a few short months ago and was bidding her home but not her pain, farewell. Her family would be on Skye when she and Robbie returned; it was enough for the present.

"Robbie," she said at length. "Will you stay in Scotland once we come back, or are you forever going to be sailing away?"

His contagious laughter made her smile.

"'Tis good to see you smile, lass. I think you've the loveliest smile I've ever seen, and I've seen a few."

"Brothers aren't supposed to say such things."

"Why not?" he protested. "'Tis the truth."

"Someday, you'll meet a lass," she teased, "and you'll tell her the same thing for different reasons."

"Not me," he boasted. "I'm staying away from the lassies. They only cause trouble for men."

"Is that so?" she said. "Now where have I heard that before?"

Rob instantly regretted his words, however, it would be impossible to avoid every sally that might bring to mind her disappointment. "I can't imagine," he said with irony. "For now, I'll settle for your smile and Mairi's, how's that?"

"'Twill do. Robbie, what did you think of Ona MacDougall?"

He snorted. "That little termagant? The besotted Kyle Campbell is welcome to her."

"I thought you might like her. She's a pleasant girl."

"She's a flirt, Kennis, I've no use for that type of lass or any lass at the moment. Here now," he handed her the spy glass, "look over there and tell me what you see."

"Dolphins," she said, delighted, watching the pair cavort in the open sea.

"Means we'll have good luck on our journey."

Kennis continued to gaze through the glass at the choppy sea and jagged coastline. "There's a galley sailing behind us."

He nodded. "Not surprising in these waters."

"Nay, Robbie, drawing close. Faith," she said, "they're raising a flag and hailing us."

"Let me see."

She drew in her breath sharply. "Oh no!"

Rob glanced at her, suspicious. "What is it, Kennis? I must see what's happening." He removed the glass from her shaking hands and peered through it. "Well, if that don't beat the devil! Looks like we're going to have a visitor. I hope you're ready for this."

"I don't want to see him," she said, adamant. "I'm going to the cabin."

Rob looked at her in concern. "Are you sure, lass? Might be a good thing."

"How do you know he's not come to see Duncan or the earl? You don't, so 'tis best that I disappear for a while. Tell me when he's gone." She ran lightly down the steps and flung open the door to the snug apartment. Hopefully, she'd be safe here. She latched the door, sat down and waited, her mind in a whirl.

What if he'd come to see her and not Duncan, should she speak with him? Surely he wouldn't venture so far on a trivial errand. Something of import had occurred and he'd come to retrieve his brother. The duke had sent him or his mother, perhaps, with a message. Her thoughts flitted from one possibility to the next while hope and denial waged a battle in her heart.

A soft tap at the door made her jump, her raw nerves on edge. She rose and pressed her hands to the door, listening. "Who is it," she said quietly, knowing who must be standing there.

"'Tis Alistair," a rich, warm voice returned. "Will you speak to me, lass?"

She paused, uncertain, wondering how far this would lead to happiness for either of them. "Why should I?"

"For good reason."

"What good reason?" she returned, hoping for the best.

She heard a low laugh. Her hackles rose. Hmph, he must be sure of her if he could laugh at a time like this. "You'll have to be more specific if you expect me to open this door."

"I have an important message for you."

"From whom?" she asked. "You can slide it under the door."

* * *

Alistair, standing outside the door, tried the latch. She'd locked it, anticipating him. He smiled. She was a bonnie lass. He strode across the deck to the steps and ran up to Rob, standing at the helm. "Rob, have you paper and ink?"

"Aye, in my cabin," he said, lifting a brow. "Why?"

"I need some right now."

Duncan grinned. "Is she giving you a hard time, my charming brother? The earl has paper and ink. I'll fetch it for you."

Alistair was impatient. "Hurry up, Duncan, I haven't got all day."

When he returned, Alistair sat down and scribbled a note. He wagged the paper in the air to dry the ink then folded it carefully. Striding back to the cabin door, he tapped again.

* * *

Kennis listened to his retreating footsteps and sat down on the bed, a bit forlorn. When the tap sounded again at the door shortly after, she rushed toward it. "Aye?"

"Here's your message." He pushed the paper under the door.

She picked up the folded piece of paper and read silently.

Kennis lass, I hardly know how to ask you to forgive me, so I'll say it plain. Will you forgive me? I know that the words I spoke to you at our last meeting were unpardonable so I'll ask again, will you Please forgive me? I've accused and berated you from the beginning, and I'm sorry for being suspicious and willfully misunderstanding what you've tried to tell me. I'll admit I've been jealous, too, of your care for your late kinsman. You must allow me to have the opportunity to say what's in my heart. I love you, lass, and I always will. Will you do me the honor of becoming my wife? I don't need the McKinnon's persuasions to marry you. I loved you long before I spoke with him at Moil, my stubborn pride wouldn't allow me to admit it. Alistair

A rush of emotion poured forth from her, releasing the agony of the last several hours and her tears flowed free down her cheeks.

"Lass," Alistair said, impatiently waiting. "Unlock the door."

"Are you sure?" she choked. Her heart pounded so hard she was sure he could hear it through the wooden door.

"Open this door and you'll discover how very sure I am."

* * *

The latch grated and he sighed in relief. For a brief moment, he feared that she didn't believe him. The still, small voice spoke truth to him. He'd listen more closely in the future. Pushing open the paneled door, he stepped inside, his heart relieved and overflowing with joy.

Without saying a word, he took her trembling figure into his arms and held her tightly while she cried, his eyes wet with tears as he laid his cheek against her soft hair. When her tears subsided, he drew a kerchief from his pocket, tipped her face upward and dried it, caressing her cheek with his fingers.

"You know, lass," he teased, "at least your face is clean this time. And there's something you still owe me, you know." She gazed at him, bewildered. "You'll learn not to look at me like that, if you expect me not to kiss you."

"You don't want to kiss me?" she said, confused.

"Poor lass, I've really muddled your brain with my ranting and raving."

"Nay," she admonished, "you must forget the past. 'Tis over."

His eyes darkened. "I can't forgive myself although I'm glad you do."

"'Twas a misunderstanding, I think, from the beginning," she said, smiling apologetically. "I asked for trouble from practically the first time I met you, and I must ask your forgiveness for being such a nuisance." She reached up and tucked the black lock of hair, irresistibly loosed from his cueue, behind his ear. She'd wanted to do that for a very long time. "And since I've forgiven you, you must forgive yourself."

"It may take a while but I promise I'll try." His expression changed and his voice lightened. "And if you hadn't made such a nuisance of yourself, lass, I might never have gotten to know you, and found myself unhappily yoked to Vanora Campbell instead. Kennis," his eyes twinkled, "about that forfeit—"

"I still owe you a forfeit," she said, smiling. "For what?"

"Don't you remember the inn at Port Eilidh when I took advantage of you? I confess, but not without purpose."

His sudden grin disarmed her. "So you admit taking advantage of me."

"And I plan to do so again," he said smoothly. "Right now."

"I wish you would," she encouraged, "and stop gabbling about it."

The gleam in his eyes brightened at her invitation. "With pleasure, my love." He gently pressed his lips to hers for a brief moment before possessing them with a fierceness that took her breath away, giving no opportunity for pause or retreat. She slid her arms upward and he pulled her closer. He lifted her from her feet, their bodies melding into one. She returned his fervent kiss, lost in his embrace. The pain and uncertainty of the previous day and weeks melted away in the comfort of his arms. She was secure in the knowledge that he'd settled in his own mind and before God that she was innocent of deceit. He was free from suspicion and through his freedom, she was completely able to trust him.

Alistair set her down. "Well, lass," he murmured, gazing into her eyes.

"You thought I loved Eavan instead of you."

"'Twas a foolish thing to believe," he admitted. "I've been blind, priding myself on my own understanding and not placing my trust in God."

"What made you change your mind?" She watched his every expression, the emotions flitting across his face. "I ran away in absolute despair."

He wore a pained expression. "I know, and I'll never forget. The stricken look in your eyes," he stared away, seeing the past, "and on your face, unmanned me. In spite of my offense, I suddenly saw myself as I never had before. I determined then and there to ask your forgiveness, even if you hated me."

"Hate you! I never have, although," she said, contrite, "I did say so, didn't I?"

"You did. It pierced my heart more effectively than any dirk ever could."

"I didn't suspect it."

"I know." His black brows drew together. "I gave you little reason to believe anything else."

She smoothed away his scowl and caressed the light scar upon his forehead with her finger. "You musn't think of it anymore."

"I'm sure I will until I learn to forgive myself more easily. You'll have to help me."

She smiled. "I will, but God can do that the best."

"Good," he smiled in return, "and I'm still waiting to hear certain words on your lips that you said to another gentleman of our acquaintance, though I hope you can say them to me with a deeper meaning."

"With all my heart, Alistair." Kennis assured him of her love with more than mere words before she whispered the long awaited phrase into his ear. "I love you." She stood in the comfort of his arms for several minutes and then suddenly lifted her head from his shoulder. "Alistair," she said. "Do you know anyone connected to Eavan named Niall? A relative, or one of his men, perhaps?"

Surprised at the question, he shook his head. "Nay, but Farrell might. Why?"

"On his last breath, Eavan said to talk to Niall. I could barely hear what he was trying to say, something about a key."

"Then we must find out when we go to Craignish. Tell me," he said, changing the subject. "Do you want to be married on Skye or at Dunolly? We've a pleasant chapel there, and many MacDougall brides have walked down that aisle."

"But I'm on my way to the Caribbean."

"Not anymore," he informed her. "You must come with me to the mainland."

"I promised Robbie I'd go with him."

"He doesn't expect you to," he said, toying with her silky hair. "Do you think I've sailed this far to let you fly from me again?" He tightened his arms about her. "Nay, lass, you'll come with me, and leave Grizel's troubles to her father, Rob and Duncan."

She gazed up at him, hopefully. "We could both sail with them."

He firmly objected. "Nay, we'll both return to Craignish where your Mother and Grandfather await, and make wedding plans." His dark eyes and rich voice were tender. "What say you?"

"But Robbie won't be there," she pleaded.

"You're not marrying Rob," he said, persistent. "I'll not wait for him or Duncan, for that matter."

"We've plenty to do in the meantime," she persuaded, "if you will."

He looked intently into her eyes. "Aye, we do. I've plans for you, lass, that don't include your brother or mine." He kissed her again, and Kennis found she was unable to resist and in so doing, agreed. "Oh, and I almost forgot. I've a wee gift for you."

Kennis gasped when she opened the case he pulled from within his jacket and handed to her. Within it lay a string of pearls, their shimmering whiteness enhanced by the black velvet lining of the box. "Oh, Alistair, they're beautiful." She threw her arms around his neck.

He grinned. "A betrothal gift for you, to wear for the wedding, if you like."

"You bought them especially for me?"

"Aye, lass, I did, before I bartered for you with the McKinnon," he teased. "I had to have some small token of my affection on hand to convince him that I wanted you." His dark eyes twinkled with mischief. "There would be earbobs and a brooch, too, if I hadn't bought you from Denoon. You see, lass, you've been mine all along."

She gave him a shove and he went sprawling. In return for her impudence, he demanded another kiss. Kennis thought it safer and wiser to exit the cabin, and said so. "You've had enough for one day, sir. I suggest that we go and share our news."

He rose from the floor. "As if they didn't suspect it already, else you'd have thrown me out on my ear."

"Maybe I should have," she said, raising her nose in the air as she walked by him.

He grabbed her as she passed him and pressed a quick kiss to her lips. Laughing, they stumbled out the door, and crossed the deck to climb the steps to the quarterdeck where Rob stood conversing with Farrell.

"Well," Rob said bluntly, "have you finally resolved your quarrel, and am I to wish you happy?"

Alistair, his hand at the small of Kennis' back, nudged her forward. "Aren't you going to tell him, lass?"

"He admitted he was at fault," she said, her imp surfacing, "and I've decided that I will honor him with not only my presence on his return to the mainland but with my hand."

Rob, Duncan, and Farrell heartily laughed. "We'll miss you on the voyage," Rob said, "but I suppose you had best appease your impatient suitor."

"Aye," Duncan agreed, "else the poor servants will suffer, and he'll be blacker than the devil. The last few days have been a torment for all of us."

Alistair withstood the teasing with goodwill. Today nothing would spoil his mood and he'd take no offense or offer one. "I wish you both the good fortune in finding a lass that will please you and make you as happy as I am today."

Rob and Duncan rejoiced with Alistair. Neither young man had plans to be tied to apron strings in the immediate future. The two young men enjoyed life and despite the sad mission that they had embarked upon, would thrive on the adventure.

Kennis waved to Robbie as she and Alistair crossed the deck and disappeared over the side of the ship to the waiting galley below. The journey to the mainland was too short for her, nestled in Alistair's arms. The lovers stood in the bow as the vessel sailed into the bay and approached the shore. Stopping at the *suidhe* where they had met the previous morning, Alistair leaped onto its flat surface and turned to Kennis. "Jump," he instructed, "I'll catch you."

She willingly obeyed and found herself in his strong arms. Happy, she sighed, and slipped her arms around his neck, clinging like the mist that enshrouded the shoreline.

The echoing voices she'd heard for so long in her dreams became clear. The words spoke of hope and love, and the fulfilling of her heart's desire. The sun sparkled on the dark waters of the loch, diamonds twinkling below the proud tower on the purple heathered hill above. The men shoved off in the galley toward the village of Kilcreag, eager to see loved ones and spread the good news about the laird and his betrothed. A wedding was pending, and all looked forward to the coming celebration.

Chapter 27

Highland Dream

The sun streamed through leafless trees, illuminating the barren track that led to the Highland village of Kilcalum.

Ahead lay burned out cottages, overgrown with dried bracken. Kennis' heart leapt with hope for the future, not only for herself but also for the McCallum clan that remained in the glen.

In the distance, the rippling waters of tiny Lochangless glistened, mirroring the intense sunlight. Her horse plodded along too slowly. She was eager to reach the village but Alistair had set a cautious pace. He sent Farrell ahead to spy out the land in the event interlopers remained, lurking in the area from the recent battle. Upon his return, her heart pounded with anticipation.

Alistair grinned. "Ready, lass?"

"More than ready," she said eagerly, returning his happy smile.

"Then let's go." He set off at a canter and she gladly followed his lead down the familiar track.

The riders burst into the clearing and to her chagrin, silence greeted them. Alistair dismounted, moved toward her and gripped her horse's bridle. "Here, love," he said, reaching for her as she came unglued from the saddle. "Where would you like to visit first?"

Kennis stood rooted to the spot. The once busy square full of playing children stood still. Today was market day and no vendors were on hand to display their wares, no cries of Buy your ale here, lads! or Ha' penny Sweets! rang out, inviting would-be purchasers. She'd known it would be this way yet hoped that by some small miracle, things might be different. In reality, some dreams are wishful thinking and must die to create room for new dreams and visions budding in a person's heart. The final healing in her soul had begun. She stood straighter, determined to cast off despair, and took the final step toward Granny Jean's shieling.

"Mistress Kennis," a gruff voice called from behind, "I'm right gled to see ye!" Davis McCallum emerged from behind the small dwelling. In his wake, faces aglow, trailed Meggie and Davy. He bowed and urged the children to do the same.

"Welcome, Laird," Davis said, beaming.

Meggie, as bold as ever, tugged on Alistair's jacket. "Did ye remember to bring us sweets, Laird?" Her eyes sparkled and her rosy-cheeked face announced her improved health. "Did Master Duncan come to visit, too?"

Alistair laughed. "Nay, lass, he's on his way to the Americas but I'm sure that upon his return, he'll do what he promised." He glanced at Kennis, smiling. "As for sweets, we've more than that to offer."

The child stared hard at Kennis and frowned. "Do I know ye, mistress?"

"Lassie," Davis admonished. "'Tis the young mistress o' Dunchalum. Ye'd best mind yer manners."

"But I dinna remember her, Da." Her tiny nose crinkled as she stared curiously at Kennis.

Kennis nodded in understanding. "It's been nearly five years, and you've grown since last I saw you, Meggie. If you'll come with me to visit Granny Jean, I'll show you what I've brought for you and the other children." Reaching out a hand, she allowed the children to lead her to the shieling. Alistair remained behind with Davis, discussing the immediate needs of the people.

Meggie released her hand and tugged on the rough wooden door. "Granny! Ye've a visitor."

Kennis entered behind her and blinked, adjusting to the semi-darkness. The peats burned low on the small fire in the center of the undersized room as they always had, and Granny Jean sat in her rocker, keeping warm by the cheery blaze.

The old woman lifted her head. "Ye're a sight fer these poor auld eyes. Come closer, lassie, an' let me see ye. 'Twas a sad day when the McCallum's left their auld home, but seein' ye here brings me renewed hope." A tear trickled down her withered cheeks and a toothless smile spread across her face. "How's yer bonny mither?"

"She's well, Granny Jean," she said warmly, kneeling by the old woman's chair. "She sends her love, and so does Robbie. I wish he could be here now but he's off on another journey."

"Aye, I heard wha' the lad was aboot," she said knowingly, "from Davis. We've much ta be thankful fer from the young MacDougall these days. Yer Da always thought the black MacDougalls a worthy lot. Noo, lassie," she said, watching Kennis with her shrewd gaze, "have ye mair guid news?"

Kennis laughed. Apparently, her kinsmen were abreast of everything. "I do, indeed. Robbie has received a temporary pardon from Argyll, and it seems there was a plot afoot to disinherit and discredit the McCallum's." Her tone was grave. "He's gone to the Americas to search out any of the men that may be alive, including my father, and the earl has papers to have them released into his custody."

Granny Jean clutched her forearm. "Guid. An' what aboot yerself, lass, 'tis a weddin' pendin' or naught?"

"Aye," she said, "in four weeks. We've already posted the banns. I'm surprised you know that, too, since we only announced it yesterday."

"Weel, ye canna expect us nae ta know, lass, after the wicked Campbell near murdered ye. Davis kept up with ye, in case ye needed air help."

With tears in her eyes, she squeezed Granny's hand. "Thank you. And now, I've come to invite you to the wedding. We'll send carts for you, and you'll stay at Dunolly for the week's festivities and the wedding celebration."

"Ew-w," Meggie squealed. "I canna wait!"

"And, I've cloth for new clothes with me today as well as taffy and a few other treats. Come, Meggie, Davy, out to the horses." Kennis rose from beside the rocker. "Help me to bring in the goods I have for all of you, and then we'll have tea and scones, and visit for a while." She exited the shieling, the children close on her heels.

* * *

"I still don't understand how you could fall in love with Alistair," Ona teased as she helped Kennis to dress on her wedding day. "He may be my brother, but he's a dour Scot, if ever one existed."

Kennis laughed. "You'll have to forgive me for choosing him, then. I can always send him to the family when he's in an ill humor, so you'll still benefit from his temper."

"I fancy we'll see him often, then."

"Ona, how naughty," Lady Grear admonished. "You know Alistair has a wonderful sense of humor when he has a mind to enjoy himself."

"You needn't worry, Lady Grear," Kennis said, smiling. "Nothing can cloud my spirits today."

"Please don't call me Lady Grear, Kennis love," she said, "you must begin to think of me as your second mother."

"I already do," she said, eyes misty. "You've been more than kind since I was thrust upon you."

"Aside from the fact that I wanted to help you, poor hurt and lost child that you were," she twinkled, "I could see that my son was rapidly losing his heart to you, nay, I believe he'd already lost it, even then."

"Well," Ona said, "aside from that, what would you think, Kennis, if I pursued a wee flirtation with your brother when he and Duncan return? I think he's very handsome." Alanna walked into the room and the two women, aware that Robbie found Ona's flirtatious behavior irritating, were spared a reply.

"Kennis, here 'tis," Alanna said joyfully. "It took awhile to press out the wrinkles, and you know I've been airing it for days. I never thought I'd see this again." She held up a blue-and-green tartan sash. A clansman had discovered Alanna's wedding chest, untouched, in the basement of Dunchalum Castle. The chest contained her personal treasures and a few family heirlooms that she'd set aside in memory of Robert, her husband.

Mairi, following in her mother's wake, was excited to be a bridesmaid and ran to embrace her sister.

Alanna placed the brightly woven strip of cloth upon Kennis' shoulder and drew it around her waist, securing the sash with the amethyst brooch Daly and Fergus recovered. She set a crown of white heather upon her golden hair which flowed unbound to the middle of her back. Then, she kissed her daughter on both cheeks. Mairi, Lady Grear and Ona followed suit.

Kennis' pale blue satin gown glittered with silvery knots of embroidered rosebuds, and matching slippers peeped from beneath the hem of the gown. Filled with expectation, her eyes sparkled like shimmering pools of seawater reflecting the luminous sky above as she clasped Alistair's gift, the pearl necklace, around her neck. Delicate pearls set in spun gold dangled from her ears and a fine bracelet adorned her wrist. Alistair surprised her with the matching pearls the previous evening when they walked in the garden after supper.

"Are you ready, my love?" Alanna asked her daughter, handing her the bouquet of heather and ribbons that matched the circlet on her head.

She shook her head. "Aye," she said, following her mother and Lady Grear out of the chamber set aside for her use as the new mistress of Dunolly House. She and Alistair would make their home for the present at Craignish, away from the family for at least their first year although she planned to visit Dunolly often. She was happy to remove to the tower house where she and Alistair had shared some of their first memories.

The women entered the foyer of the gaily-decorated chapel and awaited the skirl of the bagpipes. Mairi peeked inside and gushed. "Ooo, Kennis, wait until you see!"

"Is he there yet, Mairi?" she asked, a tinge of color staining her cheeks.

"Aye, they all are."

In lieu of Duncan and Robbie, Farrell and the Duke of Argyll stood with Alistair in front of the minister at the altar, made festive with overlapping McCallum and MacDougall tartans and garlands of greenery.

Kennis' heart nearly stopped as she saw him standing there waiting for her, the white collar of his ruffled shirt brilliant against the black velvet doublet. She began the short walk up the aisle on her grandfather's arm.

Alistair's smile grew wider as she drew near and his eyes gleamed in admiration.

"Who gives this woman to be wedded today?" the minister intoned.

John Dhu pulled her forward and clearly pronounced, "Her mother and I." He turned, teary-eyed, and kissed her cheek. He placed her soft hand into Alistair's strong, tanned one. In a dream, she moved to stand beside him and listened as he repeated his vows before her.

"I, Alistair Duglas MacDougall, now take you, Kennis Eve McCallum, to be my wife. In the presence of God and before these witnesses I promise to be a loving, faithful—"

Kennis found herself repeating her vows in the long-awaited moment. "—and loyal wife to you, until God shall separate us by death." Silently, she said her own prayer. *Thank you, God, for the miracle that you have wrought this day.* She scarcely heard the rest of the blessing but knew in her heart that she and he would adhere to their promises to one another and to God as they knelt to pray.

Alistair nudged her back to reality, grinned and stood, pulling her from the kneeler. He urged her to face him as the guests waited with baited breath.

"You may kiss the bride."

Alistair tenderly cupped her chin in his hand and stared into her eyes, seeing the warmth of his passion reflected in the sea green pools. A clansman hooted, "Kiss 'er good, Laird!" and the entire assembly burst into laughter. He looked out into the myriad of faces. "I will, lad, and gladly," he said, loud enough for all to hear. Returning to Kennis, he smiled broadly. "What say you, lass? You've married yourself to a black MacDougall, there's no turning back now."

She grinned in return. "Nay, sir, I've no desire but to go forward with you." He leaned toward her, and on impulse lifted her off her feet and twirled around. They both laughed aloud before he set her down on her feet and kissed her. The minister presented the Laird and his Lady, and the crowd cheered as they ran down the aisle amidst the good wishes of family and friends. The repeated firing of guns reverberated in the air as the McKinnons of Skye celebrated and the skirl of bagpipes led the procession to the wedding breakfast.

Songs and toasts abounded and the wedding feast was gay, and Kennis' only wish was that her father and Robbie could have been there to share this special moment. The sad memories of the past were fading. She and Alistair led out the dancing and Farrell, his best man, drew the wee Mairi, the first bridesmaid, onto the floor in the reel.

The afternoon hastened toward evening and as the guests grew merrier, Kennis and Alistair slipped out, riding to their new home at Craignish, eager to avoid the crowd and the rowdy customs that accompanied a Highland wedding celebration.

* * *

Shadows lay deep along the ancient wooded path that wound to the dark waters of the loch where a grey castle, enveloped in purple shadows, loomed high above the Bay of Craignish. Instead of the dawn breaking and unknown muses speaking, the voices of Alistair and Kennis filled the air as they watched the sun dance across the horizon, preparing to rest for the night.

The scene was familiar, one they would share now and in the future, with one another and children yet to be born. The sound of the lapping tide washed over them like the joy of their love for one another. The honeyed scent of heather floated on the breeze, mingling with the smell of fresh water and earth.

Alistair stood behind Kennis, arms encircling her as they watched the sun hide its head in the mist-covered hills. He whispered the sweet and fragrant language of love into her ear as the still, small voice of God spoke into his own, *It is good.*

The lovers confirmed His love and their own, sealing it with a kiss of promise as darkness enveloped them and the stars twinkled joyously above.

About Heart in the Highlands

The Creative Power of Faith
"Faith is the substance of things hoped for, the evidence of things not seen." Hebrews 11:1

Heart in the Highlands is the first series of the *Gallantry Inspired* imprint at Burning Rose Press, presenting elements of faith in story form. While not a Bible study, I hope that you are encouraged to have faith in God and to fulfill His purpose for your life.

I also hope that you enjoy this story because it's meant to be a fun read and the joy of the Lord is our strength (Neh. 8:10). Jesus Christ took every pain and sorrow known to man on the Cross, and when He said *It is finished*, He released us into the freedom of His joy.

On Faith

Above all things, faith is creative. God framed the world with His spoken word and poured the substance of His very nature into His creation—this means you, me and both the natural and spiritual realm that surrounds us. The earth and all it contains is a marvelous testimony of His awesome creativity.

Faith is the confident expectation that we have through Jesus Christ and the change that He brings to each person who knows Him. Faith is also tangible; the *supernatural substance* hoped for that we take hold of when we expect His purposes for our lives to be fulfilled.

What expectation do you have, what do you dream of deep within yourself? God has made a spiritual deposit in each person that He has created. That means You—so dig deep, bring it out into the open and see what wonder He has in mind for you!

One aspect of faith is the dream in every person's heart. God anticipates revealing Himself to each person and the evidence of His existence, His being, surrounds us. Heaven is open to all and the reality of heaven can be a part of your daily life. That's why Jesus came, to free us from the lie of hopelessness and the deceit of a very real adversary. We have a heavenly destiny; He has not abandoned us to an unknown or inevitable fate.

God sent the Holy Spirit to help us to understand what Jesus did for us. Through His presence, we have a relationship with God and can daily draw on His supernatural power, not only for own benefit but for those around us. We need to hear Him speaking above all of the other voices that clamor for our attention every day.

On Hearing God's Voice

What is He saying to you today? Our ways and thoughts are not like His and to have real faith and not just be religious, a mystic or a positive thinker, we must begin to think like Him.

Can we learn to think like God? Yes, and no. In part, to have faith and to think like God is a divine impartation. All we have to do is ask Him for it; the beginning of that 'new think' is when we repent and ask Jesus Christ to forgive our sins. Very simply, repentance means to change your mind and to tell Him that you are willing to hear what He is saying to you, and to do things His way when He asks. His way is better, and so much more fun than ours! It's not about religious formats and formulas, but knowing Him in a dynamic, personal way.

In the final chapter of *Highland Hope*, I have made this statement as Kennis' closing thought:

"She prayed that in the continuation of her journey, the enduring hope that drove her forward would arise stronger than ever before, to live powerfully within the reality of her long-awaited dreams."

She is waiting for God's timing in her life to fulfill the expectation of what He has promised. Like Kennis, we need more than mere hope. Being hopeful is not enough, and Kennis is learning this truth on her journey. She is learning to be patient enough to wait on God and to discover that His truths are demonstrated in amazing, unexpected ways. She experiences the move of God in her daily life and in the end, fulfills her *Highland Dream*.

In summary, faith is creative, the substance is creative, and the evidence is creative. Faith is the creative power of God waiting for release into our daily lives and into the lives of others through us. It is His will and desire to meet us powerfully in this way. When we have real faith, we are agreeing with heaven, declaring that what He has already done is now present on earth and in our midst, in you and in me.

Through this kind of faith, we're healed inside and out, and have the ability to bring healing to others. Through this kind of faith, we can move in the supernatural, miraculous power of God every day.

My Prayer for You is that you would come to know Jesus Christ in a personal way, have faith in Him in all things, and experience the person of the Holy Spirit in your life.

A Short Testimony:

As a teenager, I discovered three important yet simple things about God that many people fail to understand.

The first thing I realized was this: I could know God.

Wow. He was real, and wanted me to know Him. He was just waiting for me to understand since He had created me and already knew me intimately. No bells and whistles, no sermons, church going or prescribed prayers, rules and regulations were required.

Second, I needed Him in my life.

Desperately. And I wasn't unhappy or a bad kid. Compared to many, I had everything—a loving family, friends, all of my needs met and more, yet I knew something important was missing.

In my soul was an emptiness that I couldn't explain or understand; my heart needed filled with a *certain something* that seemed unattainable. I quickly discovered that only He could possibly fill it—and He did, to overflowing with love, joy, peace and power. I can easily say It is well with my soul! no matter what happens in my life.

Last, I knew that I wanted to know Him intimately.

Do you? I knew that He was what I'd been looking for and hadn't found elsewhere in any person, place or thing.

Knowing Jesus Christ is your answer. Just don't forget that there is a Father God and Holy Spirit to know, too. Each one is a distinct person of the Godhead and worthy of our attention and our praise.

To know and experience God, just say "Yes" with no strings attached and no conditions. You don't need to say a formal sinner's prayer. I never did! I used to wonder at the need for those prayers, and have encouraged people to just tell God how they feel about themselves—the good and the bad. Tell Him you want to get to know Him and ask Him to speak to you today.

He will speak to you in a way that you can understand and you will be on a journey like never before. However, it's up to you to decide how far you are willing to walk with Him.

For myself, after forty years (at the time of this printing), I am still running hard after Him. Each day is a new, wonderful experience and I never grow weary of His presence. He truly is the love and joy of my life, the fulfillment of all my hopes and dreams.

Author's Notes

Dear Readers,

I hope you have enjoyed *Heart in the Highlands*. Any character that bears a similarity to a real person is coincidental except for what I've noted. So for all of you history buffs and trivia lovers, please read on.

Like most authors, I've used fact and fiction to weave this story, and read an enormous amount of history but simply can't include it all. So if my geographical references are incorrect in regard to distance, travel time and location, or if I've effectively messed up your family history and not included a note in this section, you'll have to forgive me. I must lay claim to artistic license where I have "deliberately erred".

For those of you who are interested in my work and would like to be involved through reading first drafts, doing research or mapping Scotland for future stories, I'd love to hear from you!

There are always Gaelic words and expressions I'd like to use, too, and I admit that the language in *Heart in the Highlands* has been "Americanized." What can I say?!

A little history behind the story:

The **McCallum** clan was originally under the protection of Campbell of Lochow. The Malcolms evolved after two unrelated branches of the family merged, and the name changed from McCallum to Malcolm.

The McCallum's in this tale are fictional, rebels in the midst of the Campbell territory of Argyll. Isn't there some rebel in every family?!

I've also created Dunchalum, the village of Kilcalum and Lochangless. *Lochan* means wee loch, more or less, *gless* means mirror or glass, so I merged the two. It was the closest thing to *luikin* I could find, as in looking glass.

One last thing—there are slight variations of the clan motto for the MacCallum/Malcolm clan, and I combined the old and new mottos for Rob's password. The meaning of the one that I chose to use suited my purpose the best, even though the two have similar meaning. The old motto is, *Deus refugeum nostrum, God is our refuge* and the new motto, *In ardua petit, He has attempted difficult things or aims at difficult things.* The second version is, *In ardua tendit, He takes on difficult things.*

Malcolm House is also fiction, the chief of Clan Malcolm residing at Duntrune Castle, Argyll. Malcolm House is an addition, my substitution for Kilmartin Castle in Kilmartin Glen, originally a Campbell holding.

The **Duke of Argyll**, a prominent historical figure is often used in fiction and his character was easy to include in the story. This particular duke died without heirs and the title passed to another relative.

The **MacDougalls.** In 1745, Alexander MacDougall, who was called Alastair Dubh, lived in Argyll. He was married to Mary Campbell of Balcardine and had a large family—15 children! He wasn't 'out' in the '45, and I read somewhere that Mary poured hot oil on his feet so that he couldn't participate—a drastic measure that served its purpose, I suppose, but all I can say is Ouch! As a result, MacDougall lands were restored for his lack of participation. Aside from this fact, my Alistair is completely fictitious. The real Alexander did have a brother named Duncan— definitely a happy coincidence in my story—who went out in the '45.

Today, **Dunollie Castle**, the seat of the MacDougall clan, is being restored and preserved by the MacDougall Clan Society. **Dunollie House** was built in 1746 and was converted into apartments in modern times. Presently, work is being done to preserve and open the buildings to the public. Visit the MacDougall Clan online for how you can be an integral part of the restoration process at **www.dunollie.org.**

Craignish Castle was originally built by the Campbells, and MacCallums were hereditary constables although I've read that McColls, a McCallum *sept*, were hereditary constables, too. Currently, it's also been converted into modern apartments. The village of Kilcreag is purely fictional.

John Dubh MacKinnon was a real historical figure, and was 'out' in the '15 and '45. He originally lost his holdings after the '15, and had them restored at that time, not after the '45. He was instrumental in helping Flora Macdonald pass through Scotland and imprisoned for a year at Tilbury Fort after offering shelter to Bonnie Prince Charlie and taking him by ship to Maillag.

When told that King George was being generous in releasing him from prison, he became famous for the quote, "Had I the King in my power, I would return the compliment by sending him back to his own country." He did have a son, Charles; Alanna McKinnon McCallum is a fictional character.

Castle Moil or Dunakin, is a McKinnon ruin that sits above the beautiful harbor village of Kyleakin, Skye (the Misty Isle). The village of Kilmoil in the book is a fictional place.

The **Earl of Breadalbane** and his family are imaginary. The Breadalbane family at that time had 4 daughters, so I borrowed them and created a new family. Kilchurn Castle in 1745 was a government garrison. More later about the Campbell lasses, Grizel and Vanora, in later installments of *Heart in the Highlands*.

Last but not least, to live in Scotland in the eighteenth century was difficult. The Battle of Culloden was the crowning defeat for the Jacobites. The face of the nation was changing without the clan system and eventually brought on the Highland Clearances.

Altogether, it was a troubled time in Scottish history. However, the aura of romance about ancient Scotland continues to fascinate and lend itself to many charming tales today, and the Scots have amazingly 'invented the modern world.'

I hope you've enjoyed my tale with all of its fact and fiction, Thank you for reading *Heart in the Highlands*.

Go mbeannaí Dia duit (May God bless you),
Amy

Heart in the Highlands 3
About Highland Mercy

A Merciful Escape....

Grizel Campbell is in trouble again. Betrayed and imprisoned, Grizel becomes the unexpected guardian to five stolen children. Escaping her captors, she finds herself tramping through the rugged Scottish Highlands as winter approaches. How will she and the children ever manage to survive? Courage is definitely not her virtue.

Big Trouble follows after her in the form of handsome Nikolas Gage, and she soon realizes that the rough wanderer is the embodiment of her girlish dreams. Can she ever hope to win his trust and ultimately, his love? It seems that Providence has deserted her, and Forever is a long time.

An Unwilling Hero....

Mercenary Nikolas Gage doesn't have time for love. His code of honor demands that he help the lovely, beleaguered Campbell lass and her newly acquired charges. Her innocent charm tempts him beyond reason to forget the bitterness of his troubled past. With great reluctance, he agrees to escort her home, aware of the hazards involved in the wild and to them both.

Can he trust in Providence to rescue him from the new difficulties that have arisen?

A Long-Awaited Truth....

During the long, arduous journey across the Scottish Highlands and at home in Argyll, Nikolas and Grizel discover a divine purpose, and the merciful power of love.

About the Author
Amy P. Kennedy

Author and speaker Amy P. Kennedy inspires people of all ages to love life and to know God intimately.

A mom, home educator and ordained minister, she is the author of several novels, novellas and ebooks. She has taught individuals and groups for 35 years in her local church and community. A Pittsburgh native, she loves country living, and is passionate about her Divine Romance and feeding children in Burundi, Central Africa.
Facebook Page: Feed-the-Children-of-Burundi-Central Africa

Amy enjoys writing everything from blogs to novels, especially romance, fantasy and Sci-Fi, her favorite genres. Reading, playing piano and guitar, and writing songs keep her creativity flowing. Subscribe to her free e-zine for an encouraging "Byte of the Month", offers, novel updates and public events at www.mydivineromance.com or www.amypkennedy.com.

A Note from Amy: Visit Me Online

"I would love to hear from you!
At my website, MyDivineRomance.com, you will find book and character updates via Gallantry Books (BurningRosePress.com), Giveaways, Links to my blogs, Articles, and other tidbits for Readers and Writers."

Facebook Page: www.facebook.com/AmysWeb
Amy's Writing Web: www.amypkennedy.blogspot.com
Twitter Me! @MyDivineRomance
Amy's Web Store: Burundi Reflections & More
www.amyswebstore.com